KN[ ]

& [ ]

Joy Wood

A CIP catalogue record for this title is available from the
British Library

To my husband, John

If I had my life to live again ... next time I would find you sooner so that I could love you longer.

Acknowledgements

Firstly, special thanks to my amazing editor, the word wizard John Hudspith, who puts up with my endless grammar gaffes, sorts out my wayward POV's, and keeps a beady eye on the storytelling. His fabulous 'cut the fluff' directive is crucial, as believe you me, I have plenty of fluff to cut! When I'm doing something wrong he has no problem telling me, and when I get it right, his praise, reassurance and belief mean the world to me, and there's absolutely no way I could do any of this without him.

To my friends and fantastic supporters, the wonderful Gina Cardosi and Jackie Stalker who are so enthusiastic about my writing and their 'more please' always urges me on.

Special thanks to Liz Foster, Tess Doyle, Helen Stocks and Olwyn Hodgson. One memorable night in Portugal, we discussed the plot over copious amounts of gin, and the more we drank, the better the story became - I'm putting the raunchy stuff down to them!

I'm indebted to my dear friend and inspiration, Lynette Creswell – we got there in the end! Thank you so much for your great ideas, enthusiasm and loyal friendship. You have made the journey of publishing my own books an absolute joy.

I'd like to say a big thank you to Siobhan Daiko who I've never met in person, but feel like I've known forever. Your advice and encouragement has spurred me on when the going was slow. Countries separate us, but one day my beautiful friend, we will get to meet.

Prologue

The aspect is certainly stunning for a last view before death. The backdrop of the mountains is breath-taking with the sunlight colouring the rock face. But I'm not here to admire the view. I'm here for a purpose and I'm absolutely certain there's no other way. I'm about to become a murderer.

I've enticed the target here. I've had to stop thinking about a *person*, another *human being*, that's too personal. I tried 'victim' but no. This is no victim; this is just deserts. *Target* sits better with me and helps me focus on the task ahead.

I need to get us both close to the edge of the cliff, as I'll have only one chance to make it look like an accident. I step closer to the edge and clear my throat. "Let me just take a photo. It'll make a great screen-saver for my laptop."

My target sighs, "Let's move somewhere a bit less precarious, so we can talk. That's why we're here, isn't it?"

"Yeah, sure, in a minute, as soon as I've got a good shot." I hold my phone up, framing the scene, then let out a moan. "Damn, can you believe it, my battery's died. Could you take it on yours?"

I see irritation on the target's face.

My heart feels like it's on the outside of my chest, it's thumping so hard. My head is pounding too, and perspiration is dripping down my back, even though it's a bitterly cold day.

I'm going to do this, I tell myself, *I must do this*.

The target moves towards the edge, phone in hand.

"Make sure you get the full landscape," I say.

My target joins me at my side.

"Take a few," I add, "then I can choose the best."

"You should get back, you're too close to the edge," my target says.

"Yes," is all I manage as I take a step back.

This is it ... the one moment of opportunity.

One big shove ...

I can see the beautiful ravine on the target's phone.

I hear the click of the camera.

Just do it ...

I take in a great breath and lunge forward and give an almighty push with my shoulder and I have to reel back to steady myself as the cliff edge crumbles and my target topples head first over the edge.

The screams I hadn't counted on.

Terrible gut-wrenching screams and desperate agonising squeals echo around the cliffs, deafening at first, but now fading bit by bit, until faintly in the distance, only a pitiful cry.

And then no more.

1

Kathryn felt Rosa's fingers tighten around her palm. "So ... I see big change for you, Sister. I see ... I see babies, two, no three of them for you."

Her gut clenched at the mention of babies, she'd heard enough now. Although she didn't believe in this second sight that Rosa apparently had, she'd gone along with these readings as Rosa and her husband were trying to raise money for the local hydrotherapy pool for children with disabilities. Most of what she'd predicted was totally unbelievable. "Thank you ever so much," she said with a smile, hoping to bring the nonsense to a close, but there was more.

"Wait. I see aeroplane ... and Statue of Liberty."

Gosh, that's uncanny. Only last week Philip had mentioned someone at work going on a fly drive to the USA, and she'd reminded him of his promise to take her to New York.

"How exciting," Kathryn said, removing her hand from Rosa's grip, "I've always wanted to go to America, so I'll keep my fingers crossed."

"You will go," Rosa nodded, "you go with your children."

Again her tummy flipped at the mention of the one thing she desperately wanted that eluded her, and she was almost on the verge of asking about the sex of these children that Rosa could supposedly see, when the laughter of the other's in the adjacent room jolted her into her senses.

All this talk of babies was doing her no good at all. She opened her purse and handed Rosa a crisp ten pound note.

"Are you sure that's enough money, it doesn't seem very much at all?"

Rosa took the money from her and handed back her ring that she had requested to feel the so called vibes.

"Yes, is good, thank you."

"Have you any idea how much you've raised so far?"

"I not sure, Dino will add up. I know it over a thousand pound now."

Kathryn stood up, pleased to be talking about something other than babies.

"That's fantastic. I think you deserve a medal with all this fundraising you're doing."

A wave of sadness darkened Rosa's eyes, "We not blessed with baby, so we like to 'elp the children."

"Well your baking has certainly gone down well at work. The surgeons love your plum bread. Mr Barr bought three last week."

"Ah, it all good then, Sister."

She sighed, "I keep telling you, Rosa, you don't have to call me Sister, especially out of work, everyone calls me Kathryn."

Rosa shook her head from side to side, which at first Kathryn thought was in reference to not wanting to call her by her Christian name, but she saw something else in Rosa's eyes which disturbed her, and when her tiny hand reached and clasped hers, she almost flinched as her fingers had turned ice cold.

"I saw something else … it sad. Before babies, I see pain and tears, many, many tears. Your life be different soon. I see a man. This man, he change everything."

Kathryn widened her eyes in a humorous way and pulled her hand away. "I don't know who that could be then," she shrugged, "anyway, I must get off now. I'll say goodbye to the others on the way out."

Rosa followed her through the hall to the lounge. She was a tiny Italian lady, a bit of a mother hen with them all which was very sweet. Her job at St Anne's was as a cleaner, but not one of the ladies employed for deep cleaning the operating theatres after the surgical lists, Rosa was more of a keeping-the- place-tidy type of cleaner in the areas around the theatre suite like the office, tearoom, stores and recovery area.

On the short drive home, Kathryn thought about the tea and cakes, followed by a spiritual reading and wished she hadn't gone. The other theatre staff had taken part so she felt mean not joining in, but the predictions had unsettled her. Babies, Rosa had said, if only that were true. Her longstanding problem with endometriosis most probably had put paid to that, although the gynaecologist that had carried out her last operation had been optimistic. He'd managed to filtrate some dye through one of her fallopian tubes indicating that is was viable, therefore she needed to keep trying for a baby for at least a year before they could consider IVF treatment.

Ten months into the twelve and she still hadn't managed to conceive, and while her heart had leapt a little at Rosa's prediction, it quickly dropped when she thought about her comment that before the babies there would be lots of pain. And what about a man that would change everything, what on earth was that all about when she was happily married? No, the whole thing was a load of rubbish and best ignored. If Rosa could see into the future, surely she'd be predicting the lottery numbers and living on some exclusive island instead of cleaning the operating theatres of a local hospital. It was simply a bit of fun, she must think of it like that.

2

Philip was breathing heavily in his sleep. They'd just made love and it never ceased to amaze Kathryn how quickly he could drop off afterwards. According to the girls at work, the male species were all programmed the same way. Once they'd had sex, they needed to sleep.

She wished it was that easy for her. She fluffed her pillow and tried to get comfortable.

No orgasm for me tonight.

Nothing unusual there.

The waft of lemon soap hit her nostrils. After making love, Philip would always use the bidet to wash himself. Not doing so was never an option. When they were first married and not specifically trying for a baby, she would wash also, however, now after making love she would tilt her pelvis on a pillow and lie in the same position to try and assist the sperm to swim upwards for fertilisation. The time spent waiting seemed to irritate him and he would urge her onto her side so they could cuddle up. He would say that he couldn't settle any other way. Sleep was so important to Philip, and woe betide if he didn't get his eight hours.

Other couples she felt sure didn't wash after making love; they certainly didn't in any of the books she read. Most would enjoy closeness and be content to fall asleep in a loving embrace, but not Philip. He would slip on a pair of boxers after he'd washed, urge her onto her side and cuddle in. Yes, he always told her he loved her, but she yearned for a more macho approach. Just once, she'd love to have a night of sex where they made love, dozed in each other's arms, and when either of them stirred, start all over again. How good would that be? It was never going to happen, though. Philip was hardly a permanent erection kind of man, no, he was more of a once every couple of week's kind of guy, and more often than not, the initiation came from her. But she loved him very much, and that was more important surely? They were happy together, and if only she could get pregnant, then their lives really would be complete.

The tossing around the bed continued, and as she lay staring at the ceiling, she silently chastised herself knowing that she'd be a wreck in the morning and it was important that she was on her toes as it was the first theatre list of the new surgeon, Mr Dey. From previous experience she knew that it always took a little time to get used to individual operating techniques, as well as specific idiosyncrasies, and a drowsy theatre sister was not an image she particularly wanted to convey.

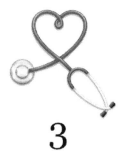

3

Fin Dey came back into his spacious lounge carrying a tray with two coffees. His sister Elsa was standing by the fireplace looking at the photographs on the mantelpiece, "Here you go, you did say you wanted it black didn't you?"

"Please, I'm cutting back on the milk."

"Whatever for?"

"Why do you think?" she said, "It's fattening."

"For God's sake, you're hardly overweight."

"That's because I'm careful. I would be if I drank loads of milk."

She took her coffee from the tray and sat down, "Anyway, dinner was lovely thank you. I can't believe you cooked that, did your housekeeper prepare it earlier?"

"No, she didn't, cheeky. I can cook and take care of myself you know."

"Can you?" She raised her eyebrows, "That would be why you employ staff then."

He laughed at her sarcasm, "I employ a housekeeper because I like to help the economy and keep the locals in work. The very same reason I employ a gardener-handyman."

"Yeah, right," she said taking a sip of her coffee. "How are you feeling about starting tomorrow at St Anne's?"

"Pretty good actually, I'm ready to get stuck in. There's quite a lot to do, though. The hospital is not performing as well as it could, but they've been awarded a huge NHS contract so I'm sure I can turn it around."

"Well if anyone can, you can."

"Thank you for your vote of confidence on the work front, if not on my domestic abilities."

She smiled back at him, "What about your surgery, you don't say much about that anymore?"

"No, I know I don't. This takeover of St Anne's seems to have taken for ever," he paused, draining his coffee, "surgery will always be my first love, but it doesn't hold the same excitement as it used to. I don't know why, but since Saskia and Christiaan's death, so much has changed." He thought for a moment about his dead wife and son. That was an understatement really, since their deaths, everything had changed.

"It's bound to be hard, Fin. I still can't believe you've given everything up in Holland and moved over here. I'm pleased, of course, but all you've ever known is living there."

"Yes, but I'll be going back frequently. I needed the change," he frowned, "once they'd both gone, I had to do something different."

"Of course you did, and I know you are going to be brilliant. It'll take time, but I've every confidence in you. Anyway, before I forget, remember to look out for my friend Kathryn won't you?"

He loved her for changing the subject. He'd exhausted his conversations about Saskia and Christiaan. One of the reasons for moving over here was a fresh start. It wasn't that he wanted to forget them, far from it. He just needed to mix with people that didn't know them both. In Holland, everyone he came into contact with knew him as a husband and father. He was pleased to have moved closer to his sister and hoped he could rebuild his life in England, well, some sort of life; there was nothing left for him in Holland.

"Did you say she's a nurse?"

"Yes, she works in theatre. She's running it at the moment as the manager is on long-term sick leave. You're bound to see a lot of her I would have thought."

"Wasn't she at your wedding?"

"Yes she was," she looked surprised, "I can't believe you can remember that far back."

"Of course I can. I can't remember much about her,

though, only being introduced."

"She was there with her boyfriend Philip who she's since married."

"Oh, right. I guess by the disparaging look on your face, you aren't that keen on him?"

"You'd be guessing right. He's a real arsehole."

"Elsa," he said sternly.

"Well he is. Why she sticks with him, Lord knows. She could do so much better."

"Is she happy?"

"She seems to be, most of the time that is, but I think she's had her moments with him. The trouble is, she's very loyal and thinks the sun shines out of his backside."

"Well surely, if she loves him, that's all that matters?"

"I suppose it is, but I don't think he deserves her."

"Why's that?"

"Let's just say I know something about him that others don't."

"Like what?"

He watched her hesitate as if she wanted to answer but then thought better of it.

"Nothing, forget I said that," she shrugged, "I can't be one hundred percent certain anyway. You'll be able to make your own mind up when you meet him. Remember I said I'd invite them round to dinner ..."

Their conversation was interrupted by Queen's Bohemian Rhapsody coming from her handbag. Only Elsa would have that ringtone. She delved in her bag to retrieve the phone and looked at the caller, "It's Nick, sorry."

As she spoke to his brother-in-law, he thought about his new role at the hospital and sincerely hoped that this move would work out well for him. A fresh start was what he needed and he was keeping everything crossed that St Anne's and England would give him that. Surely after what he'd been through, he deserved it?

4

"Are you okay love, you look tired?" Philip asked her during breakfast. He was munching on his wholemeal toast cut exactly how he liked it and only toasted on one side.

"I am a bit, yes; I didn't sleep very well really."

"I can see that, you've got dark circles under your eyes."

"Oh, thank you for the confidence boost, that's just what I needed."

He stood up and kissed her head. "Sorry sweetie, only joking. I slept really well, but then again after the night we've had, what man wouldn't."

Er ... night we've had?

The ten minutes of sex?

Kathryn rolled her eyes, "Okay, I'll let you off," she kissed him gently on his lips, "this time."

She followed him as he walked towards the hall and opened the closet. He selected his black shoes from the array of those lined up neatly alongside his other shoes, trainers and boots. All meticulously cleaned and polished in a neat row.

He sat on the hall chair and laced up his shoes, the same way he did every day, and as he stood up, he moved the chair slightly as if it had come out of its correct position. He leaned forward and kissed her cheek, "I'll see you tonight then, have a good day, and don't work too hard will you?"

As he took his car keys from the drawer, she unlocked and opened the front door for him. "I'll try not to, but today's the day the new surgeon's starting ..." she paused waiting for him to look up once he'd located his keys, but he didn't. He walked towards the door and it was clear he wasn't listening as usual. His face had switched to work mode.

"Bye then," she said, and closed the door behind him. She went into the lounge to wave him goodbye from the window as she did each morning when he left the house before her. It was a ritual his mother did that she'd fallen into also.

Once he'd driven away, she tidied up the kitchen and collected her handbag from the closet, and just as he'd done, retrieved the car keys from the drawer they'd been assigned to in the hall. No leaving car keys causally around in this house. As Philip would say, "I've seen on the television, thieves target houses with nice cars. They open the letter box and invariably see car keys on hall tables, then it's simple enough with a long rod to hook the keys and away they go."

No chance of that happening to us, Philip had it covered with the secret drawer that didn't look like a drawer. She was absolutely certain that was the reason he'd bought this particular piece of furniture as nobody with any sense would like the monstrosity.

She checked her appearance in the hall mirror, and applied another layer of lip gloss before fluffing up her fringe. *Not bad for thirty,* she smiled at herself, and then exited the house as her husband had done minutes earlier.

Nobody to wave me off though.

The journey to work was short and as Kathryn pulled into the car park, she saw Janelle one of the theatre staff nurses getting out of her car. How strange that Janelle always seemed to arrive at work the same time as she did. Every single morning she was either parked up in her car waiting, or came in behind her. It was very odd.

She waited while Janelle locked her car and joined her for the short walk to the staff entrance.

"Now then," Kathryn was dying to know how Janelle had got on with Callum Riley, one of Philip's friends from the walking club she'd gone out on a date with. "How did Saturday night go?"

"Really well," Janelle said, "We went for a drink to O'Neil's wine bar in town. Have you been?"

"I've been there with my friend Elsa, she loves it there. Did you have something to eat, the food's gorgeous?"

"No, we just had a few cocktails, and then we had an early night," she winked, "getting to know each other a little better, you know how it is."

Kathryn raised her hand jokingly as Janelle tapped in the door code, "Too much information thank you."

The warmth of the hospital hit them as soon as they walked through the door, "I guess you'll be seeing him again then?"

Kathryn knew Callum had gone through an acrimonious divorce and according to Philip he was back in the game. Maybe she should warn Janelle, but then again, she never seemed to stick to one man for long so they'd probably be well suited.

"Yes, I hope so," Janelle said, "He's going to ring me to make arrangements to meet up again. I've got tickets for the Meat Loaf tribute show at the Embassy next Friday. My friend has let me down so I'm going to ask him if he wants to come with me, unless you fancy it?"

Kathryn shook her head, "No, you invite him, that'll be much more fun. Callum's a lovely bloke and for a while he was in a pretty bad way when his marriage broke up, so it's great he's now moving on and meeting new people."

"Oh he's definitely moving on," Janelle said, "Hopefully once we've been out a few times, we could go out with you and Philip one night, maybe for a curry or something?"

"We could do," Kathryn paused; Janelle seemed to be moving along pretty quickly considering she'd only been out with Callum once, "Although Philip's not a great curry man."

"Somewhere else then. It doesn't have to be an Indian. I just thought it would be nice if we could go out together."

"It would," she lied, knowing categorically a foursome wouldn't be Philip's idea of a night out at all, and Janelle definitely wouldn't be his cup of tea. He thought if a woman slept with more than one man she was promiscuous, so with her track record, he'd have her down as the village bike at the very least.

Fortunately Janelle changed the subject, "Hey, do you know what, I reckon Callum is the man that Rosa talked about when she did that fortune telling session."

"Do you?" Kathryn pulled a face, "To be honest, I don't hold out a lot on what she said, I really don't believe in these second sights."

"Well I do. I've got a new man, and wait until you get pregnant, then you'll believe it."

"We'll see." Kathryn pressed another key code to enter the theatre changing room and didn't say any more. Although she'd told the staff about Rosa's prediction that she would have three children, she didn't let on quite how desperate she was for that to actually happen.

There was a lot of banter as the girls arrived and changed into their theatre scrubs. The staff would set theatre up for the morning's operating list, so Kathryn headed for her office to check any emails and messages since Friday. There was an hour before the new surgeon, and hospital director Fin Dey would arrive.

Kathryn thought back to Elsa's wedding and vividly recollected meeting him. He reminded her of Richard Gere, and Elsa had laughed when she'd told her that. Apparently it wasn't the first time he'd been compared to the actor.

She remembered his beautiful wife Saskia with her charming English accent. Her and Fin made a striking couple. How sad she was no longer here.

They needed to make Fin Dey welcome as he'd invested heavily in St Anne's so it was likely he'd be here permanently.

He'd bought the beautiful Manor house in Selton which he was in the process of completely refurbishing. It certainly didn't appear that money was a problem for him judging by the scale of the renovation project. Elsa had suggested she went with her one day to have a good look round, but she'd declined. It didn't seem right prying around her boss's house, even if it was her best friend's brother. Plus Philip would no doubt kick off about it.

Kathryn went into the prep room to check all the equipment and sets were ready for the surgical lists. As a theatre sister, nothing was more important than to be seen as professional and capable, but it wasn't just that, there were other more pressing reasons why she wanted to make a good impression. Mr Dey specialised in plastic surgery. He was going to be operating each Monday afternoon and bringing private cases into theatre which hopefully would ensure the hospital made a profit and they all kept their jobs. St Anne's, a small independent private hospital faced challenging times as private health insurance was the first thing to go when money was stretched. The trajectories for the next year in terms of business were steady, but at a recent marketing meeting for the Heads of Department, Matron had informed them that the hospital needed to strive for more business.

One of the male theatre practitioners popped his head round the prep room door, "Kathryn, Melons is outside asking for you with the new surgeon, Mr Dey."

"Lee," she chastised, "Keep your voice down, they'll hear you."

He grinned and winked, clearly not at all bothered about being reprimanded for addressing Matron by her nickname.

As Kathryn came out of the prep room and approached them both in the theatre corridor, she could see that the Matron, Helen Fenty had dressed to impress. Not that she ever looked a mess, she was one of those women that always wore a full face of make-up, and you could almost swear she never took it off as it was always so perfect. Her nickname, Melons Plenty, which everyone in the hospital seemed to have latched onto, suited her perfectly as she had large breasts which Kathryn suspected were more down to the skills of a surgeon as opposed to being the work of nature itself. They were accentuated by a very tight grey uniform dress, and she would insist on wearing a ridiculous frilly hat on the top of her head which she delighted in telling everyone was from her training days at Guy's hospital in London.

"Kathryn, there you are. Fin, I'd like you to meet Kathryn Knight, the senior theatre sister. Kathryn, this is Fin Dey, the new Hospital Director."

She held out her hand and he grasped it in his, "Welcome to St Anne's, Mr Dey. I hope you'll be very happy here." She withdrew her hand quickly. It felt almost like an electric shock.

How odd.

Must be a lot of static.

His eyes greeted her pleasantly, "Thank you, I'm sure I will." He turned to Helen, "Kathryn and I are old friends really; we've met before at my sister's wedding."

Well, I wouldn't have put it quite like that.

We've met before, but friends, I don't think so.

"Yes, it seems like yesterday, but it is in fact ten years since the wedding." She felt it was an appropriate time to offer her condolences, "I'm so sorry about the loss you've suffered."

His acknowledgment to the words of sympathy that he must have heard so many times was courteous, "Thank you."

His deep brown eyes, a replica of which she'd looked at so many times in his sister, were guarded, and made her feel almost awkward. Thankfully it was only for a second as Helen interjected, "Right, I'll leave Mr Dey in your capable hands then. Could you direct him back to my office when his theatre list is finished please?"

"Yes of course." Kathryn spotted Lee in the recovery area adjacent to where they were standing.

"Lee, can you show Mr Dey the male changing room please and get him sorted with some scrubs and clogs if you wouldn't mind."

Fin nodded and followed Lee. She watched him walk along the corridor. Not quite as she remembered. He looked very distinguished with his height and brooding good looks, and those eyes, absolutely wasted on a male, but there was a gloomy aura about him now which was so sad. Let's hope his move to England was going to work out for him.

She went to prepare for the procedure which was a breast enlargement which wouldn't take long. Just an open and shut case really. An incision below the breast to take out the previous implants which clearly were too small if the patient wanted an enlargement. New larger implants would be inserted and the incisions closed. A nice and easy case so she could get to know Mr Dey's operating technique.

The main thing she wanted to convey was her professionalism. Philip had warned her about getting 'up close and personal'... as if she would. She certainly wasn't expecting any perks because of her friendship with Elsa.

She turned on the taps at the scrub-up sink to start the five-minute scrubbing of her hands. As she selected a sterile nail brush, her thoughts were still on him. As if losing your wife wasn't bad enough, but to lose a child as well, how did you ever come to terms with that? To have the joy of giving birth to a baby, and growing to love and cherish it, only to have him or her taken away tragically. There couldn't be anything worse, surely?

The smell of Betadine hand scrub wafted around the scrub-up area and she took a deep breath in and tried to stifle the usual longing that occupied her thoughts every day. Her dad's saying, *Never say never,* came to mind. That's what she needed to do she told herself, be positive. One day maybe, she'd be holding her own baby.

Erin came in the prep room and opened a gown and gloves for her. She dried both her hands on the sterile towel, and discarded it carefully in the bin. As Erin tied her gown at the back, she put the surgical gloves on her clean hands feeling more positive than she'd been in days. There was no indication that her whole life was about to turn upside down, and the very principles of honesty, integrity and love which shaped the way she lived, were about to be torn into tiny little pieces.

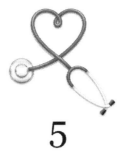

5

The breast reconstruction was going well. It was clear to see that Fin Dey was a competent surgeon. He was diligent and methodical, and when asking for a particular instrument, or surgical tie, he was polite. His pronunciation was almost flawless, and you'd have to listen hard to think English wasn't his first language.

During the dissection part of the process which is often time consuming, she found her thoughts drifting towards him standing at the theatre table with only the patient dividing them. He was very tall, and must spend endless hours exercising as he didn't have an ounce of fat on him. He didn't look thirty-nine either, although his hair greying at the temples gave him away somewhat. He had a very attractive face, but it was his intense dark eyes that were striking and made him stand out. Those very eyes that were suddenly peering over his surgical mask at her.

"When you're ready."

"Sorry?"

"I asked for mosquito forcep, when you're ready."

She quickly handed him one.

God, what am I like.

I really must concentrate.

At least he was calm and polite unlike some of the surgeons she scrubbed for who'd have gone ballistic at any lack of concentration.

The operation didn't take long, and once the new implants had been inserted, the breasts actually looked much better even though they were larger than the ones he'd removed.

As he began closing the inside of the wounds, he informed her, "Next Monday I've got a couple of cases, but just to let you know, I'll never have more than two cases each week."

"That's fine." Great, not one of those surgeons that cram too much on their lists each week and then run over into the evening. "Amy has started to develop a folder today with your requirements. It will make it easier to have the right equipment and extras ready for each case you do."

"Good, thank you." She watched him dextrously applying the steri strips to the skin incisions and handed him two sterile dressings.

"Have you got a surgical soft bra?" he asked.

They had. They were standard stock for breast surgery, "Yes, Amy's got one ready." As he was applying the dressings, she advised him, "All the swabs, needles and instruments are correct."

"Thank you, Sister," he nodded.

Their surgical masks obscured most of their faces, but his eyes looked directly at hers for a second, and for that one brief moment, her tummy did a flip as her eyes were drawn into his, almost sucked into their depths. She took a deep breath in and his spicy aftershave saturated her senses which only added to her unexpected awareness of him.

He has gorgeous eyes.

Why's he looking at me like that?

A wave of discomfort ran down her chest, as heat crept up her neck and covered her face. Quickly, she broke eye contact and turned towards her trolley. Grabbing a surgical clip, she secured the used needles onto the sticky safety device and closed it tightly. Thankfully he turned away from the theatre table to remove his mask and gloves, but even though he'd moved away from her, she could still feel a wakefulness flooding through her. How strange he had the ability to make her heart race like it did. That certainly wasn't something she was used to experiencing.

After applying the surgical bra to the patient, her and Amy both helped Lee the theatre technician transfer the patient onto her bed. As she wheeled her trolley into the sluice area and began dismantling it, Amy pulled off her face mask, and her eyes widened, "I think he's a bit of alright, don't you?"

Kathryn removed her own mask and tossed it in the bin, "He seems nice, yes."

"And single. Isn't he a widow or something?"

"I believe his is, although I don't think he's on the market so I wouldn't go getting any ideas," she cautioned.

"Oh, I'm not interested in a relationship with him, as nice on the eye as he is," Amy grinned, "I'm keen on what he can do for me." Her frown must have registered as she carried on, "At the very least I'd like a boob job, and then a tummy tuck."

Kathryn rolled her eyes, "You'll have to see if he does barrow jobs then, as I don't think your salary will run to his prices."

"No, sadly I think you might be right," Amy agreed, "Shall I go put the kettle on?"

"Yes, good idea. I'll be through in a minute, once I've cleared the trolley."

Kathryn's mind wondered back. What on earth had made her blush when her eyes met his? It wasn't like her at all. Hopefully he wouldn't have noticed with the theatre hat and mask covering most of her face.

She inwardly chastised herself, she was married for goodness' sake. Working with men was part of her job, so what was it about him that had made her heart race when he looked at her? That had never happened to her before, ever.

6

Janelle's appraisal was going well. It was much better this year with Kathryn, rather than Alison Clegg, the theatre manager. She didn't like Alison, and as far as she was concerned, she hoped she'd be off sick another six months.

It was Kathryn she liked, and she was looking forward to Avril's leaving party on Friday so she could pick her up and take them both to DiMaggio's. Her house was around the corner from Kathryn's, so she liked to give her a lift on nights out. She wasn't bothered about alcohol, she'd rather drive.

Kathryn was concluding on the appraisal, "So finally, just to say, I'm really pleased with your progress this year. You've contributed well to the theatre team, and I've appreciated your flexibility when you've changed shifts at short notice and worked over your time." She shuffled the papers neatly together, "And you've had a full year with no sick days which has been marvellous, so thank you for that."

Janelle was pleased that had been noted. There were days when she'd dragged herself to work, but she wasn't one for taking time off, she'd rather be at work surrounded by people than at home.

"I'll be recommending you for a pay rise as you've achieved all aims and objectives that were set last year, so well done."

Kathryn stood up and she followed her lead, "Thank you. A pay rise would be more than welcome, and thanks for all the nice things you've said about me, I really do appreciate it."

Kathryn smiled, "No, thank you. The reason we are successful in this department is we all work as a team. So, I like to give thanks when it's due and you have worked really hard this past year, particularly the last few months when we've been short staffed."

Janelle gave a smile which she hoped conveyed how grateful she was, and asked, "Have you got time for a drink, or have you got more to do?"

"No, I'm finished now. I've got to sign off the paperwork, and then I'll come through for a coffee. You get yours though, and can you do the theatre ordering after that please?"

"Course I will," she nodded.

Janelle left the office and headed for the tea room pleased that she'd done well, but then again anyone would with Kathryn. She was so lovely to everyone that worked there.

As she made her coffee, she remembered Kathryn's blouse she was wearing when she came into work that morning. The burnt orange was a lovely colour and it really suited her. She wanted one for herself, so she'd look online tonight to see if it was from Next. Bet it was, Kathryn bought a lot of her clothes from Next.

After she'd finished her coffee, Janelle diligently went around the two theatres ordering the stores. She liked her job. The girls were nice enough, and she didn't mind the unsocial hours they had to work. It was like a small family unit, and all the staff pulled together. She actually found it more of an escape to get to work each day. If she could afford to live alone, she would do, but she had far too many debts to manage that. Currently she lived with her mother who could be so trying and always moaning on about something, particularly, *When are you going to meet a man and get married?*

She heard it so many times and was sick to death of it. She was thirty-two now, and while not as stunning as Kathryn in the beauty department, she did scrub up well and had been told more than once that she was pretty. A permanent relationship continued to be elusive, despite the fact she was always up for sex. You'd think a bloke would want to hang onto her for that alone.

She often called at the local Number One club, where the hospital staff would hang out, and even joined the club walkers on a couple of occasions convincing everyone that she wanted to get fit, when the reality was, she wanted to meet a man and she'd heard there were a few single ones lurking at the club. She'd tried the internet, but the ones she'd met were all wasters.

Then bingo, she met Callum Riley. The fact that he was a friend of Kathryn's husband was a bonus. Or was that why she'd gone for him in the first place? She did have to work hard to get a date with him, but they'd had a fantastic night, even though a large part of the evening was spent listening to him berating his ex-wife.

They'd got on really well. There was none of those awkward silences you get on a first date, their conversation had flowed, and she was very attracted to him so didn't hesitate when he invited her back to his flat at the end of the evening. Their conversation became flirtier over coffee laced with alcohol, and once they'd finished, he asked her what she wanted to do next. The options were going home if she wanted to, or staying for sex. He didn't even try to flower it up.

"My preference is you stay. That's what I'd like you to do, but the choice is yours. The options are, you can go home now to your cosy bed with a cup of hot cocoa and a comfy quilt, or you can stay here with me." He stopped for a second as if gauging whether to say more, and then became much bolder, "I can be gentle, or fuck you hard. I can make you scream or make you cry. We can do whatever you want, and I promise you that you'll enjoy yourself."

Cocoa and comfy quilt went straight out the window, as her pussy contracted at his graphic description. She'd didn't hesitate, "I'll stay."

She remembered his sexy grin and wink as he told her, "Good girl, I was hoping you'd say that. I'm going to get us something else to drink, why don't you take your panties off and you can tell me what you like doing." He left her and went into the kitchen.

Oh my God. Remove my knickers. Bloody Hell ... should I?

Her libido made the decision for her, and she quickly pulled them down her legs and hoisted them into her handbag, but regretted it instantly when she sat again and tried to pull her short dress further down. The trouble was it looked good when she was stood up in it, but sat down it covered very little. She was still tugging when he came back into the lounge.

"Here you go, try this."

"What is it?" she asked, taking a sip.

"Whisky and dry ginger. I find it very relaxing."

He took a seat in the chair opposite her. "I'm pleased you stayed. Let's enjoy our drink and talk awhile," he smiled at her, making her tummy flutter.

I'd rather we just get on with it.

He took a mouthful of his drink, "I like to talk a bit beforehand, sort of hype up the anticipation. You really are quite lovely."

Me, lovely? What's in that drink?

"Why don't you open your legs, so I can see all of you?"

Bloody hell.

She opened her legs and her pussy clenched as he focussed on it, and it twitched even more when she spotted the bulge in his trousers.

"Now, tell me about you." He shook the ice in his glass, "What sort of sex do you like?"

"Erm ... any... I think. I don't like anything that might hurt me though."

"Okay," he nodded, "hoist your dress up so I can see all of you. And don't keep closing your legs, leave them open."

She opened them.

"Wider." She spread them wider. He really knew how to turn her on.

"Do you like giving men pleasure?"

"I do, yes." One of the blokes she'd met on the internet had said she was the best he'd had at giving blowjobs.

All this talk was exciting her, and she was becoming very moist. He really was good-looking.

His eyes dipped as he sipped his drink.

"Your pussy looks so inviting."

Her heart pumped faster and her breathing quickened.

Was she supposed to answer that?

"Are you wet?" he asked.

Yes. Soaking.

"Er...yes, I think so."

"Feel yourself. See if you are?"

She put her hand between her legs and felt her moisture.

"Yes."

"Not like that. Feel yourself properly."

She continued to stare.

God. He was good.

"Put your fingers inside."

Should I?

She slipped her forefinger deep inside herself.

"Two fingers," he instructed.

She pushed two fingers into her wetness, but it was her throbbing clit that needed attention. He read her mind, "No. Don't touch it, leave that for me. Keep moving your fingers in and out as if it's my cock fucking you."

Shit.

All this talk was really turning her on. She pushed her fingers in and out. It felt good, and her clit was pulsing.

"Tell me. On a scale of one to five, how ready are you for me to come and lick your twitching pussy?"

Ten. Twenty.

"Five," escaped from her throat.

"Really, as ready as that? His look was that of a predator about to pounce. He stood up and placed his glass on the coffee table and leisurely knelt before her. Her knees must have involuntary clamped together, but she wasn't aware she had done that, until he pulled them open. Wide.

"I'm going to make you come, and then I'm going to fuck you and you'll come again. If that's what you want me to do?"

She couldn't find any words, so nodded.

Yes, do it ... for God's sake do it.

"Spread your lips for me, so I can see all of you."

Christ almighty! She was so turned on.

She opened her labia gently with her fingers. This was a first. Her tummy summersaulted as his head moved forward. The first touch of his tongue was like a bolt of electricity and she moaned as her head fell back. He licked her gently at first, and then more firmly. His tongue felt incredible, and as he began to suck, the pleasure intensified. He gently moved her unsteady hands away and replaced them with his mouth. Her bulging folds were beneath his teeth and he was flicking her clit with his tongue. He paused and lifted his head, and she felt him push one finger deep inside her, then two, and then a third, stretching and spreading her. And then his mouth was back and he twisted and turned her clit as if his tongue was designed to do just that.

Within seconds, the first spasm of orgasm erupted and she screamed as the explosion ripped through her in exquisite bursts of pleasure, and still he kept the pressure on as she shuddered violently. It was amazing. *He* was amazing.

As she came back down to earth and was finally able to focus, he had removed his jeans and she was staring at a huge veined dick.

He placed his hands underneath her and hoisted her towards the edge of the sofa, and lifted one leg up first of all, and then the other.

"Hold your ankles," he commanded. She held onto them as he pushed her knees apart.

He sheathed himself in a second, and then positioned his penis at her slippery entrance and as he slowly slid himself into her, a guttural moan escaped from her. God, he was big. It was wonderful to have him filling her. He pushed in deeply.

"You like that don't you? Squeeze yourself around me." She tightened her internal muscles around him. It felt so good. She'd never had sex with such a big man before.

His first thrusts were unhurried. Slow in, and slow

out. He didn't attempt to kiss her at all, which fleetingly she thought was odd, but the delightful sensations he was creating from his huge dick were too exciting to worry about that.

It felt beautiful. She needed clit stimulation and didn't normally climax from penetrative sex, but with each leisurely thrust, she felt the burning emerge deep within her again. The rhythm of him moving slowly was wonderful, and as he started to increase the pace, it heightened the pleasure. He was filling her and the fullness of him was exciting her again.

"Do you want it harder?"

"Yes." She groaned.

He pushed harder, and harder still. Her pussy throbbed as the pleasure grew and increased. Still he kept the momentum going and the ecstasy was excruciating and finally exploded in an orgasm that ripped from deep within her. As she savoured the exquisite sensations, she heard his groan as he pumped his own release.

Two fantastic orgasms and she hadn't even taken her dress off.

Where has he been all my life?

The pinging of her phone brought her back to reality. It was a text from Callum asking if she wanted to meet up again at the weekend. She'd rather have seen him before that, but she was menstruating this week, so maybe Saturday night would be better.

It was great he wanted to see her again. The sex with him had been amazing so she was looking forward to more of that. With a bit of luck, this could be the start of a permanent relationship. Becoming his girlfriend might indirectly get her what she wanted which was to spend more time with Kathryn. She was such a special person, liked by everyone. All the surgeons loved her. She had a beautiful face and fantastic figure, you could put a black bin bag on her and she'd look like she was modelling it. She wished she was like her. Life would be so much better with Kathryn in it. Which reminded her, she needed to make sure that she sat next to her at Avril's leaving do. That way, she would have a much better night.

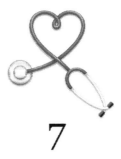

7

Kathryn arrived home from work before Philip which was good as she had time to prepare their evening meal. He loved it if she was home before him, and she knew he would have preferred it if she didn't work at all. They could manage financially if she didn't, but liked the extras that her salary could buy such as a nice car each, foreign holidays, and her desire for lovely clothes. Plus, she was too young to be at home all day on her own. If they had children, then that would have been different, but there was no point in thinking about that now and becoming all tearful. So many times she'd gone through the, *it wasn't meant to be* scenario, but it still had the power to hurt. Maybe if they could look at adoption, but Philip wouldn't consider that.

"How was your day?" she asked as they ate their spaghetti bolognaise made with wholemeal spaghetti and lean turkey mince, nice and healthy, just the way he likes it.

"Bloody awful. Keith Manning has been an absolute twat today. I know you're not going to like this, but I'm going to have to work on Saturday again."

"Oh surely not, that's the second time in five weeks. How long for?"

"Until we get finished. I would think at least until mid-afternoon."

She breathed a sigh of relief, "Oh that's alright then. It's Elsa's dinner party remember; you haven't forgotten,

35

have you?"

"Bugger," he closed his eyes for a second before re-opening them, "Do we have to go? Can't you make up an excuse; I'll be knackered by the time I get back."

"No, of course I can't, I've already told Elsa we'll be there and she wants to show off her brother."

"Brother?" he frowned.

"Honestly, do you ever listen to a word I say? Yes, brother, from Holland, he's a surgeon, remember, and the new Hospital Director." She glared at him ... if he said again he didn't remember.

"Oh yeah, right," his eyes narrowed, "Won't you see him at work, do we need to socialise with him?"

She took a deep breath in, "Yes I will see him at work, and no we don't *need* to socialise with him, but I think we should make an effort when we've been invited."

"I hate bloody dinner parties. What's she going to cook anyway?"

"I have no idea. Who cares? For once you'll have to relax your rigid healthy eating regime and try and enjoy yourself."

"You know I only like healthy food."

Yes, don't I just.

I do the food shop, remember.

"I know, but occasionally it is nice to let your hair down. A tiny bit of fat one night isn't going to send your cholesterol soaring through the roof."

He swallowed a gulp of water, "I'll have to see what time I finish work."

"Well I hope you're home on time, I don't want to have to go on my own."

You won't be happy about that.

So I know you'll be home.

They arrived at Elsa's on time despite Philip being late home. Elsa and her husband Nick owned a stunning detached house on the affluent Hawthorne Avenue. Nick opened the door.

"Hello darling," he hugged her, "Come in, it's lovely to see you."

He smiled at Philip, "Hi mate," and Philip nodded

back, "Nick." They were never going to be best friends; they were just thrown together on social occasions due to her and Elsa's friendship.

"Great to see you *both* I should have said," Nick smiled, "Let me take your coats. Elsa's in the lounge with Fin, go through."

Kathryn tapped on the lounge door more out of politeness as Elsa's brother was there. Elsa was sitting by the fireside but quickly stood and rushed over, throwing her arms around Kathryn.

"At last, I thought you weren't coming."

"We aren't late are we?" she asked knowing full well they weren't.

"No of course not, I just wanted you to get here." Elsa leant forward and kissed Philip's cheek, "Nice to see you Philip, come," she ushered them towards the roaring fire.

"I know you've already been reacquainted with Fin, Kathryn," she turned to Philip, "Philip, this is my much loved tyrant of a younger brother, Fin. Fin, this is Philip, Kathryn's husband. They shook hands, and for a second Kathryn felt a strange sensation in the pit of her stomach. It was almost a feeling of dread, as if something was about to happen.

"Hello Philip, pleased to meet you," Fin said.

"Likewise. How are you settling in, Kathryn tells me you've already started at St Anne's?"

"Yes, I've been there a week. All I can say is it's," he widened his eyes, "shall we say ... refreshingly different to anything I've done before."

Elsa interjected, "It will take time to get used to it, but I know Fin will do a brilliant job, he never fails at anything. And he's done similar in Holland so it's not as if he doesn't know what he's doing."

Nick came in carrying a tray of five bubbling crystal flutes, "I've opened a bottle of champagne. Hope that's okay to get us all started?"

They each took a drink and Nick lifted his glass, "To good friends and new beginnings," he looked at Fin, "best of luck with your new venture, Fin. Cheers."

They repeated the toast and clinked glasses.

"Please, sit down and make yourselves comfortable,"

Elsa said, "dinner won't be long."

Kathryn sipped her champagne and felt strangely uncomfortable although the conversation was relaxed. Again, she was acutely aware of Fin. The aftershave he was wearing had to be a top of the range brand, as it certainly was having an effect on her. The assault on her hormones made her feel a little dizzy each time she took a breath in. Most unusually, heat arrowed straight between her legs and her pussy clenched.

"I hear you've bought the Manor House at Selton, Fin, how are the renovations going?" Philip asked.

Hurray.

He does listen to some things I tell him.

"Not as quickly as I'd like," Fin grimaced, "but we're getting there."

Fin went on to explain in detail exactly what he was doing to the house in between sips of his drink. Her eyes were drawn to him, he really was so handsome. Both of the other males, Nick and Philip were by no means unattractive, but Fin seemed to have that charisma you can't quite put your finger on, a sort of je ne sais quoi. His hair was thick and streaked with grey, no doubt brought on by the death of his family. On most men that might look ageing, but on him, it made him look distinguished and sexy.

Wonder what it would be like to run my fingers through?

Christ! Where did that come from?

The evening was lovely. Elsa had cooked a splendid meal of chicken chasseur which should have pleased Philip, but she still noticed him scraping the sauce off the chicken.

Philip was explaining to Fin about the walking club, and then totally surprised her by inviting him to join them on any Saturday he was free. As if *he'd* be joining the local walking club.

"I'm sure Fin's too busy to be hiking at the weekends, Philip."

Fin shook his head, "Not at all. I like the sound of it. I am busy at the moment, but I'd like to give it a go some time in the future. Where do you meet?"

"The Number One club. You pass it as you drive along to St Anne's. It's the large grey building, you must have seen it?"

Fin nodded, "Yes, I think I have, it's on the right, isn't it?"

"That's it. You're welcome to join us anytime. Some people dip in and out of the walking trips and only use the club for socialising, whereas old stalwarts like myself go every week. We do a lot of fundraising for certain charities."

"Sounds great to me, and certainly something I'd like to do. I can't promise to attend weekly or anything like that, but I do like outdoor pursuits particularly walking, so if there are any long hikes in the future, I might join you on one."

Elsa turned questioningly, "I've heard that there's more drinking than walking taking place when you all go out Philip?"

"I can vouch that there's plenty of truth in that," Kathryn laughed joining it the banter.

Philip raised an eyebrow, "No, not at all. We only drink for medicinal purposes," he winked at Fin, "you know how it is, when it's really cold, you need to keep warm and water just doesn't cut it."

Fin shook his head playfully and his lips curved into the most gorgeous smile. "I know exactly what you mean; unfortunately women don't get what we men have to do."

They all laughed, and as his eyes glanced towards her, she felt her chest tighten.

I love your eyes.
The way they crinkle at the corners when you smile.

The evening was really pleasant, and despite Philip's reluctance, she could tell he'd enjoyed himself too. Elsa excelled at entertaining and it was obvious she was thrilled to have her brother there. Both her and Fin had kept them entertained with exploits of their childhood in Holland, and the mutual respect and love for each other shone through.

She'd been surreptitiously observing Fin for most of

the evening but she needed to stop as he'd caught her a few times. It was as if she had no control over her own eyes, and she could feel perspiration prickling the nape of her neck as she watched him.

He has a lovely mouth.

And such a seductive voice.

"Coffee anyone?" Elsa asked from the doorway, "I've put it in the lounge if you want to come through."

They all stood up from the table and followed her. The lounge was so inviting with the stunning décor and classic furniture. Nick must have stoked up the fire as the flames were bellowing up the chimney. Kathryn sat on the sofa next to Elsa and patted her leg, "It's been a lovely evening, thank you."

"My pleasure. I love having people round, you know that."

"Yes, and you've done us all proud tonight."

Elsa handed the coffees round and then produced a small dish of Ferrero Rocher chocolates. "Fin, just so you know, you need to grab one of these quickly if you want one, because someone in this room, not mentioning any names but follow my eyes, will eat them all if we aren't careful."

Kathryn raised her hand, "That would be me. I'm not sure about them all though," she laughed turning to Fin, "but I am quite partial to the odd one."

Nick selected one, "It's funny how Elsa buys these when Kathryn's here, yet all she gets for me is Cadbury's Dairy Milk."

Elsa tapped him playfully with the back of her hand, "They're good enough for you the way you eat chocolate," she reached forward and took one from the dish, "these are wasted on you, whereas my dear friend here loves to savour the taste. That's why I buy them."

Kathryn smiled affectionately at Elsa. Every birthday, Easter and Christmas, Elsa would give her a beautifully wrapped box of them, and she loved her for it.

The conversation continued to flow comfortably between them all and nothing seemed amiss. But something was. Kathryn couldn't put her finger on what was wrong, and was unable to acknowledge it until much later that something actually was. Sadly that was the last normal evening they would all have. None of them had any inkling of what the following week would bring, and how all of their lives were going to change irreversibly.

8

Each week, Kathryn allocated herself some office time which allowed her to do the duty rota, answer emails and order theatre supplies. Halfway through her emails, her phone pinged and she was surprised to see it was a text from Elsa's husband, Nick.

`Can u ring me urgently`

It was unusual for Nick to text her and with no kiss at the end, her stomach plummeted. Something was wrong. She quickly pressed call back and he picked up straight away.

"Hi Nick, it's Kathryn." Identifying herself was pretty stupid considering her name would come up as the caller, "Is everything alright?"

"Kathryn, thank goodness. I'm here at the hospital with Elsa. You know those headaches she's been getting, well ..." he faltered.

"What is it, Nick ... tell me?"

"They've done a scan and it's ... it's ... the cancer again, it's back. A tumour or something, I forget what they said it's called, it's in her brain."

"Oh my God. Where's Elsa now?"

"Gone to have some bloods taken. She's not good, Kathryn ... neither of us are."

"No, of course you're not, how could you be with such a shock."

"I've been dismissive of her headaches," he paused, "Bloody hell, I only came with her today as I'm on a week's leave."

"Well it's a good job you are there. I'm going to come over this afternoon as soon as the theatre list is finished, I'll come straight to the house."

"Would you? I really don't know how to cope with all of this. I don't know what to say to her."

"Who would? Look, there's tons they can do these days Nick. I know you can't think straight right now, but there are loads of treatments available." She went through them quickly in her mind, surgery, chemotherapy, radiotherapy. One of them would help Elsa, she was sure of it.

"What about Fin, have you told him?" she asked.

"No not yet, I've only texted you as I know how close you are to Elsa."

That was an understatement. Elsa was like a much loved sister to her. She rubbed her forehead, the news was devastating.

"Okay. I'm at work now so I could pop to his office," she thought for a moment and added, "but do you think Elsa will want to tell him herself?"

Nick was silent for a second obviously trying to weigh up his answer. "Probably yes. I don't know what to do for the best really."

The thought of going and seeing Fin Dey and giving him this news was not something she particularly wanted to do, she hardly knew him.

"Perhaps it's best to get her home after the tests," and then trying to inject a bit of lightness, she added, "you know Elsa, she'll soon be giving out her orders, she'll want to speak to him herself I'm sure of it."

"Okay whatever you say. We'll wait for you at home then."

"Text me when you're home and I'll leave work and come straight there."

"Thanks Kathryn, I really don't know how I'd manage without you."

She let out a deep sigh, "You won't have to, you know that. I'll see you soon, oh and Nick, I know it's hard, but try and keep as positive as you can, won't you?"

"I'll try, he said in a deflated voice, "see you soon."

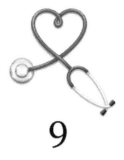

9

Kathryn couldn't concentrate. The second time she made a mistake during the hip replacement, Mr Sutcliffe became irritated.

"What's the matter with you today, you're all fingers and thumbs?"

"I am sorry, I'm just having a bad day."

"Well don't think you've got the monopoly on that. My wife's called to say she's managed to prang the bloody car."

"Oh dear, is she all right?"

"Well there's no side effect from the bump if that's what you're asking, but I can't guarantee she will be in one piece when I get home."

His sarcasm lightened the moment and the staff around the theatre table sniggered at his joke. At the end of the case, she asked Erin to scrub for the minor cases so she could get to Elsa and Nick as they'd be home from the hospital by now.

She left theatre and headed round to the Matron's office to clear it that she could leave work early. Fin Dey's office was adjacent to Helen's, and she felt a slight pang as she saw through the small glass window that he was there with his eyes fixed on his computer screen. She hesitated, should she tell him?

Helen interrupted her thoughts as her office door opened.

"Hi Kathryn, are you looking for me?"

"Yes I am. I wanted to let you know that I've got a bit

of a family emergency and I need to leave early if that's okay with you? Theatre's covered staff-wise."

"Of course it is. Is everything okay?"

"Yes fine, I just need to get home." Helen was astute enough to realise that she wasn't going to confide in her what the emergency was as she put her hand on her arm, "Right, you do that then. Are we alright for staff if you can't get in tomorrow?"

Typical Matron thinking of hospital business.

Who cares, my friend is ill and needs me.

"Oh, I'll be in, don't worry. Thanks Helen," she nodded, "I'll see you tomorrow." Conscious they were adjacent to Fin's office and if he came out, she'd have had a real dilemma, she quickly made her way back to theatres. Keeping things from him was okay if she didn't see him, but face to face, she'd have felt obliged to say something, it was his sister after all.

The traffic was busy which was frustrating. A wave of nausea reared up from the pit of her stomach so she opened the window for some fresh air. She desperately wanted to get to her friend to offer some comfort, but at the same time, she was dreading it.

Three years ago Elsa had gone through the terrible ordeal of breast cancer followed by weeks of gruelling chemotherapy. The beautiful vivacious Elsa had to succumb to the side effects of losing her eyebrows and eyelashes, and that gorgeous thick wavy hair that still to this day, Elsa said never grew back quite the same, but always looked beautiful to her. Not that Elsa could be anything but beautiful; she'd modelled in her youth so not only looked gorgeous, her overall deportment was one of elegance.

Nick met her at the door, "Thank goodness you're here, come in." He helped her take off her coat, "Just to warn you, she's not good. Reckons she's not having any treatment this time," his voice was jerky, "says she's going to die with dignity," he broke into a sob, "speak to her would you, she has to have treatment."

Kathryn gave him a hug, "Look, it's been a massive

shock. Give her time, and she will do, I'm sure of it. Let me go through and see her."

With a heavy heart, she made her way through to the conservatory. Elsa jumped up as soon as she saw her, "Oh Kathryn, thank you so much for coming," as if she was greeting a dinner guest. They hugged each other tightly, neither wanting to break free. She inhaled Elsa's unique smell, it was always the same. She never deviated from her familiar perfume.

Eventually it was Elsa that pulled away and guided Kathryn towards the sofa, "Is Nick making us some tea?"

"Maybe. Shall I go and give him a nudge?"

"No, I'm sure he will be."

Kathryn looked deep into her friend's stormy eyes, "I'm so sorry, Elsa. I can't believe the cancer's back after all this time."

"I can't either," Elsa shook her head, "I don't feel ill or anything, in fact I feel quite well apart from the headaches."

Kathryn took her hand, "And what's all this about you not having any treatment? I know you're shocked and upset, but you have to, you know you do ..."

Elsa interrupted, "I'm not having any, and that's definite. I've already been there with the wretched chemo which made me sick beyond belief, and then I lost all my hair; trust me, I am not going there again."

"Well I think Fin will have something to say about that." She thought about him sat at his desk, totally oblivious while this particular volcano was erupting, "Have you spoken to him yet?"

"No, I'm going to tell him when he's home tonight." Anxiety and apprehension glistened in her eyes, "I'm so worried about it though, he's been through more than enough since the accident, I'm dreading telling him."

Kathryn wrapped her arms around her dear friend again. It was so typical of her to be worried about how her brother would react. Her throat tightened as she fumbled to find the right words to say, but fortunately, she got a reprieve as Nick came into the room carrying a tray of tea. She pulled away from Elsa and watched as he placed the tray on the coffee table.

"Have you been able to talk some sense into her yet?" he asked, his face full of anxiety as he passed her a cup.

"Not yet no, but I'm working on it."

Nick sat on the huge sofa with them and took Elsa's hand, "Listen to Kathryn, Elsa, you must have the treatment ..." his speech faltered, clearly he was thinking of the consequences if she didn't.

Elsa shook her head, "You must both listen to me ... I'm not going to change my mind," she breathed in deeply, "I am not, and I repeat, *not* going to have any interventions. I don't know how long I've got left, but whatever time I have, is going to be spent with the people I love, and not stuck in a hospital being prodded and poked about." She sighed, "You have to both respect my wishes. I know the consequences, and while that fills me with utter despair, the thought of being pushed into something that I don't want, hurts me even more." Tears glistened in her beautiful brown eyes and Kathryn took her hand, stifling her own urge to cry. A life without Elsa would be intolerable.

"Don't get upset," she squeezed her hand tightly, "Of course we're going to support you, that goes without saying. We love you. It's just that we can't bear the thought of anything happening to you."

Elsa nodded and lowered her voice, "I know that. But it's my life, and for however long I've got left, I'm going to live it how I want to."

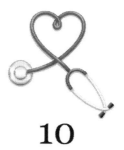

10

Kathryn could barely concentrate on the drive home. The only thing she could think about was Elsa. How could life be so cruel, hadn't she been through enough last time?

She pulled onto the drive and turned off the engine. As she sat staring at the garage door, a movement in the bay window caught her eye and she turned towards it. Philip was watching her. She'd completely forgotten he was working from home that afternoon. He moved away and she knew he'd be unlocking the front door to let her in.

She stepped inside the porch and kept her feet on the doormat while she removed her shoes. Philip's eyes watched her feet, checking that she didn't accidentally step on the laminate floor, as if she would. She'd been married to him long enough by now to know not to stand on any floor in the house in shoes, it just wasn't allowed.

"Hello sweetie," he kissed her cheek as she walked into the hall, "you're home early. I'll get you some tea."

"No tea for me thanks, I'm all tea-ed out to be honest." Still stood in the hallway, she looked into his eyes and tried to speak, but the words wouldn't come out. The tears she'd been holding back, started to flow down her cheeks and Philip quickly wrapped her in his arms, "What is it? What's wrong?" He held her tightly, kissing and stroking her hair while she told him.

"Bloody hell, that's terrible. No wonder you're upset. You say that you can't persuade her to have any treatment?"

"No she's adamant. I'm hoping Fin will be able to talk some sense into her, she's seeing him tonight to tell him."

"Well I think you'd better leave it to him then, he's medical so will be better at dealing with it than you."

What like I'm not medical?

Sometimes you say the most ridiculous things.

"You've done all you can I'm sure. Come into the lounge and get warm, you're freezing. Do you want something to eat?"

"I'm not sure I could get that much down to be honest."

"You need something, you've had a shock. I'll do you a slice of toast to nibble on. You sit there, and I'll run you a nice warm bath. I'll put the toast on when you shout that you're getting dried."

She warmed her hands against the fire, contemplating life without her beloved Elsa. It was unthinkable anything happening to her, she loved her so much. And poor Fin, what a bombshell for him after all he's been through.

You have to talk some sense into her, Fin.

She must have treatment.

Philip interrupted her dismal thoughts telling her the bath was ready. She couldn't really be bothered, but he was being kind, and it wouldn't take long. It wasn't worth saying no anyway; she hardly remembered a night in their marriage, when they didn't have a bath.

The warm soak did help and she felt better afterwards sitting at the kitchen table eating hot toast covered in Benecol. No butter in their house, only cholesterol busting margarine. She'd have preferred to have taken the tea and toast into the lounge and eaten in front of the fire, but food in the lounge had always been frowned upon by Philip. She resisted the temptation to text Elsa to see what Fin had said, as it didn't seem right to be discussing something so serious in a text. Instead she sat in front of the television with her eyes fixed on the screen, but her mind focussing on the future. The outlook was so terribly bleak without Elsa.

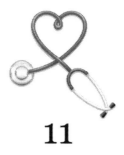

11

Amy popped her head around the prep room door.

"Ah, there you are Kathryn. Mr Dey has rung and asked if you could pop round to his office when you're free."

"Thanks, Amy, I'll be there in five minutes."

Blast, she didn't want to see him. She'd had a dreadful night and had intended to immerse herself in work today. The last thing she wanted was to spend any time with him discussing his sister. But he was the boss so she couldn't really ignore him.

After sorting out the work board, she headed for his office. Through his office window she could see him sat at his desk as she knocked. He stood up and beckoned her in.

"Hi," she smiled. It was stupid to feel awkward around him, but she did. It must only have been because of Elsa, what else could it be?

God, he looks hot in a morning.

Is that my tummy doing a flip?

"Hello Kathryn, thank you for coming round, please sit down." With an inclination of his head toward the coffee machine, he asked, "Can I get you a drink?"

"No thank you, I'm okay, but please get yours."

"I'm fine," he grimaced, "I've drunk far too much this morning anyway."

He sat down. Although she didn't know him that well, his appearance indicated that he'd had a bad night also. Immaculately dressed, he had dark circles forming below his eyes as if he hadn't slept very well. A bit like her, she guessed.

"She's told you then?" she asked.

"Yes, she's told me." His pained expression was desperately sad, "And devastated as I am about it all, I can't get over the fact she won't have any intervention," he sighed deeply, "I've tried to persuade her, but she's having none of it."

"Me too. I'm hoping she'll change her mind when she gets over the shock," she looked hopefully at him, "Do you think there's any chance of that?"

He shook his head, "No, I'm afraid I don't. It's not her usual stubbornness either, she's just determined to do things her own way. You know Elsa ..." He didn't finish the sentence.

Kathryn hesitated. She didn't know him that well so was unsure if it was appropriate to speak her mind.

"What is it?" he asked, his eyes questioning.

She took a deep breath in, "Can I be frank?"

"Yes, please do."

"I haven't slept much and I'm sure you haven't either," his gentle nod confirmed her assumption. "I've been going over it all in my mind and keep coming up with the same thing. Maybe it's her right not to have anything done, and perhaps we should support that?" She paused giving him a chance to answer, but he didn't, so she carried on, "I'm devastated at the thought of losing her. Selfishly, I want her to have treatment, but there is part of me, which thinking back to how difficult she found the whole thing last time, supports her decision." She shrugged, "Is that so wrong?"

"No of course it isn't," he agreed, "I didn't actually see her for a few months following the surgery and chemotherapy as I was on a secondment in Texas, but she visited us once she'd completed it all. And you know Elsa, apart from the colourful scarves she wore to hide her alopecia, you would have no idea she'd been through any of that trauma."

"That's her, a real trouper." They both smiled and their eyes locked for a brief second, both immersed in their own thoughts.

He raised an eyebrow, "I hear what you're saying about supporting her decision making, but as a physician, my training and ethos is to prolong life. And as her brother," he paused clearly struggling as reality dug in, "I can't bear the thought of her dying."

"I know," she agreed, "and it's hard to remain impartial when it's so close to home."

He looked so forlorn. An overwhelming urge to comfort him crept up unexpectedly. He needed a hug, someone to put their arms around him.

And kiss the tension away.

Crikey! Where on earth did that come from?

Relief flooded through her when he changed the subject, "Anyway, shall we get back to work issues? It might take our minds off things."

As if.

But worth a try.

Fin changed the tone of his voice, "This coming Friday is the disciplinary hearing of the theatre technician Gary Hicks. I've been looking through the investigation, which makes interesting reading."

"It certainly is a tricky one," she agreed, "Did you read the recommendations at the end of the report?"

"Yes I did, and I agree totally with them. We will have to dismiss him, especially as this is the third time he's messed up. How long has he been on suspension for?"

"Over three months. To be honest, it's been a relief not having him around, he really is a liability."

"Yes, I'm sure. The problem is Matron has had to go to Bournemouth as her mother has had a fall so won't be able to support me at the hearing. Shall I cancel it, or are you able to step into her shoes?"

She hesitated, and as if he sensed her uncertainty, he continued, "I do need a member of staff with me that has worked with him, otherwise his union rep might kick off. You know the sort of thing, biased without knowing him and how he works."

She didn't really want to get involved. Gary Hicks was a nasty piece of work, but she hated the fact he was suspended and still receiving full pay. Once he was dismissed, they could advertise his job which the theatre staff would welcome.

"That's fine," she nodded, "I'll sit in with you. It won't be easy though, he won't accept any responsibility for his actions, and be warned, he will say we are biased because he's gay, he always pulls that card."

"Thanks for the warning; I'll bear that in mind. Shall we meet an hour beforehand to go through his history so that I'm clear as to exactly what he's been up to? I've read his p file of course, but it would be helpful to put some meat on the bone."

"Okay, I'm not sure an hour will be enough though, we could do with a day to go through it all," she smiled.

His eyes looked directly into hers, making her feel oddly hot.

"We could meet earlier then, I've been told that the Rushley Inn does a hearty breakfast," he paused, waiting for her response.

He wasn't wrong about that. The restaurant situated round the corner from St Anne's did indeed do wonderful food, the question was, should she be eating breakfast with him? Philip would go absolutely mad.

He must have sensed her reluctance, "Or we could meet here in my office first thing, if that's more comfortable for you?"

Why was she being so silly, it was a breakfast meeting Fin was inviting her to, nothing else? "No, the Rushley's fine, and you're right, they do serve a really nice breakfast."

"Great, shall we say nine then? That should give us plenty of time I would have thought."

"Okay." She got to her feet, "Now if you'll excuse me, I better get back to theatre."

He followed her towards the door and opened it for her, "I'll see you on Friday then at nine." He smiled and her heart gave a little kick. Why did he make her feel this way? There was something about him that reached deep within her which was so wrong considering she was married. As she exited his office she chastised herself for behaving like a teenage girl with a crush. It was totally inappropriate.

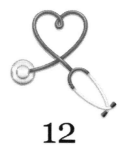

12

Kathryn's tummy was in knots by the time Friday morning arrived. It wasn't so much the disciplinary that she was going to do with Fin, it was more the breakfast meeting with him and the fact she hadn't told Philip.

There'd been plenty of opportunities during the week when she could have said something, but it had been so much easier not to. Philip had this absurd idea that everyone found her attractive, which was completely ridiculous.

"What time are you back from work today?" he asked in between spoonful's of his healthy all-bran.

"I'm finishing at lunchtime as there's no theatre lists this afternoon. I thought I might pop and see Elsa after work though." Knowing exactly what he was going to say next, she quickly added, "Just for an hour, I'll be back by the time you get home."

He put his spoon in his empty bowl, "Don't you think you should give them a bit of space? She's got her brother there now, and Nick. Perhaps it's best to leave them on their own for a while to come to terms with what's happening?"

How did I know you'd say that?

Typical, jealous of anyone taking up my time.

"It's more for me really, I want to see how she is."

"I know that, darling, it's just that you've got a lot on with your job," his voice softened, "and looking after me. I don't want it to be too much for you, that's all."

54

"How can seeing my friend be too much? I want to see her," tears were beginning to threaten, "the way things are going, I won't be seeing her much longer anyway."

Philip was always uneasy with any emotional outburst and patted her hand, "Don't get upset, love, you do what you have to do." He stood and took his breakfast bowl to the sink and began running the water.

"Oh for goodness' sake, why you insist on washing pots when we've got a perfectly good dishwasher I do not know."

"You do know. I don't want any dirty pots lined up and smelling. I'd sooner give them a quick wash and then they're done."

She stood up and opened the dishwasher to put her cereal bowl inside, which was petty as she knew he'd lift it out and wash it anyway. He did.

His next question irritated her, "Is it the time of the month, is that why you're tetchy?"

"No it bloody isn't," she snapped, "I've got a lot on at work today and my best friend has a death sentence hanging over her, so if I am a little *tetchy* today, can you cut me a bit of slack, do you think?" She glared at him and he raised his hands in surrender, "Okay, okay, I get it. I won't say any more."

"Good, please don't." She left the kitchen to go to the bathroom to clean her teeth, but the toothbrush wasn't there. Philip was still in the kitchen, disinfecting the table they'd eaten breakfast off, which was completely unnecessary as neither of them had spilled a drop, and the outsize dining mats would have caught any crumbs.

She saw the electric toothbrush plugged in a socket, and grabbed it, irritated that it was on charge yet again.

"You should have shouted, I'd have brought it to you," he smiled, "we need to charge it every day now as I read in the Mail on that health page that if it's not fully charged then it won't remove all of the plaque from your teeth."

Right, and we wouldn't want that, would we.
All that nasty plaque build-up.

She wondered into her bedroom and stared at her

reflection in the full-length mirror, pleased with how she looked. The stylish dress and short jacket was smart and business-like. She selected a pair of plain navy shoes to match the outfit, but carried them into the hall to put them on. It was easier than having a lecture.

Anything could be on the soles,
And might contaminate the whole house.

Philip whistled, "Good God, that's a bit over the top for work isn't it?"

Guilt flooded through her for not mentioning the breakfast meeting and she brushed some pretend fluff off the sleeve of her jacket.

It's not as if I'm telling any lies.
Or is an omission just as bad?

"I'm doing a disciplinary hearing so I can hardly turn up in jeans," she defended.

"You don't usually get involved in that sort of thing?" he frowned.

"I know. Helen, the Matron is off and Fin has asked me to sit in on it. With him not knowing Gary, and the fact that the union rep could challenge aspects of his work, Fin wanted someone to support him who had worked with Gary and knew his history."

She stood in front of the hall mirror putting the finishing touches to her lip gloss and he came and stood behind her. He enveloped her in his arms and nuzzled her neck, "Well I think you look far too attractive for that place," he raised his eyes suggestively, "pity we both have to work today."

She smiled back at him feeling remorseful for snapping at him earlier, "You're only saying that because you're safe," she laughed and broke away from his arms. He was all talk. They'd only recently made love so she knew that wouldn't be happening again for at least another week, and only then if she initiated it.

He sat down to tie his shoelaces, always the same way, the left first and then the right.

Don't forget the chair,
It might have moved.

He stood and adjusted the chair, "Right, you have a good day and watch the roads," he kissed her gently.

"You too," she said, "I'll see you around six."
"Is it salmon for tea?" he asked.
No, it's a cheeseburger with fried onions,
And loads of greasy chips.
"Yes, that's what I'd planned."
"Great, I'll look forward to that, then."

She waved goodbye to him from the bay window. He invariably left before her each morning as he had a long drive to the city, whereas her drive to work was relatively short.

As he reversed the car out of the drive, she waved again. For a second, an image of Fin behind the wheel flashed before her eyes with him waving back at her with that gorgeous smile of his. What would it be like seeing him off in a morning? Maybe after a night of great sex? A familiar ache throbbed between her legs.

For years she hadn't considered herself much of a goer on the sexual front. Philip could make her climax, but that was more robotic. He rubbed her clit, quite clumsily sometimes until she orgasmed. But of late, she had taken to using a spare head from her electric toothbrush and giving herself an orgasm. She hadn't ever thought of anything like that before and only ever used her fingers, but she read an article at the GP surgery in a Cosmopolitan magazine discussing orgasms from vibrators and electric toothbrushes.

She thought back to that very first time she'd used the toothbrush on herself and it had felt like her head was coming off. Her imagination went into overdrive about what an actual vibrator must have felt like, but that was something she could never have. Philip would think it was a reflection on his lovemaking.

Had she got time? She glanced at the clock in the hall. Yes, plenty. Collecting her spare toothbrush head, she went into the bathroom and eased her dress up over her hips so she didn't crease it. She lowered her panties and attached the head to the electronic handle and positioned the toothbrush onto her clit. She flicked the switch and closed her eyes.

Thank you, Philip for leaving it powered up.
The vibrations were particularly vigorous.

The image she conjured up was of a mouth and tongue delivering the sensations. The bristles scratched, but she didn't care. All she imagined was a head between her legs with hot breath on her pussy, licking and sucking her. She pressed down harder and squeezed her legs together which heightened the ecstasy. The buzzing echoed around the tiled bathroom, and she moved the toothbrush in frantic circles desperate for the release it would give her. The head of the toothbrush was giving such delicious pleasure she was forced to grab the sink for support. An eruption surged from deep within and a massive explosion burst inside her breasts and gushed down her entire body. As the convulsions tore through her, she saw a face, but it wasn't Philip's ... it was Fin.

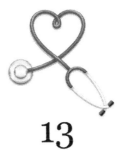

13

Kathryn walked into the Rushley Inn and saw him immediately. Fin Dey was one of those men that stood out.

God, he looks so handsome.

My tummy's in a knot.

He was watching the door as she entered and came forward to greet her, "Good morning, come and sit down. I've taken the liberty of ordering some fruit juice, but I wasn't sure if you drank tea or coffee?"

"Either, but tea would be nice, thank you."

She sat down and he handed her a menu, "Have a look and see what you fancy, then we can order and chat."

They gave their orders to the waiter, and once he'd gone, she felt slightly awkward, as if she was out on some sort of secret date.

I really wish I'd told Philip,

This doesn't feel right at all.

Fin spoke, interrupting her thoughts, "I've read everything about Gary Hicks and I think we are right to get rid of him once and for all. He certainly seems a bit of a loose cannon."

"Oh, he's definitely that, and a whole lot more. I'll be glad when he's no longer associated with us. Currently he's still on full pay which irritates the theatre staff, and me too if I'm honest."

"Yes I'm sure, but we'll dismiss him today with a month's pay and then he won't get another penny." Fin frowned, "What on earth was he doing taking a photograph of a patient on his mobile phone?"

"I really don't know; it's staggering isn't it?"

"I'm guessing he was hoping to sell the photo on?"

"Yes, I think so. He probably thought he'd make a packet from it. She is a well-known singer after all."

"Bloody fool," he cursed, "Sorry, but surely he realised by taking a photograph of a patient, he'd end up losing his job?"

"You would think so, yes. Maybe he thought he'd get so much money for selling it that he didn't care. He still denies it was him anyway so he'll sue you for unfair dismissal, and he's one of those people that spend their whole life challenging. You should hear the tales he comes out with. He makes a healthy living from complaining," she warned.

"Well, don't worry about that anymore. I've read everything about him so I intend to throw the book at him today. If he wants to take further action, then that's his prerogative, but any legal bigwig worth their salt will tell him to cut his losses, I'm sure."

"Are you going to write to the HPC and have him stripped of his ODP qualification?"

"Probably not," he shrugged, "disgusted as I am about what he's done, I feel the sacking is sufficient; I wouldn't be comfortable depriving him of ever working again. He's young, so has a lot of working years ahead of him. Hopefully he'll learn from this." He sipped his juice, "What do you think? Tell me if you feel I'm being a soft touch?

No, I don't think you're soft.

I think you're lovely.

"I think that is very gracious of you considering what he's done. He's a very lucky man."

"Would you have him stripped of his qualification?"

"No. I wouldn't want that on my conscience however much I dislike him."

"I'm pleased we agree on that then. Clearly we are likeminded," he raised his eyebrows and smiled which caused her heart to race, and the heat spread between her legs.

God, he is so gorgeous.
I wonder what he'd be like making love?
She saw his face in her mind's eye again, down there, licking and sucking, and the heat spread to her cheeks. Thankfully their food arrived and proved a timely distraction. She'd only ordered a bagel and cream cheese as she'd already eaten some cereal with Philip so she didn't arouse his suspicion. As she took a bite, she inwardly chastised herself knowing she should have said something about meeting Fin.

He paused from eating to sip his tea, "Tell me a bit more about yourself, how long have you and Philip been married?"

"Seven years ... we're very happy."
Why on earth had she added that?
When the poor man had lost his wife.
She quickly apologised, "I'm sorry ..."

"Don't be, please. Just because I'm solemn and grieving, doesn't mean everyone else isn't entitled to a happy life. I'm getting there. I think the change of lifestyle in the UK has been exactly what I needed." He smiled, "Anyway, Elsa says you're hoping to have a family in the future? That's certainly something to look forward to."

"Yes we are," her stomach churned as was usual at the mention of children, but then she remembered his loss, "I'm sorry, it must be so hard for you."

"It is, yes, but I had Christiaan for eleven years and he was an absolute joy which you'll find out when you have your own. Children enhance your life incredibly. You actually love them more than you love yourself." His face was animated when he talked about his son.

He loves children.
What a lovely man.

His face clouded over, "I can't ever replace Christiaan, but if some kind girl wants to take me on, there might be other children one day, who knows what the future holds for us all. I don't particularly want to go through the rest of my life childless." He paused for a moment, as if considering whether to say something else.

You'd make beautiful children.
Especially if they looked like you.

He rolled his eyes cheekily, "There might be the question of a little operation if I was to want any more though."

Oh no, not a vasectomy.

What's that got to do with me anyway?

The sadness was back in his eyes, "But for the moment, I need to try and do something with my very stubborn sister."

"Yes, I'm so sorry about Elsa ... sorry for you, and selfishly sorry for myself." Her voice faltered, "I can't bear the thought of ..." she couldn't finish the sentence.

"Me too, and I'm still working on her having some treatment, but I'm not having much luck. All she's focussing on at the moment is the housewarming party which she's insisting that I have."

She smiled, "That's so her, isn't it?"

"Yes, it is," he nodded, "but what worries me is she'll invite a host of single women and try and coax me into a relationship with some poor soul who'd get a shock at being landed with me."

Who on earth could be shocked with landing you?

Shocked by their good fortune, maybe.

A sharp stabbing pain cut deeply in her chest, which was silly really. It was only to be expected that a single man as good-looking as he was would eventually form a relationship.

He's so very appealing.

It won't be long before he's snapped up.

"Anyway, you're not getting away that easily. Elsa tells me she's roping you in to help with the party also."

"Oh is she now," she said, "I'm not sure if I'll be any good, I'm hardly the hostess with the mostest."

He grinned, "Don't you worry about that, Elsa is enough of a social butterfly for both of us put together." They laughed intimately, and she knew his thoughts would reflect her own. How could they possibly live without dear Elsa?

14

Fin concluded on the disciplinary, "Following a thorough investigation in line with St Anne's employment policy, the Investigating Officer has concluded that you are indeed guilty of gross misconduct, and as of today Mr Hicks your employment is terminated with this organisation."

"I-didn't-do-it, I keep telling you. This is all shit."

"That's enough, Mr Hicks," Fin warned.

"You'll wish you'd listened to me," Gary threatened.

Fin didn't bat an eyelid, and in an authoritative voice answered, "I think we're all done here now."

"We are nowhere near done yet," Gary spat. His eyes darkened with fury, "You wait and see." He turned to his union rep, "I want the stuff from my locker back."

"We'll empty your locker and forward your belongings on to you," Fin answered.

"I want to get them now," he snapped and turned to Kathryn, "Can I come to theatre with you and get them?"

"No you can't," Fin said firmly and stood up. "As I said, your possessions will be forwarded to you. Now, thank you for attending today. I will follow this meeting up with a formal letter to you outlining our discussions." He nodded to the union representative, "Thank you, Mr Summers."

Mr Summers gathered up his papers and placed them in his briefcase. Gary's face was etched with disgust as he sneered at her, "To think, I used to like you," his stare was menacing, "but now I see what you're really like. Don't think for a minute, that they're your friends in theatre because they aren't. You'll be sorry for this ..."

"That's enough," Fin interjected, "This meeting is over, please leave now." Fin walked round to the office door and held it open. Gary stood up and kicked his chair so hard it tipped over. He walked towards the door and as he exited, stuck his middle finger up at Fin, "Fuck you!"

Unperturbed, Mr Summers nodded to them both and followed him out.

Fin closed the door and came back to his seat, "He's a nasty piece of work, isn't he?" His eyes were sympathetic and she was totally surprised when he reached forward and clasped her hand, "Are you okay?"

She wasn't okay, she was upset from the outburst, but him holding her hand really had her nerves on edge.

You really shouldn't do that.

But please don't move it away.

The look in Gary's eyes had unsettled her as she hated confrontation of any sort, yet it was Fin's touch that caused her the most turmoil.

"I'm fine, just a bit shaky."

His gorgeous brown eyes looked concerned, and he squeezed her hand,

"Why don't you go straight home?"

She shook her head, "There's no need for that. Don't worry, I'll be fine." He let go of her hand and she immediately missed the warmth.

"Did you mean what you said about emptying his locker?"

"Yes. Can one of the lads in theatre to do that and I'll get the porter to drop his personal items off at his house?"

"Yes of course." She stood up, "I don't think I'm cut out for all this aggro."

"No, I can see that," he smiled sympathetically, "thank you anyway for your support. I'll make sure Helen is around for any other disciplinary meetings in future."

"Oh, I don't think there'll be any more. This place is very close-knit, and everyone works together. Gary," she paused, "he's never really fitted in."

"Did you interview him and take him on?"

"No, it was Alison the theatre manager."

He nodded, "Right, well don't worry about it anymore, it's over now. Are you sure you're going to be okay?" It was there again, whenever their eyes met, she felt a warmth flood her body. Did he feel it too?

I wonder what it would feel like to kiss him.

And have those huge arms wrap around me.

"I'm fine honestly. She headed for the door, needing to get out quickly before she had any more thoughts about kissing him, "I'll see you later." What the hell was she doing fantasising about him? She was being ridiculous.

The drive home seemed to take forever. There was no point in calling at Elsa's as she hadn't responded to her text so clearly wasn't home. Her thoughts drifted again towards Fin which seemed to happen more frequently as each day passed. She'd enjoyed having breakfast with him and remembered the warmth she experienced when he'd clasped her hand and how bereft she'd felt when he pulled it away. Although she knew it was totally inappropriate, she had to admit she was very attracted to him.

She chastised herself as she thought about Philip who loved her so much. She'd been only sixteen when she met him, and he'd been nineteen. There was no doubt they would marry, it was more a question of when, really. He'd gone to university and she'd done her nurse training, and then out of the blue her mother died. It was such a low point in her happy life and Philip had wanted them to marry so that he could look after her.

Their marriage was strong, and it was successful because of her allowing him to dominate. It just happened somehow, she was busy grieving for her mother and let Philip more or less take over. Before she knew it, he'd purchased their house, chosen the furniture, and here she was the suburban housewife. The only thing they lacked was a baby to make their lives complete.

She loved her job, though, working in the theatres at St Anne's, and liked to think she was good at it. Her hard work had been recognised when she was appointed acting theatre manager while the current manager, Alison was on long-term sick leave. Okay, so it wasn't the most high-tech hospital in the world, but she enjoyed it, and had great staff working for her.

She exited the car and locked it. As soon as she entered the front door, she was startled to see Philip in the hallway. Why had he let her use her key and not opened the front door for her like he usually did? A glance at his face told her something was wrong. He looked furious.

"Hi," she said, "you're home early, are you okay?"

"No I'm not bloody okay. I want to know what's going on between you and Elsa's brother?"

"What?" she frowned, "what are you taking about?"

"Finley fucking Dey, that's what I'm talking about. You've been out with him. I know all about it so don't bother denying it."

"What do you mean *I've been out with him*?"

"Out," he barked, "the two of you, out together, on your own. Don't insult me by playing the innocent."

She narrowed her eyes, "Who told you this?"

"Never mind who told me, I want to know what the fuck's going on?"

"Nothing's *going on*. It was a business meeting, that's all. I can't understand why you would think it was anything else." Although there was no need to explain, she found herself doing so anyway, "It isn't anything to worry about."

"Let me be the judge of that," Philip spat, "why didn't you meet at work for this so-called business meeting?"

How could she answer that? Anything she said sounded feeble.

"Look, do you think I can actually get into the house please before we discuss this any further?" She walked into the kitchen, and took a glass out of the cupboard and filled it with tap water. She took a large gulp and then breathed in deeply, "I don't know what you think is going on here," a sudden thought struck her, "how did you know by the way ... about the meeting?" she quickly added.

Philip picked up an envelope from the table, and thrust it at her. Puzzled, she opened it, and was shocked to see a photograph of her with Fin at the Rushley Inn that morning. She was smiling at something Fin had said to her, and the photograph was damming. They looked like a couple dining intimately together.

"This isn't what it looks like. We had a breakfast meeting to discuss the disciplinary this morning, for Gary Hicks. You remember, he took the photo of Phoenix ..."

"I don't give a shit about Gary fucking Hicks," he snapped, "I want to know why my wife is all dolled up for work, having a so-called *breakfast meeting* with her new boss, and doesn't think to tell her husband about it. What exactly do you think *it looks like*?"

"It was a meeting, for Christ's sake, and nothing more than that. Who would take a photograph of something so innocent? I don't understand."

"No, I don't either, but I'm telling you, Kathryn, I'm not putting up with this. Are you having some sort of affair with him? For God's sake tell me, I want to know, now!"

"Of course I'm not having an affair," she said, "why would you even think that? You know me better than anyone. I would never cheat on you, you know that."

"Then why meet him in a pub? Why not at work?"

"Simply because Gary's file was huge and Fin wanted my advice on it without work distractions."

He shook his head, "If it was all so bloody innocent, why didn't you say you were meeting him this morning?"

He had a point.

It was deceptive of her.

She sighed, "Because I knew how you'd react." She lowered her voice, "I'm sorry. I should have said something, but for God's sake, Philip, I am not having an affair. By suggesting it, you aren't only discrediting me, but Fin also. He's lost his wife and son, so he's hardly going to be chasing me, is he?"

She could see the cogs in Philip's brain going round, and at least some of the tension had left his face. She put her arms around his neck, "You know you mean the world to me," she kissed him and he didn't resist, "I would never do anything to hurt you, surely you know that?"

Although he didn't speak, he reached for her and kissed her with a possessiveness which was unusual for him. She found it quite a turn on and matched the pressure of his lips with her own, but he pulled away, "I can't bear the thought of you with anyone else. You're mine, and I love you so much."

They kissed again and the forcefulness of his lips caused an ache in her tummy. Keen for things to progress, she pushed herself against him and tightened her hold around his neck, eager for him to rip off her clothes. Just once for him to become so carried away that he couldn't wait. But that wasn't Philip. She realised long ago that sex anywhere else in the house but the bedroom wasn't doable for him.

He pulled away, "You're so beautiful, you know. I can understand another man wanting you."

She stroked the side of his face with the back of her hand and hoped her eyes would reflect how much she loved him. It was awful to see him so upset and she hated herself for causing his pain.

"No one else wants me," she reassured, "and there wouldn't be any point as I'm already spoken for."

"God, Kathryn, I've been frantic." He shook his head, "I couldn't bear to lose you."

She moved in for another kiss, but he wrapped his arms around her. She rested her head on his shoulder and hugged him tightly, hoping to give him the assurance that he needed.

"You won't lose me, silly. I love you too much."

"Thank goodness for that," he kissed her head and then almost as if the last few minutes hadn't happened, he totally surprised her by asking, "Do you want to get a bath now or after dinner?"

"A bath," she pulled away and widened her eyes, "I thought maybe you might fancy a bit more than a bath."

He looked regretful, "Maybe later. I'm so uptight about it all, it's really shaken me." He picked up the photo, "I felt sick when I saw it. Everything seemed to be crumbling in front of me." He shook his head, "Who would do such a thing, and what were they hoping to gain?"

She had absolutely no idea, but she shouldn't have met with Fin outside of work regarding a work matter, and even worse than that, not telling Philip. If the situation had been reversed, she'd have been terribly upset if she saw a photo of Philip out with a woman.

"I'm so sorry for not telling you about the meeting, it seems silly now. I'm sure this is Gary Hicks' doing. When Fin sacked him, he said there'd be trouble for me."

"Why you? You don't employ him."

"I know, but he wanted support from me and I didn't give him it."

Philip looked intensely into her eyes, "I don't give a toss about Gary Hicks, it's you I care about. Promise me you won't do anything behind my back again."

"I promise."

He took hold of her hands, "I love you so much you know."

Then why don't you want to make love to me?
We hardly ever do.

"I know you do and I love you just the same."

At midnight, long after Philip had gone to sleep, she sat at the kitchen table staring at the photograph. Why would anyone take a photograph of her and Fin, when it really was a business meeting? Nobody would, unless they had an axe to grind.

It had to be Gary Hicks. Clearly he'd spotted them together having breakfast, and decided if the hearing didn't go his way, then he would cause trouble. And he'd done exactly that by pushing the photograph through the letterbox. No doubt he was lurking somewhere watching the house for Philip to arrive home.

She'd managed to pacify Philip once he'd relaxed by giving him oral sex which he'd eagerly accepted, but it was his aversion to penetrative sex that worried her. Oral sex was okay, and he did seem to love it, but that wouldn't ever get her pregnant.

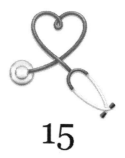

15

Fin stared at the photograph, "I'll have to speak to the police, we can't have this."

"Police!" Kathryn shrieked, "Is that really necessary?"

"Yes. Hicks has no right taking photographs of us and sending them to your husband to cause trouble. I'm not having that."

"But we don't know it's him for definite do we?"

"No we don't, but I'm fairly certain it will be, and that's why we need to inform the police and nip this in the bud right now. I'm sure they'll have a word with him, which needs doing to make sure he doesn't try anything like this again."

Kathryn knew he was right, but she didn't want any more hostility and was hoping by sacking Gary that would be the last of him.

Fin interrupted her thoughts. "This is so spiteful, what he was hoping to gain by sending a photograph of the two of us having a business meeting I'm not sure, are you?"

She shook her head, "I've no idea."

"I'm guessing the inference was something untoward going on between the two of us, I can't think of any other reason. Maybe he thought that you hadn't told Philip about our meeting and hoped it would cause a rift between the two of you?" Fin paused, "Philip did know we were meeting together for breakfast, didn't he?"

"Yes, of course he did. He's fine about it." Blast. Why had she lied? Why didn't she just come out and say she hadn't told him? Because that would mean describing Philip's jealousy, and she didn't want to do that.

"Right, then leave it with me, I'll speak to the police and let you know what they have to say."

"Okay," she agreed, and stood to leave.

"I'm seeing Elsa this evening, I'm taking her and Nick out to dinner," he smiled but it didn't quite reach his eyes, "One last ditch attempt to make her change her mind about having treatment."

"Good luck with that then. She's resolute so I don't think she will."

"I know that, and I'm almost resigned to it, but I'm going to give it one last try. I have to."

He looked so desperately unhappy, she wanted to put her arms around him and hug him tight.

She left his office and returned to theatre. The lists had finished and the staff had left for the day. As she tidied her desk, and switched off her computer, she thought about Fin and the family he'd lost.

Sadly, the way things were going, the likelihood was he would lose his beloved sister in the not too distant future, and that could be too much for one person to take. It was so unfair that his reason for coming to England was to seek solace in his family, yet his closest relative was not going to be around for much longer. If only Elsa would listen and have some treatment.

As she drove home, he was still on her mind. There was something about him that she found attractive, and that was not only a surprise, but a worry to her also. She was a faithful person, and berated herself for even thinking about him that way, but she really did like him. She thought about Philip and compared the two, but they were like chalk and cheese. Fin had a charming persona, a real man's man, and she liked everything about him. She was excited in his company; there was something about him that aroused her curiosity. What would he be like to hold, to kiss, to make love with? Did he give oral sex? It was a sure bet that he did. The very thought made her pussy twitch. No chance of that with Philip, he'd never attempted it. It was probably too physically dirty for him.

Later that evening, she was cuddling in Philip's arms watching a film when her phone pinged. It was a text from Elsa.

`Hi chick, are you free for tea on Thursday? x`

Quickly, she texted back that she was, and would meet her in the Hut at six. There were only a few eye cases on the theatre list in the afternoon so she could easily make tea with Elsa. Now all she had to do was tell Philip. She already had Avril's leaving do on Friday, so going out on two consecutive nights would irritate him.

"Who was that?" he asked kissing her forehead.

"Elsa. She's asking if I'm free for tea tomorrow night."

"You're out Friday aren't you?" he frowned.

"Yes, that's Avril's leaving do."

"Did you tell Elsa that?"

"No, why would I? If she wants to go for tea, then I'm going to meet her." *Lord knows how many more teas I'll get with her.*

"What, you're going out both nights?"

"Yes, just this once. You don't mind do you?"

"Well, I'm not overjoyed. What am I supposed to do on my own?"

"Oh Philip, you're not a child, I'm sure you'll think of something."

"But I like being with you. That bloody hospital monopolises your time anyway, so the evenings you are home, I like it to be the two of us."

"I do too, but I'm here all weekend with you. Oh, and hang on a minute though ... on Saturday you'll be out with *your* friends walking, and I'll be here on my own."

"That's different," he stiffened, "and anyway, you used to come to the club with me but you haven't been for ages."

"That's because it's boring. I don't mind the

occasional walk, but all of that drinking in pubs and back at the clubhouse puts me off. I can think of much better ways to spend a Saturday afternoon. Anyway I don't want to bang into Gary Hicks either, does he still drink there?"

"Course he does. It's his local."

"All the more reason for me not to go, then."

"Right, so what you're saying is, you aren't coming anymore while he's there?"

"No, I'm not saying that at all. I just don't want to go at the moment."

"That's stupid. You can't let him rule your life."

"He's not ruling my life. I don't particularly enjoy sitting around on a Saturday afternoon drinking. It never ceases to amaze me that you do either considering how unhealthy it all is."

Why was she goading him?

It was almost as if she was looking for an argument.

"I only drink real ale and that's okay. It's spirits that do all the damage."

"Yeah, sure it is. If you believe that, you'll believe anything."

She got up to make a drink. Philip had his mardy face on, so it was best to clear out of his way. Going to tea with Elsa had started it all, but she was going tomorrow regardless of his nose being put out of joint. He was such a Neanderthal. If he had his way, he'd have her barefoot in the kitchen preparing him meals. Or was it *barefoot and pregnant* in the kitchen? The thought crushed her insides.

16

As Kathryn entered the Hut on Thursday teatime, she was surprised to see Fin sat alongside Elsa. He stood up as she walked towards them.

What's that thumping?
It's catching my breath.

She forced herself to swallow, "Hi," she smiled and leant forward to kiss her friend's cheek.

"I'm not stopping," Fin said, "I've just dropped Elsa off as Nick's working late. She fancied a glass of wine which I'm about to get for her. What can I get you?"

"Erm, a soft drink for me, maybe a diet Coke or something like that please."

Fin headed towards the bar and she touched Elsa's hand, "How are you doing, missus?"

"Good actually," Elsa smiled, "let's wait until Fin gets back and we'll tell you together."

"Okay. I hope it's something nice, you look lovely, Elsa." She meant it. You wouldn't know there was anything wrong with her, she looked so pretty with her hair freshly styled and her perfect makeup. They chatted until Fin returned with their drinks, and she couldn't help but think he looked lovely too. There was something about him that she found so appealing.

He placed their drinks down and put his arm around his sister, "Have you told her?"

"No, I waited for you to get back."

"Right, well I'm back now. Go on then," he urged,

"tell her."

Elsa smiled, "The oncologist has offered me a chance to try a newish drug, which I've agreed to."

"Oh Elsa, that's marvellous," she hugged her, "what is it called, tell me all about it?"

"It's called Kadcyla and is showing encouraging results on those that have been taking it. It's not suitable for everyone so I'm going to be a bit of a guinea pig, but it's worth a try."

She squeezed Elsa's arm, "I'm so proud of you for going ahead with this."

Elsa breathed in deeply, "Before you get too excited," she glanced at Fin, which Kathryn suspected was because he'd instigated it all, "a word of caution, there are no guarantees. This treatment is only offered for patients' who don't want, or have exhausted the conventional chemotherapy route. It isn't a cure by any means, but I'm told it *could* prolong the time I have left."

"Well, that's good enough for me. I don't know much about it, but I'll read up on it. Is it injected, or an oral drug?"

"It's an injection every three weeks and I can get it at the Hope Street clinic in town." Elsa nodded her head toward her brother, "Fin will tell you all about it I'm sure, but not right now eh?"

As Elsa took a sip of her wine, Kathryn smiled at Fin, "I'm guessing her change of heart is down to you?"

"Something like that," he agreed, "and the big rubber cosh I bring out on special occasions."

She laughed, liking him even more for his humour, "Then all I can say is, well done, you." She turned to Elsa, "We'll have to keep everything crossed it works for you. Let's have a toast," she lifted her glass, "here's hoping that the medication puts you in remission for a long time yet, cheers." She clinked glasses with Elsa and as she went to do the same to Fin, her eyes were drawn towards his lips as he smiled.

The shape of your mouth is so sexy.
You really are very kissable.

Fin broke the spell, "Right, I'll be on my way so you

ladies can enjoy your chat." He kissed Elsa on the cheek, and then as if it was the most natural thing in the world to do, he leant forward and kissed her cheek also. It was only a light peck, but the imprint of his lips on her skin made her pulse race. She felt suddenly warm and slightly lightheaded as he withdrew, and she knew his eyes were on her but she daren't meet them. She turned her attention to her handbag for a tissue she didn't really want.

What would it be like to kiss him properly?
Taste his lips, and feel his tongue in my mouth.

Aware that Fin had walked away, she looked up at Elsa who was about to speak to her, but she stopped and tilted her head slightly.

"What?" Kathryn asked.

There was a moment's silence between them, and then with an almost puzzled look on her face, Elsa said, "He likes you, he really likes you, Kathryn."

An uncontrollable blush warmed her cheeks, "And I like him. He's a nice man, and no more than I would expect from your brother."

Elsa shook her head as if cogs were turning in her brain that she didn't want to, "I mean it, he *really* likes you. I saw it in his eyes when he looked at you."

"Don't be daft," she dismissed, "he's only being friendly." She needed to shut her up. This was terribly embarrassing, and completely inappropriate.

She picked up the menu and possibly over-played her interest in it, "What do you fancy to eat, I'm absolutely starving?"

Their conversation while they were eating was their usual girlie stuff, and Kathryn made certain that she steered the conversation well away from Fin. Once they'd finished two courses, it was evident that Elsa was becoming tired.

"Why don't I drive you home to save dragging Nick out?" Kathryn suggested.

Elsa rummaged in her bag for her phone, "No need, Nick won't mind, he's expecting a call."

As they waited for Nick to come and collect Elsa, for the first time ever in their relationship, Kathryn felt uncomfortable. She couldn't erase Elsa's words from her mind, *he really likes you.* The question was did he? It was so wrong of her to hope the answer was *yes*, but she did. She wanted him to *really like her.*

Nick arrived shortly afterwards and they all walked together to the car park. As they stood next to Nick's car, she reached for Elsa, "Come here, you," and hugged her dear friend tightly, "I'm keeping everything crossed this drug works and keeps you in remission for a long time to come." With her arm still around Elsa's shoulders, she turned to Nick, "Look after our precious cargo won't you?"

"You can bet on that," he said, helping Elsa into the car and leaving the door ajar.

"Where's your car?" he asked.

"There," she nodded towards her blue Mini parked opposite.

"Right, get in it then, it's too cold to be standing out here." He hugged her, "I guess the next time we'll see you is at Fin's housewarming party next Saturday?"

"Yes, we're really looking forward to it." She used the term *we*, but knew Philip wouldn't be, and obviously Elsa knew that too as she laughed from inside the car.

"I'm not sure Philip will be, can't you ditch him and come on your own?" Although Elsa was grinning playfully, Kathryn knew she meant it.

She arrived home shortly after ten thirty to the house in darkness. Philip would be fast asleep in bed which was his usual routine. Normal people would be having a coffee, playing about online or watching a late movie, but not him. He'd have watched the ten o'clock news, and then, come hell or high water, he'd go to bed. She was pleased tonight, though. With a bit of luck she could creep into bed and not wake him. It was unlikely he'd want to make love anyway, and that was the last thing she needed tonight. She'd rather lay and think about Fin.

17

Elsa lay awake listening to Nick's snoring. She couldn't sleep, there was too much planning to do. She'd agreed to go for treatment and convinced them that she would, but nothing was further from the truth. She had absolutely no intention of having any intervention to prolong her life. There was no way she was going through that trauma again. The physical sickness had been utterly wretched, and the thought of losing her hair and eyelashes again filled her with horror. And all for what? She'd been through it before and what good had it done her? The cancer was back, and the consultant had been very clear. This time there was no cure.

Her thoughts drifted to Paul DuToit as they did each night as she settled down to sleep. He was the special love of her life. Paul couldn't cope with her having cancer, he was all about the finer things in life, beauty, elegance, and sophistication. He'd told her so often that his two passions were her and his art collection.

They'd met years earlier when she'd gone to work at his art gallery in the city. They developed a natural affinity even though he was twenty-two years older than her. Theirs was a deep unexplainable love which had deepened with the years. They were soulmates.

He had a wife and she had a husband, but they talked very little about either of them. Their time together was very precious, and they didn't want to waste a second talking about others. They'd agreed in the beginning, Wednesday was *their* day.

They had been conducting their weekly meetings for the last two years. She'd given up her part-time job at the gallery primarily so she could spend more time with him. Nick and everyone else thought she was doing voluntary work at the gallery, but nothing was further from the truth. Her and Paul would fill their day visiting the theatre, cinema, exhibitions, or just about anything with an art association. They'd enjoy long lunches and would head back to his flat in the city and spend the afternoons together. If someone had told her it was possible to love a man without a physical relationship, she would have said that was *impossible*. But it was possible. She loved him with such intensity, and thankfully, he felt the same way about her. He adored her.

He was the father she'd lost as a child, and the brother she only previously saw a couple of times a year. When she was with him, it was as if the outside world ceased to exist.

She loved her husband Nick, but loved Paul also, and despite their meetings being only one day, they were the highlight of the week. He made her feel alive and she couldn't live without him.

When she'd been told that the cancer had returned to her brain and it was only a question of time, her first thought had been Paul. She'd been offered palliative support by way of radiotherapy, but that would only prolong her life by no more than months if she was lucky. Lucky? She wanted to laugh out loud when the oncology nurse had said that, it certainly was a bad choice of words.

Very quickly she formulated a plan in her mind and nothing was going to stop her. She already knew every snippet of information available about breast cancer and secondary metastasis, but it wasn't that she was interested in. She wanted to know about revolutionary new drugs, and once she'd found one on the internet, she explored everything she could about it. This gave her the knowledge to explain it all to Fin as if the consultant had been willing to start her on it.

The hardest part was going to be ensuring that Nick didn't accompany her to any of the fictitious clinical appointments. She'd made some little tablet bottles and filled them with different types of paracetamol, aspirin, and Ibuprofen, so it looked like she was taking a cocktail of tablets each day to counteract the side effects from the Kadcyla. She'd even bought several bottles of Gaviscon, telling Nick she needed this to counteract the indigestion which was a side effect of all the medication. She needed to keep the tablets hidden because if Fin was to stumble across them, then the game would be up. He would know immediately that none of it was real.

Nick wouldn't cotton on, though. He wasn't the sharpest tool in the box, and not one of those inclusive husbands that knew every little detail of their wife's personal habits. Nick was more of a workaholic and drinking fine wine man, totally oblivious to anything feminine such as periods, mood swings, and sexual needs.

There was no doubt he'd be devastated when she died, she knew that. He loved her, and they'd had a good marriage. He'd mourn for a while, but men like Nick quickly move on, and he would be snapped up by someone which is exactly what she wanted for him. He was a good man and deserved to be happy.

The resignation that she was going to leave this world, hurt so badly. It crushed her very soul. To know the life that she'd built, and all that she loved, cherished and held close to her heart, would soon be gone. The tiny word of three letters with a huge meaning, *die*. The fear and injustice of it all was pure agony. It was more than physical and emotional pain, it was a deep-rooted, gut-wrenching ache. Every passing moment was filled with the same question, *why me*? What did she do so wrong that she was chosen for this excruciating agony? It wasn't as if she hadn't had her share. She'd had cancer before and she'd fought it valiantly. So, why her turn again? Let someone else have it.

It was as if she was looking down from a high position at herself, and it wasn't really happening. Almost like a dream that she would wake up from. But it was real, and happening right now and she needed to manage it. There was nobody she could confide in as they wouldn't understand. Nick, Fin, and Kathryn were all begging her to have some form of treatment to prolong her life, but she wasn't going to do that. She done a good job convincing them all about the Kadcyla, and she was determined that Paul wouldn't find out she was ill. She desperately wanted him to remember her as the beautiful woman he loved.

18

Kathryn was doing the off duty in the office when a knock interrupted her. "Come in?" she said and Rosa entered carrying a mug.

"'Ello, Sister, I brought you coffee just how you like it."

"Aw, thank you, Rosa, that is kind of you." She took the coffee mug from her and placed it on the coaster next to her computer. Rosa stood in the doorway smiling. She didn't make an attempt to go, so Kathryn thought she must want something, "How are you?"

"Good, thank you. Me and Dino go to Bridlington next week on coach trip."

"Oh, that'll be nice. It might be a bit cold, though, so take plenty of layers," she smiled.

"Yes, I take my furry winter coat."

Rosa didn't move, it was almost as if she was rooted to the spot.

"Is there anything else I can do for you?"

Rosa put her hand in her pocket to retrieve something, and then moved her clenched hand towards her, "This for you, Sister."

Kathryn held out her hand and Rosa dropped a tiny knitted doll, covering what looked like a household wooden peg. It was a figure of a slender female, but with a tiny protruding belly. It was deliciously cute.

"Oh how lovely, where did you get that, Rosa, it's beautiful?"

"From my sister, I want you to 'ave it."

Kathryn shook her head, "I can't do that, it belongs to you."

"It for you. It bring you luck."

"Oh, Rosa, that's really sweet of you, but it's yours."

"I no need it. It how you say, fertilise doll... ?"

"You mean fertility doll?"

"Yes, fertility doll. You keep it 'till you 'ave baby, then I take back."

If it worked like that, why then didn't Rosa ever have children? She must have guessed the way her mind was working,

"I 'ad my womb taken away so couldn't 'ave the babies. You can do, but you need the luck to 'elp."

Should she take it? She really didn't believe in this kind of thing, but she was puzzled quite how Rosa knew so much about her desperate desire to have a baby. She certainly didn't broadcast it at work, and on the two occasions she'd needed surgery to assist the process, she'd taken leave and gone into the main NHS hospital so nobody would find out.

"Well if you're absolutely sure. It really is very kind of you Rosa, and if I do ever get pregnant, I will give you the charm back so you can give it to someone else. How about that?" she smiled.

"Yes. Keep it 'till then by your bedside. But don't lose it, Sister or it won't work."

"I won't, I promise. I'll guard it with my life. Thank you, it really is very sweet of you. I'm going to put it away now to keep it safe."

Kathryn headed for her locker and placed the tiny doll in the zip pocket of her handbag. A fertility doll was all very well, but the powers of reproduction would be tested quite heavily without sperm, and no amount of lucky charms could assist with that. She really needed to make an effort and get back on track with sex. The problem was it wasn't Philip she wanted to do it with.

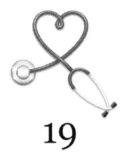

19

It was the day of Fin's party. Kathryn poured herself a glass of wine, deep in thought. She was not happy at all about Philip working that weekend and recalled their heated conversation.

"Why can't you tell Keith you have something on and can't go to Oxford?"

"It's my job that's why. You know Keith, he doesn't exactly ask."

"But it's not right. It's a Saturday for goodness' sake. You know ... family time."

"I know that but I can't get out of it. The company we're auditing want all the books sorted for the Monday morning shareholders' meeting. I haven't got a choice. I'm sorry, but I have to do it, it's my job."

She sighed, he did have a point. "How about I come with you. I can go shopping in the day and we can have dinner in the hotel when you've finished?"

"I thought you were set on the party and had bought a new dress?"

"I have, but it doesn't matter. Anyway, I could wear the dress for our dinner."

"There's no point," he shook his head, "Lord knows what time I'll get done, so I'll grab room service for a sandwich or something."

She didn't get it. Normally he would protest about her going on her own, but for some reason he wasn't, which was odd and uncharacteristic.

"It won't be the same going on my own, I'll feel like a fish out of water."

"You won't be on your own. You'll be with Nick and Elsa and they'll look after you."

"Do you know, if I didn't know you better, I'd think you didn't want me to go with you. You haven't got a woman tucked away that you're seeing on Saturday night have you?"

"Don't say things like that," he snapped, "I'd never do that to you."

"Alright, I'm only joking. So you're quite happy for me to go to the party without you, then?"

"Like I said, you'll be with friends and probably a stream of single women Elsa will have invited to tempt her brother."

Oh, I hope not.
That really hurts.

Although she was still niggled with Philip as he'd agreed to work, there was a part of her that was secretly pleased he wasn't coming tonight. It made her question why she suddenly felt unsettled in her marriage after all these years. The only conclusion she could come to was Fin. Since his arrival, she had become a different person, and Philip who she'd loved since she was sixteen, suddenly seemed less attractive, and more often than not recently, irritated her. When was the last time they'd made love? Had they since Fin had arrived? She dismissed any further thoughts in that direction as she wasn't ready to face that particular conundrum.

She stood back and looked at herself in the mirror and was pleased with what she saw. Her dress looked beautiful.

Will Fin like it?
Does he think I'm attractive?

She remembered his warm lips touching her cheek and a shiver ran through her. With a smile on her face, she reached for the new drop earrings she'd bought specially to match the dress, but the sound of the front doorbell interrupted her.

Damn, who's this? She opened the front door and

85

was surprised to see a pizza delivery man clutching two large boxes.

"Sorry for the delay, love, we're a bit short-staffed tonight." He pushed the boxes towards her.

She frowned, "I think you must have the wrong house, they're not mine. I haven't ordered pizza."

The delivery man checked the door number, "This is number seven, isn't it, seven Butler Close?"

"Yes it is, but I haven't ordered any pizza, there must have been a mistake."

"Well someone has from this address, and I need paying. It's ten pounds and there's a free bottle of Coke."

"Look, I'm trying to get ready to go out. I can assure you, I haven't ordered pizza, we don't even eat pizza in this house therefore it certainly isn't us. Maybe you've got the wrong house number."

The delivery man shook his head, "No, it's definitely number seven. It must be a prank then," he rolled his eyes, "we get them from time to time, you know people ordering loads of food and then sending it to someone's house for a laugh. But it's not bloody funny at all."

"No it isn't, and to be honest I really can't imagine anyone doing that to us," she tried to be polite and added, "maybe check when you get back with the person that took the call, it could well be they've taken down the wrong house number."

"Doubt it, but I'll check."

"I'm sorry you've had a wasted journey." She closed the door and watched him through the glass walking down the drive. Who on earth would do such a thing? Surely not Gary Hicks playing another trick? Fin said he'd spoken to the police about the photograph of the two of them having breakfast, but the police couldn't be certain that it was him that had sent it. Apparently, they'd given him a gypsy's warning about keeping away from St Anne's. Maybe this was another revengeful act on his part? She'd have to tell Fin. Not tonight though as it was his housewarming party and she was looking forward to the evening herself.

She stared again at herself in the mirror pleased that she'd been to the hairdressers and had her hair put up. It showed off her shoulders and décolletage to perfection. One last squirt of hairspray and she was ready. In ten minutes she'd call a local taxi. Her intention wasn't to arrive too early as she'd much rather get there when the party was in full swing.

There was plenty of time for another glass of wine which hopefully would help to calm her racing heart. It felt like she was going out on a first date. Before she changed her mind, she quickly poured herself one and stood in front of the full-length mirror in the bedroom for what must have been the twentieth time that evening. Good job Philip had no idea how much she'd paid for the dress and shoes, he'd go ballistic. And the fact she was stood in her stiletto shoes on the carpet would send him crazy.

Staring at her reflection, she knew the amount she'd spent had been worth every penny. The dress fitted her like a glove, and sparkled with hundreds of tiny little diamante stones glistening in the light. It was cut fairly low, which was another thing Philip wouldn't like. The thought of other men looking at her cleavage would incense him. Sadly not enough to make him overwhelmed with desire to rip the dress off her.

The days were becoming less and less that she actually went anywhere to dress up in evening clothes so she enjoyed looking at her reflection in the mirror. She'd been lucky and born pretty, rather like her mother, and had an enviable figure which she didn't have to work at. She could eat anything and didn't really exercise, but seldom put on weight. People used to say that when she had children that would all change, and she would smile at them silently thinking she'd gladly trade her enviable figure in an instant for her own baby. But that was unlikely to happen. The sound of the front doorbell interrupted her thoughts once again.

Through the glass panel, Kathryn could see Janelle from work on the doorstep. What was she calling round for? The only time she'd previously been to the house was when they were on a work's night out and she'd given her a lift. Even then though, she didn't come inside the house. There wasn't a problem mixing with the staff from work on nights out, but she didn't particularly want them in her home.

Puzzled she opened the front door, "Hello, Janelle, I'm afraid I'm just about to go out."

"Hi, Kathryn, I'm really sorry for disturbing you. I'm after a favour. You know you said I could borrow your copy of *The Disappearance,* I wondered if I could have it tonight?" She grimaced, "I'm visiting my mother in hospital and she asked me to bring her something to read. I remembered you said it was a fabulous book and that I could borrow it."

"Oh, right, yes of course you can," she opened the door to let her in and closed it behind her, "Come on through."

Janelle followed her into the study and Kathryn's eyes drifted upwards to the bookshelves, "It's here somewhere. Normally I could put my hand straight on it, but it looks like Philip has been tidying up." She rolled her eyes at Janelle and turned to look the large bookcase. As she continued flicking across the vast array of books on the shelves, she asked, "I'm sorry to hear your mum's in hospital, what's the matter with her?"

Janelle sighed, "They thought it might be an ovarian cyst so they took her down to theatre for laparoscopy, but they ended up having to remove the ovary."

"Oh the poor thing, is she doing okay?"

"Yeah, she's fine, fed up sitting around though, so I said I'd see if I could get a good book for her. I hope you don't mind me dropping in like this?"

"Of course not," Kathryn glanced at her watch, "you only just caught me, though, I'm heading out now."

"Yes, you look lovely. Where are you off to all dressed up?"

She didn't really want to let on where she was going, but it seemed silly not to say anything dressed as she was.

"I'm on my way to Mr Dey's housewarming party. You've heard me talk at work about my friend Elsa," Janelle nodded, "well she's Mr Dey's sister."

"Oh, right. Yes, I've heard you talk about her. You're not driving are you?"

"No, I'm about to order a taxi."

Janelle shook her head, "Don't do that, I can drop you off."

"Aw thank you, but there's no need. I wouldn't want to put you out."

"Don't be daft, it's no trouble. Where does he live?"

"Selton. He's bought the manor house there."

"No problem then as it's on my way to the hospital, mum's in the General."

"Are you sure? Normally I'd be going with Philip but unfortunately he's had to work. Ah, here it is," she located the book and handed it to Janelle, "I ought to be making a move really, I'll just get my bag if you absolutely sure you don't mind dropping me off?"

"Of course I don't mind. Could I use the toilet quickly before we go?" Janelle asked.

"Yes, it's on the left," Kathryn pointed towards a door and watched as Janelle placed the book on the hall table. She collected her bag from the bedroom and checked herself in the mirror again while she waited.

*

Janelle locked the door and stared around the elegant bathroom. Not only did Kathryn always look fashionable and chic, she clearly had stylish taste in décor, too. The bathroom had a huge enamel bath with ornate chrome taps, and delicate sparkling tiles covered the walls and shower cubicle. Everything was black and cream and the bright decorative towels added a perfect finishing touch.

She'd never seen Kathryn with her hair like that before and it really suited her. She was beautiful anyway, but looked stunning this evening. And that dress had designer label written all over it, *I wonder how much that set her back?*

Quietly, she eased open the bathroom cabinet noting the array of products and medications. She spotted some Elemis creams and took each of the small bottles out one by one, memorising the labels so she could buy similar for herself. She peered in the shower and noted the shampoo and conditioner that Kathryn used, making a mental note to purchase some for herself to see if she could tame her own curly hair. The sink cabinet held no surprises, only

Kathryn would have perfumed cleaning products and disinfectants.

She flushed the toilet and ran the tap before opening the bathroom door. Kathryn was in the hall with the front door open and she was fiddling with her key in the lock.

"Sorry to keep you waiting, I've not made you late, have I?"

"No, of course not," Kathryn smiled, "You know what these do's are like, you never want to be the first to arrive."

As she was about to walk out of the front door, Kathryn nodded towards the hall unit, "Don't forget the book. Your mum will be disappointed if you turn up without anything for her to read."

"Oh, yes, what am I like? I'd forget my head if it wasn't screwed on." She retrieved the book and followed Kathryn out as she locked the front door and pulled her trolley bag along towards the car.

Kathryn gestured towards the boot, "Shall I put my bag in the boot?"

"Yes, here let me." She took the overnight bag from Kathryn's hand and opened the boot, "Gosh, how long are you staying for, a week?" She mockingly lifted the bag as if it was weighed down with bricks.

Kathryn laughed, "I couldn't decide what to wear the morning after a bash such as this, so I've got a bit of allsorts in there."

They both got into the car and Janelle asked, "Are there many of you staying overnight?"

"I'm not entirely sure. I'm guessing just Elsa, her husband, and me as far as I know. Elsa feels sorry for me because Philip's away and I'm on my own. They suggested picking me up, but they live nearer to Selton so it didn't make sense for them to come all the way back here for me. That's why I said I would get a taxi."

She fastened her seat belt and waited until Kathryn did hers before she started the engine. Kathryn continued, "Elsa's not keen on me coming back to an empty house after the party either, so it was easier not to argue and agree to stay overnight."

"Doesn't Mr Dey mind? It must be a bit awkward with him being the boss at work?"

Kathryn frowned, "Mmm, I know what you mean, and yes if I'm honest I do feel a bit odd about staying. But if you knew Elsa, you'd see I have no choice. Once she makes up her mind about something, nothing will change it."

During the drive, Janelle's senses were overwhelmed by Kathryn, "What's the perfume you're wearing, it smells lovely?"

"It's Jo Malone. Philip bought me it for my birthday."

"It's really nice. Which one is it? I might treat myself to some."

Kathryn delved into her bag and produced a small bottle, "It's Pomegranate Noir, but I've got the body crème on as well so that makes a difference. It's all about layering, so the assistant said," she sniggered, "I can still remember the look on Philip's face when she told him the price."

"It smells gorgeous. I think I'll get some as long as you don't mind me copying you."

Kathryn shook her head, "Of course I don't. Isn't there a saying about copying being the sincerest form of flattery?"

"Yes, something like that," she agreed.

They chatted on about work on the short drive to Selton. As they approached the manor house Janelle noted several expensive cars parked in the vast grounds, and a pang of envy churned inside her. How good would it be to attend an event like that? Kathryn was so bloody lucky.

Kathryn undid her seat belt and passed the bottle of perfume to her, "Take this and try it. Perfumes can smell differently on each of us so you want to make sure it's what you want before you buy it."

"Are you sure? I won't use much, honestly, just a squirt or two."

"Use as much as you like, as long as you leave me some," she joked, "you're back at work on Monday aren't you?"

"Yes unfortunately," she pulled a face, "I'm dreading it, I've enjoyed a few days leave."

"Have you seen much of Callum while you've been

off?"

"Yes. We've been out a couple of times."

"That's great. It must be going okay then?"

"Oh yes, more than okay."

"Good, I'm really pleased for you both. Right," Kathryn squeezed her hand, "thank you for the lift, it's really kind of you. Are you going to visit your mum now?"

Janelle glanced at her watch, "Yes, I'll go straight there."

"Well I hope she gets better soon." Kathryn exited the car and leant forward giving a glimpse of the most perfect cleavage, "Okay, I'll see you on Monday then."

"Will do. Have a lovely evening won't you?"

"I'll try. Just let me get my bag out of the boot before you drive off."

She waited and waved as Kathryn made her way to the house. Even her walk was graceful; she could almost be a catwalk model the way she held herself.

Janelle put the car into gear and the wheels screeched on the gravel as she made her way out of the drive. As she paused to check the road, she sprayed a generous amount of Jo Malone on herself. The car was filled with Kathryn and smelled beautiful. During the drive, she thought about the party and all the men and women dressed in their finery. How she wished she could have spent the evening in Kathryn's company. Now that really would be marvellous.

Instead, she entered the drab end semi where her mother was sitting watching TV with a generous amount of red wine in a glass resting on the coffee table. She looked up at Janelle, "Hello, love. Was Asda busy, you seemed to have been ages?"

"I had a good look around the clothes and tried a few bits on."

"Did you get anything?"

"No, nothing floated my boat," she lied, "anyway, I'm going straight up, so I'll see you in the morning."

"That's a shame. Mr Selfridge is on in a minute. Don't you fancy watching that with me?"

"Not tonight, I've got stuff to do. I'll see you in the morning. Night."

The last thing she wanted was to sit with her mother. She wanted to go to her room and try and put her hair up like Kathryn's. It looked beautiful and she wanted to see if it suited her like that. One day she vowed, her and Kathryn would go to a swanky do *together*. They'd be able to dress themselves up to the nines, drink plenty of the fizzy stuff, and enjoy each other's company like mates do. They'd have such a good time. Maybe a day at the races, that would be good, or possibly a summer ball. How fantastic would that be? Then at work she'd be seen as Kathryn's *friend*. So all she needed to do was make that happen. It couldn't be difficult.

She took the bottle of Jo Malone, sprayed the room and breathed it in. the alluring sent made her heart race and her chest flush with heat. Before she knew it, she was lifting her skirt and stroking the bottle up her thigh.

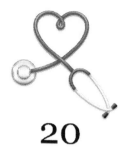

20

As Kathryn approached the door of the Manor House, it opened and Nick greeted her, "Hello gorgeous. My, my, don't you scrub up well." He wrapped his big arms around her, "I was just nipping out for a crafty cigar but you've caught me and saved me from the perils of all that nicotine."

She laughed, "You'll be in trouble if Elsa catches you."

"Yes, you're right," he grinned as his looked past her, "Where's your taxi?"

"A friend gave me a lift."

"Oh, that's good. Here, let me take your bag."

They walked a few paces down a spacious hall before he stopped to open a cupboard door and put the bag inside, "It'll be fine there until you're ready to go to bed. I'll bring it up then for you. Come on, let's find the others."

As they made their way through the impressive atrium, she gazed in awe at the imposing staircase facing them

"Has Elsa been responsible for the design all of this?"

"Well, that's what she tells me has been taking up all her time, so I have to believe her," he joked.

"Gosh, it's incredible. She has such flair doesn't she, it's absolutely stunning."

"Yep, I'll give her that; she has got excellent taste," he winked, "come on, then, follow me if it's a party you're looking for."

They headed towards the direction of the noise, and entered an enormous kitchen where caterers were busy in the food preparation area.

"Don't mind us," Nick said as they passed.

The span of the kitchen must surely equal the ground space of her modest bungalow. It was huge. She followed Nick towards the open bi-fold doors and into a marquee that had been erected against the house and stretched into the garden.

She saw Elsa straight away, talking to a small group of people with her hands gesticulating, no doubt in relation to one of her entertaining stories.

Typical Elsa,
The life and soul of any party.

Elsa quickly excused herself from the people she was with and came towards her, "Hello my darling," she kissed her cheek, "you look absolutely stunning Kathryn, doesn't she Nick?"

"Yes, I've already said that. You both do, and if I wasn't already spoken for," he shook his head from side to side, "I'd not be able to choose between the two of you."

Nick's voice had a slight slur to it, which Elsa quickly picked up on,

"Honestly, how many have you had? It's still only early you know."

"Aw, don't be getting cross with him Elsa, it is a party. Anyway, you look pretty good yourself, and from what I've seen of the house, you've done an amazing job."

Elsa linked her arm through hers, "I'm so pleased you like it, I'll show you round properly later. Come on, let's find Fin. He's sober, or at least he was the last time I saw him."

Kathryn grinned at Nick and he saluted her playfully as they walked away. They were going to find Fin. That gave her heart a kick.

The marque was fabulous. It had been intimately decorated with subtle lighting, and judging by the warm air, heated also. The floral arrangements strategically placed on podiums were stunning, and the soft background music was classical, adding a nice touch.

Elsa manoeuvred her towards a small bar area in one corner of the marque. There was a bartender in attendance, and some of the staff were organising what looked to be a stunning banquet. The whole event was spectacular and as she gazed around at all the guests in their finery, she felt excited at the prospect of the night ahead. How lucky was she to be part of such a lovely evening. Now, where was Fin?

It was almost as if she felt him before she saw him. Although he was engaged in conversation, his eyes met hers, and again just as his sister had done, he excused himself and walked towards her.

Handsome didn't even come close to Fin wearing a dinner suit. If her heart rate quickened earlier at the prospect of seeing him, it now accelerated to dangerously fast.

Oh, my God!

Is he for real?

"Hello Kathryn," he kissed her cheek. It was only a social kiss, but to her it felt so much more. Even the courteous touch of his hand on her arm made her feel giddy.

They pulled apart and he smiled warmly at her, "I'm so pleased you could make it, you look beautiful."

Do I?

Really?

"I wouldn't have missed it for the world," she smiled as chastely as she could and then politely added, "I'm so sorry Philip couldn't make it, he sends his apologies."

"Please don't worry, Elsa has explained. He's working away, isn't he?"

"Yes, I'm afraid so. He's been summoned to a firm that's likely to be going into liquidation on Monday, so the accounts have to be done."

Why was she talking about Philip? He was the last person she wanted to discuss this evening. Good job he wasn't here as he'd be on edge all evening and urging her towards leaving at the first opportunity.

Elsa chipped in, "Fin, would you get Kathryn sorted with a drink please, I need to say hello to someone. Excuse me for a moment both of you." She watched Elsa walk in the direction of a couple of women stood on their own, which poured cold water on her excitement. She crossed her fingers they weren't single.

Fin took her arm, and led her towards the bar, "What would you like to drink?"

You.

Straight.

"A dry white wine would be nice please." Better to stick with what she had been drinking, she didn't want to mix her drinks and end up with a huge hangover tomorrow.

As Fin chatted to the barman, she couldn't help but appreciate his attractiveness. There was such a handsomeness about him and an air of sophistication. He laughed at something the barman said, and then he turned to look at her. Their *eye-meeting look* was becoming rather regular. Good job he had no idea how she felt about him.

He took her drink from the barman and walked towards her smiling so nicely, she could almost believe he found her attractive. *You look beautiful* he'd said when he greeted her, did he really think that?

I hope so.

Because I so want you to think I'm beautiful.

Their fingers touched as he passed her the wine. He had large hands and she felt overwhelmed by his masculinity. Her nipples tightened and heat curled in her stomach. God, it was warm in here.

He cleared his throat, "I need to speak to you privately but now isn't the time really. Do you think when everyone has gone home, you and I could sit down and have a chat?"

"Of course. Is it about Elsa?"

"No, not really. It's more about you and I."

You and I at work?

Or you and I having sex?

She took a huge gulp of her drink, "You and I? Do you mean about work?"

"No, definitely not about work. Let's leave it until later shall we? Oh look, here's Elsa back now," he smiled lovingly at his sister, "we were just talking about you."

"Really, what about me? Remember, tonight is a no talking about Elsa's health night," she smiled but her expression indicated she meant it.

Fin gave her a loving squeeze, "No, nothing to do with your health, I promise. I was telling Kathryn how much of this beautiful house is down to your wonderful taste."

"Well, left to you, or any man for that matter," she raised an eyebrow, "it most probably would have ended up cream and white everywhere."

"What's wrong with cream and white," he asked, "you can't ever fall out with it?"

"It's boring and bland," she said, "nobody has cream walls and white doors anymore."

Fin rolled his eyes, "Is that right? On that note, I think I better go and circulate." He kissed his sister affectionately on the cheek, and Kathryn couldn't help wishing it was her receiving it.

As he walked away from them, she felt herself missing him.

What does he want to talk to me about later?
If it's not work or Elsa, what else could it be?

Kathryn spent the evening circulating and thanking her lucky stars again that Philip wasn't there. She enjoyed the opportunity to chat freely without him huffing and puffing about it not being his sort of thing. She covertly observed Elsa, and for someone that wasn't well, she was displaying remarkable powers of resilience.

The food was splendid and delivered efficiently by the outside caterers. The delicious array of cooked meats and fish dishes were laid out in a display that was a sin to delve into. Everything was scrumptious and all were served with the corresponding wines as accompaniments.

But she couldn't eat. Her stomach was too busy churning at the thought of Fin with one of the surplus women who appeared to be there without partners. Most of the guests did appear to be couples, but the sight of a lone female she spotted speaking to Fin was like a dagger piercing her heart.

Get a grip, Kathryn.

He doesn't belong to you.

Nick and Elsa stayed close by for most of the evening. She'd loved to have spent more time with Fin, but as the host of the party he was kept busy.

She returned from the bathroom and found Elsa with Nick and it appeared he was getting a telling off.

Kathryn interjected, "I can't believe Fin already has all of these friends Elsa when he's only been here a few weeks."

"Ah, don't be fooled," Elsa said, "not many here are actually *friends*. It's more about networking and bringing more business to St Anne's. You'll know the surgeons, of course, but there's also a selection of GP's here and I believe senior staff from the local radio station and newspapers. Apparently he's going to be commercially advertising the hospital to bring in more business."

"That sounds sensible, although it's hard to think of a hospital as a commercial business."

"Fin reckons that's the way forward. There are also some bigwigs from various charities, and I think he's joined some sort of Freemasons group for businessmen. So that's who most of them are."

Nick drained his glass, "Come on then my darling little matchmaker, exactly how many single women have you invited to this bash?" His glazed eyes drifted around the marquee, "There seems to be a few here on their own."

"Only a couple Nick, but surprise, surprise," she widened her eyes, "you've managed to spot them."

Elsa lowered her voice as if she was about to disclose a secret, "I think it's time Fin got back into the dating scene. Men are no good on their own, are they, Kathryn?"

Don't.

Just stop it, Elsa.

She forced herself to smile, "Hey, leave me out of your matchmaking would you."

It was nearing midnight and tiredness was beginning

to take its toll. Kathryn couldn't blame that entirely on the alcohol. Her feet ached in the ridiculously expensive stilettos which she'd bought on impulse to match the dress. Even when she was buying them she'd thought of him.

She'd circulated and engaged in conversations with some of the surgeons from work, chatted with the GP's she'd been introduced to, and even been polite to a couple of single women Elsa had insisted she met. However, what wouldn't be obvious to anyone else in the room was her internal antenna fixed on Fin. She surreptitiously watched every woman that he engaged with and each time she heard him laugh with one of them, her tummy twisted in protest.

Please don't like any of them.
I couldn't bear it.

By now, she was feeling light-headed and extremely intoxicated. She silently willed everyone single one of them to go home so she could be on her own with him.

What was it he wanted to talk to her about? He said it was about him and her. He wouldn't have any idea how she felt about him, surely? It was only a crush after all. She'd remembered reading about such feelings in a magazine. A reader had written about an attraction she'd felt towards her brother-in-law and the reply had firmly stated to keep herself busy, never spend time alone with him, and do not ever let him know how you feel.

So, she kept her thoughts about Fin to herself. Who could she share them with anyway? The problem was, initially her feelings were quite chaste about him, but of late they'd taken on much more of a sexual connotation. The depth of her erotic fantasies was hard to fathom, and she wasn't sure how to handle them. Since she'd met Fin, she was masturbating more and more.

I bet he gives great oral sex.
With that delicious mouth of his.

It was a huge relief when Nick and Elsa approached, interrupting her train of thoughts, "I'm going up to bed now sweetie as I'm feeling a bit tired," Elsa said, "Nick's not coming yet, though, so he'll be around to bore you to death for a bit longer."

"You're such a meanie to him," Kathryn grinned, "he'd never bore me to death." She put her arm around her friend, "I should go to bed really. I've had far too much to drink and need to lie down."

"No, you stay a bit longer." Elsa playfully looked over her shoulder, "You can fill me in tomorrow on any of the women Fin's been chatting to." She placed her empty glass down, "Oh, I've just thought, you don't know which room you're in yet. Do you want to come up with me and I'll show you where it is?"

Fin appeared from nowhere, "It's alright. I can show Kathryn where her room is if you're going to bed."

"Okay. Nick's put her bag in the hall closet."

"Fine. I'll see to it."

He turned to Nick, "Another one for the road, mate?"

"Why not?" Nick replied.

"There is no road tonight, Fin, we're staying here remember?" Elsa chastised, "And don't you be plying Nick with loads more alcohol when he's already had enough. I'm not having him snoring all night long. I've got to sleep with him, you haven't."

"Thank goodness for that," Fin laughed and Kathryn loved the way his eyes crinkled at the sides. He really was so gorgeous.

He kissed his sister, "I'll say goodnight then and see you in the morning."

Her and Nick were saying goodnight to Elsa when a male guest tapped Fin on his arm and whispered in his ear.

"Will you excuse me for a moment?" Fin smiled and walked away into the house. Damn. He keeps disappearing.

She continued to chat to Nick but he kept getting her drinks, and she really needed to draw the line.

"No more, Nick. I've had far too much. I haven't felt this drunk in years."

"Good. That's what parties are all about."

She rolled her eyes, "Remind me of that in the morning when I'm nursing a thumping hangover, will you?"

Her internal antennae kicked in once more as Fin approached behind her. She didn't see him initially, but the tiny hairs on the back of her neck prickled. It was almost as if her body knew he was close by.

"How we doing here, you two?"

"Fine," Nick answered, "but I think I'm ready to call it a night now. How about you, Kathryn?"

"Yes, I think that would be wise. You're such a bad influence; I've had far too much to drink."

Fin smiled, "It's thinning out now and there are only a few stragglers left so I'll go and give them a gentle push. Can you stay and help me, Kathryn, you know, a woman's touch and all that?"

"I'm really not sure how good I'd be at drawing things to a close," she said, "you'd perhaps be better on your own."

"Nonsense. Come on, take pity on me and we'll round them up together. Are you going to give us a hand, Nick?"

"No, count me out. I'm ready for some shuteye so I'll say goodnight." He kissed her cheek, "Don't be letting Fin keep you up longer than you want to either, Kathryn. He can be a bad influence. I know all about his university days."

"Thank you for that, *Dad*," Fin rolled his eyes, "enough said."

Nick winked, "See you in morning, then," and walked away.

"I really think I should go too, Fin. I'm dead on my feet and have had too much to drink really."

"Don't go yet," he pleaded, "I need to speak to you remember. It won't take long. Do you want to get some water? I tell you what, why don't you grab us both a coffee and go and wait for me in the sitting room, I won't be long."

Yes, coffee, that would be good.

Anything to stop the burning need simmering away inside me.

21

Kathryn wandered into the kitchen intending to make them both a coffee, but the housekeeper Elaine offered to make it for her. She should have said no when asked if she wanted a liqueur in it, but she didn't.

She chatted to Elaine for a while about the success of the party and explained how she worked with Fin and her relationship with Elsa. Eventually, Fin came back to the kitchen.

"That's the last, thank goodness."

She handed him a mug of black coffee, "Before you turn your nose up, it's got a liqueur in it."

"Ah, you certainly know the way to a man's heart, Sister Knight. Let's go sit in the lounge and we can have that chat."

She followed him into an elegant sitting room. It was decorated in the same sophisticated style of the other rooms and while the table lamps were bold in design, they brought an intimacy which made her tummy flutter. He gestured towards the settee, "Please have a seat."

She placed her coffee on the occasional table next to the sofa, and sat down. When he sat down next to her, awkwardness kicked in and she mumbled, "It certainly has been a fabulous party, you must be really pleased."

"Yes, it's gone much better than I envisaged. I wasn't terribly keen initially but Elsa was right, it has been a great way of getting to know people who we may need in the future." His took a sip of his coffee, "I'm hoping I've convinced a couple of the GP's to refer the private patients to us as opposed to the opposition over the bridge."

A tap on the door interrupted them, "Come in."

The housekeeper popped her head around the door, "All done and locked up. If you don't need me for anything else, I'll say goodnight and let myself out."

Fin stood, "Thank you, Elaine, your car's outside, isn't it?"

"Yes, closest to the door."

"Good. You get off then, and thank you so much for your help tonight."

"My pleasure. I'll be here first thing for breakfast."

"Brilliant. We'll say goodnight then."

Elaine nodded at them both, "Goodnight."

Kathryn smiled at the woman, hoping she didn't think it's odd that she was in the lounge with him while everyone else has gone to bed.

The door closing added to her anxiety. They were all alone now.

Don't be stupid.

He doesn't know the effect he has on you.

She stifled a yawn, "What is it you wanted me for, I really ought to be getting to bed?"

Fin sat down again and took a deep breath, "Okay, but give me five minutes."

He took a sip of his coffee, "This is a little awkward so I thought I'd say what I have to say tonight, and if you don't feel the same way, then hopefully we can put this conversation down to too much alcohol."

Why wouldn't she feel the same way?

They both wanted the best for Elsa?

"Go on?"

She watched him take another deep breath in, "Are you happily married?"

Jesus.

Why's he asking that?

"Yes I am, very." She narrowed her eyes, "What's this all about?"

The urgency she saw in his mesmerising brown eyes made her chest tighten, "I'm really attracted to you, Kathryn, so much so that it's taking me all my time keeping my hands off you."

Bl-oo-dy Hell!

He does like me.

"You shouldn't be talking like this. I am very happily married, you know that."

"Do I?"

"Yes of course you do. You must do."

"I don't know anything except how attracted I am to you. I've wanted you since the first time I saw you in theatre. Can you remember that day?"

Yes she could, vividly. It was the day he turned her life upside down. The day that desperately wanting a baby came second to desperately wanting him.

She raised her hand, "Please don't say any more."

He ignored her plea. "So am I to understand that you don't feel there's anything between us?"

Lie.

Don't admit anything.

She shook her head vigorously, "I don't want to have this conversation. You're an attractive man and there's an air of vulnerability about you because of what you have been through, but that's as far as it goes."

His stare was penetrating but he didn't speak so she continued, "You're Elsa's brother and I want to be friends, but you're also my boss."

"That's how you see me is it," he drawled, "as Elsa's brother and your boss?"

No I see you naked,

And making love to me.

"Yes."

"And it's no more than that?"

"No."

"Well I never had you down as a liar Kathryn Knight but that's exactly what you are." He tilted his head to one side, "You feel it too. You want me as much as I want you. I see it in your eyes every time you look at me."

"No. I don't. You're imagining it. I'm married."

"Do you think that if you keep saying that often enough, it's going to alter the way you feel?" he frowned.

"It has to. I really don't want to have this conversation. I *can't* have this conversation. We must stop now and as you said, put it down to the alcohol and forget we even discussed it."

He nodded, "Fine. If that's what you want, then yes, we'll have to. But it doesn't stop me wanting to take you upstairs right now and make love to you."

"Stop it. Stop talking like that."

"Why?" His voice became guttural, "What's wrong in telling you that I want to remove that sexy dress you're wearing, and then peel off your underwear. I'm desperate to kiss that beautiful body of yours, everywhere."

Shit. Shit. Shit.

I want you to.

"But you don't want that," he raised any eyebrow, "so you say."

He abruptly stood up, "I'd better show you to your room then."

Yes, that's what she must do. Go to her room.

And close the door.

Lock it if necessary.

Her mind was working overtime as she followed Fin into the hall and watched him take her overnight trolley bag from the closet where Nick had stored it earlier. The silence between them was awkward, and she cursed the amount of alcohol she'd consumed as it had given her a brain fog. She needed to speak, but all she could visualise was him *removing the sexy dress and underwear* and making love to her.

They mounted the stairs and she counted each step to focus on anything but him. Her mind was struggling to assimilate their conversation. He felt the same way. He *did* find her attractive and wanted her. But he was single and she wasn't. She must remember that.

She glanced sideways at him, but he had what appeared to be an enforced straight ahead look.

It is so very tempting.

I want him so much.

They walked across the landing. Was it her imagination, or were they both walking slowly?

This house was seriously huge. As they passed yet

another bedroom door, Fin broke their silence, "That's Nick and Elsa's room and you're around the corner."

They turned onto another landing and the tension intensified between them. Maybe it was the thought of what could happen inside the bedroom, but she mustn't go there. She tried to lighten the moment, "Gosh it's so big everywhere. How many bedrooms do you have?"

"Nine, but one of them next to mine I've had made into a dressing room, so technically there's eight."

"It's a beautiful house. You really have done a terrific job."

"It is rather lovely, isn't it? My bedroom is that one there," he nodded towards the big imposing bedroom door facing them.

Take me in there. Please.

Undress me.

"And yours is right here" God, did he have to put her next to him? How cruel was that. She'd spend half the night fantasising about him lying naked next door. She thought of her electric toothbrush, glad that she'd brought it.

"Oh right, thank you." They stood at the door to her room. This was completely new territory for her. She'd never felt such an acute longing for a man before.

He put the trolley bag down and pulled the handle up so that she could drag it in rather than carrying it as he'd been doing.

I don't want to go in on my own.

Come in with me.

"Okay," he said, "I'll say goodnight and trust you'll have a good night's sleep."

Their eyes locked and she could see a glint of a gold fleck as they glistened with desire. If ever the saying *come to bed eyes* fitted anyone, it was him.

"You know where I am if you need anything." His eyes flicked towards his bedroom door before returning to hers.

I do need something.

I need you.

"Thank you." It was all so polite on the surface, but simmering below was acute sexual tension. She could feel it, the heat down below, the tightness in her stomach.

She placed her hand on the handle of the bag to take it from him, but he quickly placed his own hand over the top of hers, trapping it. Their gazes drifted simultaneously towards both of their hands resting on the handle. The heat of his hand on top of hers felt almost as if it had been warmed around a hot cup of tea.

"I could bring it in for you?" he suggested huskily. The air around them was thick and heavy. It had become a life-changing moment. The words he'd used may have said that he'd take the bag inside the room, but his meaning was something totally different. He knew it, and she knew it. The question had nothing to do with him bringing the bag inside. He was asking if she wanted *him* inside. And she did.

Inside the room, inside the bed,
And inside of her.

"Or ..." his eyes looked searchingly into hers, "you might want to go in on your own ... while you still can." Her gaze was drawn again to his hand still trapping hers, and then her eyes returned to his gorgeous brown eyes glimmering with need.

Her tummy flipped with excitement. She wanted him so badly. Just one night, that's all. Could she?

Yes. A thousand times, yes.

Now, before I change my mind.

She pulled her hand away from the handle and swallowed the lump at the back of her throat, "Yes." His eyes flashed darker, almost black with arousal, which she hoped hers mirrored, "Please. Bring it in for me."

He broke their gaze and leant forward to open the bedroom door.

Tonight she was going to give in to the overwhelming need she had for this man. Tomorrow she'd worry about the consequences.

He closed the solid door behind them and pushed her against it. With his huge hands holding her forearms, his face moved towards her with such speed, she barely had time to think. All logic disappeared as he cupped her head and brought his mouth down on hers. Their lips synchronised and moved effortlessly together. It was hardness meeting softness. His muscular body was as hard as steel against her.

Not once did he pause. His mouth relentlessly devoured her, and she matched his ferocity. She couldn't breathe, but didn't want to. His huge arms enveloped her, and hers seemed to have a will of their own as they wrapped themselves around his neck as if that would bring them any closer together.

She met him kiss for kiss, nipping, sucking and biting. Desire swept over her. He felt amazing and she wanted to ride the tidal wave of lust that was making her insides shudder.

He was first to break contact and rest his forehead on hers. His chest heaved and it took a second before he groaned, "Tell me to stop."

She cupped his head and stared into his eyes. He was right. She should stop him right now. She wasn't the sort of woman to have an affair.

He whispered, "We should stop now ... while we still can." But she didn't want him to stop. Not now she'd tasted him. She wanted more. She wanted all of him.

She put a finger on his lips to silence him, "Please don't stop... I want you. Let's just have tonight together."

He took her hand and brought it to his own mouth and kissed her palm before walking backwards towards the bed pulling her with him.

"I want you so much too," he groaned as they effortlessly sunk onto the bed.

He frantically removed her dress and her underwear as he'd promised he would. His eyes consuming her naked body delighted her, "God, you're so beautiful," he sighed and the longing in his eyes thrilled her.

He removed his own suit carelessly discarding it on the floor.

She sighed with pleasure as he began the exquisite exploration of every inch of her body, and as his tongue followed the shape of each breast and sucked her nipples, she wanted to explode. The licking and sucking continued with his delicious tongue running over her sensitive breasts and alternating with his thumbs circling her hardened nipples.

"I want to taste every bit of you," he hissed, and a groan escaped from her lips as his attention left her breasts and moved lower towards her silky wetness. She wasn't sure if she parted her legs, or they fell apart of their own accord, but she writhed and squirmed as she felt his hot breath before sliding his tongue into her.

The slick sound of his tongue rolling in and out of her wetness, and his strong arms on her hips was a delight. Her fingers curled around the covers and her head tipped back as she savoured completely new sensations. She'd never experienced anything so exquisite. His mouth found her sensitised clit which throbbed and pulsated as he flicked it with his tongue causing ripples of pleasurable sensations to build. It was incredible. Her hips lifted of their own accord as she relished every second of his hungry mouth on her. One flick and then another from his magnificent tongue, and then several more as he devoured her.

She heard a long groan as he drank her in. He sucked hard, and with one long, merciless pull of his mouth on her clit, she screamed. Her orgasm erupted, and wave upon wave of sensational torture lifted her up and carried her along as her body contracted, and still he lapped her with his tongue until her convulsions ceased. Oh, God, she'd come in his mouth.

She welcomed the weight of him as he moved his body onto hers. His gorgeous lips were consuming her mouth again. The taste of herself on him excited her and she weaved her fingers through his hair as she met his need with a newfound desire of her own. Long, slow, mind-blowing kisses, each one seducing her beyond reason. His mouth was compelling.

His erection pushed against her thigh and she yearned to feel him deep inside her.

He breathed out, his beautiful eyes smouldering, "You're sure about this?"

She silenced him with another long intense kiss, "Yes," she said, "but I want to touch you."

"Later, I need to be inside you."

She spread her legs and felt him at her entrance. Still he continued to kiss her. The feeling of his lips on hers and then him breaking away and searching her face caused the heat in her already hot pussy to burn.

He reached down and gently eased himself into her, sealing his body fully with hers. A guttural groan escaped from him as she forced her hips upwards, anything to get more of him. He slid in deeper and an uncontrollable moan of pleasure escaped from her lips.

She wrapped her legs around his back and her fingers dug into his shoulders as he pulled out and surged back in, setting a blistering pace, thumping into her, her flesh rippling with waves of pleasure.

Their joining went deeper than physical pleasure. His lips grazed everywhere; along her jaw, over her throat, and then back to her lips. He murmured thick hot words in his native Dutch tongue which she didn't understand, but guessed their meaning and they thrilled her.

"You're incredible," he breathed against her mouth, "I knew you would be."

"Oh, Fin." She called his name, over and over as the pressure mounted. Her needy pussy tightened around him. They fitted together so perfectly.

"Open your eyes," he demanded hoarsely.

Slowly her eyelids opened.

"I want you to see me, and know what you do to me."

Her hands went to his hair, his face, and then to her breasts, where she squeezed and moaned for him. He pushed back into her, all the way, and he held it there. He felt so big inside.

"You're so beautiful, Kathryn," he said and she pushed her breasts together, nipples puckered and tight, aching for his mouth.

He took both nipples into his mouth at the same time and sucked hard. She dug her heels into his back and writhed against his cock. "Harder," she said, and he needed no more encouragement. He pulled his head away from her breasts and she let go of them, spread her arms and clutched the covers as he fucked her, building up to a steady rhythm that sucked her insides with the most amazing feeling.

His hand eased her right leg over his shoulder and he plunged deeper. The rhythm was sensational. She felt perspiration on his brow, above his lips and on his chest. Or was that coming from her?

She inhaled him. The speed of the thrusts increased and she felt the emergence of a second climax pulsing through her. Their beautiful rhythm continued until finally the volcano erupted, and as the blissful convulsions surged through her body, he roared loudly as he pumped hard and fast into her with brutal force.

22

Kathryn was still drowsy as she spotted the sunlight creeping underneath the drapes. It was the morning after the night before. Her and Fin has spent all night making love and dozing in each other's arms. Each time they'd woken, he'd slid into her again and again.

Reality kicked in. Now she was going to have to endure breakfast with him, Elsa, and Nick. How the hell was she going to do that? Thank God he'd crept out of her room and she hadn't had to wake up with him next to her.

She'd been unfaithful to her husband. What happens now?

If she left straight away this morning and headed home, Elsa would become suspicious, and she couldn't cope with anyone knowing what she'd done, least of all her best friend. Worse than that though was seeing Fin. The man that had shown her how beautiful lovemaking could be. He'd made love to her so tenderly, as if they had all the time in the world. Now she had to face him in the cold light of day. How quickly could she get out of this house and back to her own where she could think?

She showered and washed her hair. Nausea was coming and going in waves and she couldn't decide whether it was because of her actions of the previous evening, or the generous amount of alcohol she'd consumed. Either way, she felt lousy.

A gentle tap on the door startled her ... please not

him.

She remained on the stool in front of the dressing table mirror where she'd dried her hair, "Hello?"

"Hi hon, can I come in?" Elsa asked sweetly. A wave of relief washed over her and she slowly released the breath she was holding.

"Course you can." She stood up smiled as her beautiful friend entered her room looking stunning as usual, as if she'd spent the last two hours in a beauty salon.

"Good morning. How are you?" she asked Elsa.

"I'm fine honey, what about you, did you sleep okay?"

Sleep?

No, I fucked you're brother all night long.

"Wonderful," she lied, "it must have been all the wine I had, I was out like a light."

"Good. It's hard sometimes sleeping in a strange bed. Are you ready for some breakfast? Fin's waiting downstairs and I'm warning you, his housekeeper will have made enough food for the feeding of the five thousand," she laughed.

"Oh God, I'm not sure I can eat any breakfast," she said, placing her hand on her tummy, "to be honest I'm contemplating getting a taxi home."

"No, don't do that. We'll take you home. What time is Philip back anyway?"

"Lunchtime hopefully. He said yesterday he was going to get the earliest train he could."

"Right, then you'll want to be there when he gets home so let's grab something to eat and then we'll get off. You ready now?"

"Yes I am." As she closed the bedroom door she silently cursed. If she'd have known she was going to spend the best night of her life making love with Fin, she would have worn something much more attractive than trousers and a top for the morning after.

Do I look okay?

What's he going to say to me?

As she walked down the stairs, her tummy was doing summersaults at the thought of seeing him again. The man that had held her, kissed her, and made love to her so passionately. She could still feel him. It was as if he'd left an imprint inside her. Her pussy clenched when she remembered his mouth and that delicious tongue flicking away at her.

He was sitting at the table reading his newspaper as they walked into the dining room, and got up straight away as soon as they entered. He kissed Elsa first and then he kissed her cheek also. Heat warmed her face as she recalled those sensational lips that had given her a first incredible orgasm.

They took their seats at the table.

He's even more handsome now.

I wish we could go back and do it all again.

"Did you sleep alright?" he directed his question at Elsa. He knew she hadn't.

"Fine," Elsa answered, "Where have you got that mattress from? No, don't tell me … it'll be way out of our price range. She looked at Kathryn, "Was your mattress comfy?"

Kathryn wanted to laugh out loud. If Elsa knew the comfort of the mattress was the last thing she'd noticed last night.

"Oh yes. It certainly beats anything I've ever slept on." She felt herself blushing and hastily took a gulp of water. Fin was watching her. Not in an obvious way, but she knew he was. She felt hot and flustered. Images of him naked on top of her flashed before her eyes; of her squeezing her breasts together. She needed to get away. This breakfast was the worst nightmare imaginable.

Maybe I could say I feel ill.

No, he might offer to drive me home.

The housekeeper was unobtrusively bobbing around, and placing food in the centre of the table so they could help themselves. The talk was about the success of the previous evening. Fin had explained that at the crack of dawn, the cleaners had arrived and taken care of the surplus mess. Nobody would have any idea looking around the house that morning that there had been a party at all.

She fiddled about buttering a slice of toast and watched Fin turn to Elsa, "Are you in a rush to get off this morning? I wondered if you fancied a walk around the village?"

Elsa shook her head, "Not today. I've got some bits to do and Kathryn's keen to get home as Philip's coming back. Is it alright if we get straight off?" She smiled as she took a sip of her tea, "Will you be okay on your own, Billy no mates?"

Fin grinned and his gaze turned towards her making her tummy plummet, "What time is Philip coming back? I could run you home later if you'll take pity on my being on my own all day, and come for a walk?"

Her guts wrenched. She didn't want to be discussing Philip with him, and certainly didn't want to spend any more time in his company.

A walk? Christ!

I need to get away from him.

It was an effort, but she kept her voice light, "Sorry, I'm not so sure what time Philip's back, but like Elsa, I've a few bits to do." She wasn't convincing and she knew it. It felt like she was in some sort of dream and this wasn't really happening. Being in close proximity to him had her nerves in tatters. He was staring at her which made her feel even more edgy.

Elsa was busy spreading marmalade on a slice of toast, and she prayed that she wouldn't be able to spot any tension between her and Fin.

She smiled at Elsa, "So I'll tag along with you two if that's alright," she silently pleaded for it to be soon.

"Of course it is, we'll drop you off."

Elsa turned to Fin, "You're welcome to come and spend the day with Nick and I. We aren't doing much, so could be persuaded to go for a pub lunch later, I've heard that the Kings Arms is rather nice, or we could go to good old Francine's?"

Fin drained his glass of orange juice, "No need to alter your plans. I'll catch up with a few bits that I've been putting off. I've got plenty of paperwork and boring stuff like that to do, and I'd best be around when they come to dismantle the marquee. I'll be fine on my own, honestly."

Elsa looked lovingly towards her brother and affectionately touched his arm, "It must be hard without them."

Kathryn's insides churned at the reference to his late wife and son. They'd spent the night making love when he was still in mourning and she was married? How could they? It was all wrong.

Get out now.

Run if you have to.

She tried the oldest trick in the book, "I'm really sorry, but I've got a splitting headache and feel a bit queasy, I really think I need to get home." And as if to reinforce her need to leave, she stood up, "I don't want to spoil your breakfast so I'll call a taxi."

Nick wiped his mouth on his napkin, "Of course you won't, we're done now anyway aren't we Elsa?"

If Elsa had wanted to stay, Nick standing up gave her little choice. She could have protested, but thankfully she didn't. Her eyes did widen though, as if to say why such a rush.

"Okay, looks like we're off then," she shrugged, "you going upstairs to get the bags then Nick?"

Elsa turned to her, "You definitely had too much last night if you feel so rough," she chided good humouredly, "Tut, tut, tut, what would Philip have to say about that?"

The inference was about Philip's dislike of women and alcohol which stemmed from his own mother being a virtual alcoholic, but she really didn't need reminding of it today of all days. She'd betrayed her husband in the most terrible way, and desperately wanted to be on her own to think about what she'd done.

"You're right, I had far too much to drink."

That's why common sense went out the window,

And I spent the night with your brother's cock inside me.

She turned to Nick, "I'll come up with you. I only need to collect a few bits from my room and I'll be ready." She was aware Fin was watching her closely, but she quickly moved away and followed Nick up the stairs.

She rushed into the en suite and splashed cold water on her face. Anything to cool her down. She fastened her overnight bag and took a couple of deep breaths in and out as she walked along the landing to Nick and Elsa's room.

Nick was waiting for her, "All set?"

She nodded, "I think so. I'm so sorry about breaking up breakfast."

"Don't worry, I'm ready for the off. To be honest, I'd rather have got a taxi home last night, but Elsa insisted we stayed. I prefer my own bed. I know Fin's loaded and his beds are top of the range, but I still prefer my own."

She nodded in agreement, "I know exactly what you mean," and then as if to draw suspicion away from anything between her and Fin, she added, "but it's been nice, I did enjoy the party last night."

"Me too. Fin certainly knows how to throw a good bash."

As they came downstairs and into the hall, Fin and Elsa were talking but their heads turned towards them as they reached the bottom of the huge staircase.

"How are you feeling now?" Fin asked.

What could she say? *Well, after a full night being unfaithful to my husband, I feel pretty lousy actually.*

"I'm okay. Maybe too much wine as Elsa says." She tried to make light of it, but he would know there was nothing physically wrong with her.

Elsa flung her arms around Fin giving him a great big squeeze, and then he shook Nick's hand. Kathryn stood transfixed, how was he going to say goodbye to her?

She needn't have worried. He innocently held her forearms and kissed her cheek, but even that felt like a volt of electricity, "Take care then Kathryn, hopefully if you're well enough, I'll see you at work tomorrow. I think we have a meeting booked first thing, haven't we?" There was no meeting first thing, but she knew by his eyes that statement was a covert way of telling her they would talk tomorrow at work.

She didn't answer about the meeting, but dismissed any thoughts of being off sick, "I'll be fine tomorrow I'm sure. It's just a bit of a headache, nothing a rest and a good night's sleep won't cure."

Say something about the party.

It's expected.

She smiled, "Anyway thank you for a brilliant party."

Nick had opened the front door, and she welcomed the fresh air on her as she felt hot and knew it was likely her face would reflect the heat rippling inside her.

"I'm pleased you enjoyed it, I did too." A cheeky glint flickered in his eyes, "I often find that parties with a lot of pomp and ceremony can sometimes turn out to be long boring evenings, whereas something a little less formal, like last night, can offer much more pleasure and satisfaction."

Jesus Christ!

She was beetroot now.

Elsa was chastising Nick for something so thankfully wouldn't see her blush. Breaking eye contact, she looked down and reached for her trolley bag. Fin did too and as their hands touched, she pulled away quickly as if she'd been burned. She recalled grappling with the trolley bag last night outside her bedroom and look how that ended up. He obviously recalled it too as his lips formed a sexy grin which made her pussy throb unexpectedly.

"Shall I take it while you get in the car?"

She didn't argue. Distancing herself from him was exactly what she needed. Fin walked slightly behind her and she knew his eyes were on her neck and ass. The same neck he'd nibbled and bitten so provocatively until she'd begged for more from him. The same ass he'd slammed against all night long.

As she settled herself in the back seat of the car, she let out a deep breath. She fiddled with her handbag so she didn't have to look at him stood alongside the car, but she knew he was looking at her.

Nick eased the car into gear, and she raised her head to wave goodbye.

"It really was a fabulous party wasn't it?" Elsa said as she waved to Fin with both her hands.

"Yes it was," she agreed.

"You had a good time, didn't you?"

Oh yes, I had a really good time.

You're brother's skill at oral sex is just heavenly!

"Yes, I had a lovely time."

She recalled him nibbling her ears and whispering endearingly, Kat as he brought her to the brink over and over again. She wasn't sexually experienced as she'd only ever been with Philip, but she knew that Fin was an accomplished lover. And during the night as they'd dozed in each other's arms, not once had he got up and used the bidet.

23

The crisp sunshine warmed Kathryn's bare legs through the conservatory window. Sunday was normally one of her favourite days of the week, but not today. She finished her coffee and stared out at the cold dormant garden. Philip was due home shortly and she'd slept with another man.

What happens now? If he'd been unfaithful to her, she'd want him to leave. No, she'd *make* him leave.

I'll have to tell him.

Don't be bloody stupid.

Infidelity wasn't the only dilemma whirling around her head. She couldn't continue to work with Fin now so she'd have to give up her job. But how could she suddenly announce she wanted to leave St Anne's? Philip knew how much her work meant to her so to quit would not only surprise him, it would throw up all sorts of questions that she wouldn't be able to answer.

What the Hell am I going to do?

It's such a bloody mess.

The banging of Philip's car door interrupted any further thoughts about her predicament. Her knotted up tummy clenched even tighter if that was possible. Right, this was it then.

She placed her cup in the sink as she walked through the kitchen and into the hall. He was coming through the front door and greeted her with a loving smile, "Hi, darling." Bottled-up tears scratched the back of her eyes. What had she done?

She rushed forward and wrapped her arms tightly around his waist.

I've let you down.

I'm so sorry.

He held her for a few seconds, before pulling away, "Hey, that's a nice welcome, are you okay?"

"Yes, I'm fine."

"Why are you in your dressing gown?"

"I've had a soak in the bath and wondered if you'd feel like going out for something to eat?"

"Are you sure that's all," his eyes searched hers, "you look really pale?"

"Of course I'm sure."

"You didn't have too much to drink last night did you?" His eyes narrowed accusingly, "Is that why you want to go out, for a big fry up or something?"

"Not at all. I just thought I'd see what you fancied doing."

He placed his car keys in the allocated drawer in the dresser, "I'm not bothered to be honest, but if you really want to go out, I'll take you."

"No, that's fine. I can easily make us something. How was it anyway?"

"A bloody nightmare. I'm shattered with it all."

"You must be, what with the audit and the travelling. Have you eaten?"

"Yes, at the hotel before we left."

"Okay. I'll go and put some clothes on if we're staying in."

He caught her arm, "Actually, can you sit down for a minute before you get dressed. I've got something to tell you."

"That doesn't sound good," she scoured his face, "what's the matter?"

"Let's sit down first." He led the way into the conservatory and sat down on the sofa. She took the adjacent chair and tightened her dressing gown around herself. It suddenly felt cold.

He took a deep breath in, "Keith has announced the firm are having to make redundancies and warned me that I'm likely to be one of them."

"God no," she shook her head, "I can't believe it."

"Me neither," he shrugged, "even if I'm lucky enough to escape it this time, it's likely they'll be making more cuts next year."

"Is it only you, or will there be any others?"

"Martin and Greg have been warned too."

"That's awful, they've both got young children."

"I know. It's a massive blow. It sounds like there'll be a few of us."

She sighed, "What's the criteria for redundancy, do you know?"

"They're currently looking at that but it's not like it used to be, last one in, first to go out. Seemingly it's more about a selection of employees. So they'll have to pick someone nearing retirement age, someone newish, and an equal amount of female and male." He scratched his head, "It was one big bloody surprise, that's for sure."

"Martin and Greg went with you, didn't they?"

"Yes, us three and Keith."

"When did Keith tell you? Don't say he made you work yesterday with this hanging over you all?"

"No, the crafty sod didn't do that. We did all the work until late last night and he told us at breakfast this morning. We'll find out more when we go in tomorrow."

"So you're not on the definite list?"

"*Probable* I think was the word he used."

The news really was a massive blow and put a whole new slant on her leaving St Anne's now. It was no longer a consideration, she wouldn't be able to.

She moved to sit next to him on the sofa and took his hand, "Listen, this isn't the end of the world. As long as you've got your health, that's what's important."

Although his eyes were downcast, he gave her a weak smile, "You're right, but it's such a bloody shock. None of us had any idea."

She squeezed his hand, "Of course it's a shock. You've worked really hard for the firm and don't deserve this."

He curled a loose strand of her hair behind her ear, "What did I ever do so good that I got someone like you, eh? Most women would be going hairless by now."

I need to support you.

Especially after what I've done.

She breathed in deeply, "There's no point getting upset, is there? You're a brilliant accountant, and you'll get another job quickly enough, I know you will. Anyway, you haven't even lost your job yet. Let's wait and see. As Dad always says, it's never over until the fat lady sings."

"Yeah," he nodded, "and we are luckier than some. At least you've got a job. So it's a waiting game now to see what tomorrow brings."

He squeezed her leg and stood up, "I'll go and empty my bag and put my dirty stuff in the wash basket and then you can tell me all about the party."

Trust me.

You really don't want to know.

24

Kathryn was up early for work. Had she actually slept at all? The heat of the shower and the rough sponge seemed to act as a buffer for her nervous energy and she took longer than normal washing. In less than two hours, she'd be seeing Fin again. What was she going to say?

Fin, I've never had sex like that before, you were amazing.

This must never happen again, I'm sorry but I love my husband.

The aroma of coconut shower gel lingered as she stood naked in front of the bathroom mirror. As she gently massaged body cream into her breasts, she thought of Fin, naked, on top of her and loving her in a way which she hadn't known existed. She could feel herself becoming aroused again. Her nipples burned and her clit throbbed. Why was it that she could go for weeks without sex and not even bother satisfying herself, yet one night and two orgasms later, she wanted more? Hadn't she read in some magazine that the more sex you have, the more you want?

Oh, God, I so want you again.

No, not that, she mustn't go there.

She placed the towels on the radiator knowing full well Philip would move them. No wet towels in the bathroom. He would have them in the tumble dryer in five minutes flat. Not for the programmed thirty minutes, though. Ten minutes only is all they need, to save on the electric consumption.

She was drying her hair in the bedroom when Philip came in and walked towards his wardrobe, "What time will you be home today, do you know?"

"Not that late. There's a list on at two o'clock," she couldn't bring herself to say it was Fin operating, "so no later than six I would have thought."

"That's good. I'll have some news by then no doubt."

"Let's hope it's not redundancy and you escape it this time, you never know."

Answering her was impossible for him as he was occupied selecting a work shirt from those lined up in colour order, two white, two light blue and two cream ones. Each one was hanging on an identical black coat hanger and facing the same way on the rail.

He selected a white shirt and turned towards her, "Martin's lent me the James Bond DVD, Spectre. I thought we could watch it tonight. I know you like Daniel Craig, don't you?"

I did, but I've got a real fantasy now.

Daniel Craig has paled into insignificance.

"Yes, I like his films. We'll enjoy that. Is quiche and salad ok?"

25

Only thirty minutes to work and Kathryn would see him again. What would he say to her? Was she just a one-night stand? What was *she* going to say to him?

As she approached the hospital, his black BMW was in his reserved parking slot, flashing at her like a beacon, *I'm already here*. Her heart was thudding as she found her own space in the staff car park. She pulled the handbrake on and cut the ignition. No Janelle today. That was a first.

She pulled the sun visor down and used the vanity mirror to quickly add some lip gloss. Fin was still dominating her thoughts as she entered the female changing room, and almost stumbled over Rosa who was busying herself cleaning the floor with a huge duster.

"Morning, Sister, how you today?"

"Good morning, Rosa, I'm fine thank you, and you?" She opened her locker and put her handbag inside. Blast. The last thing she needed today was Rosa's beady eyes scrutinising her. Rosa was far too perceptive and might sense her anxiety.

"Me, good. Mr Dey bin round bright and early. He want me give you message. Says you to go to his office." She shook her head, "He not look 'appy."

"I'll go and see him shortly. It'll be some sort of problem that's come up regarding the theatres no doubt."

Kathryn selected some theatre scrubs from the shelf and proceeded to take off her top and put it on a hanger.

As she pulled the blue tunic over her head, she could feel Rosa's eyes boring into her back, and knew it was only a matter of seconds before she would speak again.

"I think Mr Dey is the man I saw, Sister, the *man that change everything.*"

"I really don't think so Rosa," she dismissed, injecting firmness into her tone, "Mr Dey is grieving for his late wife and he and I are work colleagues. He would be mortified if anyone heard you talking like this. And please remember that I'm also married."

"Yes, you married, and he sad for losing wife, but he want you. And you want him," she tapped her nose, "I see it. It true."

"No, it isn't true at all," she said, acutely aware she was protesting too much but needing to stress the point, "so please, no more. This is just how rumours start."

"Okay, okay, Sister," she raised her hands, "I say no more. I think you and 'im 'ave scopato and now the black is going to 'appen."

"Scopato?"

Rosa grinned, "You know," she made a circle with her thumb and forefinger, and pushed her other forefinger through it, "sexy man and woman."

Kathryn felt her cheeks warming, "Stop it, Rosa," she snapped, I've heard quite enough now."

Kathryn unlocked her office door and the first thing she noticed was a single Ferrero Rocher chocolate balanced on the keyboard. Oh, my God. Fin must have left it for her. He'd have a duplicate key for her office so would have used it when he came to theatre this morning and given Rosa the message.

Warmth flooded through her. He'll have remembered that first dinner when Elsa had told him how much she loved them. They were a delicious passion of hers and it was so sweet of him to leave one for her. But by doing so, he'd made everything so much harder.

What's he done that for?
Does he want more from me?

Her head was beginning to ache as she switched the

computer on. Ten more minutes and then she'd go and face him, but not just yet. She sat down at her desk.

She couldn't resist bringing the chocolate to her lips. Not to unwrap and eat, it was more a tactile gesture because he was the last person to touch it. What was going to happen when she came face to face with him? He must feel something for her to have left her a chocolate, surely?

She placed the chocolate in the desk drawer and made her way into theatre to secure the day's operating list on the wall, and proceeded to the prep room to write the names of the staff on duty on the whiteboard. It was the senior staff member's duty to allocate the workforce to a particular task for the duration of their shift.

The staff started to filter in one by one, and she was grateful for the distraction by asking each of them about their weekend.

Putting off going to straight Fin's office was juvenile, but nerves got the better of her. She busied herself in the prep room checking the instruments and supplements were ready for the scheduled operations that morning. Everything was ready really but she was avoiding stepping out into the corridor and bumping into Rosa again. How had she deduced that her and Fin had been intimate when she was only just coming to terms with that herself? Yesterday had been a terrible day trying to keep Philip's spirits up and her own guilt hidden, and as unhappy as she was about his possible redundancy and the effect it would have on them both, at least it deflected from the real reason she wasn't herself.

The prep room door swung open, and Janelle came bursting in, "Morning, sorry I'm late. There's been a pile up in Bank Street causing huge tailbacks."

"Oh dear, has anyone been hurt do you know?" Amy asked.

"I'm not sure. There's an ambulance and fire engine there, though, so you do wonder."

"What an awful start to the morning for somebody," Kathryn said, "let's hope it's not too serious."

Janelle reached for the theatre list, "Anyway, every cloud has a silver lining so they say," she grinned, "because

I was running late I nipped in the front entrance, and Mr Dey spotted me. I thought he was going to tell me off, but instead, he widened his eyes and smiled at me. I scooted past him quickly though so he didn't have chance to say anything," she laughed.

"Janelle," Kathryn chastised, "you know he doesn't want staff coming in the front entrance. Now he'll tell me to have a word."

"Well if he does, tell him I'm ready to take my punishment any time he wants to give it." She winked, "I can't think of anything better than a good spanking from that lovely man!"

Kathryn rolled her eyes, "Thank you, that's quite enough of that. I'm nipping round to see him now as according to Rosa, he's looking for me. I've done the work board and put you to scrub up for Mr Sutcliffe. Maybe a long orthopaedic list will take your mind off any spankings."

Kathryn popped into the theatre changing room. Great, Rosa wasn't in there. No more dallying now. It was time to face him.

The dull ache in her head amplified to a pounding throb as she stared at her reflection in the small mirror above the sink. Did she look any different? Was it evident she'd spent the best night of her life having sex with a man that wasn't her husband? That same man she was now going to have to tell that it could never happen again between them, when deep down inside, she wanted nothing more than to repeat the whole thing over and over again. She gave herself a quick squirt of perfume and headed for his office.

As she walked through the hospital foyer, her legs felt like water. The receptionist greeted her, "Hi, Kathryn, did you have a nice weekend?"

Yes. I spent Saturday night having passionate sex with your boss.

So I'd say it was a pretty nice weekend.

"I did, thank you. The nice weather helped. I know it's winter, but it seemed so mild. How's Lilly, is she over her cold?"

"Yes, thank goodness, she's back at school today so normal service is resumed."

Kathryn was about to reply when she felt him behind her. There was no need to turn around to look as her senses told her without any doubt that he was standing there. She took a deep breath in and savoured his gorgeous smell.

That aftershave is divine.

Who needs foreplay?

"Ah, Kathryn, there you are." She turned and found herself looking directly into his striking brown eyes. The very same eyes that had gazed beautifully into hers as he'd entered her for the first time and pushed himself slowly inside her until she accepted all of him. Oh, God.

"Good morning," she smiled brightly at him. Nerves got the better of her and she mumbled the first thing that came into her head, "Have you had a nice weekend?"

Of course he has, stupid.

Shagging a married woman.

"I had an amazing weekend, thank you, but do you think we could get a move on, I have another meeting shortly and really need to prepare for that. Shall we?"

Amazing!?

God, me too.

He indicated with the folder in his hand the way forward and the receptionist smiled at them both. She would have no idea of the sexual tension between them.

They entered his office together and he moved towards his desk, "Would you like a coffee?" He looked edgy, nervous.

"I'm fine thank you. I haven't got long I'm afraid."

"We'll have as long as it takes as we need to get this sorted," he said, "please, take a seat." She gratefully sat, her knees felt like they might buckle any second.

He sat down too and she stared at his tie knot, which was ridiculous when they'd been so intimate, but she was scared to look directly into his eyes. She was frightened what she'd see there.

He was staring at her though, "How are you?" he asked.

Guilty.

I feel like crap.

"Not good," she swallowed, "terrible if I'm honest."

She lifted her eyes to meet his, and her heart melted at the level of concern she saw, "Yes, I guessed as much."

"I keep thinking it's a dream that I'll wake up from. I can't believe what we did."

"I take it this has never happened before?"

She shook her head, "No, of course it hasn't. I feel wretched. Philip doesn't deserve this."

"You shouldn't be so hard on yourself," he said, "none of it was planned."

"Wasn't it? I keep thinking back to you telling me that you wanted to speak to me alone that night. Were you thinking about... you know, us having sex?"

His voice softened, "I've thought about nothing else since the day I met you," he said dryly, "but my intention genuinely was to find out if you felt the same way," a rueful smile curved his mouth, "which apparently you did."

I did. I do.

And I loved every second of it.

"But this can't go anywhere, surely you realise that, I'm happily married."

His dark brows arched, "In my experience, *happily married* women don't have affairs."

"Please don't say that," she pleaded, "and it's hardly an affair. It was ... a one-night stand; people have them all the time."

His mouth twitched, "I'd like to think it was much more than that Kathryn, and you know it was."

The way her name rolled off his tongue with a slight trace of accent sounded beautiful. Her throat constricted, "What do you expect me to do? It can't go anywhere."

"I don't *expect* you to do anything other than being honest so we can at least discuss what happened between us." She tried to interject but he lifted his hand, "let me finish. I didn't think when I lost Saskia that I would ever want another woman again, so this ... this attraction between us is equally as hard for me to deal with as you. I've tried to ignore it, and in normal circumstances a married woman would be completely off my radar, but I can't help the way I feel." She watched his Adam's apple move as he swallowed. "I want you in my life."

"Please stop this. We can't have this conversation."

"Why not? It meant something to you, I know it did."

It meant the world to me.

But it can't go anywhere.

It would be easy to say it was the best night of her life, but she couldn't, "It was lust, pure and simple, which we gave into. Let's put it down to too much alcohol like we said."

"What if I don't want to do that? What if I want more?"

"There is no more, can't you see that? We have to put Saturday night behind us and forget it ever happened. I know that won't be easy with working together, but that's how it has to be."

Even though the heat between my thighs is saying otherwise.

Even though I'd love to lie down on your desk and do it all again.

His jaw tightened, "That's how *it has to be* is it? Aren't you even going to consider my feelings?"

"Oh, come on, you know as well as I do, we can't pursue this. We did say it was just for one night," she reminded him.

"If I remember rightly, *you* said it was just one night, I don't recall saying any such thing." His dark eyes were far too intense.

She sighed, "Look, because of what happened between us, I did contemplate leaving my job to make things easier. Unfortunately when Philip returned yesterday, he told me that it's likely he's going to be made redundant so I have no choice but to stay here. That's why I think the best thing we can do is try to get back to some sort of professional footing."

I can't be with you.

This is how it has to be.

"I am so sorry," she continued with a thickness in her throat, "*deeply* sorry about all of this, but surely you didn't think after one night we could be together."

"I don't know what I thought," he shrugged, "I had

hoped we'd be having a discussion about what we *both* want, but it appears you've closed the door on that."

I can't consider what you want.

There's no point, this has to stop now.

"I have to. You must be able to see that? I'm so ashamed about what I've done and really would like to try and forget it." Her eyes pleaded with him, "Do you think we can find a way to do that?"

It was evident by his expression that her request wasn't what he wanted to hear. He paused, and the quietness between them stretched until a noise from the corridor disturbed the silence. She watched his chest rise as he took a deep breath in, "If that's what you want, then yes, we'll have to at least try. We can't have you *ashamed*."

"Fin, please ..."

He interrupted her, "I think we're done now."

She could hear bitterness in his tone, and his accent suddenly seemed more pronounced as he continued, "What happened between us is clearly *regrettable* as far as you're concerned. So," a thunderous cloud of sadness passed across his face causing her chest to constrict, "as it's evident that it isn't me you want, then, yes, you are quite right, we need to move on."

She blinked back the tears that threatened and swallowed the growing lump in her throat.

But I do want you.

I'd love to feel like that again.

He pushed back his chair and got to his feet. He was dismissing her. Even though she wasn't going to leave Philip, for some bizarre reason she wanted him to ask her to, which was completely irrational. But what had been rational since he'd walked into her life?

She stood also and gave him a weak smile, "Thank you," before turning towards the door and letting out a relieved breath.

Get out of here, keep walking.

One foot in front of the other.

Her hand was resting on the door handle and she almost made it out, but his voice stopped her, "One other thing."

She turned her head to look at him, and his normally

handsome face looked slightly distorted, as if he was in pain.

"From now on, may I suggest that you and I are never alone together?"

Confusion must have been evident on her face as he added, "Because if we ever are, I'll be tempted to take you in my arms and make love to you again, and believe you me, if that happens, I'll not let you go a second time."

26

The morning dragged and Kathryn's insides were in turmoil. *I'll not let you go a second time,* he'd said.

I don't want you to.

But I can't be with you.

The confrontation with Fin had left her tummy in knots so she knew eating lunch would only aggravate her already delicate stomach. She left the others eating in the tearoom and went into the prep room to check the instruments and extras for the afternoon list.

As if things weren't bad enough, Fin had two surgical procedures that afternoon. Why couldn't he operate on a Friday or something like that? Any other time, but not the day after the weekend she'd spent a night in bed with him.

Today, she wished herself a thousand miles away. She didn't want to be part of his operating list at all but Janelle was scrubbing for him for the first time, and although she was an experienced scrub nurse in general and orthopaedic cases, she wasn't used to plastic surgery.

As part of theatre's training and development programme, they'd always had a senior member of staff scrub in for the first time when one of the staff nurses worked with a new surgeon, so she had no choice really other than to stand alongside to support her.

She stared at the two procedures on the theatre list for that afternoon. On most occasions, surgeons either bought the services of a junior doctor from the local hospital, or used St Anne's resident medical officer to assist them for the larger cases. It was quite a skill to be able to assist a surgeon during a complex surgical procedure, and nurses did sometimes have to step in which normally she wouldn't hesitate to do, but she prayed he'd have an assistant that afternoon otherwise it would be her supporting with him and she couldn't, not today.

Please let him bring someone to assist.
No, don't let him bring anyone.

Janelle interrupted her thoughts, "Are you okay, you didn't have any lunch?"

"I'm fine. I'm not that hungry really. I haven't had chance to tell you as you were scrubbed this morning when I told the others, but Philip's likely to be made redundant."

"God, that's a bummer, I'm sorry to hear that. Will he get any redundancy pay?"

"Not as much as we would like I'm afraid. Fortunately we don't have a massive mortgage or any debts, but it's still awful. He'll find out more today, but even if he does escape the redundancies this year, it sounds like there'll be more next year."

"Bloody hell," Janelle pulled a face, "good thing you've got your job here, and at least you don't have any children." And totally oblivious to the pain those words caused, she continued, "You know what I mean, more mouths to feed and all that."

Kathryn thought of how much she wished she did have other mouths to feed, but now wasn't the time or the place, "You're right. We can manage on my salary but I'm hoping he's not out of work for long. Philip's not the stay-at-home type at all," she frowned. "Anyway, let's talk about this afternoon's case, are you okay with it all? I've checked the instruments and supplements, so we've got everything ready."

"I'm fine, I'm pleased you're with me, though," Janelle replied, "at least until I get well under way. Then if I'm doing okay, you can leave me to it. Please don't go far, though," she grimaced, "I don't want a telling off from Mr Dey if I'm a bit hesitant and unsure."

"He won't tell you off, everybody's got to learn. I'll

have a quick word with him beforehand and explain I want you to learn plastics."

"Would you? Thanks, that'd be great. I'm quite looking forward to being up close and personal with him, though I have to say," Janelle grinned, "he's so gorgeous, and it's a waste him being single and all that."

Keep your hands off.

He's not single.

Kathryn scowled, "What are you like Janelle, honestly."

They headed to the tearoom where Fiona had made them all drinks. Kathryn positioned herself facing the door, waiting for him to come down the corridor.

The talk was about the new television series the night before with graphic sex scenes which the majority were surprised had even been aired on terrestrial TV. Kathryn hadn't seen it so didn't join in. She'd enough sex scenes of her own to think about.

Although the theatre entrance was concealed from where they were sitting, when it opened, she knew instinctively it was him. The tearoom was at the end of a long corridor and she watched every step as he made his way towards them all. His strides almost seemed in slow motion to her, and in those short seconds, her heartrate increased dramatically. He might have looked handsome in his expensive navy blue suit, but the image in her mind was his taught naked body.

I remember him filling me.

And calling my name as he spurted inside me.

"Hi." Was that her voice sounding normal? "Have you brought an assistant with you?"

"No, I'm afraid not. I tried but couldn't get one. Apparently the ward doctor's tied up with an admission at the moment but says he should be free in about an hour. Is there anyone here that could assist me for the first case?"

Me, if you're nice.

But not if you're horrible.

"Yes. Janelle's scrubbing for you today and she's done loads of scrubbing in general theatres, but not plastics. I was going to scrub and stand alongside her, but I could assist you and help Janelle at the same time?"

"That sounds like a plan. I'll get my theatre scrubs on and be with you in a few minutes."

"Fine, can I get you a coffee?"

"No thank you." He nodded curtly and walked into the male changing room adjacent to the tearoom.

He's switched to being the boss.

And I've breached my employee position.

*

Janelle had scrubbed up and was in the prep room preparing the sterile trolley for the abdominoplasty procedure. Kathryn was alongside her, scrubbed also.

Amy was the circulating nurse for that afternoon's list and was opening sterile extras onto the trolley.

"What order does he use the blades in?" she asked Kathryn.

"A size ten for the main incision, and a fifteen to fashion the umbilicus."

She attached the blade to the scalpel handle and placed it in the receiver to hand to Mr Dey when he was ready to start.

Kathryn looked at Amy, "He'll want Chirocaine, two point five percent when he's closing so if you could have it ready to give to Janelle when she asks."

Through the glass partition on the door of the prep room she saw the patient being taken into theatre by the technician and the anaesthetist. Amy went through to help transfer the patient from the trolley onto the operating table.

"Have you got everything?" Kathryn asked her.

"I think so. If not I'll yell out for Amy to get me it."

"You'll be fine. Mr Dey is quite easy to scrub for."

"I'm glad you're assisting him. I'd hate to have to assist and manage my trolley as well, although I know you do it regularly."

"Ah yes, but I've been working in theatres a lot longer than you so I'm used to it. When it's a procedure you haven't done before, it's best to concentrate on your trolley and the surgeon. At least Mr Dey is slow and methodical so there'll be no dramas. Unlike Mr Hurst."

"Oh God, no. He's got chaos tattooed on his forehead," Janelle sniggered.

Once the patient was positioned and the Anaesthetist had given permission to start the surgery, Amy held the prep room door open for them and they squeezed through, careful not to let the trolley or themselves touch anything. Any contamination would mean a rescrub and the whole preparation process starting again.

The operation began by Mr Dey making an incision to the patient's skin and dissecting the abdomen. Janelle watched Kathryn. Her dexterity was evident as she was swabbing the area he was cutting, and offering him the diathermy when a small vessel wouldn't stop bleeding and needed cauterising. Kathryn reached up to the sterile handle and moved the light so that there was a better view inside the patient's abdomen.

"I didn't ask you to do that," Mr Dey snapped at Kathryn.

"Sorry. I thought it might help you see a bit better."

"I'll let you know when I want you to move the light."

Kathryn's eyes widened above her mask and Janelle gave her a 'what an arse he's being' look.

Janelle concentrated on attaching swabs to a holder and placing them near Kathryn's hand so that she could use them to swab the area to keep a bloodless field. That way Mr Dey would be able to see where he was dissecting. It was the boring part of the operation and her mind started to wonder.

I bet it's not that long before he gets snapped up, he really is quite hot. Wouldn't it be fantastic to go out with him? How good would that be? Imagine being his girlfriend, you'd get plenty of respect then. Nights out in swanky restaurants and trips to the theatre, and I bet he's amazing in bed. You could tell he'd be ace at that.

It's not unheard of for doctors and consultants ending up with nurses. I bet Kathryn wishes she wasn't married to that knobhead Philip. If she wasn't, Mr Dey most probably would be after her like all the other males who seemed besotted with the darling of the theatre suite.

His irritation with Kathryn was becoming more noticeable, "I can't see where the bleeding's coming from. Can you swab there? No, not like that. Give me the suction." She watched, puzzled as he snatched the suction out of Kathryn's hand.

What the hell is the matter with him? He couldn't have a better assistant than Kathryn. She could almost do the surgery herself she was that good at it. Why was he being so horrible to her? It was unusual to see her standing tensely as she was always so laidback. Maybe her theatre crown was slipping? It would be a first for her not to be liked.

Being the ultimate professional, Kathryn didn't lose her cool, though. She carried on trying to assist, but interestingly didn't speak to Mr Dey. It was unlike her as she always was so chatty with the consultants. Yes, there was a place for quietness during the operation which they all understood. Nobody would be laughing and joking during the crucial dissection part of the surgery, but when they were closing the wound, generally the banter would begin.

The operation was time-consuming, but Kathryn had been right, there wasn't much to it. Janelle was pleased with herself that she'd had everything to hand as Mr Dey had requested it, and she hadn't made any mistakes.

As the operation was drawing to a close and Mr Dey began removing the retractors, the theatre was suddenly plunged into silence when the background music stopped. The only sounds were the noises of the anaesthetic equipment signifying all was well with the unconscious patient.

Amy went over to change the CD and paused to select one from those lined up on the shelf. Matron purchased an eclectic array of music to suit each surgeon's individual preference, but more often than not, the surgeons didn't specify a particular CD. Most were content to go along with whatever was playing in the background, with the exception of one or two of the older consultants who sometimes asked for the music to be turned off.

"Can we do a final count Amy please?" Janelle asked.

Her and Amy began counting the swabs, needles and instruments on her trolley. Ensuring they were all accounted for was standard procedure of the scrub nurse to ensure nothing was left inside the patient. As she and Amy finished the count, the harmonious voice of Harry Gardia came on. She liked this one.

"Are you sure you want me, am I right for you? Show me you love me, and I'll show you, I love you too."

"For Christ's sake, switch that racket off." Mr Dey barked.

Amy moved across theatre to turn it off.

"You are the answer to my dreams, now everything's perfect so it seems."

"I said off. Did you hear me? Switch the damn thing off, now."

"Okay, okay," Amy replied, pressing stop on the CD player, "it's off."

Janelle couldn't see the whole of Kathryn's face as part of it was obscured by her theatre mask, but she could see her eyes which mirrored her own. What was going on? Why was he being so nasty?

Better try and keep him sweet, "The swabs, needles and instruments are all correct, Mr Dey."

"Thank you, Janelle. Are you taking the next case?"

"Yes, if that's okay with you."

"Fine." He looked at Kathryn, "Can you see if the ward doctor is free to assist me for the next case."

God, how cutting was that. He might have well have said he didn't want Kathryn to help him anymore. She didn't flinch though and looked at Amy, "Could you ring the ward and see if Doctor Singh's free? If he's still tied up, can you ask Fiona to come through and assist Mr Dey for the next case please?"

He spoke again to Kathryn. "You can go now. Janelle and I can finish up here."

Talk about being dismissed. There were only the last few sutures to do and the dressing to put on but it couldn't have been more obvious he wanted rid of her. How odd? It was stupid to feel pleased, but she was. Kathryn was held in such high esteem by everyone, it was refreshing to see someone who didn't seem to like her that much.

What she needed to do now, was try really hard with the next case and see if she could make a bit of headway with him. Who knows what that might lead to?

27

Kathryn's mood was irritable as she pulled into the drive. She'd been stuck in roadworks operating a convoy system, and typically her turn for the passage through was much longer than anyone else waiting. From now on, she'd find another route into work as she couldn't face that again.

She locked the car and walked towards the front door. *That was one helluva day.* Fin had been a bastard. Their conversation had clearly hurt his male pride. What did he think she was going to do, for Christ's sake, leave her husband after one night of sex?

Janelle had told her Fin had been fine with Dr Singh assisting him for the second case, and had even asked for some music to be put back on. Not the Harry Gardia CD, though.

She'd sat in her office wondering if he might try and catch her as he left theatre to apologise for his obnoxious behaviour, but he didn't. He changed from his scrubs into his suit and left. She couldn't decide whether that made her angry or relieved.

Philip was waiting for her in the hall as she opened the front door. His expression said everything.

"How was it?" she asked, slipping off her coat and hanging it up in the closet.

"Bloody awful. I *am* on the list of redundancies. Can you believe that after all the effort I've put in? What a shit company."

"It's terrible, and so unfair when you've worked so hard. I'm really sorry." She put her arms around him and hugged him tightly. He felt familiar, unlike the newness of Fin's arms. "Any idea about redundancy pay?" she asked, pulling away.

"Not that much because I haven't been there long enough. I reckon eight measly grand if I'm lucky."

She raised her eyebrows, "That's better than nothing, I suppose. It'll tide us over until you get something else."

"*If* I get something else. There are thousands of men and women my age looking for work, so it's not going to be easy."

"I know, but we need to stay positive, and you're not old," she frowned, "I don't class thirty-two as old."

"I do. All companies are interested in these days are young graduates so they can pay them less."

"I'm sure there'll be someone out there that will want experience. We've just got to get cracking with letters and applications. You'll have all the time in the world to do that once you've left work."

"Thanks for reminding me."

"Don't be like that, you know what I mean. Did they say when you'd have to finish?"

He shook his head, "It's not immediate by the sound of things."

"That's good then. It gives you time to look around and see what's available."

They walked into the kitchen together and she washed her hands ready to prepare their meal. As she was drying them, she remembered, "A sudden thought came into my head driving home, a sort of lightbulb moment if you like."

"Oh bloody hell," he lifted the salad drawer and quiche out of the fridge, "I'm dreading what you're going to say next."

She rolled her eyes, "I thought that maybe you could set up freelance. You know, become independent and offer your services to companies and do some short-term contracts."

He frowned, "Who do you think would employ me doing that?"

"I don't know, you'd have to do your research, but it's worth thinking about. You always hated working at Bemrose & Carr anyway, so why not have a go at branching out on your own?"

"I'd prefer to work for a company with good employee benefits rather than setting up on my own and not getting holiday or sick pay."

"Mmmm, yes, there is that I suppose," she agreed, turning the oven on to warm the quiche.

She began chopping up the salad, "I'll get this sorted and we can chat over dinner."

"Okay. I've just got to make a quick phone call."

As she plated the quiche and put it on the table along with the salad bowl, Philip reached for a bottle of wine from the rack.

"Good idea," she said, "I could do with a drink. Are we allowed on a week night, though?"

He raised his eyebrows, "Sarcasm is the lowest form of wit you know."

"And the highest form of intelligence, remember." She was pleased to see at least he was smiling. It was such rotten luck losing his job, especially as he worked so hard. He never missed a day, and did loads of unpaid work from home. It really wasn't fair.

They sat opposite each other at the dining table. He poured the wine and handed her a glass, "You'll need this when I tell you what else has happened."

"Oh no, what now?" she put a slice of quiche on his plate and he reached for the salad bowl.

"We've had a wreath delivered to the house."

"What?" Her eyes darted rapidly around the kitchen.

"It's not here," he said, "I didn't accept it."

"I don't understand."

He shook his head, "I don't either, but some bloody nutcase has sent a wreath to us. I felt quite sorry for the delivery girl when she tried to hand it to me and I said nobody had died. She checked all the details, though, and she had your name."

"My name?" *That is creepy.*

He reached in his pocket and handed her a small

card, "I kept this but told her to take the wreath away."

As she looked at the writing, bile rose up in the back of her throat, *Night, night, sleep tight*. She shuddered, as if someone has walked over her grave and immediately Rosa's words sprung to mind, *'the black is going to happen'*. God, this was horrible.

She threw the card down, quickly, as if it burned her fingers.

"The sick bastard."

"Who?"

"Gary, bloody Hicks, that's who. It'll be him doing this, like the pizza delivery."

"What pizza delivery?"

Damn, she'd completely forgotten to tell him. Fin had dominated her thoughts since Saturday night. Even the prospect of Philip's redundancy had faded into second place.

She explained about the pizza delivery and watched his expression change from curious to annoyed, "Why is this the first time I'm hearing about this?"

"Because it's the first time I've had chance to tell you. Yesterday when you came back, you dropped the bombshell about the redundancy, so it slipped to the back of my mind."

"You had all day to say something," he challenged, "that's three things, the photograph, a wreath, and now you're telling me about a bloody pizza delivery. I can't imagine why you didn't say anything sooner." He glared before taking a huge gulp of wine.

She rubbed her forehead with her fingers as if that would miraculously soothe the headache she'd had all day. "I was hoping the pizza delivery was a mistake, but put like that, it is worrying. I'm certain it's Gary Hicks doing all of this, though." She paused for a moment, "Does he still go to the Number One on a Saturday?"

"Every week," he nodded, "he's always there, and he does the walks. But I thought you said the police didn't think it was him that sent the photograph?"

"They didn't, but who else could it be? It's someone that wants to cause trouble and he did threaten to."

"I'm not so sure," he shrugged, "this sort of thing isn't

really his style."

"His *style*? How would you know what *his style* is?"

"I know him from the club. He's okay really."

"Rubbish. He's not okay, he's a bloody menace and this needs stopping. Pity I'm not at work tomorrow to let Fin know."

Philip's expression was vacant, so despite telling him yesterday about her plans, he'd clearly forgotten.

"I'm on a day off and going to the spa with Elsa, remember? It'll have to be Wednesday when I speak to him."

"It might not be Gary, you know," he said completely ignoring her reminder about her day out, "you haven't any evidence, so you need to think carefully about playing detective and pointing a finger at him."

"Don't be stupid," she snapped, "I'm not playing detective. If I was, I'd be trying to find out why you're defending him, he's hardly a friend."

"I never said he was, but I still don't think it's him."

"Who else could it be, for God's sake? I can't think of anyone apart from him who'd be doing all of this."

"I don't know," he shrugged, "but he's talking about emigrating so he's obviously moved on."

"Good. That's the best news I've heard all day. I'll speak to Fin on Wednesday and hopefully he'll be able to get to the bottom of it."

"Will he? He didn't *get to the bottom* of who sent the photo? Did you tell him on Saturday night about the pizza delivery?"

Erm, no.

We had other things on our minds.

"No. I didn't think his party was the time or the place. I'll tell him at work."

He raised his eyebrows, "Maybe you should look a bit closer to home who might be doing all of this."

"What do you mean?" she frowned.

"It could well be one of those other weirdo's you work with."

"What are you talking about, *weirdo's*?"

"That shirt lifter Lee for one, or that man eater Janelle."

"They aren't *weirdo's* at all," she said through gritted teeth, "that's your warped mind. I can assure you, neither of them would be playing these sorts of tricks. It's Gary Hicks, I know it is, and I'm sure Fin will sort it once he finds out."

"Are you? I'm not so sure."

"What makes you say that?"

"Something Nick said."

She sighed. She loved Nick to bits, but he could be a bit of an old woman.

"What has Nick said?"

"He says Fin's not exactly all he seems."

I can vouch for that.

But then again, neither am I.

"In what way?"

"He reckons he's essentially a businessman wearing surgeon's gloves. Apparently every decision he makes has pound signs attached to it. If there's nothing in it for financial gain, then he's not interested. Nick said he's charming when he wants to be, but ruthless and has a dark side. Seemingly he'll tread on anyone that gets in his way."

"What's wrong with that?" she defended, "That's what business people are like. That's how they succeed."

"I know. I'm just saying, don't get your hopes up he'll sort things. It doesn't sound like a wreath and a pizza delivery will be top of his priority list while he's running his *empire*. I don't think for one minute he'll be interested in what's happening in this house."

He's very interested in what's happening at this house.

Only not in the way you're suggesting.

"Shall we try and eat some of this," she sighed and reached for more wine.

The rest of the evening was spent with Philip enveloped in his thoughts about his future employment and looking online for opportunities, while she sat in front of the television having no idea whatsoever what was on the screen.

The wreath was playing on her mind. It was terribly unsettling. The pizza delivery had been bad enough, but the wreath was horrible. What would Fin make of it? The thought of speaking to him caused a flutter in her chest.

Don't be alone with me.

I'll not let you go a second time.

Was it only two nights since they'd been together? It seemed an age ago. What was he doing right now? Her clit twitched as she fantasised about him making love to her, caressing her with that gorgeous mouth of his, and calling her name over and over again as he reached his climax.

How was she ever going to make love again to Philip after him? She'd strategically placed a box of tampons in a prominent position in the bathroom in case he had any ideas. That might stall things for a while as he wasn't the most highly-sexed man, but even though their lovemaking was sporadic, and of late almost non-existent, he'd smell a rat if it *never* happened.

She couldn't put off making love indefinitely, so how was the situation going to be resolved? Everything was different now she'd had a taste of what making love could be like. She wanted more of that, not wham bam thank you, ma'am, and a dousing in the bidet.

28

Elsa was sprawled out on a lounger at the day spa, "This is just what the doctor ordered. Thanks for coming with me today."

"No need to thank me," Kathryn smiled, "anything is better than a day cleaning the house and doing the washing. I wish you'd let me pay for myself though, I feel awful being here and not contributing."

"Don't be bloody daft. Who else would I want to spend the day with? I've got vouchers galore to spend here, Nick has no imagination where birthday and Christmas gifts are concerned, it's either perfume or spa vouchers."

"Bless him, Philip's not much better. Men, they're useless aren't they? Why don't they use a bit of imagination? There's a stack of female sales assistants only too willing to help in the major stores, yet they seem to repeat the same gifts year after year."

She rubbed some Vaseline on her lips, "At least Nick gets you Spa vouchers, Philip would never think of anything like that. He takes the easy way out and asks me what I want, and then takes me shopping to buy it so I never get a surprise."

"What we need is someone like Fin," Elsa smiled, "now there's a man that has romance as his middle name. He spoiled Saskia rotten. He would think nothing of whisking her to New York for a few days, and the jewellery he bought for her was stunning. He seems to be one of those blokes that just knows what makes a woman tick."

Kathryn's tummy plummeted, which was ridiculous. Fin didn't belong to her, so she shouldn't feel jealous at the mention of his wife.

She couldn't resist, "How long were they married for?"

"Oh, ages." Elsa paused for a moment as if calculating the number of years in her head, "Twelve years I think. Christiaan was eleven when they were killed, so yes, twelve years or thereabouts."

Kathryn kept her voice light, "Were they madly in love?"

"I guess so. Saskia and I weren't ever close so she wasn't one for confiding in me, but Fin was happy and it was obvious he adored her."

"Fancy losing her *and* his son, life is so cruel, isn't it?"

"Yes it is, but he's coped amazingly well with it all. I think the move to the UK has helped, and he's certainly throwing everything at St Anne's." She paused and a weary expression passed across her face, "My illness has upset him, though, I know it has."

Kathryn touched her arm, "It's upset us all. We can't bear you being poorly. How's it going anyway? What's the latest from the oncologist?"

"Not much. He seems pleased, but they don't say much these medical types," she winked.

She smiled at her dear friend, "But he's happy about the way things are going? You don't say much."

"Because there isn't much to say. Everything's as expected at this stage, he reckons, so that's good enough for me."

"Great, I'm pleased. I want us to be sat here a year from now drinking Prosecco, and saying thank God it's all over and behind you."

"Yeah, that will be good," Elsa replied, but not convincingly.

"You're sure you're okay?"

"I'm fine. I'm a bit tired, but the nurse said I will be for the next few months. It's all part and parcel of it."

"I guess you will be and you'll just have to go with it. Once the treatment is finished you'll gradually get stronger each day, and before you know it, you'll be back to your old self. Your hair looks lovely by the way. Has there been any mention about losing it again?"

"No, the oncologist said I wouldn't this time so I'm thrilled about that. Anyway, enough about all of that nonsense, we're here to enjoy ourselves and relax. I'd rather talk about the bit of gossip I have."

I bet you would.

Anything to deflect from yourself, you poor soul.

"Go on then, I'm listening. What gossip?"

"It's about Fin. He'd kill me for saying anything, but I know you won't let on you know."

Kathryn stiffened, "No, I won't say anything, what about him?"

"He's taking your Matron out for dinner this weekend?"

Kathryn's stomach lurched, *no*. And totally oblivious to the explosion erupting inside of her, Elsa carried on, "He's playing it down, reckons it's just dinner, but I'm hoping."

No, not Melons.

Don't take her *out, you're mine.*

"What's she like," Elsa asked, "do you reckon she's his type?"

The green-eyed monster lurking inside, reared its ugly head and thumped her, but she forced herself not to react outwardly, "She's nice enough, but I've no idea what his type would be."

"I don't either since Saskia. He likes good-looking women, though, and he used to be a real player in his younger days, so I'm guessing that now he's asked a woman out to dinner, he's ready to get back in the game."

No. Please, nobody else.

You belong to me.

She kept her voice steady, "Do you think he's been with anyone since he lost his wife?"

"I doubt it," Elsa shrugged, "but who knows. You know what men are like; they have to empty their sacks regularly."

Kathryn giggled, "Honestly, what are you like."

"It's true. Their blood supply only runs to two organs in their bodies, their brains and their dicks, and as we all

153

know, never at the same time."

She laughed outwardly at Elsa's wicked humour, but inwardly she was seething at the thought of Fin with anyone but her.

Elsa swung her legs onto the floor, "Come on, let's have a swim before our lunch."

Lunch? Waves of tightness gripped her abdomen. Elsa wouldn't have any idea about the effect her innocuous announcement would have, but food was the last thing on her mind right now. She felt physically sick as she followed her towards the pool.

Bloody Melons.

I knew she was after him.

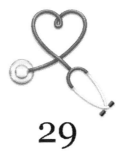

29

Kathryn was sitting with the staff in the tearoom having lunch as the theatre door opened and Fin walked towards them. Had it only been four days since their night together? Four long days and four long nights that she'd craved him, and relived every touch and every orgasm over and over again.

First thing in the morning as she opened her eyes she thought of him, and at night in bed, he dominated her dreams. Thank goodness no one would have any idea about the internal Catherine wheel whirling away inside her as he paused in the doorway looking incredibly handsome in his dark suit and snazzy tie.

I've missed you.

So much.

"Hi," he smiled at them all, "how was this morning's list?"

"Fine," she replied, "the last patient was cancelled as Dr Staves didn't like the sound of her chest so that's why we've finished on time."

"That makes a change for you all, then. At least you'll all get your lunch rather than the hurried sandwiches you usually have to grab."

"Yes, it does make a change." She paused wondering why he'd come round to theatre, "Did you want me for something?"

"I came to let you all know," he glanced at the others not just her, "I'm having an arthroscopy on my knee next

Tuesday. Liam Sutcliffe's doing it for me. I thought I'd better come and warn you as I'm not the best patient."

Act natural.

Don't let anyone see you're concerned.

"Oh dear, I'm sorry to hear that. What have you done to your knee?" she asked, and then quickly added, "if you don't mind me asking?"

"Nothing specific this time. It's an old skiing injury that flares up every now and again. Liam's going to give it a quick wash out and have a look at the cartilage ... well, so he says." He pulled a cheeky face and she wanted to kiss him for his humour.

She smiled back at him, "Let's hope that does the trick. It's probably a bit of debris floating around, that's all."

"Yes, I hope so," he nodded, "my problem is I'm a bit of a wimp when it comes to having surgery."

"You and most of the male population, Mr Dey," Fiona interjected.

"It's a man thing," Lee joined in, "women don't understand how we males are about displaying weakness. We're macho, so it's not in our makeup to be ill or needy."

Fin's eyes crinkled at the edges, "Quite," which had the others sniggering.

Oh my darling,

I want to look after you.

"So you'll be off work for a while?" she asked distraught that she wouldn't catch a glimpse of him each day. Even now she dreaded the weekend and not seeing him for two whole days.

"Only for a couple of days, I'll be back after the weekend."

You live alone,

Who'll look after you?

She wanted to rush up and put her arms around him and tell him she'd take care of him personally, but instead she joked, "Well, you've come to the right place, we'll take care of you, I promise."

"I'm banking on it," he grinned. "I'm pretty hopeless when it comes to having an anaesthetic," he widened his eyes, "which is absolutely ridiculous I know. It takes me back to a pilot I operated on once who was terrified of surgery and almost called it off, much to the amusement of staff when you think about people's fears about flying and crashing. He told me that he loved flying planes as he was in control, and it was relinquishing that control by putting yourself in the hands of others that frightened him, and I think that's what it is for me."

They were a captive audience listening to him. He had such charisma, and by saying those few words, he'd made his own fears sound completely rational.

He continued, "That's why I thought I'd come round and let you know so that if there's a kind soul amongst you who wants to take pity on me and hold my hand as I go off to sleep, then I'd be grateful."

Me. I'll do it.

I'll hold your hand, and I won't let go.

Lee sniggered, "That'll be me as I'm usually on anaesthetics for Mr Sutcliffe's list," which brought a huge laugh from the others.

"Thanks for that," Fin rolled his eyes, "how very reassuring."

Janelle joined in, "At least you'll see how the hospital runs from a patient's perspective. Surely that's got to be a positive?"

Shut up, Janelle, the man's nervous.

He's hardly going to be interested in customer care.

"Ah, yes, that's a point which I must admit, I hadn't thought about in the midst of all these nerves," he grinned. "Right, on that note, I'll get back to work. Have a good afternoon."

She watched each step he took as he walked away down the corridor to the theatre exit.

I'll take care of you.

And kiss you better.

Janelle kept her voice low, "I'm more than happy to hold his hand while he goes off to sleep."

"Yeah but it's not just his hand you want to hold," Lee laughed.

Laughter erupted in the tearoom which annoyed Kathryn. She stood up and took her plate and cup to the sink, "Thank you. I think that's quite enough now. Let's try and behave like professionals shall we, he is our boss after all."

"Yeah," Janelle said, "that's the problem. He's not old and ordinary like you'd expect a boss to be, he's young and hot, and needs someone to take care of him."

Kathryn squeezed some washing up liquid into the sink. "Why don't you go and check the order of this afternoon's list with the ward, and Lee can you check the pharmacy delivery please?"

The image of Melons Plenty with Fin was bad enough, but Janelle and him together didn't bear thinking about.

After she'd washed and dried her lunch dishes, she went to her office and busied herself printing off the theatre numbers for the week. As she opened the drawer for a paperclip, she spotted the Ferrero Rocher chocolate Fin had left the Monday morning after their night together.

She took it out and opened its golden wrapper. Was the significance of leaving a chocolate because he hoped they'd have a future together, or was it just a thank you for a fantastic night of sex? There was no way of knowing as he'd been horrible that morning in his office and in the afternoon when she'd scrubbed to assist him. Yet he'd been lovely today when he came round to tell them about his op. Maybe he was a bit of a charmer when he wanted something as Nick had implied to Philip?

She popped the chocolate in her mouth and savoured the delicious flavour on her taste buds, sucking it slowly to make it last. An image sprung to mind of his gorgeous mouth sucking her. God, she wanted to feel like that again. How could she have ever thought that one night would be enough with him? Maybe because before him, she had no idea that sex between two people could be so beautiful.

The shrill sound of the telephone interrupted her daydream, and as she reached for the receiver she remembered she'd forgotten to tell him about the wreath.

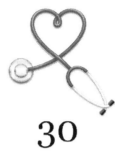

30

On the morning of Fin's surgery, Kathryn arrived at work earlier than usual. She hadn't been able to sleep thinking about him coming down to theatre as a patient.

Since their night together, things weren't the same between them. How could they be when they'd broken the boundaries? That relaxed friendliness of his first days had quickly evaporated. He was polite towards her, and she to him, and nobody would have any idea of the tension between them, but it was there.

As she headed towards her office, her thoughts were on making sure his surgery went smoothly. Whatever had happened between them, she needed to put their relationship to one side and act professionally.

She unlocked the office door, and her eyes were immediately drawn to the computer. Perched on the top of the keyboard was a Ferrero Rocher chocolate.

He's been here already.
And he's thinking about me.

She swiftly removed it and put it in the drawer before anyone saw it. It was only a little touch, but one that lifted her spirits and lightened her heart as she wrote on the whiteboard where the staff would all be working that morning. She'd put herself to scrub for Fin's knee procedure, and as a courtesy, he was the first patient on the list. *That's why he's here so early.*

She put Fiona down for recovery although there was no way she was going to let anyone else wake him. She wanted to be the first person he saw when he opened his eyes after his anaesthetic. No need to say anything to the staff just yet though.

Janelle came into the prep room, "Hey Kathryn, Rosa's hovering outside. I've told her to go but she's still milling around on the corridor with a duster saying she's waiting to see you before she goes."

Damn. The last thing she needed this morning was one of Rosa's predictions, she had enough on thinking about Fin.

She sighed, "Right, I better go and speak to her."

As a member of staff was coming down to theatre for surgery, she needed to adhere to the hospital policy and have all ancillary staff removed to ensure complete confidentiality. She'd rostered only trained staff on that morning, so wanted to make sure Rosa would be long gone by the time Fin was wheeled down.

She found Rosa dusting in the recovery area, "Morning Rosa, are you about done?"

"'Ello Sister. Yes, I done. I came in early like you tell me."

"Thank you, I appreciate that. You get yourself off now and I'll see you at the normal time tomorrow."

Rosa nodded, "Would you like me make coffee before I go?"

"No thank you, not this morning. We've got an early start so we'll grab a coffee later."

"Okay. I bake a cake and left it in tearoom. Make sure you 'ave some as you losing weight with the worry."

Trust her to have noticed she'd lost a bit of weight. What worry, though? Someone must have mentioned Philip's job, but there was no point in discussing that with her. Best to get rid of her quickly.

"I'll have a piece later with my coffee, and I know the others will be thrilled as they love your cakes. Thank you."

"Okay," she nodded, "cake make you strong," she lowered her voice to barely a whisper, "you need to be strong, Sister. The sand is running out of the glass."

Jesus Christ! What with the wreath and Rosa, she might as well hang herself now and be done with it.

"I've got to dash as we're starting shortly. I'll see you

tomorrow."

"Okay, I be 'ere at usual time tomorrow."

"Lovely. We'll see you then. Bye."

Kathryn's walk was almost a trot to get away. She was going to have to speak to her privately. She couldn't have all this gloom and doom every time she saw her, it was far too unsettling.

Fiona returned from pre-operatively visiting the patients on the ward scheduled for surgery that morning, "I felt almost nervous going into Mr Dey's room to say hello and that I would be waking him up from his anaesthetic. It's daft I know as he's a patient like any other at the moment, but with him being a consultant, and the boss as well, I felt a bit stupid going through the usual jargon. It was almost like I was on a test telling him not to worry, and that I would be the first person he would see when he came round from the anaesthetic."

"Well it's a good job you did," Erin answered, "at least he can see the patient experience for himself, and the fact that he's anxious he won't remember what you said anyhow. I feel a bit sorry for him really. He's brave telling us he's nervous rather than acting all macho about it."

"Is he tucked up in the bed?" Janelle asked Fiona.

"No, he's sat in the chair, but he's got his gown on ready. I must say, he's the only bloke I've ever seen that looks good in a hospital theatre gown."

I wish I could give him a hug.

And tell him everything will be okay.

Lee came through to the prep room, "The anaesthetist's here, so are we ready for me to send for Mr Dey?"

"Yes, we're ready. I'll go and get scrubbed," Kathryn replied.

Look after him, Lee,

He's scared.

Kathryn's tummy tightened as she glanced at Fin unconscious on the theatre table. He looked so exposed and vulnerable attached to the anaesthetic machine with an airway jutting out of his mouth. There were hundreds of patients that passed through theatres each year, yet they all paled into insignificance next to this one.

She carefully prepped his knee with iodine ready for the surgery, and attached the sterile drapes with equal care.

The exploration of Fin's knee was uneventful as he'd predicted. Using the arthroscope with a camera attachment, Mr Sutcliffe dexterously shaved a piece of cartilage and gave the knee joint a washout which was visible to them all on the TV monitor. At the end of the procedure, the surgeon injected some local anaesthetic into the knee joint to help with any subsequent pain from the instrument invasion. The whole process took no longer than thirty minutes.

Once the surgical procedure was complete, Kathryn elevated Fin's leg by his foot so Mr Sutcliffe could apply the wool and crepe bandage around his knee and down to his ankle.

Lee wheeled the bed in as she was pulling off the adhesive sterile drapes and she reached for a blanket off his bed and covered him.

"This blanket's cold, Janelle. Could you go and get one from the warmer."

She pushed her used trolley towards Erin. "Would you mind getting rid of this for me while I take Mr Dey into recovery please?"

Erin took the trolley from her, "Shall I give Fiona a shout?" she asked looking puzzled. Kathryn knew why, she rarely recovered a patient these days.

"No I'll take him through. They should be finished next door shortly, so Fiona will be around to recover that patient."

With Lee and the anaesthetist, she helped transfer Fin onto his bed, and by that time Janelle had returned with a warm blanket. Kathryn placed it next to his skin, pulling the edges around his neck.

There, that will keep you snug.

You'll be cold when you first wake up.

Once the anaesthetist was satisfied Fin was breathing unaided, they transferred him to the recovery area.

Kathryn applied a pulse oximeter probe to his finger

and gently attached the blood pressure cuff to his upper arm. Still he slept.

He looks so peaceful.

I wish he was mine.

She took the monitor readings and transposed his observations onto the recovery sheet. He was fine, and the beeping of his heart on the monitor assured her that all was well.

His skin appeared even darker against the white hospital sheets, as if he'd been on a Caribbean island for a couple of weeks, and her eyes traced the edges of his thick wavy hair curling around his ears, which she itched to stroke.

Fin coughed and spluttered almost expelling the airway. She eased it gently out of his mouth, "It's alright, Fin, you're just waking up. The operation's all over."

Tears surfaced, and she swallowed so she didn't make a fool of herself. He already meant more to her than was decent, but in a vulnerable position like this, she wanted to take care of him, "Take a deep breath in for me."

He must have heard her as he breathed in deeply before his eyes fluttered open. It was a second or two before he looked at her standing beside his bed.

"Hi," he croaked.

Her heart melted, "Hi to you too."

"Am I dreaming, Kat, or is it you?"

Please don't use that name.

It reminds me of us making love.

"Yes it's me. Try not to speak, just keep taking some nice deep breaths. The operation is all over, everything went well. You're in the recovery room."

He was quiet for a moment, and then he asked, "I thought Fiona was going to look after me?"

"She's busy with another patient, so you'll have to make do with me waking you up."

"Mmm, best offer I've had all day. We should make that permanent."

Yes, we should.

If only.

"Well I hope you're not going to wake up from too many anaesthetics."

With his eyes closed, he smiled knowingly at her deflection, "I meant we should make it permanent, you waking me up each day, but then again," he opened his eyes and looked at her, "you know that don't you?"

"You're talking nonsense from the anaesthetic. Try and sleep it off. I'll keep you here with me in the recovery room for the next thirty minutes or so, and then I'll send you back to your room. Everything's fine, all your obs are normal."

"Are they? How's my blood pressure?"

"It's fine."

"Really? I am surprised. It's usually sky high if I'm anywhere within a metre of you."

"Fin, stop it. Someone will hear you."

The sound of heels clicking on the floor interrupted them both, and Kathryn looked up to see Melons approaching the recovery bay.

Get lost. I'm taking care of him.

He doesn't need you.

"Ah, the patient's out of theatre, how's he doing?" she asked approaching the bed, "Well done, Fin, it's all over now. We'll take you back to your room and get you a nice cup of tea."

"He's not ready to go back yet!" Kathryn snapped.

"Why ever not?" Melons glanced at the monitor, "His obs look okay. He'll be more comfortable in his room."

"The anaesthetist hasn't been out to see him yet so I'll keep him a bit longer. I'll send him back to the ward shortly."

He's stopping here with me.

He was mine long before you.

"Alright then," she shrugged, clearly miffed as she squeezed Fin's hand, "I'll see you when you get back to the ward, the worse bit's over now." She smiled that sickly lipstick smile of hers.

Fin nodded to her, "Great, I'll see you shortly then, Helen."

She watched Melons totter away, and turned to Fin, "You're honoured, she doesn't usually come round to recovery to see anyone." She watched his face for a hint of anything between the two of them.

"I think she's only showing a matronly concern, which is very nice of her."

Yeah, sure it is.

You know, and I know, it's a lot more than that.

31

Elsa had insisted Fin stayed with her following his operation. She'd browbeaten him into it, but he'd only agreed to two days and was sticking to that despite her protests. Maybe that was a good thing though considering how inquisitive he'd become. She knew he could catch her out about her treatment in an instant if she slipped up.

She loved being on her own with her brother. Nick had made a fire before he left for work making the lounge warm and cosy as the inclement weather blasted against the window. It reminded her of her and Fin's childhood in Holland and their mother, who had loved a real fire roaring up the chimney. They'd have drinking chocolate with marshmallows floating on the top, and all three of them would sit together wrapped in woollen throws playing I spy or various other daft games.

"When are you seeing the oncologist again?" Fin asked, stirring his coffee.

"Next week. It'll be the usual blood tests first, and then see him to find out how things are."

"What day next week?"

"Why?"

"I'd like to come with you ... to find out how things are going." He took a sip of his drink.

"I prefer to go on my own, but thank you anyway." A peeved look passed across his face, prompting her to remind him, "Remember at the beginning, when I said I'd go through with this treatment if I could do it my way?"

"I know that," he sighed, "and I'm trying to respect your wishes, but my medical background does make me somewhat curious. Surely you understand that? There's no harm in me coming with you once to find out how things are going, is there?"

"No harm at all, but as I've said dozens of times, I don't want any interference. You have to let me deal with this my own way. Nick respects that, and so should you."

"Well he would wouldn't he. It's easier for him to pretend it isn't happening."

"That's not fair and you know it," she snapped, "Nick's being very supportive. Just because he's not weeping and wailing all the time, doesn't mean he doesn't care. He's the rock I can rely on, and that's all I want."

Fin took a deep breath in, "And all *I* want is to speak to the oncologist face to face to see how you're doing. It's hard, you know, having to stand by and not being at the appointments with you."

"I know it is, but this is the way I want it, so let's leave it shall we? I'm not changing my mind." Her *not another word* glare must have done the trick as he didn't press any further. She changed the subject, "Anyway, moving swiftly on, are you making any progress with the hospital matron, what's her name, is it Helen?"

"Yes, but I told you, it was only dinner," he paused as if considering how much to divulge, "to be perfectly honest, it was more a business dinner as we spent most of the time talking about work."

"Oh lovely," she scoffed, "I bet she was delighted you'd taken her out."

"You could be right," he rolled his eyes, "I'm taking her out for Sunday lunch to make up for it, and I'll make sure that St Anne's is well and truly off the menu this time."

"I would do, if you want any more dates with her," she warned, "anyway, are you going to spill the beans how you feel about her?"

"Definitely not," he grinned, "one word and you'd be organising a wedding planner."

"Now there's a thought," she smiled, "go on, give me something, do you like her? Can you see things continuing?"

He shook his head dismissively, "She's nice enough, but there's no chemistry there."

"There might be if you let things progress. I know you, stiff upper lip and all that. You're young and should have a woman in your life. Saskia would want you to move on."

"I know she would. We'll have to see," he sighed, "I should make more of an effort, but the trouble is, I've been out of this dating scene for too long."

"All the more reason to get back on it, then," she coaxed.

"I am trying, but one thing's for certain; you'll be the last person I'll be discussing my love life with." He narrowed his eyes, "I hope you haven't told anyone Helen and I went out for dinner, the last thing I need is a load of hospital gossip?"

She shook her head, but didn't look him in the eye.

"Elsa," he frowned, "who have you told?"

"No one, why would I? Anyway, I don't know anyone you work with so I'm hardly going to be discussing who you date."

"You know Kathryn."

"Yes, well, she's not likely to be gossiping about you. She's the soul of discretion, and anyway, she's got enough on her plate at the moment to be thinking about your love life."

"Why, what's happening with her?"

"Philip's likely to be made redundant."

"Oh, yes, she did say. Has he got anything in the pipeline?"

"When did she tell you that?"

"One day at work she was discussing it."

"Really?"

"She didn't say that much," he shrugged, "does it matter?"

"No, of course it doesn't. I'm just surprised she's mentioned it really, that's not like her at all. Anyway," she continued, "she wants him to set up in business on his own, but he's not very keen."

"That's easier said than done I would have thought.

There's so many people doing that, they can't all be successful."

"I'm sure you're right, but he won't even try. That's typical of him, though, how he ever got her to marry him, Lord only knows. He was batting well above his level when he got her, I can tell you."

"Don't you think they're happy?"

She shrugged, "You'd never know from Kathryn, she's very loyal to him. They were childhood sweethearts and all that, but I think I said once before, he whisked her down the aisle while she was grieving for her mother, and now she's stuck with him."

He raised an eyebrow, "Not everyone is as cynical as you. I'm sure she loves him very much."

"I'm not. I think he's a control freak, and she lets him get away with it. I've never really been keen on him."

"Kathryn doesn't strike me as a shrinking violet. I can't imagine her putting up with someone who doesn't treat her properly."

"Trust me, you don't know him, and she doesn't see his faults."

"I'm sure you're seeing the negatives because you don't like him. Besides, she's your friend, not him."

"Yes, and I love her to bits. She's the sister I never had. Anyway, would you mind if I went for a quick nap, I'm a bit tired and could do with a lie down?"

"Of course not. Can I get you anything?"

"No thank you, I'm okay, and you're the patient here remember. Give me an hour and I'll be fine."

Elsa lay on her bed thinking of Fin. The thought of leaving him on his own after all he'd been through losing Saskia and Christiaan, crushed her. It might help if he had a woman in his life, that would at least make the grieving easier. She had been hopeful about this Helen woman, but listening to him, she sounded very much like a dead end.

Kathryn sprung to mind. What a pity she was married, they'd be ideal for each other. Fin already had a soft spot for her, she could tell, but who wouldn't; she was such a lovely person.

She recalled telling Kathryn over supper that Fin

liked her, which had embarrassed her and she'd become all uptight.

She sighed. Much as she'd like to imagine them romantically linked, there was no point when Kathryn was well and truly joined at the hip to Philip.

Another niggle reared its head and prevented sleep from coming. During her conversation with Fin, she'd managed to deflect from the hospital appointment, but how long could she keep that up? He'd asked which day she was attending the clinic, but she knew that if she'd given him a fictitious day, he might well have turned up. He seemed to accept for now her refusal to allow him to accompany her, but she knew him. Fin was tenacious; he always found a way to get what he wanted.

*

Fin sat in Elsa's lounge pondering their conversation. So it didn't sound as if Kathryn was deliriously happy in her marriage. Good.

Elsa had been quick to ask how she knew about Philip's possible redundancy. He could vividly recall their meeting in his office when Kathryn had given that as a reason she couldn't leave St Anne's.

Hurray for redundancy. The last thing he wanted was for her to leave. Every morning when he woke up, she invaded his mind and last thing at night it was her that he saw. Much as he tried to suppress it, he eagerly searched for her at work each day, even though when he did see her, jealousy gnawed away at his insides because he couldn't have her. But to not see her wasn't an option he wanted to even consider. She was like a drug he shouldn't want, but had an overwhelming desire to have.

The sexual chemistry between them had been amazing. He'd had one brief fling since Saskia's death, but that was really grieving sex, whereas with Kathryn, it was so much more. She'd been so receptive to him, and despite it being their first time together, it was no one-night stand. They'd made love. There was no doubt alcohol had played a major part, and she possibly wouldn't have let things go that far sober, but she had, and he couldn't get that night out of his head.

On the Monday morning in his office following the party, he wasn't sure what to expect, but his mind had been jumping ahead about all sorts of ways they could be together. He didn't want an affair, that wasn't his style, but he wanted her. Disappointingly, she'd dismissed their night together and wanted to forget all about it. That hurt. He knew she had feelings for him, she wouldn't have responded the way she had otherwise, but she was loyal, and as Elsa had said, she wouldn't leave her husband.

He was working exceptionally hard physically and mentally trying to put her out of his mind, but every time he saw her, he wanted her, especially in that sister's uniform she wore for meetings. There should be some sort of enforcement of a strict dress code for theatre staff. The theatre blue scrubs she wore he could just about manage, but seeing her in that little navy number with its tight belt around her waist and its hem sitting nicely on her knees, fulfilled every fantasy he'd ever had about screwing a nurse. Each time he saw her in it, he had the urge to rip the frilly white hat off her head and release her gorgeous thick wavy hair, hitch the dress up, and fuck her senseless over the nearest desk. He couldn't decide if she wore stockings underneath it, but if he ever found out that she did, he wouldn't be able to contain himself.

He recalled waking up from the anaesthetic and she was the first person he saw. He'd felt so exposed on the bed with her stood next to him, but seeing her only intensified his need. Not only for sex, either. He wanted her in his life. But she didn't want him. She wanted her husband; she'd made that perfectly clear.

He tried to shrug off his thoughts about her as he did each time she invaded his mind. He needed to concentrate on his sister. She certainly looked okay, but his scientific brain wanted more detail from her. As always, though, Elsa was in control and plainly wasn't going to discuss her treatment which really frustrated him. He knew that if he rang her consultant, Angus Meadows, he wouldn't divulge anything to him due to patient confidentiality, but he might say more if he could accompany Elsa to one of her appointments. The problem was her forbidding that. So for the moment, he was at a lost as to how he could find out anything more. He needed to, though, because something wasn't quite right.

32

It was the final meeting of the Heads of Department before Christmas in the boardroom, and the last agenda item was the Christmas Ball the following Saturday. Kathryn couldn't keep her eyes of Fin at the head of the table with Melons Plenty to his left. If she didn't stop twittering around, topping up his water and hanging onto his every word, she'd be over there.

Where she should be.

Touching his leg under the table.

Fin was speaking, "So I'd like to thank everyone in advance for their contribution towards the planning, particularly Helen who has done a sterling job," he glanced at Melons and she gave him a sickly smile.

Bitch.

I hate you.

"And I sincerely hope that the staff and their guests have a wonderful evening. I think that's everything for now. Any questions?"

Sarah Smith, Head of the Outpatients department had one, "I've still got reservations about this free bar. I'm worried that some of the younger staff may take advantage."

"Me too," agreed Mark Davis, Head of Catering, "My lot aren't to be trusted on any night, even paying for alcohol, let alone getting it for free."

Fin nodded, "I can appreciate your concerns, however, the whole purpose of the event is to reward the staff for their hard work. I think perhaps the best approach would be for all of us to keep a watchful eye on the staff in our own departments, and any we think are getting carried away, have a quiet word. I could send a memo out also regarding expectations if you think that will help?"

Kathryn didn't contribute verbally in the meeting. She couldn't care less what anyone drank, in fact, getting drunk seemed a good idea right now if it made her forget him. Not once since that morning in his office had he made any reference to their night together. He'd obviously taken her at her word and put it out of his mind. He might have been a bit flirty following his surgery, but that was the anaesthetic. Since then any interactions between them were either a hello on the corridor if they passed each other, and very much a surgeon-nurse relationship when he was operating.

Was I just a fling?
Don't you want me anymore?

She still needed to tell him about the wreath. Maybe now after the meeting would be a good time. When everyone was gone and she could be alone with him. Her heart rate accelerated.

*

Fin was concluding the meeting, "If there isn't anything else, we'll leave it there." He stood up, "I'll get that memo out before the end of today."

The Department Heads started to shuffle out. Kathryn turned to him, "Could I have a word please?"

Not in that Sister's outfit. Unless the words are fuck me now.

"It'll have to be quick, I've got a lunchtime appointment."

"It won't take long."

"Fine. Do you want to come to my office?"

Christ. Get a grip.

"No, I can tell you now if you like?"

As the others filed out, Mark Davis reminded him, "Don't forget, the Bellamy's rep is due at three thirty today. I know you wanted a quick word with him."

"I won't, thank you. I'll be round later."

Mark closed the door and they were alone. She

174

looked pale. Had she lost weight? Maybe something was wrong between her and Philip?

He sat down again. Not right next to her, he chose a seat apart. Being too close to her wouldn't be wise the way he was feeling.

"What is it?"

"You remember the photograph sent to Philip of the two of us at the breakfast meeting?"

"Yes."

"Well, since then, a couple of other things have happened."

"What other things?" he frowned.

"I've been sent a pizza delivery to the house that I didn't order, and more disturbingly I've been sent a wreath with *night, night, sleep tight* on the card."

"I see. Do you think it's Hicks?"

"It has to be. I can't imagine anyone else would do this to me."

Bastard. He wants sorting doing this to her. "He hasn't been in touch or anything since we sacked him?"

"No. Philip's seen him, though."

"Philip?"

"Yes. Gary's a member of the walking club."

"Has he said anything to Philip?"

"He says not."

"And do you believe him?"

"Of course I do, he's no reason to lie. He's reluctant for me to suggest his name to the police, though."

"Why's that?"

"He thinks it's unlikely Gary would do any of this. On the occasions he sees him at the club, he reckons he's quite jolly and is talking about emigrating."

"I think that's for the police to decide, don't you?"

"That's why I wanted to bring this up at work. I was wondering if I should ring them from here ... you know with this starting out as a work issue?"

"Meaning you don't want Philip to know?"

"No, not at all. I think it is Gary, so it's best to sort it at work really."

"Best for you, is that what you're saying?"

"Best for everybody," she emphasised, "if it isn't him,

then the police will confirm this and there will be no harm done."

He frowned, "Why are you frightened to stand up to your husband? If someone is playing mischievous pranks on you, then you need to find out who it is, and if that means the police interviewing Hicks, then so be it. I don't see a problem."

She took a deep breath, "Can I contact the police through work, that's all I'm asking, not an analysis about my marriage?"

"I'm not *analysing* your marriage, Kathryn, far from it. I think if someone was performing malicious acts against my wife, I'd point the police straight in the direction of any suspects. Quite frankly, I'm at a loss as to why Philip is reluctant to do so."

He was beginning to think Elsa was right, she said Philip was an arsehole.

"Thank you for your words of wisdom on matrimony, maybe you've forgotten what it's like being married and not wanting to upset your partner?"

Ouch! That stung. "Are you deliberately trying to provoke me?"

"No, of course not."

"Then I suggest that you get the hell out of here right now and do whatever you think is best."

She shook her head, "I wish I'd never asked. I don't know why you're being like this with me."

"Don't you? Haven't you any idea why I'm *like this* around you?"

She must have seen something in his eyes that scared her. As quick as a flash, she scurried towards the door and almost reached it, but he quickly covered the distance between them and stood in front of her barring her way. There was no disguising the flash of excitement in her eyes, the spark of something between them which she tried to dismiss, "This is about work and not ... not about us," she flustered.

He lowered his voice, "It's always about us," and then almost through clenched teeth he added, "And didn't I warn you not to be alone with me?"

"We can't avoid each other all the time when we work

together."

Now her cheeks were flushed and it took all his control not to ravish her right there.

"Don't you think I don't know that? Christ almighty, Kathryn ... every single day I'm reminded we *work together*. Have you any idea how hard that is, knowing you're going home to another man each evening when you leave here?" Frustrated by her silence he barked, "Have you?"

His eyes were drawn to her beautiful neck as she swallowed. Those perfect lips that were begging to be kissed. He wanted to feel them on his so much, it hurt.

His control flew out of the window. He took hold of her upper arms and pulled her to him and kissed her hard. It was a punishing kiss because she'd challenged him, because she was with another man, because he wanted her so badly. She pushed herself onto him, as eager as he was and he felt her fingernails clawing his head. He couldn't get enough of her, and moved his lips frantically against hers, exploring with his tongue and she sucked at it and bit his lip. The fact they were against the door in the hospital boardroom was completely forgotten. It was just him and her. His senses screamed he wanted her ... until reality kicked in. *She doesn't want you, she's with somebody else.*

He pulled away, "No," he breathed heavily, "no more. Not like this." He gritted his teeth, "I'm not playing second fiddle to another man again."

Her face was now etched in misery and he wanted to kiss her all over again to take the hurt away. She narrowed her eyes, "Are you ... with Helen now?"

"No," he snapped, before reminding her, "Not that it's any of your business."

Why would I? She's not you, and it's you I want.

A look of relief passed across her face, and it suddenly came to him where she'd got that information from. He took a deep frustrated breath, "Let me guess, Elsa?"

Were they tears in her eyes? It wasn't any of her business about Helen, what he did in his own life was up to him. She didn't want him. It still knotted his gut to see her upset though, like a knife stabbing into his abdomen and then twisting itself round to cause the maximum pain.

Her beautiful eyes scrutinised his face, as if she was noting every facet, as if she wanted him to fuck her again. He needed rid of her before he did something to relieve his throbbing dick. He fumbled behind his back, and the fresh air flooded into the room as he opened the door, killing the moment between them like water dousing a flame. She moved past him and quickly left the room. What the hell just happened?

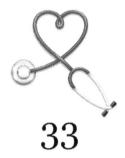

33

"We're all done, Kathryn, theatre's all set up for tomorrow. Are you about ready?" Janelle asked.

"I've got a couple of other bits left to do, so you get off. I'll not be long."

"Is there anything I can help you with?"

"No thanks, I'm fine honestly. I've a few emails to answer and then I'm off home."

"Okay, if you're sure. I'll get off then as I'm going to Callum's."

"Oh right. How are things going?"

"Great, I really like him."

"Good, I'm pleased he's finding a bit of happiness."

"Yes, although his divorce does seem to have scarred him, he's very bitter. He doesn't say much about *us* though, has he mentioned anything to you or Philip about me?"

"No, although I haven't seen him lately. I'll ask Philip, but you know what blokes are like, talking about relationships is not what they do. Their conversations are more like, this is a good pint, or did you watch the game last night, that sort of thing."

Janelle laughed, "Yeah, you're right. Mind you, there are some things in our relationship I'd rather Callum didn't discuss," she winked.

Kathryn widened her eyes and laughed, "If he's been bragging about that, Philip's keeping shtum."

"That's a relief then," Janelle smiled, "by the way, I

was thinking about asking Callum to fix up that night out for us all, if you still fancy it?"

Christ, I can't think of anything worse.

"Err, yes. I tell you what; I'll get Philip to sort something out shall I?"

I'll not mention it to Philip and hope it dies a death.

"Great, it will be nice all going out together as a foursome."

"Right, you get off then so you're not late. Don't forget it's an early start in the morning."

"No, I won't. Rosa's hovering around still, shall I tell her to go?"

"Yes, would you," she rolled her eyes, "I don't particularly want her here in the afternoon, but she had an appointment this morning."

"Yes, so she said. Okay, I'll tell her to get off now."

"Thanks, see you tomorrow."

Minutes later there was a knock on the office door and Rosa appeared, "Is okay I go now, Sister?"

"Yes, of course. You get off. Thank you."

"Are you staying? Would you like cup of coffee?"

"No thank you, I've got my water." She nodded towards the bottle standing next to the computer.

"I go home then. Mr Dey be round when I go, you see."

She knew what Rosa was implying and wanted to curb it, "I think he'll have gone home by now."

"No, he not gone home. He wait 'till we all go, then he come round and see you."

Rosa's creepy smile made her feel uneasy. She should really speak to her about this constant innuendo and speculation, but couldn't be bothered right now. It was late and she was tired.

"I really don't think so," she answered firmly, "but you get off, and thank you again." She watched Rosa close the door behind her and breathed a sigh of relief. No further mention of *the black ahead,* thank God.

Was Fin still in the building? She was still upset about the way he'd spoken to her this morning in the boardroom. Not the kiss, though, that was heavenly. He'd kissed her with such passion and she'd met him with the same intensity. If he'd have asked, she'd have ripped her knickers off right there and then. Her pussy clenched imagining him inside her one more time. Blood rushed to her pelvis at the thought of them screwing on the boardroom table. It was wrong desiring him the way she did, but she couldn't help it.

What excuse could she have for going round to reception and seeing if he was still in his office? Just to see him before he left for the evening.

Don't go there, Kathryn.

You'll regret it. And you know it.

She switched the computer off and decided to check the theatre was set up for the gynae list in the morning. The changing room door to the outside corridor slammed indicating Rosa had gone.

A glance around the pristine theatre reinforced the fact that she had good staff. They'd ensured everything was ready for their early start the following day. Her ears pricked up as she heard the theatre entrance door open, and she peered through the frosted window on the swing door, out onto the corridor. Rosa's prediction had been right. Fin was poking his head in her office.

Her heart leapt. She eased the door open, "Are you looking for me?"

"Ah, yes," he walked towards her, "I was hoping you were still here." She should leave the theatre and step out onto the well-lit corridor, but she stayed in the darkness and let him walk towards her, her heart thumping madly. He came through the theatre door, letting it swing shut behind him. It was intimate with only the corridor lighting reflecting through the small windows on the double doors. Too intimate really. She tried to calm her breathing as his eyes locked onto hers.

He tipped his head slightly to one side, "I wanted to apologise about earlier."

She swallowed the lump in her throat. "There's nothing to apologise for."

"Yes there is." He reached forward and gently stroked her cheek, "I was short with you this morning and I'm sorry." He breathed in deeply, "It's such a mess. You're not free I know, but it doesn't stop me wanting you. I've tried," he screwed his face up, "so bloody hard."

He looked tortured and it crushed her, but it wasn't just despair she saw in his eyes.

She wet her lips, "We mustn't."

Something shifted in his expression and there was a raspy edge to his voice as he asked, "Is that what you want? Tell me to go now, and I will. In fact, you'd better say it quick because if you don't, I'm … I'm going to fuck you senseless right on this theatre table."

Heat bloomed between her legs and her face burned for him. She was glad of the darkness.

Do it, Fin … please, do it.

Right now. Fuck me senseless.

The air around them was thick as she stood and held her ground. Speech was impossible. Their gazes held and she saw the heat flare in his eyes, "Hell, I have no control around you." He captured her jaw with both of his hands. She couldn't have pulled away if she'd wanted to as his grip was so firm. His lips glided across hers, hard and punishing and she met his force. His arms moved tightly around her as he pressed himself against her, and she relished his hardness pushing against her tummy. His need excited her and she wrapped her arms tightly around his neck. He felt so good, and smelled divine. How she loved kissing him, nibbling him and tasting him. Right now, she was exactly where she wanted to be.

He reached for the bottom of her theatre tunic and she raised her arms so he could lift it over her head, exposing her crimson bra. They continued kissing, while she quickly undid the tie at the side of her theatre scrubs. She stepped out of them and stood proudly in front of him in her bra and knickers. There was no thought that anyone could walk in, all that was in her mind was dealing with the desperate need she had bubbling away inside of her.

He lifted her up, and her legs automatically clasped around him as they continued kissing. He walked a few paces and eased her gently down onto the operating table. The piece of equipment that she earned her living from, at which she'd stood opposite him so many times with a patient between them. But she didn't care. She wanted him inside her. He leant across and continued kissing her, it was as if he couldn't get enough of her, nor she him. He pulled away and eased her bra down around her waist exposing her breasts to him and she felt her nipples tighten. His gorgeous lips took a nipple into his mouth and she moaned as her pussy throbbed. He treated the other nipple to the same teasing flick of his tongue, and as he sucked, she pulled his head onto her and squirmed against him.

"Oh, god," she said, and heard herself begging, "Please Fin ..."

Fuck me.

Fuck me hard.

He pulled away and reached for her panties, tugging them down her legs and over her feet. It felt as if she'd been hypnotised as she met his eyes and saw his need. He lifted one of her legs by her calf, and laid it gently in the gynae stirrup attached to the table, and then did the same with the other one. She should have felt self-conscious being so blatantly exposed with her legs in the stirrups, and her femininity explicitly on display, but she didn't. It turned her on. Watching his eyes stare at her pussy excited her. He moved away slightly and she saw him sit on the portable chair that the gynaecologist would use to sit between a woman's legs as he performed surgery. Fin manoeuvred himself forward towards her on the chair and reached for the theatre table remote control. He lowered the bottom of the theatre table downwards so he was sat between her legs with her exposed pussy right before him and she almost orgasmed from him being so intimately close. Then the oral onslaught began. The first touch of his mouth on her sent pleasure ricocheting up her tummy and through her breasts. To have Fin's head between her legs, and his tongue licking her folds over and over again was incredible. She felt his tongue glide along her silky wetness and groaned for more.

He slid one finger inside her, and then two, stroking deep, which added a whole new layer to her pleasure. She felt another finger slide in, as his tongue pressed harder on her clit. Her eyes drifted towards this delicious man sat between her legs sucking her. Her breasts were swollen and aching for his touch, which turned her on incredibly,

183

and her heart hammered out a rhythm all of its own, faster and faster until her body felt like a live wire.

She called his name, "Fin, Fin, God ... ," as the most exquisite waves of pleasure rippled down her body, stiffening her limbs as ecstasy radiated out of every pore. Her head rolled from side to side and her entire body shook as she rode the waves of orgasm and still he kept his tongue and fingers working simultaneously until she begged him to stop.

As she slowly came back to reality, he stood and kicked the chair away, before reaching for the remote to bring the bottom of the theatre table upwards to a level where he could climb on. He unzipped himself and eased himself on top of her, "You're beautiful when you come, Kat." He entered her with a forceful thrust, and slid in easily as she was so wet from the incredible orgasm. The feeling of him filling her was exquisite. He withdrew slowly, and then thrust higher, and then higher still. Her legs were starting to ache from being raised, but she didn't care. The lithotomy position with her legs in the stirrups gave him deeper access, and he pounded into her, over and over again. The pleasure was mounting once more as he buried himself deep inside her. His throaty Dutch words were coarse in her ear, words she'd never heard before but nevertheless intensified her longing and heightened her arousal. She tightened her hands around his neck, as his hot breath heated her skin. The sensation of him sucking and biting her neck tingled down her spine, and she felt her eagerness building again.

"I can't get enough of you," he breathed huskily, reaching for her clit. His fingers pressed hard and moved the sensitive nub backwards and forwards, "God Kat, what you do to me."

The sensations seemed even greater because of the position of her legs. He slid his hardness back into her and filled her over and over again. The pleasure was excruciating. She let go, crying out and riding the waves of ecstasy, and simultaneously his release came and he groaned and jerked as he poured himself into her. His guttural roar, thrilled her, and she realised that much as she loved receiving pleasure, the joy was much greater giving it to him.

Silence enveloped them. Still on top of her, and still inside her, he kissed her gently on the lips, "Are you okay?"

She smiled, "I am, but my legs aren't, they've gone to sleep." He lifted himself off her and gave her such a sexy grin, "You should have said." He gently lifted one leg down and then the other, and passed the blue theatre scrubs to her. She eased herself off the table, fastened up her bra and quickly pulled the tunic on which covered most of her, while he straightened himself up and tucked his shirt in. Had he really had sex with her without even removing his clothes? How bad were they?

They stood inches apart and he shook his head, "I feel like a hormonal teenager having sex in any available place." His face became more serious, "I did warn you not to be on your own with me."

"Yes, you did."

And I'm glad.

Because that was amazing.

She felt awkward, and wanted to escape, "I need to shower."

"Yes, of course." He looked weary, "We can't keep doing this. It isn't me."

"No, I know it isn't. It's not me either. Go Fin ... go now. This shouldn't keep happening between us."

There wasn't anything else to say. They'd given in to lust, but she still had a husband to go home to.

She picked up her knickers and walked out of theatre towards the changing room barefoot and without her scrub trousers. It felt uncomfortable that she now had to shower so there was no evidence on her of another man when she returned to her husband. Being unfaithful was the worst thing in life as far as she was concerned and she hated herself for allowing it to happen again.

She dried herself after her shower and put on her outdoor clothes ready for home. Fin's lovemaking dominated her thoughts as she picked her dirty theatre tunic off the floor and threw it in the linen basket. She needed to go and retrieve her trousers and theatre clogs so nipped back into the theatre suite and was amazed to see Fin sat in the tearoom.

"Gosh you frightened me. What are you still doing here?"

He shrugged, "Waiting for you I guess."

"I've got to go."

"I know. Come and sit down for a minute." He patted the chair next to him.

I need to go home.

But I want to stay with you.

She took the seat, "What is it?"

"We can't carry on like this, Kathryn ... *I* can't carry on like this."

"No. We can't."

"Every time I see you, I want you. Yet I feel so bloody guilty."

She sighed, "Take what *you* feel and multiply it by a thousand!"

He nodded sympathetically, as if he understood how she was feeling, "Tell me. What is it you want?"

"I don't want anything." She shook her head, "I feel so bad about what I'm doing. It's terrible and not fair. I do want you," she looked into his eyes, "badly, but I don't want an affair, I'm not like that. I hate what I've become." His face etched with rejection made her gut ache, "I'm sorry, but that's the way it is."

He stared at her before speaking. He had a habit of doing that, as if he was weighing up precisely how much to say. "Then there's no more to be said." He stood up, "I'll say goodnight and let you get home."

She watched him walk away, and an overwhelming urge hit her right in the middle of her chest. She wanted to run, grab his hand, and leave with him. He disappeared around the corner and out of sight, making her feel bereft. Was it possible to love two men at the same time?

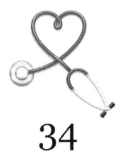

34

Elsa sat at the desk in the study which had belonged to her mother. It didn't really fit in with the modern contemporary furniture she had in the house, but it held such special memories. As she stroked the leather inlay, she recalled how her mother, an avid letter writer used to sit at it most days, and occasionally would allow Elsa as a child to use it. It was a special treat for a young girl, and made all the thank you notes and birthday cards she'd been encouraged to write, that bit more special if she could sit at her mother's beautiful writing desk to compose them.

Today was not a good day for using the desk. Her intention had been to secretly plan her funeral while Nick was out for a meal with some colleagues after work, but that was easier said than done. She wanted to ease the burden on him and Fin when the time came, but to actually put anything down on paper was too difficult. It was admitting that death was looming, which it was, but to actually plan for that was too much.

She'd scanned the loss, grief and bereavement booklet the Macmillan nurse had given her, and even though she recognised she was in the *accepting* stage of dying, it wasn't that clear cut. It was going to happen, there was no doubt about that, but accepting seemed the wrong word somehow. Maybe *reluctantly accepting* summed it up more appropriately.

How do you begin to organise your own funeral? Planning parties wasn't a problem for her, she'd hosted that many over the years, so could do it with her eyes shut. There was a certain irony in that statement; her eyes would well and truly be shut at this *event*.

She scanned the *Planning a Funeral* section in the booklet. Did she want to be buried, or cremated, did she want flowers or donations to charity, and what hymns would she like to be sung in the church? Who cares? She didn't want to die let alone plan her funeral. It wasn't fair. Why her? She wasn't even forty for fuck's sake.

A sharp pain shot up her neck and she took a deep breath in. The physical pain was becoming much worse in her spine, and there wasn't a day now that her head didn't throb relentlessly. Each daily activity such as bathing, walking, driving, or even laying down, required a cocktail of tablets to manage. Some days when the pain was particularly bad, she'd look at the painkillers and wonder if she should take the lot and be done with it. That would be the easy way out, but she wanted to hang on to the little bit of time she had left. She loved life too dearly not to.

On Wednesday she'd met with Paul and he'd taken her to an art exhibition of a new contemporary artist. She'd tried to be interested and chirpy, but the outing had been a significant challenge. Maybe it was the combination of the tablets she'd consumed that morning, as well as the rapid advancement of the disease. She was terribly weary, and much as she'd tried to disguise it, Paul knew something was wrong with her. She'd been able to pass it off as a virulent virus she was recovering from, which he'd accepted, but it had confirmed to her that their special Wednesdays together were almost numbered.

It wasn't only the pain she had to cope with. The cancer cells were affecting her brain. She knew some of it was the tablets making her feel fuzzy and lightheaded, and she had been advised that she might become forgetful. The medics had even warned that in some cases, advancement of cancer would result in changes in her personality. Seemingly the most docile person has the ability to become aggressive as the disease takes a greater hold on the brain cells.

Some days she toyed with the idea of sitting down with Nick, Fin, and Kathryn and explaining what she was going through so she'd have their support and not have to do this all on her own, but she always talked herself out of it. It would be too much for them. They wouldn't let her *die with dignity* as the pamphlet discussed. They'd proven that when she initially told them she didn't want any interventions, and they'd badgered her until she reluctantly agreed to treatment which she'd had to lie about. For now they still believed her, but as each day passed, it was becoming more difficult to keep up the pretence.

She closed the drop leaf of the desk and locked it. It didn't matter what the brochure said, she couldn't do it. Nick would have to make any decisions when the time came.

A salty tear rolled down her cheek as she sat down on the settee. She reached for the throw and wrapped it tightly around herself. It consoled her, rather like a child with a comfort blanket. Thoughts of her funeral had upset her and she desperately wanted to eradicate any images of dying from her mind. She needed to be normal, even if it was only temporary. She blew her nose. Who could she speak to that would lift her spirits if only for a short while? She reached for her mobile and pressed Kathryn's number, praying she'd be there.

"Hi hun, it's only me, have you five minutes to chat or are you busy?"

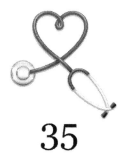

35

"You don't like going to the Number One," Philip challenged Kathryn as he ironed a perfect crease along his shirt sleeve.

"I know I don't. It's just that Janelle mentioned she was going and asked me to go today."

"What, Callum's latest bit of stuff?" he frowned.

"Yes, Janelle from theatre."

"The man-eater?"

"She isn't a man-eater, where have you got that from?"

"You said she was always on the internet meeting blokes."

"I never said she was *always* on the internet. I may have mentioned she'd been on it and out with a few men."

"That smacks of desperation to me."

"Don't be daft. Loads of people are internet dating, it doesn't make them man-eaters. Anyway she's mentioned going out with us as a foursome a couple of times now which I've managed to dodge out of, but she won't give up on it. So I thought meeting up at the club for a drink was better than a whole night out together."

"Funny how you'll come to the club for her, but not when I ask."

He was right about that. The Number One club had never been somewhere she liked, but she'd gone on occasions. She used to like walking but hadn't been on one of the club walks for ages, which thankfully he didn't appear that bothered about lately. He used to always be pushing her to go, but of late had stopped asking. It was as if he'd given up and seemed surprised when she said she was going with him today.

He folded down the ironing board, "I've just realised that Janelle's the one Callum calls his fuck buddy."

"Oh, charming."

"You know what I mean ... a friend with benefits."

"Yes, I get your drift, thank you. That can't be right, though. According to her, he's worried Mandy will be difficult with access to the children if she thinks he's met someone permanent, that's why they keep things quiet."

"Yeah, right. If you believe that, you'll believe anything. If he has said that, which I doubt very much, it'll be to string her along. He's not interested I'm telling you."

"Then he should be up-front and tell her he doesn't want a relationship."

"He has. He's been honest with her from the start, but she doesn't get it. You ask her if they ever go out together, and the answer will be no. He doesn't take her anywhere. When he does see her, it's a takeaway at his and the sex Olympics afterwards. Trust me, that's what's happening, not the relationship she's conjured up in her mind."

"Well he's bringing her to the club today, so that must mean something."

"Yeah, that he's caved into pressure," he said cynically. "I bet we don't see her there again with him. He's on about ditching her anyway as she's a bit needy."

She shook her head, "Honestly, men. I feel sorry for her, she seems to really like him. I wished I'd never agreed to go now."

"Me too. I'd prefer to go on my own rather than get stuck with them."

Yes, you would.

You don't seem overjoyed at me coming, either.

As soon as she told Janelle she'd be there today, she regretted it. She'd rather be spending the day with Elsa like she often did on a Saturday. Elsa worried her. She sounded cheerful enough on the phone yesterday, but she sensed through all the jovial chatter, she was down. It was only to be expected that the treatment would take its toll, but it had upset her. Next week they were going to have a shopping day which she knew would lift Elsa's spirits. They always enjoyed their girlie days together.

Hours later, she sat in the dreary Number One and took a gulp of the wine that Philip has begrudgingly bought. God knows why, the prices were cheap enough in the club. It was most probably because she asked for a large one, but she needed something to get through this silly foursome get-together.

Philip had barely acknowledged Janelle, which made her cross and meant she was stuck on her own chatting to her. She saw enough of her at work and had hoped today they'd be more of a foursome and laugh and talk together, but looking across at Philip chatting to Callum, she realised that wasn't going to happen.

Janelle leant forward, "I'm so pleased you came today."

"Me too," Kathryn lied, "I haven't been here for ages."

Janelle glanced around the room and pulled a face, "This place could do with a bit of a make-over really couldn't it?"

"You're telling me," she agreed, "it's looked like this as long as I can remember."

"Never mind, at least next Saturday we'll be in the glitzy ballroom at the Gables. Are you looking forward to it?"

"Yes, I suppose so. The trouble is, these Christmas work functions can be a bit of a let-down, last year's was nothing special, if you remember."

"Yeah, but that wasn't at the Gables. I think this year will be much better." Janelle took a sip of her drink, "I was wondering whether to invite Callum, what do you think?"

"Erm, I'm not sure," Kathryn hesitated, remembering the conversation with Philip earlier, "is it something he'd like to go to? I wouldn't have thought a ball is a bloke's idea of a good night out."

"Mmm, you might be right. Philip's going though, isn't he?"

"Yes, he comes with me every year."

But I wish he wasn't.

I don't like the thought of Fin and him in the same room.

"I probably will ask Callum, maybe you can help me persuade him to come?" Janelle grinned.

Kathryn took a sip of her drink to avoid answering.

"We're starting to do a lot more together," Janelle continued in a much lower voice, as if she didn't want anyone overhearing, "I think I already told you, he's been worried about things getting back to that ex-wife of his, and her being spiteful with the children."

"Yes, you did, but Callum's a good-looking bloke, so it's obvious he wouldn't be on his own for long."

"You're right, but I have to respect his wishes. He doesn't want to broadcast our relationship; he's worried it might look like he's moved on too soon with a new partner."

"New partner? I thought it was causal between the two of you?"

"No, it's serious, but we're trying to play things down. We spend a lot of our spare time together," she glanced across at Callum, "I know he doesn't look the type, but he can be quite romantic when he wants to be, he took me to a lovely hotel in the Dales last Saturday."

"Gosh, you've really surprised me, I had no idea you were that close. I thought you only met up occasionally."

"That's what Callum prefers people to think, so keep it to yourself until he is ready to go public, would you?"

"Yes, of course."

"I think it's best for now. We're going to give it a few more months, and then it will be time for me to meet the children." She pulled a face, "I'm not looking forward to that, though, as I'm rubbish with kids."

She must live in a fantasy world.

Either that, or Callum's telling porkies.

"I wouldn't worry about that. The children are only young, and you're a nice person so I'm sure they'll take to you."

"Aw, that's a nice thing to say, thank you."

Kathryn reached for her handbag, "Anyway, excuse

me for a second while I pop to the loo, would you?"

She headed towards the ladies toilet in the foyer. As the bar door closed behind her, she physically jumped as she came face to face with her nemesis. It was almost as if he knew she would come through the door at that very moment. It had crossed her mind she could run into him at the club, but she'd hoped that wouldn't happen, however, there in front of her stood Gary Hicks with a supercilious smirk on his face.

"Well, well, well, if it isn't Sister Knight, long time no see. How are you?"

She glared at him, "Fine."

Get lost, Gary.

I don't want to speak to you.

"How's things going at the fun farm?" he widened his eyes enquiringly.

"I don't think that's got anything to do with you."

"I'm only asking. I can take an interest, can't I? I did work there."

"You left, remember."

"And you didn't try and stop it, *remember*. I expected more from you, Kathryn."

"Did you really," she dismissed, "it just goes to show."

Anger flashed across his face, "There's no need to be so fucking high and mighty. It's not easy living on benefits."

"I'm sure it isn't."

He smirked, "But you'll know all about that soon." She must have looked puzzled as he continued, "With Phil going to lose his job and all that."

How the hell does he know?

And why is he shortening Philip's name?

There was no point in rising to the bait. "I don't think that's any of your business. And the fact you're unemployed has nothing to do with me, so you can stop playing those ridiculous pranks. I'm *not* responsible for your sacking."

"Yeah, well the jury's still out on that," he sneered, "and as I've told the police, I'm not the one playing tricks on you."

"Well someone is."

"Let's hope you find out who, then. There's some sick people out there you know, maybe it's someone who doesn't like Phil, he's not everything you think he is."

Again he was abbreviating Philip's name. Philip would hate it if he was here, he couldn't stand anyone calling him Phil, even though she actually quite liked the shortened version. What was he on about anyway that Philip wasn't everything she thought he was? What did he know?

"I can't see why anyone would have a grudge against ... *Philip*," she emphasised his full name, "only someone very sick in the head would spend time and money doing those stupid things."

"Yeah, well, you never quite know how people get their kicks these days, but like I said, it isn't me."

"Why is it I find that hard to believe?" she sneered.

He shrugged his shoulders, "I'll look forward to an apology when you do find out who's the actual culprit."

There was no point discussing it further. It was him, she knew it was. He was just clever enough to escape the police. Anyway, why was she even talking to him?

"Get lost, Gary, and keep well away from me. I'm warning you, if there are any more tricks I'll be informing the HPC, and they'll most likely revoke your registration to practice at all."

She hurried away, but typically he had to have the last word, "Nice to see you too, Kathryn. Hope to see you on one of our walks again soon."

She didn't turn back. He'd be the last person she would be walking with. Quite why Philip gave him the time of day she didn't know but she was going to tackle him about it. Gary Hicks was nothing but trouble and she didn't like his negative inference about Philip at all.

As she stared at her reflection in the mirror in the ladies toilet, her first thought was she would need to tell Fin she'd seen Gary. Warmth flooded through her at the thought of an opportunity to speak to him alone.

What was he was doing right now while she was stuck at some stupid club house? She recalled making love with him at his house the night of the party when they'd devoured each other's bodies, and then at work in theatre with her legs in stirrups. God, how she wished she was having sex with him right now, and to have an afterwards so they could share intimacy like lovers do. A flush appeared on her face which she patted with powder to reduce. It took a few minutes before she was satisfied that nobody would spot her high colour and she could make her way back.

She hated confrontation, and as if the clash with Gary Hicks hadn't been bad enough, to add insult to injury, when she got back to the bar, Philip was sat talking to him at a neighbouring table. Fury erupted within her. He knew the problems Gary was causing and should be supporting her, not talking to him as if they were the best of friends.

As she approached Janelle and Callum, she couldn't help but feel that Philip had been right and Janelle was instigating their relationship. Callum didn't look at all attentive, in fact he looked almost indifferent, which was sad. What was she hoping to gain by fabricating their relationship?

Kathryn sat down and Callum asked, "Would you mind if we got off now? I'm picking up the kids early tomorrow and taking them to Filey."

"Gosh, it's a bit cold for that isn't it?"

He laughed, "Yes, it would be for the beach, but it's my sister we're going to see, she lives there."

"Oh right," Kathryn smiled, "I had visions of you building sandcastles wrapped up in coats, hats and gloves with an umbrella shielding you from the rain."

Philip appeared at their table, "Anyone ready for another drink?"

"Not for us, mate," Callum replied, "we're ready for the off."

She stood also, "I'd like to go too, Philip." The confrontation with Gary Hicks had upset her, but watching her husband chatting with him had infuriated her.

Philip looked puzzled. She knew he'd have preferred to stay, but he must have seen the determined look on her face as he didn't protest.

They all walked out to the car park together, and stopped at Philip's car. She turned and smiled at them both, "I'll see you on Monday at work, Janelle, nice to see you Callum. Enjoy Filey tomorrow with the children."

Callum smiled back, "Thanks I will. See you at work, mate," he nodded at Philip.

Once inside their car, she couldn't contain herself, "What on earth have you got to be talking to Gary Hicks about? You know the trouble he's causing with all these pranks."

Philip started the engine, "I've told you, he swears it isn't him."

"He's going to say that, isn't he? You should be ignoring him, not cosying up to him like he's your new best friend."

"I have to speak to him, we do go hiking together and I'm not going to ignore him because of some stupid mistake at work."

"Mistake? Are you mad? Is that what he told you, that it was a mistake? If you believe that you're a real mug."

"Do you mind not calling me a mug; you're not at work now you know."

"For God's sake, he's a trouble causer. Don't have anything to do with him."

"I don't need to take orders from you about who I speak to. He's a friend and has found it hard to get work since leaving your place."

"He didn't leave, he was sacked. And what are you talking about him *being a friend*. Please don't tell me you are actually socialising with him?" She glared at him, but he ignored her and continued driving which infuriated her even more. "I don't think it's too much to expect a little support from my husband."

"That's rich," he snapped, "I support you all the time. I spend half my life waiting for you to come home from that ... shithole at night."

"That *shithole,* pays us a good salary so we can live."

"Yeah, well maybe you ought to look for a different job somewhere. One where you don't have to work the ridiculous hours you do, and lets you be at home in the evening when your husband gets in."

"Oh, I see what this is all about. Poor Philip on his own. Do you realise how pathetic that sounds?"

"And do you realise how much that place dominates your life? What with that and Elsa, I might as well be single, I spend that much time on my own."

She threw her hands up, "I don't believe I'm hearing this. All I asked is for you to give Gary Hicks a wide berth, and now I'm in an argument about my job and my best friend." He didn't respond so she carried on, "And don't be thinking Gary Hicks sees you as a *friend*."

"What's that supposed to mean?"

"He's bad mouthing you. I can't remember what he said exactly, but he implied I didn't know you properly, as if you've got some sort of hidden side. Now you tell me what that's all about?"

"I've no idea. Who cares anyway? Do you think we can shut up about Gary fucking Hicks, I've had enough talking about him for one day?"

"So have I. And as far as I'm concerned, you are being disloyal to me by having anything to do with him."

She stared out of the window. How the hell had a trip to the Number One ended in a full scale row about Gary bloody Hicks. Anger had flared in Philip's eyes when she mentioned that Gary had implied he wasn't everything she thought he was. Good. Hopefully that meant he'd steer well clear of him now.

Thankfully when they got home, Philip went into his study which gave her a much-needed break from him. It was daft, she knew, but she really didn't like him at that moment. It was unlike them to row, they rarely did. Possibly it was a build-up of testosterone in him, she couldn't remember the last time they'd made love. Not that she wanted to, well, not with him anyway. There was a time when making love to him totally dominated her life, but not anymore. All thoughts of getting pregnant had well and truly gone off her radar.

An image of exactly who she did want to make love to came into her mind, and a sharp throb of need arrowed between her thighs that she wanted to see to, but it was hard with Philip in the house. It would have to be a bath as he wouldn't come in the bathroom while she was having a soak. Not Philip. No bathing together for them. But to make absolutely certain, she popped her head around his study door, "I'm going to have a bath before starting dinner."

He turned from the computer and his eyes told her he'd regretted them falling out too, "Okay. I'll be through myself in a minute after I've finished reading this document for work. Do you want me to do anything?"

"You can peel some potatoes if you like. I won't be long."

It was late afternoon and dark outside, and the warmth of the bathroom made her all the more turned on. She lit two scented candles and filled the large bath as full as she could with loads of bubbles. She slipped out of her clothes and immersed her sensitised body in the warm soothing water, easing herself against the back of the bath with her head supported on the tiles.

Her hands glided across her skin, and she gently tweaked her nipples which made her pussy pulsate. She moved her fingers downwards and with her forefinger, gently stroked her clit. She would have preferred the hard vibrations of her toothbrush but she couldn't use that with Philip in the house.

Circling her clit felt so good. Excitement was bubbling within, and with a bit more pressure, she'd easily come. She visualised Fin's mouth brushing against her stomach with his tongue dancing around her bellybutton. The ecstasy of one of his fingers slipping deep inside of her, and then two, and as his fingers moved deeper, his thumb speeded up and circled her nub. She imagined his dark head moving between her legs, and his gentleness as he slowly licked her swollen lips, before moving his tongue onto her clit.

She rubbed her fingers backwards and forwards frantically. She was virtually there and the anticipation made her feel like she was suspended from a great height, until the pleasure burst in her breasts and tingled down her tummy. Still she rubbed, harder and harder, biting her lip to avoid crying out, grasping every last sensation of pleasure and desperately wishing it was Fin delivering it.

36

Elsa was pleased to see Fin again. He kept dropping by after work to check on her. Nick was still working and she was happy just sitting with Fin in the conservatory with some music in the background. He'd tell her what he was doing at the hospital, and it was clear to her that he'd made a great start. But that was Fin, if he was asked to build a rocket and fly to the moon, he'd do a better job than anyone else.

She knew he was only staying until Nick came home so she wasn't on her own and she loved him for it. Today, he seemed relaxed flicking through the local newspaper so she thought it was an opportune time to ask him about something that had been niggling away at her. It would be interesting to see if she got anywhere with him, though.

"Would you give me an honest answer if I asked you a question?"

He put the newspaper down and looked at her, "That very much depends on the question," he smiled widening his eyes, "if it's about my personal life, then no."

"No, it's not about your personal life," she paused and could see the relief written across his face, so went in for the sucker punch, "well not really. It's about Kathryn."

"What about Kathryn?"

She didn't miss him swallowing.

"Remember the night of your operation when you stayed over?"

He nodded.

"I couldn't sleep and came downstairs to make a drink, and when I passed your bedroom door, I could swear I heard you call out *Kat*. I wondered if you were dreaming about her?"

He frowned, "Why on earth would I be dreaming about Kathryn?"

"That's what I was wondering?" *And why Kathryn was asking questions about you the day we went to the spa together.*

"I have no idea what I was dreaming about, but the anaesthetic gases can stay in your system for at least twenty-four hours, so if I did call out, it would no doubt be the after effects of the anaesthetic." He shrugged, "As for Kathryn, I have no idea why on earth you would think I'd be dreaming about her." He lifted the newspaper back up in front of his face, as if dismissing any further comments.

"Because I think you like her."

"I do like her, but I don't dream about her I can assure you," he answered turning the page of the newspaper but not looking directly at her.

"Are you sure about that?" she probed.

"Quite sure."

"There's nothing going on between the two of you, then?"

That got his attention. He put the newspaper down on his lap, "Of course not. Kathryn's happily married."

"I know, but in my experience a wedding ring doesn't prohibit an affair."

"Well, in mine it does. I'm not interested in pursuing a relationship with a married woman, end of, so let's say no more on the matter."

"You're lying, I can tell. Ever since you were a little boy, you've had a nervous twitch beneath your eye when you're not telling the truth. Mum could always tell, and right now, I can too. There is something going on between you and Kathryn, admit it."

"Correction, there is nothing *going on* between us. She loves Philip and wants to be with him, you've said that yourself often enough."

"Oh Fin, don't ever take a lie detector test will you. Do you think by answering you aren't having an affair, I'll believe you? Let me try and be a little more direct. Are you currently having a relationship with Kathryn, you know the type I mean, quickie sex, a secret shag ..."

"That's enough, Elsa."

"Well, are you?"

She watched Fin breathe in deeply. The last person he would want to tell would be his sister. He knew how close her and Kathryn were so he'd be reluctant to speak about the two of them. But she knew her brother. He would want to unload and work it all out. Fin was a problem solver.

"Do I have your word this conversation is between you and I?"

"Of course."

He placed the newspaper on the table and folded his hands in his lap, "Then yes, Kathryn and I have become ... close. But she loves Philip so it's a non-starter."

"And how do you feel about that?"

"Dejected, disappointed, sad ... all of those."

"So it's more than a fling on your part, is that what you're saying?"

"I'm saying a relationship is out of the question. She won't leave Philip and I have to respect that."

"You're right there, she'd never leave him. Kathryn wouldn't be able to live with herself if she did that. To be honest, I'm absolutely amazed she's attracted to you at all," she widened her eyes, "not that you aren't gorgeous, of course, but this isn't like her, she's devoted to Philip. You must be very special to have broken through that strict moral code she lives her life by."

She saw some of the tension leave his face. Almost as if she'd given him a ray of hope, even though she hadn't really.

"So what's the state of play at the moment," she asked, "do you meet secretly?"

"Hell no, she keeps her distance, which to be honest is what I asked her to do."

"So what about you and the matron, Helen? Are you not pursuing that?"

He shook his head, "She's a friend, someone to take out occasionally really. She's hinting at more though, but

I don't want to raise her hopes."

"Do you think if Kathryn wasn't around, you'd be interested?"

"No," he dismissed firmly, "to be honest, Kathryn has shown me that I'm ready to move on. I thought when I lost Saskia, that was it and I'd never find anyone again. But now I know I'm capable of a relationship, it's just so bloody unfortunate that the person I want, is in love with someone else."

"Oh Fin. I really am sorry. I love Kathryn to bits, she's so easy to love. I'd like nothing more than to see the two of you together. I'd like to know you're happy before …"

"Before what? Don't start getting all melancholy on me now. I'm expecting you to be around for a long time yet, so when I do meet someone in the future, you'll be here to share that."

If only. Why was life so shit?

"I hope so too. I'd like to know you were settled."

He must have seen something in her eyes, "Hey, what's that look for, you're feeling okay, aren't you?"

"Yes of course I am. I want you to be happy that's all, especially after what you've been through. I know," she winked, "shall we lighten things up a bit, how about a gin and tonic?"

"What about your medication, should you be drinking with it?"

"Finley Dey, who is the eldest here?"

He threw back his head and laughed, "You are, bossy boots."

"In that case, dear brother, mine's a large one."

"Okay, your wish is my command," he grinned as he stood up.

"And don't be sticking loads of ice and tonic in it. I want to taste the gin."

"Would I?"

As he went over to the drinks cabinet and selected a bottle of Bombay Sapphire, she asked, "One more question, and then I'll shut up."

"Only the one then," he raised an eyebrow, "I think I've answered enough for today."

"Are you in love with her?"

He paused, as if needing time to digest the question, "Maybe I am," he answered despondently, "who knows?"

Her insides churned. How bloody unfair. Fin, her gorgeous brother could have almost any woman he wanted, yet the daft bugger falls in love with the one woman he can't have. Yes, for the second time that day she concluded that life was indeed shit.

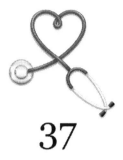

37

Fin had discretely booked a room for the night at the Gables Hotel so he was there early to welcome staff as they arrived for the Christmas party.

A glance around the function room confirmed the hotel had done a terrific job with the all the colour-themed decorations. He looked up at a huge net securing dozens of balloons to be released at some stage during the evening, which should be fun. The whole objective of the evening was for staff to have a good time as he'd always worked on the principle that well-looked after staff were productive staff, and tonight was a reward for their efforts.

In the short time since taking over at St Anne's he'd seen the small private hospital steadily making a profit and the trajectories for the following years were encouraging. Making money thrilled him more than performing the surgery he'd been trained to do. He knew he was the right person to turn St Anne's around and fortunately he had the capital to do so. Years of careful investments, property development and a hefty insurance pay out on his dear wife and son had made him wealthy beyond anything he could have dreamt of at university.

His thoughts were interrupted by the arrival of Helen looking lovely in a deep purple dress, and he greeted her with a warm embrace. She was alone which surprised him as she was an attractive woman so must have had plenty of men she could bring. He hoped she didn't think that because they'd been out together a few times, there might be something in the future between. He didn't want to embarrass her in any way and had been clear that he wasn't looking for a relationship, which she appeared to understand. However, in his experience, women invariably had a different agenda to the one they admitted to.

Staff began to arrive, and Fin welcomed them individually, assisted ably by Helen. They circulated, making sure they greeted everyone, and smiled warmly at the spouses or plus one's. All the time his senses were finely tuned to Kathryn's arrival. He'd not exactly lied to his sister about his relationship with her, but he hadn't told the entire truth either. He didn't respect that she was married and spent most his time plotting ways he could be with her.

This overwhelming desire for a woman was completely new to him. He'd loved his wife very much and could still remember their heady days of being in love and getting married, and despite them both being career focussed, he could recall their absolute delight when Christiaan came along. Their relationship had been fulfilling, but very steady, so these new-found feelings he had for Kathryn were completely alien to him. She was the card hand you couldn't win, or that elusive lottery jackpot. Virtually unobtainable, yet still he craved her.

He felt Helen's hand on his arm, "Fin, have you a moment? Jim's just given me some bad news which I'm worried might spoil the evening."

He moved her away from the others, concerned about what Jim the porter had said as she looked quite shocked. She glanced around to make sure she wasn't overheard, "Jim says Dr Elahi has been killed in a road traffic accident in Italy."

Christ. He didn't know the anaesthetist Mul Elahi that well, but nevertheless was shocked to learn tragic news about a well-respected colleague that worked with them all.

Helen continued, "Apparently Jim's daughter is at

the same school as Dr Elahi's daughter, so she heard about it through friends, but the news hasn't filtered through to others yet. I don't know what you think, but I feel it's best for Jim to keep it under his hat for tonight, as upsetting as it is, there's no sense in informing staff when there's little we can do about it."

"You're right," he nodded, "we'll send our condolences to the family on Monday when it's official. Do you want me to go and speak to him?"

"No, I'll go over and let him know you agree and to thank him again for not discussing it."

"Okay, you do that, and when you come back I'll get you another drink. It really is terrible news."

Two of the admin girls approached him and introduced their partners and he chatted politely with them but his internal antenna was on high alert. Would Kathryn bring Philip?

Helen returned and joined in with the chatter which he was grateful for as it gave him the opportunity to covertly watch the door. He checked his watch, where was she? He glanced again at the table where the theatre staff were sitting in case she might have slipped in and he'd missed her, and noticed Janelle holding court. There'd certainly been a transformation in her this evening. She'd put her hair up in a style similar to the way Kathryn had worn hers on the night of his party, and it appeared as if she'd dyed her mousy-coloured hair a shade lighter. She must have been waiting for someone because even though she was laughing and joking with her colleagues, she frequently glanced towards the entrance.

He sensed Kathryn's arrival seconds before he physically saw her. She stood in the doorway and took his breath away in a fitted black dress that clung to her in all the right places. She'd left her gorgeous blonde wavy hair loose, which he'd not seen since it was splayed out on the pillow the night he'd first had sex with her in his house. He remembered how beautiful her hair had smelled, like a ripe peach, so clean and fruity.

While some outpatient staff and their partners

chatted to him and Helen, he nodded attentively trying to look involved, but he was acutely distracted. Common sense had told him she'd bring Philip, but jealousy gnawed away in his stomach at the sight of him helping her remove the little white furry wrap she was wearing. He wanted to be the one taking it from her.

His eyes were riveted to her bare arms in the short sleeve dress. How can a woman's arms be so alluring? She looked stunning as she walked gracefully towards a table that the theatre staff had taken up. He watched as Janelle retrieved her handbag from the vacant chair next to her, indicating it was spare.

The other theatre girls all looked lovely too. None of them were by any means unattractive, but next to Kathryn they looked ordinary. Kathryn radiated elegant beauty and had a figure many would die for. An image of her naked body flashed before him causing an inappropriate twitch in his groin.

"Fin," Helen interrupted his lustful thoughts, "do you think we can get that drink, I think everyone must be here now?"

"Yes, of course, sorry, what can I get you, the same again?"

"Another dry white wine would be nice. Do you want me to come with you?"

"No, you stay here, you're doing a great job," he winked, "you're a natural at all this." He did like Helen, she was a lovely young woman, but not for him. The woman he wanted was standing metres away with her bloody husband.

Eventually he made it to the bar having been interrupted along the way by several members of staff. It was nice to see everyone enjoying themselves, they were good staff and very loyal to St Anne's. He'd been impressed with the work ethos of the hospital; it seemed to be one big family. Yes, there was an odd one or two that needed HR to keep an eye on, but on the whole, it was a good hospital with an excellent reputation within the local community.

As he stood at the bar waiting to be served, he turned to let someone pass with their drinks, and almost banged into Philip stood directly behind him. Despite his deep-rooted jealousy, he had to be pleasant to him as he hadn't done anything other than be married to the woman he wanted for himself.

"Hello Philip," he reached out to shake his hand and the lie slipped easily off his tongue, "pleased you could come."

"Thank you, it's nice to be here," his eyes glanced towards the main hall, "it certainly is a great venue for a party."

"Yes, isn't it. Have you been here before?"

"No, I can't say I have."

"Me neither, but Elsa tells me the food in the restaurant is to die for, and they do excellent bar meals."

"Really? We'll have to give it a try sometime." There was a tiny awkward pause as they didn't really have anything in common, but thankfully Philip filled it, "How is Elsa?"

"She's doing okay, thank you, quite tired, but that's only to be expected with the treatment."

"Yes, Kathryn did say." He paused as if deciding whether to carry on with what he wanted to say next, and then surprised Fin by continuing, "Actually, I wouldn't mind having a word with you sometime," he frowned, "it's a little bit difficult though as it's about Kathryn."

"Kathryn?" Fin didn't need to feign concern, "Is everything alright?"

"Yes, it's about the effect Elsa's treatment's having on her. She's not herself at all."

"In what way?" He shouldn't be asking, but he wanted any snippet of information he could get about her.

Philip grimaced, clearly struggling to say any more which was understandable; they weren't friends by any stretch of the imagination. He seemed to have thought better about discussing his wife further, "Maybe some other time perhaps," he glanced around, "I don't think this evening is the right time to talk."

"No, of course not, but I know how fond Elsa is of Kathryn so if there's anything troubling her, I'd like to help."

"Thank you, I appreciate that."

Fin's curiosity couldn't leave it there, "I seem to remember you talking about the hiking trips you do, maybe I could join you one weekend and we could chat then?"

Philip nodded, "Sure, we could do that."

Fin reached in his jacket pocket and handed him his business card, "If you give me a ring, we can fix something up. My weekends are less hectic these days so a bit of exercise in the fresh air would be most welcome."

"Sounds good to me," Philip smiled, "I'll do that."

"Great, I'll look forward to it. Right, I'd better get Matron her drink or her mouth will be completely dry with all this meeting and greeting she's doing. Enjoy the evening."

He turned his attention to the barmaid as Philip moved away to the other end of the bar. So, Kathryn was behaving differently because of Elsa, or was it that? Maybe her behaviour had changed because of the two of them? *God I hope so. Let her be unsettled in her marriage.*

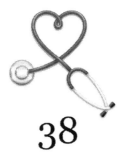

38

It seemed an eternity since Kathryn had arrived, when in fact it had only been just over an hour, but Fin couldn't resist any longer. While he'd played the part of a good boss circulating and making small talk, his mind was occupied by one thing, *her*. He approached her knowing she was as aware of him as he was of her. She did a great job of perfecting the look of being polite to the boss.

"Good evening, Fin. What a fantastic party, everyone seems to be having a great time."

"Yes, isn't it? Are you enjoying yourself?"

"Sort of," she nodded, "but I'm trying to keep a watchful eye on the staff. A free bar and theatre staff don't go that well together I'm afraid." The most beautiful smile curved her lips, and all he could think about was kissing her senseless.

He smiled, "Let's hope they slow down and eventually stall."

"Let's *hope* you're right," she grinned.

"Anyway, I'm sorry to have to break up the party, but I wonder if I could have a quick word with you?"

A wave of anxiety passed across her face which he didn't like to see, so he quickly added, "I've some news about a member of staff which I wanted to let you know about."

Relief was quickly replaced by a look of concern as she registered exactly what he was saying, "Oh dear, I don't like the sound of that."

"It won't take long," he glanced at the theatre crowd, "where's Philip anyway?"

She arched her eyebrows "Long story. He's nipped out to help a friend jumpstart his car but he'll be back shortly. I'm afraid these parties aren't really his thing so I think he was pleased to be able to escape to be honest."

"Him and me both then," Fin replied as they made their way out of the main hall. He wanted to touch her desperately but knew people would be watching and he didn't want to draw attention to either of them.

They stood in the foyer which was perfectly appropriate as there were several members of staff moving about to use the toilets and popping outside to smoke.

"I'm sorry for dragging you away."

"What is it? Is it bad news?"

"I need to tell you in private," he put his hand in his pocket and produced a sheet of folded paper which he handed to her.

He raised his voice slightly, "Could you look at this for me please, it's my speech for later. Check if you're happy with the section about the theatre staff."

Her puzzled expression made him lower his voice, "My room key's inside, room 1101."

The implications of him having a room registered, "I can't. Someone will notice I've gone."

"They won't. It won't take long. Please, just go and I'll be there in a minute or two."

"Why can't you tell me here?"

Lust, pure, potent and powerful pumped through his veins as he took a deep breath in, "Because it's not only the news I want to give you."

Heat flashed in her eyes. Thank God their desire was mutual. She turned away from him clutching the blank piece of paper and elation kicked his groin, knowing that in minutes he'd be inside her. Excitement scorched through him as she made her way to the stairs.

He made himself visible, circling around the venue and nodding to a few members of staff before making his way discreetly towards the stairs himself.

Nobody would know he had a room booked at the

hotel and he wouldn't be gone long anyway. The way he was feeling right now, ravishing Kathryn would take less than a minute.

He used his second key card and opened the door, and there she stood in the dimly lit room. She'd closed the curtains and lowered the lights, and the sight of her eyes inviting him inside the room, and inside her, was incredibly erotic.

The door clicked shut behind him as he walked forward and pulled her towards him. He kissed her hard, plunging his tongue into her mouth as his dick throbbed with need for her.

"Fin," she murmured in between kisses.

"God, Kathryn," he groaned as he hoisted her black dress up, pleased to see she'd already removed her panties, "You look beautiful. I want you so much."

His fingers touched her soft and wet pussy and she groaned and shivered. She was ready for him, and he was hard as hell. He wanted to eat her, drink her, smell her, lick her, but there wasn't time. He eased his dick out. He didn't want to fuck her standing up, but they hadn't the time to get into bed, remove their clothes and savour their lovemaking. It was going to be urgent and quick.

He buried his lips in her thick lustre of hair and inhaled her, murmuring hot words in native Dutch, and then English, "This won't be slow," he groaned, rubbing his hard dick against her moist clit.

"Who wants slow?" she breathed, taking hold of his dick and working it.

He filled her with his fingers and was rewarded by a deep guttural moan, "Hurry up, Fin, I need you right now."

There was a dresser unit next to them, and he turned her and leant her over it. He hoisted her dress up higher and lust surged through him as he gripped her perfectly ripe ass. He used his leg to move hers wider apart and plunged into her.

"Yes," she moaned as he rammed hard, holding her hips and stretching her wider each time he pushed.

"Squeeze me," he demanded, and he moaned as she clenched her pussy tightly around him.

She felt incredible as he set a thrusting rhythm, spurred on by her gasps. His fingers glided over her moist clit and her breathing became louder as she groaned and held on to the dresser. He sank his teeth into her neck, "Come for me, Kat, come for me." He fucked her hard and harder still until he felt her body jerk around him as she screamed her release, seconds before a hoarse growl escaped from his own lips as he pumped his seed inside her, groaning Kat, Kat, over and over again.

He pulled her into a standing position and eased her against the wall, his heartbeat thumping. Their damp foreheads touched as they both steadied their breathing. Her beautiful red lips were swollen and her face was pink from their frantic sex. He kissed her gently, "I wasn't too rough for you?"

She shook her head, "No, I loved it," she smiled, "but we have to get back before someone notices."

"I know," he said, pulling on his trousers, "I'll go first to give you a chance to sort yourself out."

"Do I look that bad?" she asked cheekily.

"You look gorgeous to me, but others might think you look like a woman who's just been shagged."

"They'd be right then," she sexily rolled her eyes, "shagged beautifully I might add," she giggled.

He loved her laugh, it was infectious, "Thank you for that, Sister Knight, I'm pleased you enjoyed it."

"You're welcome, Mr Dey. And I did, enormously."

He hovered around the foyer waiting for her to emerge from the stairwell. A few people were around but most were in the main hall where the music was thumping away. He nodded to a few, again making sure he was visible. Not that anyone would have noticed he'd been absent judging by the look of some of them. He was beginning to agree that the free bar hadn't been such a good idea.

Kathryn walked nonchalantly towards him as if she'd stumbled upon him. It was evident she'd done her makeup as she was back to her stunning self. She looked so sexy, and remembering her screaming his name as she

215

climaxed, made him want her all over again. He couldn't get over his desire for sex with her, it definitely was a first for him having sex and then wanting it straight away again. But that was how she made him feel. It was as if he needed to put his mark on her all the time. She might belong to someone else, which was initially a huge problem and totally against his moral compass, but he'd thrown that out of the window long ago.

"Hi, Kathryn, are you having a nice evening?"

"Yes, thank you. It certainly is a lovely party. Well worth all the effort, are you enjoying it?" she questioned with a gleam in her eye.

"I am, so far it's well exceeded my expectations," he winked.

"Did you really have something to tell me?"

"Ah yes, I almost forgot. It is bad news I'm afraid, about a colleague of ours."

"Oh dear, who, what?"

"I don't know any more details, other than Jim the porter told Helen that Dr Elahi has died in a car accident in Italy."

Kathryn's hand went up to her mouth, "Oh God, no. I can't believe it. That's terrible. He has young family, did you know?"

Fin shook his head, he didn't know, but he was distracted remembering the awful moment when he'd been given the tragic news about his wife and son. The total disbelief that they'd lost their lives while he'd been operating on a woman wanting bigger breasts. His loved ones wiped out by some stupid idiot that had gone out after work, got smashed, and then decided he was fit to drive home.

Kathryn must have realised his despair as sympathy filled her eyes, "Are you alright?" She placed her hand on his arm and his eyes were drawn to the slenderness of it. He stared, not because he didn't want her touching him, he wanted that all the time, but the slight gesture had a dramatic effect on him. At that precise moment, the loss of his wife hit him hard and he had an overwhelming urge to pull her into his arms, hold her tightly, and tell her exactly how she made him feel.

She quickly withdrew her hand, "Sorry. It's such a shock."

"Yes, we've told Jim not to say anything for tonight. I didn't see the point in upsetting everyone. I hope that was the right thing to do?" He wanted her approval that his instinct was correct.

"I think it was," she agreed, "the staff will know soon enough. It makes you realise though how short life is, doesn't it?"

The silence between them stretched until she spoke again, "I'd better be getting back."

But neither of them moved. They stood, looking deeply into each other's eyes. To anyone passing by, they were two people, a boss and an employee having a conversation, but to them, it was intense, as if nobody else mattered except the two of them cocooned in their own little world.

"I want to be with you," he whispered, "you must know that."

"No," she shook her head, "don't say any more."

"I can't help it, Kathryn, it's the way I feel."

"Please don't do this, not here, not now. Someone will hear you."

"I don't care. Christ, I don't know who I am anymore," he swallowed hard, "I want you in my life. Leave him ... please ... leave him."

"I can't. You have to stop this. I need to go."

He closed his eyes slowly and opened them again, "Tell me if there's a chance of a future for us together."

"This isn't the time or the place," she whispered, shifting uncomfortably.

"I don't care. I need to know."

"And I need to get back."

"Just tell me, yes or no," he pleaded, "yes, there's a future for us together, or no there isn't."

He regretted speaking out, but he'd started now, "It's not that difficult," a wistful tone came into his voice, "yes or a no?"

The transformation of her beautiful face from happy to tense was solely down to him. He knew he shouldn't be pressurising her in public, however, he'd done it now and as he stared, willing her to answer, Helen interrupted them, "There you are, Fin. Hi, Kathryn. Are you ready to say a few words and present Rosa with the flowers?" She looked at them both and must have sensed something wasn't quite right, "Unless you'd prefer me to do it?"

He didn't want Kathryn compromised in any way so deliberately turned away from her and towards Helen, "I'll come now. I've just told Kathryn about Dr Elahi and it's clearly upset her."

Helen gave her a sympathetic look, "It's terrible, isn't it. He's got young children I believe."

Kathryn nodded, "Yes, he has teenagers but also two very young ones, nine and seven I think."

"Do you think you'll be alright now?" he asked Kathryn, cursing Helen for butting in.

"I'll be fine, it's been such a shock, I think I'll probably call it a night."

"You'll stay for Rosa's presentation though, won't you?" Helen asked and turned to Fin, "Shall we get on with it?"

He nodded to her, and turned to Kathryn. She wasn't getting away that easily when he'd bared his soul, "You haven't answered my question?"

"No, I haven't." She'd turned pale and he hated himself for causing that, but now that he'd asked, he wanted an answer.

"I'd like to know," he pressed.

"Maybe we can have a chat on Monday?" She didn't give him chance to respond and turned to Helen, "Rosa has no idea she's going to be thanked for all her fundraising, it'll be such a surprise."

"It's the least we can do when she's raised so much," Helen smiled.

"She's going to be thrilled to bits. Right, I'll let you two get on with it then," Kathryn quickly moved away and he watched her walk towards her table.

Helen looked sideways at him, "Tell me it's none of my business if you want, but what question have you asked that you need an urgent decision on tonight?"

Blast Helen for interrupting at such a crucial moment. He scowled, "It's about promoting her permanently when Alison comes back. I'd like them to do a job share with one of them taking on more of a training and development role in the hospital."

Helen raised her eyebrows, "Well I think Alison may have something to say about that."

"It was just an idea," he replied, ignoring the surprised look on Helen's face and wishing she'd shut up. She wouldn't, "I can't believe you've asked her that at the same time as telling her an anaesthetist had died. That seems a little bit crass to me."

"Yes, probably it was," he snapped as he turned and made his way towards the stage. As far as he was concerned, the whole evening had been crass. He'd been ridiculous pressurising her to leave Philip, but he was so frustrated. He wanted her in his life. He wanted to take her out to dinner and go away for weekends, sleep with her at night and wake up with her in the morning, yet there was no chance. That privilege was afforded to her husband while he was forced down a route of opportunistic sex whenever they could. He didn't want that, he wanted more. That yearning was becoming stronger each day to the point of domination from waking up each morning, to going to bed at night. Things couldn't go on the way they were, he had to bring it to a head.

39

Fin gave his speech thanking the staff for their contribution and buoying them up for another year's hard work, and then called Rosa to the stage. Both Rosa and her husband had raised a substantial amount of money towards the local hydrotherapy pool and he was pleased to be able to publicly thank them, and judging by the enthusiastic applause, the staff seemed to share his sentiments.

By the time he'd come off the stage, Kathryn had gone. He'd surreptitiously watched Philip who'd managed to find his way back to the party, put the furry wrap around her shoulders and felt a tightening in the pit of his stomach as he placed his arm around her waist. He hated Philip Knight at that moment; he couldn't bear the thought of his hands on her. He wanted to be the only one that touched her, not her husband.

Where the hell had he disappeared to during the party anyway? Supposedly starting a friend's dodgy motor. Maybe *he* was having an affair? Wouldn't that be an irony?

The sex tonight had been amazing, but frustrating at the same time. He didn't want their lovemaking to be rushed; he wanted it to be leisurely. This whole affair wasn't right. He knew he couldn't have her, but when had *couldn't* ever stopped him before? All his life he'd prided himself on his decision making and tonight he had to make another. He needed to find a way for Kathryn Knight to be his. He was uncertain at that precise moment how, but he was going to do everything in his power to make it happen.

He mingled with staff until he thought it an appropriate time to leave. They'd have a better time without the boss around so he found Helen to make his excuses.

"I'm going to call it a night, Helen. They've closed the free bar so they'll have to pay for their drinks if they want any more."

"That's good then as there's one or two that have had more than enough." She reached for her handbag, "I'm ready to go myself now. I'll get reception to call me a taxi, how are you getting home?"

"I've got my car and haven't been drinking so I can take you home if you like."

He only offered as he didn't want to draw attention to the fact he had a room at the hotel for the night.

She frowned, "I've seen you drinking, haven't I?"

"Only tonic with ice and lemon. I tend to have that and people assume I'm drinking gin. It saves a lot of *why aren't you drinking, or go on, one won't hurt you.* I see tonight as more of a business evening so I prefer to be sober."

"Okay, if you're sure, I'll get my coat. I won't be a second."

They walked out of the main hall and into the foyer and while he waited for Helen, Janelle staggered out of the ladies toilet. Clearly she'd slipped through the net on keeping an eye on staff drinking too much at the free bar.

She lunged forward and he caught her, "Steady ... are you alright?"

"Yessss, I'm fine, Mr Dey, thank yooooo."

"You don't look fine to me, you look as if you've had one too many."

"I've only had a few, you said we needed to enjoy ourselves."

"Yes, but not to the point of getting plastered."

"Pardon me? Who's plastered? I can take my drink."

"Sure you can. How are you getting home, is someone

with you?"

"Nope, only me on my ownsome. Hey, nice speech by the way," she gave the biggest hiccup as Helen joined them clutching her coat with a stern expression on her face.

"Janelle, you've had too much to drink by the look of things?" she accused.

"Not you as well, Melon, oops, I mean Helen."

Fin looked at Helen, "I think we better drop her off home, don't you?"

"Absolutely," she agreed, linking her arm in Janelle's, "come on, Mr Dey's going to give us a lift home."

He helped Janelle in the back of his car and strapped her in before coming round to the front and sitting next to Helen.

"Where do you live, Janelle?" he asked turning on the ignition.

"Landsmore Close."

He frowned, "Where's that?"

"I know where it is," Helen said, "I'll direct you. It's probably easier to take me home first though otherwise you'll be doubling back on yourself."

He sensed by her tone that Helen was disappointed. Had she been hoping he would have gone back for coffee? He was relieved that fate had intervened; he'd love a coffee and a shed load of other things, but not from her.

"Right," he agreed "I'll do that."

The journey to Helen's at that time of night didn't take long. He pulled up outside her house, "Thanks for this evening, it was down to you that it went so well."

"Nonsense, it was a joint effort. Anyway, you've had to foot the bill so I'd say the success of the evening is largely down to you."

He smiled, "Long as it went okay, that's the main thing. I want the staff to feel valued."

"Oh we do," Janelle piped up from the back, "very valued, it was a fab night." He turned his head slightly and looked at Janelle, and then back at Helen, "I think I'd better get her home. The last thing I want is a drunken woman throwing up in the back of my car."

"Hey, what drunken woman are you talking about? I'll have you know I can take my drink." She hiccupped again.

He rolled his eyes at Helen, "I'll see you on Monday. Remind me where I'm going, would you?"

"Turn right at the end of the crescent, and then right again onto the main road. Keep going for about three miles until you see the Crow's Nest pub, then take the left onto Landsmore Close."

"That's great, I'll find it. Thanks again."

Helen smiled and her eyes flicked to Janelle sprawled on the back seat, "Good luck with that."

He raised his eyebrows good humouredly, "Thank you." He watched until he'd seen her go in the front door before putting the car in gear and pulling away.

✳

It was going well so far. Janelle thought about her bedroom makeover with the new trendy blinds, the intimate bedside lights and the sexy silky sheets, and excitement spurred her on. She looked at Fin in the front seat and injected more of a slur into her voice, "Are you hungry?" she asked, tossing a hiccup in.

"No, I can't say I am."

"I'm shtarving. Can we shtop off for something to eat?"

"I don't think so."

"Aw. Food's good when you've been drinking."

"That's why the hotel put on a buffet, didn't you have anything?"

"Caaaan't remember."

"I think the best thing right now is to get you home and to bed."

"Ah, bed, yesh, that shounds good."

"You can sleep it off then. Have you got someone at home waiting for you?"

"No, if I had, I'd have brought him with me tonight."

She pretended to be asleep, slumped on the back seat. As they approached the Crow's Nest, she sat bolt upright, playacting at being dazed and looked out of the window, "Oh, that didn't take long." She threw in another fake hiccup and looked at him through the mirror, "It ish very kind of you to bring me home, you really didn't have to."

"I know I didn't, but I wanted to make sure you got home safely. You shouldn't drink to excess when you're out, you leave yourself wide open to problems."

"What short of problems? I knew everyone there tonight, nobody would hurt me." She slumped back down.

"Of course *they* wouldn't, but when you had left the safety of the hotel and headed for home, anyone could take advantage of you. Which house is it, by the way?"

"The one next to the big camper van."

He pulled in front of her house and applied the handbrake but left the engine running, "There you go then," he turned round in his seat, "make sure you drink plenty of water so you're not too ill tomorrow."

"I'll be fine, nothing that a few black coffees won't short out. Would you like to come in for a coffee?"

Thank God her mother was visiting her sister for the weekend.

"No thank you, I'd better get off."

She cleared her throat, "Do you think you could walk me to my door? I'm not sure I'm shteady enough to make it on my own."

She could see by his expression he didn't want to, but nevertheless, he switched off the car engine and released his seatbelt. He came round to her door and helped her out. She purposely went limp and put her arms around him for support.

"Ooooooh, thank you."

She dragged her heels to make things more difficult, and after a few seconds of hoisting her down the drive, he made it to the front door.

"Key?" he asked.

"What?"

"Your key, to get in."

"Oh, that key." She opened up her handbag and fumbled inside, "Here it ish." She wound her arms back around his neck and giggled, "Are you sure you don't want a teeny weeny cup of coffee?"

He removed her arms and pushed her towards the

wall, holding her there with one hand while he unlocked the door. She went floppy again so that when the front door opened, he had to use both hands to support her.

"I'm starting to feel a bit shick," she groaned, "could you help me inshide pleashe?"

She watched his chest rise as he inhaled a deep breath, "Come on then." He supported her weight as she pushed herself against him and eased her into the narrow hallway. The front door closed on the latch behind them.

Kerching!

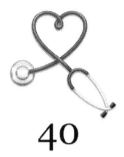

40

It was Monday morning, two days since the Christmas party, two long days Kathryn ached for him, and she was kissing him like she'd never wanted to stop.

Kathryn had come into work much earlier than usual, leaving the house before Philip so she could see Fin. They were in one of the consulting rooms in the outpatients department and the outside world was shut out by the drawn blinds at the window. She was half naked against the door but nobody could get in if they tried as he'd locked it.

"I hate the weekends and not seeing you," he breathed.

"I know, I know. Shushhh."

She kissed him again and felt him release her bra. She loved the feeling of his delicious mouth trailing down her neck and smothering her breasts as he devoured her. He sucked hard on her nipple, and her head rolled back onto the door, eagerly anticipating the delivery of the same pleasure to the other breast. He reached for the tie at the side of her scrub trousers and, excited as he made her feel, she needed to call a halt.

"Stop. Fin, we've got to stop. We can't …"

He raised his head, "I can't stop," he said and continued to try and untie her. She put her hands on top of his, "You'll have to, I'm menstruating."

He pulled a face, "Tell me you're joking … not that?"

She loved his obvious disappointment, "Yes, *that*,"

she said and widened her eyes, "but it doesn't mean you have to suffer too much."

She gently manoeuvred him so that he was leant against the door and reached for his trousers to unzip him. She released his dick and slowly started stroking him, enjoying his hardness, before dropping to her knees. She inhaled the cleanliness of shower gel as she took him in her mouth. He placed one of his hands on the wall to steady himself as she started unhurriedly, wanting to please him, and teasingly licked the tip before taking all of him into her mouth and sucking down the shaft. She wrapped her hands around his dick and fed him in into her mouth, sucking as hard as she could. Sexual power surged through her as he groaned her name ... *Kat, Kat*, over and over again as she continued plunging him deeply in and out of her mouth. She loved giving him pleasure and hearing his guttural moans.

Now his hands were in her hair, tugging, guiding her mouth over his cock, pushing it deep. Kath gagged and pulled away.

"Fuck, Kat, I'm going to come," he said, and she opened her mouth and looked up at him.

"Not in your mouth, I want to come over your tits. Hold them for me."

Oh, God, she was so hot right now.

She cupped her breasts, the nipples hard and taut, and gave them up to him as he jerked his cock fast. The first spurt hit her neck. The next splashed across her chest warmly and the sparks flew through her as Fin cursed and trembled and emptied himself down her front.

He reached for her arm and pulled her up to his level. His seed glistened over her chest and her nipples ached to be touched. With both hands, he massaged her breasts, smoothing his cum onto her skin, tugging at her nipples. A needy moan escaped her lips. She wanted more of this.

"Wear me all day. Don't wash," he ordered.

Words failed her, he was so hot. *She* was so hot. She'd never experienced anything like this before.

"I won't," she said, "I promise."

"You're stunning you know," he said and kissed her gently; a warm and loving kiss that she returned with simmering passion, their tongues caressing before he pulled away and went to the hand basin.

With her heart pounding and her pussy on fire, she slipped her bra on and he raised his eyebrows, "How I'm expected to do a clinic after that I really don't know. I'll be reliving that delicious mouth of yours all day."

"You should think yourself lucky," she laughed, lifting the theatre tunic over her head, "I'll be carrying the evidence *all day*."

"Exactly what I wanted," he grinned and started to wash his hands, "anyway, what time do you think you'll be done tonight?"

"We've only got one theatre list this afternoon with you not operating, and only small cases, so probably about six. Why?"

"We need to continue where we left off Friday night and look at the future," he dried his hands and moved to the window to open the blinds, "I've got a meeting at the Eastleigh after my clinic here today, but I'll be coming back. Give me a ring in my office when you've finished and everyone has gone and I'll come round to theatre and we can chat."

His eyes had challenged her, as if to say *I'm not going to go away*. She wasn't going to argue anyway because today would be a much better day knowing she was going to see him at the end of it.

"Okay," she nodded, "I'll ring you."

"Good girl. Oh, and before I forget, I'll be away for the next few days, I'm flying to Holland tomorrow."

She already hated the rest of the week now which he must have sensed as he reassured, "It's only a short trip. I'll be back on Friday after I've seen my accountant and lawyer."

"I'm off Friday, so it'll be Monday when I next see you then," she pointed out.

Six whole days not seeing him.
That's far too long.

He raised his eyebrows, "All the more reason for us to have that chat."

Despite knowing he'd be coercing her to look at the future as he'd done on Friday night, she didn't argue.

Pressure was the last thing she needed right now, but rather like a naughty child that misbehaved to get attention from a parent, she welcomed any contact from him. She didn't have answers to give him, least of all the one he was looking for, however, she wanted to see him regardless. He was beginning to mean that much to her.

She reached for the door handle, but he stopped her, "Hey, before you go, tell me, is Rosa a little bit puddled?"

His turn of phrase amused her, "That's debatable," she grinned, "why?"

"I was talking to her on Saturday night after the presentation for her charity work. She was very sweet and delighted with the flowers, but then she put her hand on my arm and with a really serious face said, *the sun is setting*. What's that about do you think?"

"I've no idea, but I wouldn't worry," Kathryn said, "she's crackers. She reckons she can see into the future. I've had warnings of, *the sand is running out of the glass,*" she widened her eyes humorously, "and *the black is ahead*. It's all very weird and I've no idea what she's talking about. She's retiring in February, did you know?" He nodded so she continued, "We need to look at whether we replace her, or have the theatre cleaners do the rest of the suite. She was originally moved from the wards by HR due to a back injury as they wanted her on light duties, so she potters really, but with her retiring soon, there's never been a great push to send her back."

"Right, yes, that sounds like a plan. Can you discuss it with Helen?"

"Yes of course." She reached again for the door handle, "What did you say to her by the way, when she said the sun was setting?"

"I told her yes, but there'll be another sunrise tomorrow, God willing."

She loved his humour, "Good for you. I've been putting off having a much needed quiet word with her about all this doom and gloom. The trouble is, I'm a bit of a chicken as this gypsy stuff scares me."

"I didn't realise you're easily scared?" he smiled playfully.

"I am of her," she giggled.

"And what about me, do I scare you?"

"No," she laughed, "not very much anyway."

"You should be scared ... very scared. I can be a beast if I don't get what I want."

"Is that right?"

"Yes, so any attempt to remove me from your body could result in consequences."

"Really? Mmm, I'm wondering if it's worth washing then, just for the hell of it."

"Tut, tut, tut, you'd better get out of here now Sister Knight before I show you exactly how scary I can be," he winked.

"Promises, promises," she laughed as she opened the door clutching a folder which had nothing in it at all, but it looked business-like and gave her a legitimate excuse to be alone in a room with the Hospital Director.

She returned to theatre as the staff drifted into work, all reminiscing about the staff ball. Kathryn informed them about Dr Elahi's death but most of them already knew via social media. She put a collection bag in the tea room for contributions towards flowers for his wife. She knew St Anne's would send some from the hospital, but she wanted to make more of a personal gesture from the theatre staff as they'd actually worked more directly with him.

The day dragged relentlessly and she spent most of it clockwatching until she would see Fin again. She thought of him as each minute ticked by, savouring him on her skin, and blushed at the audacity of the man.

After lunch, she let half of the staff go home as they were only running one theatre that afternoon for minor cases. At five thirty when the last patient was in the recovery room, Kathryn headed for the tea room making drinks for them all.

Janelle had scrubbed for the cases, and Kathryn had put herself down as the theatre circulator. Circulating required little concentration, which suited her as she preferred to daydream about Fin rather than boring surgical procedures which she'd seen a thousand times.

Crikey, she really must have it bad. She relived their

morning over and over again, and an image of Philip coming all over her appeared in her head. God alive, he'd pass out if she suggested that. Not that she would, sex with him was unthinkable when she had Fin.

Janelle flopped down on a seat as Kathryn waited for the kettle to boil, "Am I glad that's over," she sighed, "I'm not sure why Mr Vince was in such a rush today, are you?"

"Something to do with a presentation he had to attend this evening," Kathryn answered, "I think it was at his son's school, that's why there weren't any major cases on his list."

"Oh, right. Remind me not to scrub for him again when he's in a rush, will you?"

"Yes, he did seem a bit irritable I have to say."

"Irritable? He was bloody awful. I think half his trouble was he wanted you to scrub for him. Why didn't you do any of the cases?"

"I'd come on this morning and have awful cramps so I didn't feel like standing at the table. I am sorry, I should have relieved you."

"Don't be daft. It was fine. There wasn't that much, it's just him, he's a pain in the neck when he's in a hurry."

"Yes, he is. Mind you he's not much better when he's not rushing," she grinned.

Erin came in and she sat down next to Janelle, "That was a better Monday. Where's Mr Dey today, do we know?"

"He's at a meeting in the city this afternoon," Kathryn replied, stirring the drinks she'd made. She placed them on the coffee table in front of Janelle and Erin and sat down with hers.

"Must be important then," Erin said, "it's not like him to miss a Monday."

"No it isn't. It's something to do with the Eastleigh Hospital, I think he's bought shares in it, or maybe he's bought it outright, I'm not sure."

Janelle frowned, "How do you know about his business dealings, I thought it was his sister you were friendly with?"

If only you knew.

I'm wearing him all over me.

"It is Elsa that gives me snippets, I think he's quite a private person really."

Erin turned to Janelle, "Your face Janelle, you look almost accusing at Kathryn. What is it? Are you worried she might be trying to pinch him off you?" She took a sip of her coffee, "Oh, but then again, he's not yours is he," she said sarcastically, "much as you'd like him to be."

Janelle pulled a face "Ha, ha, very funny."

Kathryn took an exaggerated breath in, "If you don't mind, Erin, have you forgotten something?" she lifted her left hand up and wiggled her ring finger, "I am married, remember?"

"Sorry. It just made me laugh the way Janelle turned on you."

She didn't like the way the conversation was going as it was a bit too close to home. "Shall we try and be a bit more respectful, he is our boss and probably still grieving for his wife and son. I don't think he belongs to anybody, least of all anyone in theatre."

Janelle put her mug down on the table and smirked at them both, "Well that's where you're wrong," she folded her arms smugly, "I don't think he's still grieving at all."

"What makes you say that?" Erin asked.

Almost as if she knew she was about to hear something she didn't want to, Kathryn had an uneasy flutter in the pit of her stomach.

A shout from the patient recovery area interrupted the conversation, "Can someone check some post op for me please?"

Erin stood up, "I'll go," she turned to Janelle, "but I want the juicy gossip when I come back."

Kathryn didn't like gossip and was close to telling her to shut up, but at the same time she wanted to know exactly what she meant by Fin not grieving for his wife.

"I wish I hadn't said anything now," Janelle continued, "Erin's like a dog with a bone, she'll not let it drop."

Yeah, like you want her to stop.
You're bursting to say something.

"Why did you then? You know what she's like." She

kept her voice light and asked, "Anyway what exactly are you implying?"

"I was about to ask you both to guess who brought me home from the Gables the other night."

Despite the voice screaming in her head, *don't go there, leave it alone,* she shook her head, "I've no idea."

Janelle's expression smacked of a cat that had got the cream, "Who do you think?"

Please God, not him.

She frowned, "Not Mr Dey?"

"Yep, the very man himself."

You're lying.

"Really."

"Yes, *really.* We've become *friends,* she lifted her fingers up and made air quotes. "He took me home, and," she cocked her head to one side, "well, you know."

Kathryn's chest tightened. No she didn't know ... she didn't want to know. It was unthinkable.

He wouldn't.

Not with her.

A voice cried inside of her, *she's lying, she must be.*

Her heart began pounding, and her throat tightened so much, she almost choked. She swallowed, "Are you serious?"

"Yes. Don't look so surprised, we are both single."

"But what about Callum?"

"What about Callum? He's too hung up on that ex-wife of his so I'm not hanging around forever. I'd rather pursue Fin to be honest."

Oh, I bet you would.

You bitch.

With smug written all over her face, Janelle carried on, "Between you and I, he's a real stallion and mad for oral sex," she paused as if considering, "I suppose it must be better when you're circumcised."

Janelle looked questioningly at her, as if expecting confirmation that oral sex was better without a foreskin. It was a good job she hadn't eaten because at that precise moment Kathryn felt she might throw up.

She knows he's been circumcised.

She's not lying.

233

The tightness in her chest was crushing and the stabbing pain continued somewhere around her heart, *God, no.* She had to get away quickly before Janelle realised her despair.

Keep your face blank.

Don't give anything away.

Her stomach rolled as if it had been on the high seas, and it took every bit of strength to remain impassive, "That's quite a surprise I must say," she mumbled, and stood up before she totally dissolved, "I'll go check on them in recovery, they must be about done by now."

She placed her coffee cup in the sink and made her way to the recovery area. Fiona was handing the patient over to the ward staff, and Erin was tidying round, so she quickly headed to her office and closed the door. It felt claustrophobic as she leant against the door, and she had to remind herself to breathe in and out, in and out to try and get some oxygen into her body.

No, she silently screamed. Why would he have sex with Janelle? He was hers. For Christ's sake, he was still all over her body. She struggled to hold back the tears.

Don't cry.

You must stop shaking.

She needed to control herself, at least until they'd gone. She had to hang on until then.

Pull yourself together.

You can't let her see you're upset.

There was a tap on the door and Kathryn turned and opened it.

"The patient's gone back to the ward now, is it alright if we get off?" Fiona asked.

"Course it is," she was on autopilot, "have the drugs all been checked?"

"Yes, I'll take the keys round to the ward on the way out."

"Okay, I'll come down." She walked with Fiona down the corridor to the tea room with shaky legs and clogs that felt as if they had lead weights in them. Janelle and Erin were sitting waiting. She needed rid of them quickly so she could get in the shower, "Are you ready for the off?"

They stood up and Erin asked, "Is it a seven thirty

start tomorrow?"

"Yes, it is."

Was her voice sounding normal?

Erin turned to Janelle, "Am I still okay for a lift home with you, I can't wait to get the juicy gossip?"

"What juicy gossip?" Fiona asked.

Janelle rolled her eyes, "I wish I'd never said anything now."

Why did you?

What a cow you are.

She put the bright voice on again, "You all get off then, I'm going to take a quick shower before I go home."

"Wouldn't you rather get a shower at home, or better still a bath?" Fiona asked, "That shower in our changing room is awful."

Fiona was right about that, but she needed to remove every trace of him from her body.

"I've got a quick errand to run on the way home so I'll freshen up here."

Please all of you, just go.

Let me be alone.

She watched all three of them disappear into the changing room and sat back down in the tea room. A couple more minutes and they'd be gone.

She listened for the changing room door to slam behind them, and then headed in there herself. She turned the shower on and quickly ripped her scrubs off and stepped inside the cubicle. The water was hotter than she liked to the point of almost scalding, but she didn't change the temperature. She was ice cold and rubbed at her chest furiously with shower gel to the point of hurting herself, desperate to remove every last trace of him. It was more symbolic than anything. To physically wash him off her skin took only seconds, but to rid herself of the guilt would take so much longer.

The first sniffle started which she didn't try to hold back, and then the next, until finally she was sobbing her heart out. She leant her head against the cold tile and watched as the droplets of her tears mixed with the water and flowed down the drain. What a fool she'd been. *What a great big bloody fool,* she sobbed.

41

Each mouthful of food during dinner was an effort; it could almost have been sawdust she was eating. Philip placed his knife and fork together on his empty plate and she watched as he took a deep breath in.

"What's the matter, you've hardly touched your food?"

Kathryn looked down at the half eaten salmon fillet on her plate that she'd picked at. It was lovely of him to cook a meal after her shift, but food was the last thing on her mind after Janelle's disclosure. She put her own knife and fork together, "Sorry, the meal's lovely, I'm just not that hungry."

"What's wrong?" he sighed, "you look like you've got the weight of the world on your shoulders."

"Nothing. I'm a bit down that's all."

"Down about what?" he asked, "a baby, or is it Elsa?"
Not quite tonight.
But I'll have to go for the baby.

"I am worried about Elsa but I'm sure after the treatment she'll be fine. It's more the baby issue," she lied, "I've got an appointment with the consultant next month and I know he'll suggest the IVF route as we haven't conceived naturally."

She knew he wasn't ecstatic about the IVF route, but then again what was he ever ecstatic about? He never seemed as keen as she was about having a baby. It would be too much disruption in his orderly life no doubt.

She went for her well-rehearsed verse she'd repeated often enough in the past which would deflect from what was really bothering her, "It's so hard. Most women get pregnant with the blink of an eye, yet I've got all these hurdles to climb."

"I hate to see you so upset," he reached for her hand, "I want you to be happy, you know that, don't you?"

"Yes of course I do. And I am happy," she reassured, "but when I start thinking about going through life without a child, it tears me apart."

It was ridiculous talking about having a baby when her heart had been torn to shreds, but she couldn't let him know what was really upsetting her. None of this baby talk would surprise him as he'd heard it so many times the last few years, it was only lately that she hadn't mentioned it. She'd been far too distracted by a serial womaniser.

He stroked her hand with his thumb, "You'd be a great mother, you deserve to be one. There's no one better than you."

The tears she was holding back started to flow down her cheeks and she tried to hold on, but a sob escaped. How could she have betrayed him when he cared for her so much? She reached in her pocket for a tissue as Philip got up and come round to her side of the table and hugged her, "Hey, don't cry, I can't bear to see you so upset."

She tried to control herself, but the tears flowed relentlessly. He pulled her up to a standing position and held her tightly as the sobs continued. She felt so wretched.

Eventually, she pulled away and blew her nose, "I'm sorry, I don't know what came over me."

He kissed her head, "Look, I know I'm not overawed by the idea of IVF, but maybe if you get some information so we know a bit more about it."

I know all about it,
But you've always resisted.

"Are you sure? You've always been so emphatic that it isn't what you want."

"I know," he nodded, "Let's get the information and we'll take it from there."

"I can't believe you'll even consider it," she started to

sob again, "thank you."

sob again, "thank you."

"I don't want to see you this upset, but we need to take it steady, okay? Remember, my job's not secure so if I lose that …" he didn't finish the sentence.

"If you do, we'll deal with it."

He lifted her chin and kissed her, "You know how much I love you, don't you?"

"Yes, and I love you the same."

He moved away and picked up the plates, "I'll wrap the salmon in foil and take it outside to the dustbin so the smell doesn't linger in the kitchen."

What was he like? Only Philip, having discussed a momentous decision that would affect them both, would be twittering on about the smell of fish in the kitchen.

She got up and started to clear the rest of the table. Although her tummy rumbled from lack of food, she felt quite queasy. She's made such a massive mistake betraying Philip. How could she have done that, and with such a bastard? He didn't deserve it. He was a good man who loved her dearly, and she'd behaved terribly.

She must now focus on getting her marriage back on track and devote herself to him and any children they might have in the future. She remembered a time when having a baby was the only thing that consumed her life. That seemed such a long time ago, before *he'd* come along, lifted her up and then dropped her from a great height. Tears filled her eyes again.

I hate you.
And what I've become.

She pictured him sat in his office this evening waiting for her to call so he could pop round to theatre. He'd have a long wait. Thank goodness he was going away tomorrow, that meant at least this week she wouldn't have to see him. Quite how she was going to face him again now she knew what he was really like, she didn't know, but what she did know was Fin Dey was history now and her future was with her husband.

42

Elsa sat in her conservatory painting her fingernails. There was something quite therapeutic about applying nail polish. She'd selected a pretty coral pink colour from the vast array of nail varnishes she had, and as the aroma of the varnish filled the air, she considered how many more times she would paint her nails.

Each day was becoming more difficult than the previous. The agony in her back was becoming intolerable now. It would be so easy to lie down and simply sleep. Death was hovering like a thick black cloud around her, and very soon it would envelope her. She took a few deep breaths; she mustn't cry and spoil her make-up.

Her head throbbed. When was the last time it didn't hurt? She couldn't remember. Her brain was slowing down now and she was having difficulty with recall. Was she supposed to be meeting Paul this Wednesday, or was it this week he was on holiday? She'd forgotten to order some flowers for Nick's secretary despite telling him she would. Nick had made her feel really bad when he told her he'd reminded her a dozen times to place the order so they were delivered to the office as a surprise for her fortieth birthday. It was a simple phone call yet she'd forgotten. Mild forgetfulness the booklet labelled it.

Since then, she was writing herself reminder notes each day to keep up. Why me, she asked herself again for the hundredth time. She wanted to stay here and live her life, a normal life free from illness. She was too young to die.

Anger raged inside her at the injustice of the disease. The previous day there was an old lady in front of her at the cash machine fumbling around and taking forever to withdraw some money. Irritated, she'd found herself huffing loudly at her slowness. Why couldn't she trade places with her and she could be the one dying? The old dear had had her life and was surely in God's waiting room whereas she should have years ahead of her. It took all her resolve not to go and shake the woman, and recalled the information she'd read that her behavior could become aggressive.

Nick was carrying on as if things were normal and was far too jolly these days. How different would he be if he knew he was going to lose his wife very soon?

Fin was asking all sorts of questions which she had to keep dodging. He'd figure it out soon enough though, he was too sharp not to. Thankfully at the moment he was pre-occupied with Kathryn. What were they both like? Who'd ever have put the two of them together even if it was an affair? She'd figured out rather quickly that something was going on between them. When they were in each other's company, it was like a heat radiating between the two of them. Both of them had tentatively spoken about each other to her. Kathryn had asked questions about Fin's late wife, and Fin had been asking if Kathryn was happy with Philip. Even though she'd sussed it all out, it had come as a surprise.

She desperately wanted to tell Kathryn she knew all about the two of them, secretly hoping that she might confide in her, but her gut instinct told her that was unlikely. Kathryn would be absolutely mortified that she had any inkling. Elsa's fear was that she'd be so embarrassed about it, she would keep away. She loved her dearly and needed her in her life for what little she had left. It wasn't as if Kathryn and Fin could be together anyway. She'd never leave Philip. Still, the fact that she'd had an affair was shocking. She'd have gambled her last pound Kathryn would never betray Philip. He'd always been the great love of her life. Philip says this, Philip says that … if only she knew what her precious husband was really like. Maybe she did? Could she have found out and was seeking solace with Fin? No, she would have said, surely?

She opened her car door and sat down inside. What had the nurse said, fatigue can severely limit a person's ability to function. She'd certainly hit the nail on the head there. A trip to town was an effort but thankfully her cocktail of analgesia was kicking in. There wouldn't be many more shopping trips so it was best to enjoy the day as much as she could and not let on she knew about her and Fin. If Kathryn wanted to confide in her, then that was fine, otherwise there was nothing to be gained by letting on she knew. That might result in losing her when she needed her most of all, and she couldn't bear that.

*

Kathryn took a sip of her latte, but it was too hot so she placed the cup back down on the saucer. Jocelyn's was one of her and Elsa's favourite places and they always called in when they went shopping.

Today she was determined to find out how her friend actually was. It was ages since they'd had a girlie day out and she'd missed her. Elsa looked okay, lovely in fact, but then again she was always so perfectly groomed, she wouldn't let on if she was finding the treatment a struggle.

Kathryn smiled, "Before we shop, I want to know how you are and what the consultant has said."

Elsa gave a sort of *here we go again* smile, "It all sounds good, but you never know with those medical lot, present company excepted of course."

"Of course," she agreed, "go on."

"Dr Meadows says I'm responding well to the treatment. He calls it part remission, but he wants to see some sort of reading in my blood come down below a mystical figure, whatever that means."

Kathryn wasn't sure either, bloods weren't her forte, but she was pleased it all sounded hopeful. "That's good then, so how are you feeling? It's hard to tell how you really are as you always look beautiful and well."

"Do I? That's a relief then, all the money I'm spending on cosmetics is obviously worth it." She smiled and touched Kathryn's hand, "I'm okay, honestly. I do seem to sleep a lot though, as I keep telling everyone."

Kathryn stirred her latte, "That's a small price to pay I would have thought. The main thing is you're getting better, I was worried for a while back there."

"I know you were, and I'm so sorry for putting you all through it."

"Hey, it isn't your fault," she punched her arm playfully; "you were worried and panicked at the thought of more treatment. Fortunately for us all, you saw sense."

Elsa rolled her eyes, "I couldn't really do any other with my bossy brother now could I?"

Kathryn's antenna went up at the mention of Mr Shag 'em all, "No, I don't suppose you could." She needed to get off the subject of Fin, the mention of him was like a knife stabbing her tummy and twisting around.

"What are you looking for today, anything specific?"

"I need a nice dress for Nick's firm's dinner and dance. I'm not sure if I'll go, I'll see how I feel. If I don't have a nice new dress to wear though, I definitely won't," Elsa laughed.

"Like you haven't got a wardrobe full of beautiful dresses."

"Ah, but I've worn them all before. I'll have a look anyway, I might not buy."

"Yeah right. You not buying would be a first."

Elsa smiled and took another mouthful of her coffee, "Anyway how's things with you? If I dare say, *you* look a bit tired and not at all like your usual self, are you okay?"

"Yes," she gave her best smile, "busy at work, that's all."

"My workaholic brother's not pushing you too hard is he?"

No, he's only screwed me.
Physically and mentally.

"No, nothing like that. I love my job."

"What about you and Philip, are things okay there?"

Kathryn tilted her head, "What's made you ask that?"

"Nothing. I was wondering if it's not your work, maybe it's his job? I know the redundancy must be a worry for you both."

She breathed a sigh of relief. For a split second she thought Elsa knew something. "Philip's not his self, that's for sure, so yeah, that's been putting a bit of a strain on us both."

"So it's nothing else?"

"No. What else could there be?"

"I don't know," Elsa shrugged, "you would say if there was anything wrong?"

"Of course I would, but there isn't. I'm fine, honestly."

"That's good then. I know Philip can be a bit … difficult at times."

"Yes he can, you're right about that," she laughed, remembering how many times she'd confided in her friend about his behaviour.

Elsa spooned the froth from the bottom of her cup, and nonchalantly asked, "Do you love him?"

"Bloody hell," Kathryn reeled back, "where's that come from? Of course I love him."

"I don't mean anything by it," she dismissed, "it's only that he seems to control certain aspects of your life … it must bother you."

"That's not true. I know it sometimes comes across that way, but he doesn't." She paused for a moment, struggling with the urge to offload, but not wanting to betray her husband by gossiping about him. "Things have been a bit tricky lately though."

"In what way *tricky*? Tell me," Elsa urged.

"I'm sure you don't want to hear all about my marriage."

"Why not? I've heard about it before."

"Not this you haven't."

"What is it?" Elsa raised her eyebrows enquiringly, "Tell me. If something's bothering you, I'd like to know. I might be able to help, you know, two heads and all that."

Kathryn hesitated before taking a deep breath in, "I've made a huge mistake that's all."

"What sort of mistake?"

"One I deeply regret. Honestly, I'd rather not say. I'm really not ready to talk about it." She drained her coffee cup.

"Gosh it sounds serious. In my experience, that look on your face can only mean one thing. Is this mistake involving another man?"

Yes, there *had* been a man.

Please don't let him have told you.

I couldn't bear that.

The enquiring look on Elsa's face indicated she didn't know, but there was no point in confiding in her about how Fin had betrayed her. It hurt too much and he was her brother after all so she was bound to defend him. She'd no doubt tell him off for behaving so despicably, but where would that leave the two of them? Elsa was going through enough at the moment, the last thing she needed was any more stress.

She swallowed the lump at the back of her throat, "I lost my head for a while, that's all, but thankfully I saw sense before it went too far."

"That's so unlike you. Are you finally realising that you can do better than Philip?"

"Stop it Elsa," she chastised, "I know you aren't that keen, but he is my husband and he does love me."

"That's debatable," Elsa mumbled.

"What do you mean by that?" Alarm bells were ringing, this wasn't the first time she'd heard this sort of inference. Gary Hicks had implied similar.

"Nothing," Elsa dismissed, "it's just that he pursues his own interests and you simply fall in with him."

"I want him to be happy, there's nothing wrong with that."

"You're so lovely though, and I think he holds you back. You could have anyone you want."

"But I don't want anyone else," she insisted, "I'm happy with Philip."

"Is that right? What's troubling you then? It must have been someone special to turn your head?"

Thank God she has no idea,

What a despicable bastard her brother is.

"I thought he was, yes."

"So there's no chance of anything further developing between you?"

"No definitely not," she tried to sound indifferent, "I'm married and that's what I need to focus on now. In fact, tomorrow I've got a special evening planned for Philip and I, so I must pick up a few goodies from Marks and Spencer before we go home. Shall we make a move, or do you fancy another quick coffee?"

A voice from the distance interrupted them, "Yoo-hoo."

Kathryn knew the voice so well and tensed at the familiarity of it.

"Christ no," she muttered under her breath as she turned around to see Janelle heading towards them.

Get lost, Janelle.

I loathe you now.

She watched her manoeuvre herself around a couple of tables and eventually reached theirs, "Hi Kathryn, how nice to see you."

She forced herself to be polite, "Hello Janelle, are you doing a bit of shopping?"

"Yes, I've got a few birthdays coming up that I need presents for. They always come at once, don't they?" Janelle smiled and half turned towards Elsa with an expectant look on her face.

Kathryn did the necessary, "Elsa, this is Janelle who works with me in theatre. She's one of the staff nurses."

And your brother's latest shag.

His preference is two of us on the go at the same time.

Janelle stretched her hand out and Elsa took it, "Hi Elsa, pleased to meet you. Mr Dey's your brother isn't he?"

Elsa nodded, "That's right," but didn't elaborate any further, so Janelle continued, "I've heard Kathryn talk about you at work and your various exploits."

"Oh really," Elsa replied widening her eyes at Kathryn, "What does she know? Will I have to kill her?"

Kathryn laughed in good humour at the joke, but needed to get away. She couldn't stand to be in Janelle's company a minute longer. All she could see was her and Fin having sex together. He must be insatiable knocking the two of them off at the same time.

"We'd ask you to join us but we're leaving now," Kathryn apologised.

"Oh that's a shame. Are you sure I can't persuade you to have another coffee, my treat?"

I hate you, and I hate Fin.

As if I'd sit and have a coffee with you.

She looked down at her watch, "I'm sorry, we haven't got long and have got quite a bit of shopping to do." She gave Elsa a look that said, please don't contradict me.

"That's right," Elsa agreed, "we really ought to make a move, we been here ages. We'll have to take a rain check on the coffee?"

"Ok, no problem. I think I'll stop and have one though as that's why I came in here," she said.

"You do that," Elsa replied, "and grab one of their delicious cakes. They're fat free so you'll be fine."

The joke amused Janelle as she laughed, "In that case then, I will."

Elsa smiled, "Anyway, it was nice to meet you."

"You too," Janelle answered, "I'll see you on Monday at work then Kathryn, enjoy your day."

She gritted her teeth, "Okay, you too."

As they left the coffee shop, Kathryn whispered, "I'm not kidding you, every time I turn around, she seems to be there. Honestly, it's getting ridiculous. It's almost as if she knows everywhere I'm going to be."

Elsa frowned, "She probably does then. Do you tell her what you're doing on your days off?"

She thought for a moment, "Sometimes at work we discuss what we are doing at the weekend, so I might have said something about shopping, but she would have no idea that we meet in Jocelyn's."

"You don't put it in a diary then?"

"Only in my calendar, but that's on my phone, she wouldn't see that."

"She wouldn't be the first person to access someone's phone when they weren't looking. Is it password protected?"

"No it isn't. But she wouldn't do that," she considered, "why would she?"

"I don't know," Elsa shrugged, "you haven't been exchanging texts with this mystery man have you, and she's reading them?"

"No, definitely not."

"Maybe it's a coincidence then?"

"Yeah, probably, but it is very odd. I'm going to give her a wide berth in future. She's becoming a bit of a stalker," she rolled her eyes, "it's a good job she's not a bloke or I would be worried."

"I'd be more than worried if I was you, considering the coat and boots she's wearing are identical to ones you have at home, and her hair is dyed the same colour as yours. I think she's morphing into you." She shook her head, "It's no good looking at me like that, I'm telling you, there's something very odd going on with her."

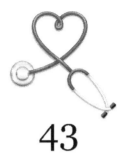

43

Janelle sat in her bedroom reflecting on the day. Kathryn and Elsa believed she'd opportunistically bumped into them in town, which was good. Sadly though, they hadn't stayed with her for coffee. It was disappointing that despite trying on several occasions, she couldn't get Kathryn to go shopping with her. Every single time she asked, she always made an excuse that she was busy.

She fancied a pick-me-up and opened the bedside drawer for a packet of cigarettes. Hidden amongst the ten or so cigarettes, was a half smoked spliff. She opened the bedroom door and called downstairs to her mother, but didn't get a reply which meant she was still out. She opened the window to ventilate the room and lit the joint, inhaling deeply and enjoying the euphoric kick it gave to her system. Now she could think.

Her efforts to get close to Kathryn hadn't worked out as well as she would have liked. She thought this business with Fin might have worked in her favour, but despite knowing Kathryn wasn't one for gossiping, she hadn't expected her indifference when she'd told her about him taking her home after the St Anne's ball. Surely having sex with a consultant was worth something more than a surprised look and a disbelieving shrug of the shoulders? The fact that she barely acknowledged it was disappointing. She had hoped Kathryn might see her in a different light as the potential girlfriend of the bloke that pays her salary.

Another thing that annoyed her was Kathryn had stopped going to the walking club. She used to go there regularly with that dickhead Philip. The only reason she'd joined herself was to get close to her. Gary Hicks had signed her in initially, and she used to go with him when he worked at St Anne's, but she'd eventually joined the club herself and cursed at the rip off joining fee she'd paid which was completely wasted now.

Initially she didn't mind as she'd met Callum there, but she hadn't seen him for well over two weeks. He'd made up a feeble excuse not to go to the St Anne's ball with her, and sent a text saying he was busy and would be in touch soon, but she sensed he was giving her the big heave ho. Again that hadn't gone exactly to plan. She liked him, and the sex was awesome, but he was too casual and non-committal. He wouldn't take her anywhere, and she'd tried to get out on a foursome with Kathryn and Philip to somewhere nice, but that hadn't come off either. Instead they'd finished up at the club which had been pretty dismal and they'd all ended up leaving early.

She exhaled smoke of the window. How lucky Elsa was to be out with Kathryn for the day. Although she was envious, a smile twitched on her lips knowing their cosy shopping trips wouldn't last forever. Kathryn had mentioned at work that Elsa was having treatment for breast cancer secondary's, so she'd looked up the drug, Kadcyla, on the internet and deduced that it probably wouldn't prolong her life that much.

Good, she'd be dead soon and out of the way.

She'd made the right noises to Kathryn about Elsa benefitting from the treatment, even making up an obscure story about someone she'd heard of having the same drug. Yes, Elsa not being around could work in her favour. Kathryn would be upset and vulnerable after she popped her clogs, leaving the way free for her to step in and offer support. That way she most likely would become an exclusive friend.

Let's hope she dies, and then her and Kathryn could have a whale of a time. Not only shopping, they could have lunches out, weekends away, and maybe even go on holiday together. How fantastic would that be? Pity about that tosser she was married to. Her euphoric state dampened a little when she thought about Philip Knight getting in the way. The cheeky bastard had warned her at the club not to get any ideas about Callum as he'd been through enough. Who the fuck did he think he was talking down to her as if she was some sort of slapper. He'd be sorry about that. Right now, she was biding her time, but she had enough on him to have Kathryn reaching for the divorce papers before he could say decree nisi.

Feeling reassured, she went back to her bedside drawer and right at the back, hidden behind a book, she found her silver bullet vibrator. She opened her jeans and pushed them down to her knees. Now she had her own secret thoughts to bring herself off to, life was sweeter all round. She conjured up the image of Fin Dey, and heat travelled through her. She switched the vibrator on and pushed it home with a sigh.

44

Kathryn finished off the fruit salad with chopped apple, and gently mixed the fruits together, adding orange juice and sugar. She tasted the juice to make sure it was sweet enough, and placed the bowl in the fridge. She hadn't cooked what she called a proper meal for ages and knew Philip would appreciate her efforts.

The smell of the chicken casserole wafted around the kitchen, and the vegetables were stacked in the steamer ready for when Philip got home.

It was getting dark earlier than usual she noticed as she closed the kitchen blind. The events of the last week had flooded her mind all day. How had she ever been unfaithful when she loved Philip? She was disgusted with herself and vowed tonight she'd make things right. It had been so long since they'd shared any intimacy. Not since she'd first been with Fin. Her thoughts turned inevitably to him. It had been lust, pure and simple, and he was history now. Tonight was about making things right with her husband.

The thought of getting things back on track in her marriage made her feel more positive, but the niggle at the back of her mind persisted. Elsa had said it was *debatable* that Philip loved her. What a strange thing to say. Afterwards when she challenged her on exactly what she meant, Elsa had been dismissive saying that if Philip loved her so much, why didn't he let her off the leash occasionally. That was daft; she wasn't on a leash at all.

Why did she have the feeling that Elsa wasn't telling the truth and was implying something about Philip she didn't know? What was that all about? It wasn't as if she'd been the first either to hint at something either. Also, she recalled Gary Hicks had made a vague comment about Philip not being all she thought he was. Why would they both say things like that? Philip was a good husband, he'd shown that by agreeing they could look at IVF when she knew deep down that wasn't something he was keen on. To her, that proved what a big man he was. Unlike the bastard who'd ripped her heart to shreds.

The sound of the doorbell interrupted any further thoughts. She approached the glass front door irritated to see two women on the doorstep, one of them wearing a police uniform.

Oh, not now for Christ's sake.

Haven't they heard of the telephone?

They must be here about the pizza delivery and the wreath. She opened the front door, "Hello."

"Mrs Knight?" the policewoman enquired.

"Yes."

"I'm WPC Moss, and this is Tina Turner, a Family Liaison Officer. "I wonder if we might come in for a moment please."

Tina Turner? How unfortunate.

I wonder if she sings.

"Is it about the pizza and the wreath?"

"No, it isn't. Perhaps we can talk inside?"

They'd better be quick, she didn't want her evening spoiled. She sighed, "Of course," and opened the door to let them in and closed it behind them.

"This way please." She'd decided to take them into the lounge as the kitchen smelled of the food cooking, but wasn't going to offer them a seat. She wanted rid of them.

"How can I help you?" she asked.

"Would you like to sit down, Mrs Knight?"

The policewoman looked concerned, and she couldn't for the life of her think why, but thought it best to sit. Tina Turner sat beside her on the settee, and the policewoman sat in the armchair. Why did the policewoman take a deep breath in? Was it something

253

about her dad? *Please no.*

"I'm afraid we have some bad news."

She knew it.

It was her dad.

"Is it my dad, is it his heart?"

"No, it's not your father, it's your husband. There's been an accident."

"My husband ... Philip? What's wrong ... is he alright?"

"He's been in an accident on the cliffs at Gannet Heights. It appears he lost his footing and fell over the edge."

"God, no, how awful ... it's a massive drop ... how could anybody ... where is he. Is he at the hospital?"

"I'm sorry to have to tell you Mrs Knight, the accident was fatal. Your husband died from the fall."

"I'm sorry ..." she shook her head from side to side, "I don't understand?"

"It appears that your husband slipped on the cliff and sadly has died from the fall."

Died? Philip? There must be a mistake. She'd only waved him off this morning.

Tina Turner spoke, "We can appreciate this is tragic news and a terrible shock for you, is there anyone we can call?"

They must have the wrong person. Philip wasn't even going to Gannet Heights today.

"I think there's been a mistake," she cleared her throat, "Philip wasn't going to Gannet Heights today, he was going to High Bridge Falls with the rest of the walking group, he told me that this morning."

Yes, that was it, they'd got the wrong man. Someone else was going to get this tragic news today, God help them.

"I'll ring him," she suggested, "although the signal's not always good. I'll get my phone."

She attempted to stand but Tina Turner held onto her arm, "Don't worry about that now. I think it's best if you sit down for a while longer."

The policewoman continued, "It is your husband Mrs Knight. We've retrieved his wallet and been able to identify him from his driving license. We will of course need you or a member of your immediate family to confirm that formally, but that can wait. You mentioned your father earlier, perhaps we could contact him for you?"

Philip dead? He couldn't be dead, he's only thirty-two. Thirty-two year old men don't die. They don't fall off cliffs. That happens on films and in books. He's got the rest of his life in front of him. They were going to have dinner together and make love. They were going to try for IVF.

Her head was spinning, this couldn't be happening for real. She'd wake up shortly.

Where had the cup of tea come from she was holding? The policewoman said her father was on his way. How did they know where to contact him, did they have his address? She knew she couldn't have given them it because right this minute, she couldn't remember it. Maybe they'd used her mobile phone to contact him? Her head throbbed.

Some time later, she wasn't sure how long, she heard the front door open and muffled whispers in the hall. It must have been the policewoman talking as Tina Turner was sat alongside her.

The lounge door opened, and never had she been more relieved to see anyone than her beloved dad. She stumbled towards him and he held her in his huge comforting arms.

"They say Philip's dead," she cried, "he can't be, there must be a mistake, he only left a few hours ago." Tears streamed down her face, blurring her vision, and her sobs gained momentum, "He can't be, Dad ... tell me he isn't."

His familiar arms tightened around her and she sobbed onto his shoulder. She held onto him, scared to let go. If she moved she'd have to respond and she didn't want to. They'd got it wrong, they must have.

Eventually her dad pulled away, "It's alright love, sit down. You've had a terrible shock." He eased her towards the sofa and as he sat next to her, she wrapped herself around him, "There, there, my darling, I'm here." He stroked her hair, "Can you manage a drink of tea, it'll help."

"I don't want tea, I want to see Philip. Can we go see him?"

"We will, sweetheart, but not right this minute."

"I want to see him, Dad," she insisted, "I don't believe it's him. They've got the wrong person, I'm sure of it."

Her dad held her. She looked at the armchair where Tina Turner was sitting. She couldn't remember the policewoman leaving, but she must have slipped away as she wasn't there anymore.

She lifted her head, "What time is it?" she asked her dad.

"Quarter past six."

"He'll be home shortly then, you see."

She cuddled into him again, "Any minute now, he'll walk through that door, I know he will."

Come home, Philip.

Please.

She heard a phone vibrate and Tina Turner excused herself and left the room, clutching her mobile.

"I wish she'd go dad, I don't want her here."

"Shush, love, she's only doing her job, she'll go soon I'm sure."

Minutes later, Tina returned with another tray of tea.

"The police have contacted your mother-in-law, Mrs Knight, and she's on her way now."

Kathryn looked at her dad, "How's Shirley going to get here, she doesn't drive?"

"Don't worry about that now," he soothed, "someone will bring her or she'll get a taxi. Now come on, drink this tea and let's sit awhile and try and make sense of things."

Kathryn lost track of time, she may have nodded off cradled in her dad's arms, she wasn't sure. The doorbell rang and Tina got up to answer it. Seconds later, Philip's mother burst into the lounge.

"Kathryn, oh, God, Kathryn, I came as soon as I could."

Kathryn rushed towards her and hugged her tightly.

She felt every bit of her pain, "I can't believe it, Shirley... I'm hoping any minute now, someone will wake me up."

They held onto each other. They were never close, but at that precise moment, they shared an overwhelming sense of loss. Eventually, Shirley pulled away and blew her nose.

"Come and sit down, Shirley," her dad suggested, "here next to Kathryn and I'll get you a drink."

"Thank you. A black coffee would be nice with some sugar in it please."

Tina Turner stood up, "Please, let me get it."

"You'll stay here with us tonight won't you, Shirley?" Kathryn asked.

"If you're sure, I'd like to, as long as I'm not in the way."

"Of course you're not in the way, you must stay. It's too much of a shock to be on your own."

Shirley reached for her hand, "Was he on his own?" she asked but didn't wait for an answer, "I don't understand what could have happened. He was an experienced walker, he wouldn't take risks."

Kathryn couldn't speak. She didn't have any answers.

Her dad intervened, "We don't have all the details, only that the ground was wet from yesterday's rain and Philip must have misjudged the conditions. He's obviously gone too close to the edge ..." he didn't finish.

"But why the need to go close to the edge? I don't understand."

"Maybe he was taking a photo?" Kathryn said, "he often used to do that."

At what stage when you fall do you realise that you are going to die?

She started to cry again, "Poor Philip. I don't understand how he was on his own. It's a walking group. Where were the others?"

"I don't know, love," her dad patted her hand, "we'll get some answers tomorrow." He turned to Shirley, "We have to go to the police station in the morning to formally identify Philip."

Shirley started to cry again, "I'd like to come with

you," she looked at Kathryn, "if that's alright?"

Kathryn nodded her agreement. What was the point in saying no? Philip was gone, it didn't matter how many of them went.

45

The man lifted the white sheet and folded it down to his chest. Kathryn noticed how starched the sheet was as it lay like cardboard and covered Philip's torso and the rest of his body.

She stared at the almost porcelain face of her husband. He looked like one of those Madame Tussauds waxwork figures. There wasn't a mark on his face, not on the bit she could see. Most of his head was obscured with a sheet wrapped around it, maybe part of it had been crushed in the fall. Was his body bruised? Had he broken any bones?

She'd witnessed death many times as a nurse, but usually the last thing done for a deceased patient was an hour or so after they'd died when they were still relatively warm, so she wasn't used to seeing someone like this. One thing was certain, the saying that the deceased looked relaxed wasn't true, Philip didn't look relaxed at all. Although she knew it was her husband, it didn't really look like him. His eyes were closed, and somebody had smoothed his hair flat to his forehead which wasn't the way he wore it. He wouldn't be happy about that. He always spiked the front up with gel.

She clung onto Shirley and heard her dad answer questions confirming it was Philip. Her eyes burned with the silent tears streaming down her face.

I betrayed you, my love.
Thank God you didn't know.

Travelling home seemed a blur. She'd kept her eyes closed as if that would block everything out, but time still moved on. It didn't stand still because her husband had died; the minutes and hours ticked away regardless. Yesterday at this time, Philip was still alive. The endless tears which had only abated momentarily started again.

Thank goodness she had her dear dad. He fussed around with drinks and food which Kathryn refused and eventually he decided something stiffer than tea was in order, and raided Philip's wine collection. She knew that would suit Shirley as she was more than partial to anything alcoholic. Philip detested her excessive drinking, but he was no longer here to criticise.

Kathryn liked the feeling the wine gave her. It made her less tense, almost as if none of it was happening even though she knew it was. Shirley tentatively broached the subject of the funeral. She couldn't think about that today. Philip was dead, and no amount of floral tributes would help. The pain was intolerable. It was almost as if someone had a hand inside her and was squeezing all her internal organs tightly. It hurt that much.

The wine made her feel drowsy and she agreed when her dad encouraged her to have a lie down. Shirley announced she wanted to walk to the high street shops for some food. What was that all about? Why would you want to walk to the shops, for goodness' sake? Her son was dead and she going grocery shopping.

Kathryn left her dad and Shirley to it. She wanted to be alone and went to the bedroom to lie down. She took one of Philip's jumpers from the drawer for comfort, and held it close to her as she got into bed. As she closed her eyes all she could see was his waxwork face and his flattened hair, and the ache inside that she wouldn't see him anymore was intense. But more than that was the guilt flooding through her. Not only would she have to live the rest of her life without her beloved husband, she'd have to live with what she'd done.

The continuous ringing of the telephone woke her. She heard the muffled voice of her dad, no doubt warding off some kind soul offering their condolences. She turned on her side to block it out.

A few minutes later her dad tapped on her bedroom door, "Are you awake love, Nick's on the phone?

Her eyes welled up again at the thought of Elsa and Nick. They'd be so shocked. More tears escaped and ran down her cheeks; how could there be any left?

"It's alright, Dad, I'll come," she sniffed and blew her nose.

I wonder why Nick's ringing and not Elsa?

As she sat up, her limbs felt heavy and she wished she had a phone by the bedside so she didn't have to leave the comfort of her bed, but Philip wouldn't hear of a telephone in the bedroom. As far as he was concerned, the bedroom was for sleeping and he didn't want disturbing during that time. Their phone was an antiquated hall one.

She opened the bedroom door and her dad had the receiver covered with his hand, "He's been trying to ring your mobile but it's going straight to answerphone."

"I'm not sure where it is right now, it's probably still in my bag. I'll find it after I've spoken to him." She paused, and looked directly into her dad's eyes, "Does he know?"

Her dad nodded, "Yes, I've told him."

She took the receiver and sat down on the hall chair, "Hello Nick."

"Kathryn," his voice sounded tense, "Your dad's just told me. I don't know what to say, it's a massive shock. I'm so sorry."

"I know, Nick, I still can't believe what's happened. It's a nightmare."

"Is your dad staying with you?"

"Yes. He's fussing around, bless him, it can't be easy for him. I'm sure it's brought Mum's death flooding back."

"I'm at a loss to know what to say. I feel for you all. What a terrible accident, Philip knows ... knew, those cliffs so well. It's unthinkable he'd slip."

"That's exactly what I keep saying. Dad says it'll be all the rain we've had softening the soil."

She needed to speak to Elsa. The sound of her

friend's voice would have her in floods of tears, but she didn't care, "Is Elsa there, can I speak to her?"

There was a long pause, "Are you still there, Nick?"

"Yes ..." his intake of breath was audible to her, "Elsa,"... the line went quiet again.

"Is everything alright? What's the matter?"

She heard him clear his throat, "That's what I was ringing you for, but after your dad told me about Philip..."

Please, no more bad news.

Don't let Elsa be poorly.

"What is it, is she alright?" Even though the telephone separated them, she knew instinctively something was wrong.

"She's in the hospital. I couldn't rouse her this morning so I rang an ambulance," she heard a stifled sob, "she's unconscious, Fin's with her now. I've only stepped out to ring you," another sob escaped; more gut-wrenching this time, "I knew you'd want to know."

"No Nick, no," she cried, "this isn't happening."

"The doctors have told us to prepare for the worst," he cleared his throat, "I'm not giving up, though ... I can't."

His distress was too much to bear, "I'm going to come over."

"Don't do that. I'll ring you when we know something. Fin's trying to speak to her consultant; hopefully he can shed some light on what's happening."

"Yes, I'm sure he'll be able to," she considered the vast experience of a consultant oncologist, "he'll know all about the medication she's been taking and how to treat any side effects."

She cursed herself for not finding out more about Elsa's treatment. She'd been far too distracted by her womanising brother. "They'll probably have some sort of reversal drug, you'll see." Her mind was working overtime. It must be some sort of reaction. They will have something to help, surely.

"Which hospital are you at Nick, the General?"

"Yes, we came through A&E."

"What ward?"

"Devonshire, but please don't come Kathryn," she heard him swallow, "she won't know you're here, and you've had a massive shock. I wasn't telling you to bring you over ... I just wanted you to know because of how close you both are."

"I'm coming Nick, I want to see her."

Almost as if he wasn't listening, he carried on, "Fin wanted her to be moved to St Anne's, but the nurses have advised she stays here. That's what I don't understand. They said she's in the best place for the ..." he sobbed, "end ... end of life care. Why would they be talking like that, I don't get it?"

"No, I don't either. I'm putting the phone down now, and I'm on my way. I'll be there shortly."

As she ended the call, two sets of concerned eyes stared enquiringly at her, "Alright, love," Shirley raised an eyebrow, "not more bad news I hope? I was going to make you something to eat."

"No, I don't want anything," she turned to her dad, "can you run me to the hospital? Elsa's been admitted today in some sort of coma."

"Dear God, no. Of course I will darling, let me get my jacket."

She knew what was coming. Philip's mum was never one for keeping quiet.

"I really don't think you should be going out, Kathryn, and certainly not to the hospital. You've got more than enough on at the moment."

"I'm going, Shirley. I need to be there, she's my friend." She was spared discussing the situation any further by her dad coming back with a coat for her, "Come on, love, put this on, it's cold out there."

"Should you be driving when you've been drinking wine?" Shirley asked him.

"The wine was more for Kathryn," her dad dismissed, "I only had a glass so I'll be fine."

Kathryn couldn't remember the actual journey to the hospital as her mind was occupied with Philip and Elsa.

Was this her punishment?

She'd been unfaithful and this was the price.

Despite encouraging her dad to wait in the car, he went into the hospital with her and in the lift to

Devonshire ward. At the entrance he asked, "Are you sure you don't want me to come in with you?"

"No Dad, honestly, Nick's there. You wait for me downstairs in the cafe."

He placed his hands on her forearms, "As long as you're sure."

She nodded, "I'm not staying long. I just want to ... I don't know, maybe hold her hand and will her on. I'm hoping by now the doctors will have sorted out what's wrong with her and given her something." She forced a bit of a smile, "You see, she'll be sat up in bed giving Nick his orders."

He kissed her cheek, "Alright sweetie, you know where I am then. Take as long as you need."

The walk down the ward was slow.

Keep going, one foot in front of the other, she repeated to herself.

The staff nurse at the nurses' station looked more glamour model than anything else with her kohl eyeliner, sculptured cheek bones and glossy lipstick. Kathryn knew that to a medical professional, she was just another patient's relative. It was all in a day's work for a busy nurse.

"Hello, are you here to see Mrs Fowler?"

Nick must have told her she was coming. She hesitated. She didn't want to go straight into the room as she knew with absolute certainty she'd be in bits when she saw Elsa. She wanted a few minutes to compose herself.

"Yes I am. I wonder if you would you be kind enough to ask Mr Fowler to come outside for a moment please?"

"Of course I will," the nurse replied, "would you like to wait in the family room so you have some privacy, there's nobody in there at the moment." The staff nurse nodded to a door at the left which Kathryn made her way to, listening to the background noise of a busy hospital ward. Her husband was dead, but everything carried on as normal.

She sat down and fumbled for one of the endless tissues she now seemed to have up her sleeve. Minutes later Nick appeared, looking exactly as she expected he would, distraught and devastated. She stepped forward into his arms as if her life depended on it.

"I'm so sorry, I can't believe Philip's dead," he said, his voice breaking. They held each other, both locked together in simultaneous pain. She was grateful for his huge arms holding her ... without them, she very well might fall.

Eventually he pulled away, "Do you want to sit for a minute?"

He took her arm and led her towards a well-worn visitor chair.

She wiped her eyes and blew her nose, "How is she? What have the doctors said?"

His chest heaved as he inhaled and attempted to speak, but he faltered each time.

"It's okay," she reached for his hand, "it's all a massive shock."

His voice croaked, "I feel so bloody helpless. I should have gone with her for the treatment," he sniffed, "I left her to it and I should have been there."

"But that's the way she wanted it," she reassured, "don't blame yourself."

She reached for the tissue box strategically placed alongside the magazines on the table. He took a handful and wiped his nose, "I can't stand seeing her like this."

"I know," she soothed, "what have the doctors said?"

He cleared his throat, "They're saying she's ... end of life," his red eyes, full of despair questioned her, "I don't get it. Why when she's been having the treatment? Why put her through all of that if she's ... *end of life?*"

She shook her head sympathetically, "I wish I knew. I don't understand either."

He was doing his best to hold on and choked back his sobs, "You don't have to do this you know, she won't know you're here."

She squeezed his hand, "I want to, Nick. I need to see her."

"Are you sure? You've lost Philip," he shook his head, "you shouldn't even be here."

Her eyes filled again at the injustice of it all, and Nick put his arm around her and pulled her towards him, "You're such a good friend," he kissed her head, "not only to Elsa, but to me as well. We *both* love you, you know."

She rested her head on his shoulder, "I know you do, and I love you both too."

How could this be happening? Her beloved husband was dead and her dear friend in a coma. Nausea was coming in waves and she kept deep breathing out of her mouth to calm herself. Her limbs felt heavy and fear choked her, she didn't want to live without either of them.

Why, God, why?

A tear escaped which she caught with the back of her hand. She sat up straight, "Come on, let's go see her."

She held his hand and they walked together into the side ward. The hospital bed dominated the tiny room, and there was a low humming noise coming from the ripple mattress.

Elsa was covered with a crisp white hospital sheet with only her beautiful head protruding. Her hair was spread out all over the pillow, and Kathryn knew she'd be mortified with it all messy like that. She looked so peaceful, as if she was just sleeping, which at the moment she was. But death was knocking on the door, Kathryn could smell it. Her hand tightened around Nick's.

Oh, Elsa, I'm missing you already.

A slight movement at the side of the bed brought her out of her trance, and she turned her head towards it. It was Fin. She'd never seen him unshaven before, and his skin was so pale, it was almost grey. His brown eyes, normally so warm and vibrant, were dull and guarded.

His voice was low and gentle, "Thank you for coming. I'm very sorry for your loss."

She nodded. What was there to say? Philip was dead, and in front of her stood the bastard she'd betrayed him for, and as if that wasn't bad enough, next to him was her dearest friend at the end of her life. There were no words.

Kathryn left the hospital an hour later knowing she wouldn't see her friend again. Nick confirmed the following morning that Elsa had died just after midnight.

How was it possible that within two days, she could lose her husband and best friend?

Knight & Dey

You were right, Rosa; the sand has well and truly run out of the glass.

46

Due to the ongoing police investigation, she couldn't set a date for Philip's funeral. They'd prepared almost everything from the type of coffin to the hymns they'd have at the service, but still had to wait for his body to be released. Her dad spoke to the police each day, and each day they said the same, as soon as their investigation was complete they would contact them. Quite what investigation they were doing Kathryn had no idea. Philip had slipped and lost his life. What more was there to investigate?

Elsa's funeral had been arranged and Kathryn was determined to attend despite her dad trying hard to persuade her into staying away.

"They'll understand, love; you've just lost your husband. Nobody will expect you to be there."

There was no question of her not attending. She wanted to be there for her friend who she loved so much. It was going to be hard, and she had no idea how she was going to get through it, but she was determined she would.

She still didn't know what had gone wrong with Elsa's treatment? Why was she taken from them so quickly? Why hadn't the medication worked, had they warned her it might not and she'd kept it from them?

Despite saying she would attend the funeral, on the actual day her resolve began to waiver. She'd told Nick she would be attending, but she wished she hadn't.

As she sat at the dressing table and applied the finishing touches to her makeup, the mirror didn't lie. She looked gaunt and no amount of blusher could disguise that.

A gentle tap on the door interrupted her thoughts. Her dad came in looking rather dapper in his dark suit and black tie, "We need to be thinking about making a move, love. Are you okay?"

She stood and took her black coat from the bed, "As good as I'll ever be. The sooner we get there, the sooner we can come home."

"We don't have to ..."

She interrupted him, "I want to Dad. I *need* to go."

"Alright love, but remember, we can turn away and come home at any time."

"I know that." She took his hand, "And I promise, if I'm not up to it, you'll be the first to know."

He caressed her chin, "I'll be watching you very carefully Kathy May, and if I think it's becoming too much, we'll be out of there."

The use of her pet name was a blast from the past, and reminded her of her idyllic childhood. He kissed her cheek and she loved him for it. Loved him for being there, loved him for taking care of everything, and loved him because he was her dad.

Elsa's service was fitting. Kathryn stared at the framed photograph of her dear friend staring at the congregation from the top of the coffin. Beautiful, vibrant Elsa, laughing and so full of life. She listened as the vicar told them she had been taken from them far too early, as if they didn't already know that. Her heart ached for her friend she loved so much and wouldn't see again.

She cried for Elsa, and she cried for her husband. How could life be so cruel? She should never have betrayed her husband with Fin and still felt this was God's punishment for doing that. She clung to her dad as if her own life depended on it.

Once the service was over, she watched Nick and Fin shake the vicar's hand and proceed out of the crematorium. She didn't want to follow as the congregation was doing as she couldn't face the man she'd betrayed her husband with.

"Can we go out the way we came, Dad do you think?"

"I don't see why not. Come on, do you want to go home now?"

"I'm not sure. I want to get out of here though."

They edged out of the pew and walked to the back of the crematorium. They followed the others out, but didn't join the queue of those waiting to offer Nick and Fin their condolences. Her dad looked lovingly at her, "Shall we get straight off and go home for a nice cup of tea?"

It would be much easier to leave, but she wanted to see Nick. She didn't want to go home and drink endless cups of tea and stare at the walls. She wanted to remember Elsa and be close to Nick. If this nightmare hadn't been happening to her, she would have made sure she was with Nick, supporting him today. But then again, that would mean being close to Fin, and she didn't want to be near him ever again. She'd betrayed her husband, and Fin had betrayed her. What do they call it, Karma?

Love, respect, and sentiment dragged her back to Nick's house. Elsa was everywhere. She fondly remembered all the dinner parties, the girlie nights, the coffees, the afternoon teas, the wine. Her eyes drifted to the walls, and on each one was photographic evidence of the once vibrant and alive Elsa.

Out of the corner of her eye, she covertly observed Fin talking to everyone. She didn't want to look at him, but it was as if her eyes had a will of their own and were drawn to him.

User.

Bastard.

Nick came over and hugged her tightly, "Thank you so much for coming, Kathryn. I never thought you would under the circumstances."

He let her go and shook her dad's hand, "Hello Jack, thank you for coming and bringing Kathryn."

"No need to thank me. To be perfectly honest, I didn't want her to come, with all the stress she's under herself, but she's like her late mother, stubborn to the core."

"Thank you, Dad," she rolled her eyes, "I am here you know."

Her dad smiled lovingly at her, "I'm only making a point to Nick that I didn't really think it wise for you to be here under the circumstances."

"I know, but I wanted to come." She turned to Nick, shaking her head, "I couldn't have stayed away," she faltered for a second before catching her breath, "and I'm really going to miss her."

Nick clasped her hand, "You and me both. I'm so pleased you are here. But what about you, how are you bearing up? I still can't believe what's happened."

Tears started to prick her eyes, but she managed to hold them back, "I'm okay," she shrugged, "you know what I mean. It's hard, but I'm hoping we can sort things out soon and have the funeral."

"I hope so for your sake, it's something we have to do." He turned his head, "Fin's around here somewhere, I know he wants to speak to you."

No. She didn't want to speak to Fin. He was the last person she wanted to see. She'd underestimated exactly how much being near him would unsettle her.

"Please don't bother him, Nick," she put her hand on her dad's arm, "you were right, it's too much, I shouldn't have come. I'll use the bathroom if that's alright and then we'll get off."

"Course it is, I'll wait here for you."

She turned away towards the lounge door, but it was too late, Fin blocked her way. He managed to look as if he'd stepped out of a shop window in his dark suit and black tie, and her breath caught in her throat at how handsome he looked, even though she could see he'd lost some weight around his face, and his skin was pale. Whatever had happened between the two of them, she knew he would be suffering at the loss of his sister. As he leant forward and kissed her cheek, her body betrayed her and she felt the same desire she'd always felt for him. Although she hated him, she yearned for him to wrap her in his arms.

"Hello Kathryn, I'm so pleased you came." His eyes

clashed with hers so deeply, she felt almost like she was drowning. "We would have all understood if you hadn't."

You need to speak, Kathryn.

Move your mouth.

"I wanted to come. She meant so much to me ... well, to us all." She had to do something to escape his intense glare.

"I don't think you've met my father have you? Dad this is Fin, Elsa's brother," and quickly added, "and my boss at work," hoping it would put some formality on her relationship with him.

"Fin, this is my dad, Jack Simpson." She watched her dad shake Fin's hand, the very hand that had brought her such pleasure.

"Pleased to meet you, Jack, thank you for coming and bringing Kathryn."

"No problem at all. I met your sister several times, she was a lovely young woman, taken away far too soon."

She couldn't stand it any longer, being close to Fin was just too much. She hated herself for still having feelings for him, and for what she'd done.

Get away from him.

He betrayed you.

"If you wouldn't mind excusing me for a moment," she turned to Nick, "I hope you don't mind me going, I'll use the bathroom and then we'll get off."

"Of course not. I'll get your coat for you."

She bolted out of the lounge and up the stairs to the bathroom. Great, now she could go home. She'd be safe there and not have to be in the same room as him. How could she look him in the eye when he'd been having sex with her and Janelle at the same time? He was disgusting.

She washed her hands in the sink, and splashed her face with cold water. As she dried herself with a towel, she looked at her reflection the huge mirror that dominated the wall and acknowledged it did her no favours at all.

Oh well, nobody to look nice for now anyway.

She opened the door and jumped ... Fin was standing there.

"I need to speak to you," he said.

"Not now," she dismissed.

"Please." He took her arm and almost dragged her across the landing.

"What are you doing?" she shrieked, "Take your hands off me." She tried to pull her arm away, but he held on and almost catapulted her into Elsa's spare room and closed the door behind them. He let go of her arm but stood with his back to the door so she couldn't escape.

"For God's sake," she spat, "we can't be in the bedroom together. What the hell will people think?"

"I wouldn't have thought anything to be honest at my sister's wake and with you grieving for your husband."

"You need to move so I can get out of here. I can't spend any time with you."

"I know that. I'm not asking you to stay, I only want to express my condolences like any normal person."

"You have done. Now can I go?"

"Of course you can," he shook his head slightly, "I'm puzzled, as to why you are looking at me as though I'm some sort of a pariah. At the hospital on the last day with Elsa, I know you'd just had the news about Philip, but you looked at me as though I was something you wiped off the bottom of your shoe. It hurt." His eyes softened, "I thought we meant something to each other?"

"No," she snapped, "you and I were a stupid fling which I bitterly regret. Now, if you would move out of the way, I'd like to go."

"*Stupid fling?*" He looked questioningly at her, but he didn't move from his position, "I'm sorry you feel that's all it was."

He shook his head again, and then said in a gentle tone, "You're right, it isn't appropriate right now. But we will need to talk sometime Kathryn, when you're ready."

Anger flared within her, "We won't be talking at all ... ever. As far as I'm concerned, I wish I'd never met you."

"Why are you being like this?" he scowled, "I understand you are grieving for Philip, but your hostility towards me ..."

"Don't you dare talk about him," she interrupted, "he's twice the man you are, and don't even think about attending his funeral," she glared at him with hatred in her eyes, "I don't want you there, do you hear me?"

Bewilderment was written all over his face, but she didn't care, "I know all about you and Janelle. She told me what you got up to the night of the Ball. Yes, you might well look shocked that I know all about your dirty little secret. You disgust me. How could you. What was it, some sort of game, which of the theatre staff are up for a quick shag with the Hospital Director?"

"Now you listen here," his grip tightened on her arm, "I have no idea what sort of nonsense Janelle has fed you, but I can assure you, nothing has happened between her and I. She's lying." Black eyes blazed at her, "Why the hell would I do anything with her?" he asked incredulously, "She's a member of staff for God's sake."

"So? I'm a member of staff but it didn't stop you shagging me." She glared defiantly at him knowing he wouldn't have an answer for that.

"You and I are more than that Kathryn," he said through gritted teeth, "but I think it probably *is* time for you to go now. You've said more than enough."

Fury flashed in his eyes as he opened the door wide for her, and she went through it and didn't look back. Tears threatened which she held in check as she walked down the stairs and saw her dad come into the hall.

"There you are, love. I was about to send a search party out for you."

"I'm here now, Dad, can we get off please?"

"Course we can. Here, I've got your coat, put it on as I can hear a wind getting up out there."

As he helped her on with her coat, Fin came down the stairs. Her dad spotted him, "Ah, Fin, we're going now. Would you be kind enough to let Nick know?"

"Yes of course I will."

"And once again, sincere condolences for your loss."

"Thank you. I appreciate it. He shook her dad's hand, and then his eyes found hers, "Thank you again for coming, Kathryn, I'm sure it's been a really difficult day for you."

She nodded her head as no words would come.
Difficult day?
You have no fucking idea.

274

She shouldn't have come. It was bad enough grieving for her dear friend, but to have to listen to Fin's lies, was too much. Why would Janelle make it up? She said he'd been circumcised and there was only one way she could possibly know that. But what did that matter now? She was mourning the husband she loved, and didn't give a toss about Finley Dey, the serial philanderer.

47

Kathryn sat in the conservatory with her Dad drinking tea. Her eyes rested on the cup and saucer in her hand. What was the British fascination with tea? A sudden shock, an accident, or any bad news, it seemed a cup of tea was obligatory.

The doorbell interrupted her thoughts. Her dad put his newspaper down and got to his feet, "I'll get it love, you sit there."

Every time she heard that piercing ring, she expected something unwelcome. She recalled the pizza delivery and the devastating news of Philip's death, and a shiver ran through her remembering they'd had the delivery of the wreath also. What an irony that was. It was almost as if someone had known there was going to be a death.

Rosa knew.

She saw the black ahead.

Her dad came into the lounge with a man accompanied by the policewoman that had been there the day they'd told her about Philip's death.

"Good morning, Mrs Knight, I'm Inspector Glen Edge and I believe you've met WPC Moss. I'm sorry to interrupt your day, but I have some questions that I hope you'll be able to answer for me."

"I have asked if it can wait until after the funeral, darling," her dad said, shaking his head.

"It's fine, Dad," she reassured, and gestured with her hand, "please take a seat."

"I'm sorry it can't wait," the inspector said, "I know this must be a very difficult time for you."

She nodded, "What is it? What can I help you with?"

"Prior to your husband's death, we understand you were the subject of some mischievous pranks, a pizza delivery, and I believe a wreath was delivered to the house?"

"Yes, that's right. I notified the police and they were chasing it up," she shrugged, "they didn't get back to me though."

"I didn't know any of this, Kathryn," her dad cut in, "why didn't you say?"

"There was nothing *to* say, they were just pranks."

"Pranks? A bloody wreath? I'd hardly call that a – "

The inspector cut her dad off with a raised hand. "I believe, Mrs Knight, that you suspected someone you used to work with you, is that correct?"

"Yes, that's right. Gary Hicks, he used to work at St Anne's but he was sacked for gross misconduct."

"Why are you bringing this up now?" her dad asked.

The inspector looked directly at her, "I am sorry that we have more bad news, but I'm here to inform you that your husband's death is being treated as suspicious."

"Suspicious? What do you mean?" Kathryn asked, "Philip lost his footing and tumbled over the cliff," she looked accusingly at the policewoman, "that's what you told me."

"Yes," the inspector agreed, "but we now have reason to believe it may not have happened the way we first thought. We currently have a person in custody helping us with our enquiries."

She couldn't believe what she was hearing. The nightmare was getting worse.

"What are you talking about? Who's in custody? Who do you have *helping you with your enquiries*?"

"I'm afraid I'm not at liberty to discuss that at the moment."

"Why not? What exactly are you suggesting?" She shook her head vigorously, "That my husband may have been pushed off the cliff?"

"I am sorry, Mrs Knight, I know it must be

frustrating, but I'm afraid at the moment, all I can say is, this is the line of enquiry we are pursuing."

The penny suddenly dropped, "Why were you asking about Gary Hicks? Is it him in custody?"

"As I said, at the moment I'm unable to discuss that. As soon as I am, I will of course keep you informed."

"It's Gary, it must be. Look, I know him; he isn't capable of doing anything like that. The mischief yes, but nothing like you're implying. He was friendly with my husband, so would hardly be likely to push him off a cliff."

She turned to her dad, "This is ridiculous. Gary Hicks may be a lot of things, but he wouldn't do that," she paused and turned back to the inspector, "that would be classed as murder, surely?"

He didn't acknowledge her question, "There is another matter we'd like to speak to you about," he glanced at her dad and back towards her, "but preferably on your own, Mrs Knight."

Her dad couldn't keep the irritation out of his tone, "What now? This is all very upsetting for my daughter. I think she has enough on at the moment."

"It's fine, Dad," she reassured, "it'll all be some sort of mix up. How about you go and make everyone a drink. I'm okay, honestly."

Her dad took a deep breath in, "If you're sure." His expression told her he was unhappy about being dismissed, but nevertheless, he asked politely, "What can I get you both to drink, tea or coffee?"

"Coffee would be fine, thank you," the inspector said without even asking the policewoman, and once the door closed behind her dad, he cleared his throat, "In light of the new evidence, I need to ask if you were aware that your husband was in a relationship with Mr Hicks?"

"Relationship? I'm not sure if you'd call it that," she dismissed, "they weren't best friends if that's what you're implying. They just met up on these walking jaunts. In fact, I told Philip to give him a wide berth because of my job at St Anne's and having to sack him."

He was staring intently at her, "I'm not talking about a relationship based on friendship, Mrs Knight. I'm talking about a sexual relationship."

"What!?"

She shook her head, "That's not possible."

This was becoming ridiculous.

Philip, with a man. Never in a million years.

She didn't want to be disloyal, but in light of the absurdity of the allegation, she needed to speak up, "Philip's actually homophobic to be truthful, he detests gays."

The inspector's voice softened as if he was talking to a child, "We do have evidence that your husband has been conducting a sexual relationship with Mr Hicks, and we also have a witness stating that your husband was not alone on the cliff the day he died. We believe the person he was with, may have pushed him to his death."

Her head felt mushy and she couldn't comprehend the information she'd been given. She felt far away from reality, as if she was an observer watching the current nightmare unfolding further.

Philip *pushed to his death?*

Philip *conducting a sexual relationship?*

She felt sick.

He couldn't be. He loved her. No, he couldn't be gay.

She could hear somebody sobbing, "This can't be happening," and then she heard it again more loudly the second time before she felt two huge familiar arms wrap tightly around her, "You're alright love, I'm here."

48

Janelle watched as Melons Plenty walked down the corridor towards the tearoom where they were all having a quick drink prior to the list starting.

Melons had been keeping a watchful eye on theatre since Kathryn had gone off. Every morning she pottered round in those stupid clippety-clop shoes. While Janelle acknowledged it couldn't be easy having the manager and the deputy manager off at the same time, Melons was really irritating, popping round all the time. The staff were all pulling together and doing okay without her interference.

"Good morning," Melons smiled, "not such a busy day for you today with only the one theatre running, thank goodness."

Janelle smiled back, thinking how bloody clueless she was. The orthopaedic list they had on that morning was massive and sure to run over, so as usual they'd most likely miss their coffee breaks, and be taking turns to try and get their lunches.

"I'm in my office all morning, Erin," Melons continued, "so if there are any problems, give me a ring and I'll come round."

Erin agreed she would, and then Melons turned to her, "Janelle, when the theatre list is finished, would you give me a ring. Mr Dey and I would like to see you."

"See me? What for?"

"I'll explain later. Ring me when you've finished

would you, please."

"Okay," she nodded.

What on earth did Melons Plenty and Mr Dey want to see her about? It sounded official; perhaps it was some sort of promotion or maybe a pay rise? She'd been doing her best to support Erin in Kathryn's absence, so it could be she was going to get an interim payment for her loyalty. Or even better than that, she might be promoted to a senior staff nurse role in theatre. That would be amazing.

It was a long morning, but as soon as the theatre list had finished, Janelle eagerly rang the Matron's office asking if it was convenient for her to go round. Melons told her to head towards Mr Dey's office and she'd meet her there.

As she was washing her hands in the changing room, the door opened and Rosa came in, "There you are, I bin waiting to see you."

"I'm in a bit of a rush, can it wait?"

Rosa reached into her pocket and pulled out a thin silver bangle, "I give you this, Amy says is yours."

"Where did you find that?" Janelle asked, drying her hands, "I knew I'd lost it but wasn't sure where I'd last had it."

Rosa pointed to the portable rack for storing the theatre scrubs, "I pulled stand out to mop and it behind there."

She took the bracelet from Rosa, "I'm pleased to have it back. I can't think how it got there though."

"You must 'ave dropped it when you was getting changed."

"Yep, you're probably right. Well, thank you anyway."

She attempted to move towards the door, but Rosa caught her hand and whispered, "The bracelet ... it told me ... you go away soon?"

Janelle frowned, "No, I'm not going away anywhere. Unless going to Nottingham shopping for the day, counts," she widened her eyes jokingly.

"Si, you be going away soon. I see it when I 'ad the bracelet."

She shook her head, "No. I'm definitely not going anywhere. I wish I was though, a break would be nice. You didn't see a holiday for me did you?" she grinned, trying to deflect from the intensity of Rosa's beady eyes.

Rosa shook her head, "No, not 'oliday. You leave here though," she nodded her head ... "soon."

"I can't afford to leave here even if I wanted to," she dismissed. "Right, you'll have to excuse me," she opened the door to the outside corridor, "I'll catch you later."

As she walked along the corridor, Janelle pushed all thoughts of Rosa's predictions from her mind and pondered about the meeting ahead. No doubt Melons was there to go through the new responsibilities of a senior role once Mr Dey had given her the news?

Excitement kicked in as she tapped on Mr Dey's door and was asked to go in.

"Have a seat, Janelle," Melons instructed.

She sat down opposite Mr Dey with the desk between them. Melons was sat to his left. Neither of them looked that happy. They weren't smiling or anything.

This is an odd way to give someone good news.

Mr Dey looked up from whatever he was reading and she thought how cold his eyes looked.

"I've invited you here today, Janelle, to give you an opportunity to explain your actions to me."

Actions? What's he on about?

"Sorry," she frowned, "I don't understand."

"I'm talking about the rumours you've been spreading about you and I."

"Erm ... I'm not sure what you mean."

Shit. Who the fuck's told him?

"Are you not? Let me spell it out for you then. I believe you have been telling people the night I took you home from the Christmas ball, when you were intoxicated, I had sex with you."

Christ, he looks so pissed.

"No. I haven't," she shook her head, "why would I do such a thing, when that never happened?"

"It's a relief to hear you say *it never happened*, but that's not good enough. You see, I *know* you've told people we had sex, and to be frank with you, I'm beyond angry. That particular night, I took you home to make sure that you were safe. This is a terrible way to repay me."

She shuffled in the chair.

God, how awful is this. I'll have to go for the fancying him tactic.

She screwed her face up, "I may have suggested something went on between us. The girls in theatre know that ... well, I like you, so ... I probably got carried away with the moment. I am sorry."

"You're sorry are you? You've tarnished my name, and my reputation, do you think sorry is enough?"

Hell, he's furious. I'll have to go for the tears.

"I don't know what else to say. I didn't mean any harm." She forced the tears to come, and as they rolled down her cheeks, she directed her next comment to Melons, "It just got out of hand. I live a pretty mundane life and I was exaggerating. I do that sometimes ... you know, make out it's more exciting than it is. I live with my mother, and haven't got that many friends outside of work."

Melons slid a box of tissues towards her. She took one and wiped her eyes, "Who told you anyway?"

"That's irrelevant," he snapped.

Melons interjected, "I'm appalled that you would do such a thing. Mr Dey is an honourable man. This has come as a great shock to him ... to us all."

Go for the big apology. Hang onto my job.

She blew her nose loudly, "I don't know what more to say. It was a white lie that got out of hand," she sniffed, "I really am so sorry. I'm not going to lose my job over it, am I?"

"I hope not," Melons replied, "but that's very much up to Mr Dey."

He spoke again, "When Kathryn returns, I will be speaking to her about your work ethic and conduct in this particular case. It's to be hoped that she will speak up for you and you can cling onto your job."

She nodded. She would need to see Kathryn before she returned to work, she couldn't lose her job.

I'll go see her and take her a gift to butter her up.

Melons spoke again, "May I suggest that in the first instance you write a letter of apology to Mr Dey for spreading these vicious lies, and also let it be known to your colleagues that you made the story up. That I feel is the least you can do."

She nodded, "Yes, of course."

"Was the theatre list finished when you came round?" Melons asked.

"Yes, the staff are finishing their lunches then setting up for tomorrow's list."

"Then I suggest that you go back round now and explain to them exactly why you have been sent for today."

"I will do." She turned to Mr Dey, "I don't know what else to say, only that I am sincerely sorry."

"I think Matron's suggestions are a start. Please ensure that you speak to *every* member of the theatre staff that you have shared this ridiculous story with. I don't want any of them in any doubt that this allegation is a complete figment of your imagination."

"Yes," she nodded, "I'll do that."

He looked really angry as he finished, "I'll speak to you again when Kathryn returns to work and I've had chance to discuss not only this incident, but your development review and contribution to the theatre team. Then I'll make a decision regarding your future at St Anne's." He nodded his head brusquely, "You may go now."

She gave what she hoped was a feeble, *please forgive me smile,* and scurried out of his office back to theatre. Writing an apologetic letter was the easy bit, but telling the others she'd made the whole thing up was going to be bloody hard. She'd be a laughing stock.

An earlier voice replayed in her head, *you go away soon.* Was losing her job what Rosa was going on about? Shit, she needed to get to Kathryn quickly and get her on her side before Mr Dey got chance to speak to her.

49

Christmas came and went. Kathryn's dad had been marvellous insisting they went out to eat on Christmas Day and Boxing Day as there weren't any festivities at the house. A pile of Christmas cards she hadn't even looked at lay in a box. Her dad had opened them all, sifting out the sympathy cards for her to read, and grateful as she was for all the beautiful floral tributes from so many friends and colleagues, she was glad when the last of them died and she could throw them out.

The police investigation was ongoing therefore they wouldn't release Philip's body for burial. Her dad hadn't left her side since Philip's death and they rubbed along nicely, almost like an old married couple.

Nick kept in regular contact, and she looked forward to his visits. He would call round after work a couple of times a week and she got used to him sitting and chatting with her. She knew he was feeling the loss of Elsa, and they sought comfort in being together.

Trying to get her dad to go back to his own home, was a significant challenge, however, she had finally managed to get him to go to his bowls club, but he'd only agreed because Nick was sat with her.

She put a coffee down for Nick and sat next to him on the sofa, "I feel like I'm sixteen again. Bless him, he's talking to me as if I'm about to leave school and start work. Everyday it's a different piece of advice, honestly, today he's told me I need to think about putting money aside each month out of my salary so I can have a nice holiday."

Nick smiled, "Maybe there's some sense in that."

"What, despite the fact I've told him Philip had life insurance and I'll be receiving a pay-out," she laughed and Nick grinned also.

"Is he staying until after the funeral?"

"I can't imagine I can shift him before then," she sipped her coffee, "it's taken me all these weeks to get him to go to the bowls club, and even then he says he'll be back by nine."

"Don't knock it. You're lucky, my house is empty and I hate going home to it at night. That's why calling in here helps. By the time I've seen you and got home, the evening isn't quite so long."

"That's why you must call in here as often as you want to." She touched his hand, "It will get easier, it just takes time," she rolled her eyes, "well, that's what they tell me anyway."

He pulled a face, "I've been going through things in my mind lately, imagining all different things."

"What sort of things?"

"Daft things really. I've started to question Elsa going to the gallery every Wednesday, and wondering about Paul DuToit. I don't suppose you noticed he was at the funeral?"

"No, I didn't, that day is a bit of a blur to be honest."
But I remember Fin's face,
However hard I try, I still see him.

She shook her head, "There's nothing odd about him being there, though. They've been friends for years."

"No, it would have been odd if he hadn't have come. It's just that he looked so upset. Distraught, in fact."

"They were close, Nick, it was no more than that."

"I know that deep down, but I can't help wondering ..." he left the sentence unfinished.

"Stop right there, you dafty," she slapped his thigh playfully, "Elsa wouldn't do anything like your mind is racing ahead and thinking. She loved you and you loved her. I know she wouldn't betray that."

He shrugged, but at least he was smiling now, "You're

right. I'm being stupid. I've too much bloody time on my hands so I'm making up stories in my head and burdening you, as if you haven't got enough on."

"Don't be worrying about that. I'm gradually coming to terms with everything. It's an odd situation though. Most women fear their husband going off with another woman, yet mine chose another man."

There was a silence between them, and she was surprised when he blurted out, "Elsa had her suspicions about that you know."

"What, about Philp being gay?" She turned her head, "I can't believe that. Why didn't she say?"

"She saw Philip in Manley gardens one lunchtime with a bloke. They were sat in the flower gardens alone, which she thought was odd. If it was two blokes sat on a bench having their packed lunches together out in the open, I don't suppose she would have thought anything of it, but it seemed strange they were hidden away in the flower gardens of a local park." He paused, possibly gauging her reaction.

"Go on."

"She said she thought they may have been kissing."

"How long ago was this, can you remember?"

"I can't to be honest, not that long though. Even when she told me she wasn't certain. She said they were pulling away from each other when she first saw them. Her instincts told her they'd been kissing."

"Oh, Nick. I can't believe she kept that from me."

"I guess she didn't want to cause trouble between the two of you."

"I wish she'd told me. I feel such a fool. I knew she wasn't ever so keen on Philip, but now I see she had good reason."

"She loved you so much and wouldn't want to hurt you. Especially with something she only *thought* she saw."

Tears welled up in her eyes, and Nick put his arm around her, "Hey, come on, I wish I hadn't said anything now."

"It's not your fault," she sniffed, "I miss her, Nick, and I miss Philip. I'm mad aren't I, missing him?"

"Don't be silly. You lived with him for all those years

and loved him. Those feelings don't go because he did something wrong."

"I'm sure you're right," she sighed, "I'll just be glad when the funeral is over. I want to move on now and put this all behind me."

"I know you do. And you are moving on. You're doing brilliantly. It's great you finally have it sorted for Monday. That's a move forward."

"Yes, isn't it? It's been far too long and drawn out."

"Any news on the investigation?"

She shook her head, "Nothing. The liaison officer rang me again yesterday. It's the same old story, they can't prove Philip was pushed, but they want to trace the person who was seen with him near where he fell."

"I don't know why he hasn't come forward. It does make you wonder who it was and if they have something to hide. There's been a load in the press about it. You would think that if the person had stopped to talk to Philip and it was all innocent, they'd want to help the police, wouldn't you?"

"Yeah, but like I've said before, hard as it is to come to terms with Philip losing his footing, I still believe that's the likely explanation, and they did find scenic photos on his phone. Gary Hicks is out on bail, but I've never believed he was capable of that anyway. The tricks yes, but not pushing someone over a cliff."

"He's admitted the pranks though, hasn't he?"

"Yes, that was him, and he told the police about his relationship with Philip. I think he was scared to death when he was questioned and spilled the beans."

"It's all a mystery though, but at least they have released Philip now so you can have the funeral."

"Yes, but I'm dreading it."

"I'm sure you are," he squeezed her hand, "but don't forget, I'm going to be with you every step of the way. I know you've got your dad, but you've got me also. I'm going to be right by your side, Elsa would want me to."

She hugged him. "Thank you; you really are such a good friend."

"And you're a good friend to me. The best actually," he kissed the top of her head, "oh, before I forget, hotshot

Fin can't make the funeral, reckons he's away on business."

Her tummy plummeted at the mention of his name. Good, he'd listened to what she'd told him.

"I never expected him to. He didn't know Philip that well."

"No, but he knows you. He's always asking if they are any further on with finding out what happened to Philip, but I don't know why he's so concerned if he can't be bothered to attend the funeral. I'm pissed off with him to be honest, and I've told him what I think, but he won't change his mind."

"Please don't bc falling out with him. I really didn't expect him to come anyway. I'm sure Matron will be there representing St Anne's."

"I won't say anything else, but I am bloody angry with him. Sometimes he can be so elevated. What's the point in showing concern and asking how you are, if he's not going to support you?" He shook his head, "Who's so busy they can't take time off to attend a funeral, eh? He knows how much you meant to Elsa," he smiled, "I'll tell you what, he'd be going if she was still here, I can tell you."

Oh, yes, definitely. Elsa would be chivvying him along, there was doubt about that, but Kathryn was hugely relieved, she didn't want him anywhere near her. The last thing she needed was reminding about what she'd done. But it wasn't only that. Despite everything, there was a part of her that still wanted him.

"He has lost his wife, son and now his sister, so I think we can cut him a bit of slack, don't you?" Why she felt the need to defend him, she didn't know.

"Maybe you're right," he nodded, and grinned, "he's still an arsehole, though."

Oh, he's much more than that. Fin Dey was the world's biggest arsehole.

50

Kathryn agreed to a break in Scarborough with her dad before she returned to work. He'd been right, walking along the cliff tops and enjoying the sea air had been cathartic. It was the last day of the break and she was sitting enjoying the view across the sea, waiting for her dad who had walked down to the town centre. She suspected he didn't really need anything, but was giving her a bit of time on her own. He'd been such a support to her, quite how she would have got through the last few months without him, she didn't know.

The life that she'd previously known was over now. All the dreams for the future were gone. Babies, children and grandchildren weren't going to happen, not with Philip anyway. How she was supposed to behave, she really wasn't sure. She mourned Philip as her husband, but he hadn't been the man she thought he was. He'd had a hidden life and they'd lived a lie.

Once she'd got over the initial shock of him being gay and the subsequent anger, she tried to forgive him for his infidelity. It wasn't easy, but there was little point in taking the high moral ground when she'd been no better herself and broken their marriage vows too. Daft as it seemed, she forgave herself a little knowing they'd both been unfaithful.

One thing that had come out of it all was her determination never to allow a man to dominate her again. In any future relationship she was going to be an equal. The old Kathryn had gone now, and the new one was going to be much more assertive.

After an extensive police enquiry, they still hadn't found any conclusive evidence that Philip had been pushed off the cliff deliberately, despite a strong suspicion that he had. He'd been walking along, supposedly on his own, however a witness had seen someone with him, but that person never come forward. The liaison officer had told her the case remained *open*.

Gary Hicks had an alibi for the day that Philip died. He'd been with another walking group far away from Gannet Heights. However, in view of the mischievous pranks, he received a police caution. He'd admitted to the police that he and Philip had been engaged in sexual activity, and Kathryn had quickly deduced that the Saturday walking trips and the one occasion when he'd left the St Anne's party 'to start a mate's car' had all been meeting up with Gary for sex. It seemed so obvious now, but at the time she hadn't suspected anything. Most probably she'd been distracted by her own wrongdoings.

Philip's funeral had been a quiet affair in the small village of Coden where he'd grown up and his mother still lived. Shirley was planning the grave stone and Kathryn was quite happy to let her. Vaguely she recollected her saying it would take six months for the ground to be ready for a gravestone, hopefully by then she'd have her life back in some sort of order.

She thought about the funeral and how difficult it had been, but she'd got through it with her dear dad and Nick. Bless Nick, she'd have understood if he couldn't have faced it following his own personal trauma of losing his wife, but he was there for her. He was her last bit of her beloved friend she could cling to. He reminded her of the good times and the closeness her and Elsa had shared, and it was good to remember that amongst all the sadness.

Fin didn't attend, which was a relief. It would have

been terrible to be reminded of what she'd done with him on the day she buried her husband. He sent flowers, of course, with a card which simply read, *thinking of you*. She *thought about him* much more than she wanted to really, yet he was another one with a hidden life. He was never hers but they'd been lovers, and he'd had sex with Janelle at the same time. Probably he thought that was fair game, she was married after all and going home to her husband each night. Maybe he wanted to have someone else also. Irrational as it was, she missed him and thought constantly about him.

Her dad returning interrupted her thoughts, "How you doing, sweetie?" he sat down on the bench next to her, minus any shopping.

"Fine," she smiled, "really, I'm doing okay. This break has done me the world of good, thank you, Dad." She leaned forward and kissed his cheek, "I'm quite looking forward now to going back to work, if I'm honest."

He shook his head, "I still think it might be too soon. You can stay off longer, people will understand."

"No, I need to go back, I've got to do it sometime."

"Yes, but it's not that long since the funeral."

"I know, but Philip has been dead months now, so I've had chance to get used to things."

"I'm not sure about that, grief can be a long process. You and Philip were together a long time, it takes a while to get over something like you've experienced, if indeed you ever actually do."

She knew by the look on her dad's face he was thinking about when they lost her dear mother. She took his hand, "There won't ever be a good time to go back. However long I leave it, I still have to work."

"True, but I think we need to let the hospital know you need more time. How about we speak to Fin? He's high up at the hospital isn't he?"

She smiled at her dad, how she loved him, "Yes he is *high up* at the hospital, but he'd be the last person I would discuss needing more time off with."

"Why? He seemed quite a decent bloke to me, what bit I saw of him that is. I'm sure he'd understand that you need more time."

"I'd speak to the matron if I was going to ask for more time off. But I don't want it, Dad. I need to get back and be busy. I love my job, and I know it will do me good to get back."

"Well, as long as you're sure. Promise me though, that if you don't feel right, you will come home and give it a few more weeks?"

"I promise. Come on, let's head back to the hotel to get ready for dinner, I'm starving. She wasn't, but wanted to get her dad off the subject of not going back to work. She needed to. It would do her good to use her brain again and mix with her colleagues. Hopefully that would bring a much needed purpose back into her life. She'd missed that. It was the only reason she was going back. *What other reason could there be?*

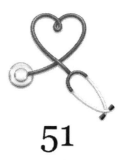

51

Kathryn looked around the kitchen. After the morning spent cleaning every inch of the place, you could eat your dinner off the floor. It would certainly pass Commander Philip's inspection.

She thought of him less harshly these days. Coming to terms with her marriage being a sham and the fact that he'd been a closet homosexual had taken a while, but she was much stronger now.

She'd had time to analyse things and realised how controlling Philip had been, but couldn't work out why she put up with it. Her only conclusion was her desire for a baby was at the forefront of her mind and dominated any rational thinking.

Why she hadn't realised he was with Gary Hicks all those days allegedly walking and the late nights supposedly working, she couldn't fathom.

Until this point, she'd never thought very much about the sexual act between two men, but since finding out about Philip, she understood now his reluctance to make love to her. He did used to, but he never put much into it, and had taken sex with another man to show her what lovemaking should be like. She mustn't think about that though, it still had the power to hurt.

Philip had been cosseted away in a heterosexual marriage, which suited him. Nobody suspected anything, least of all her, but now it was so obvious. Yet despite everything, she knew he loved her very much, and she had loved him. Not enough though, otherwise she wouldn't have embarked on an affair.

Her dear dad had told her to hang onto the many happy memories that she'd shared with him, and not to waste too much time on negativity. The key he said was to move forward, and tomorrow she was going to do exactly that. Go back to work, and see how she felt after a few weeks. *No hasty decisions,* her dad had said, *take your time, and sleep on it.* The trouble was she couldn't sleep as *he* haunted her dreams every night. Fin Dey, honourable on the outside, but really a philanderer of the highest degree. When she'd gone to the clinic for sexually transmitted infections to get checked out due to Philip's homosexuality, she questioned in her mind if she did have an infection, it could well come from Fin as he was putting it about by all accounts. She hated him so much and couldn't see how she could stay at St Anne's indefinitely and see him each day when he'd just remind her of her stupidity.

The front doorbell interrupted her thoughts; it still had the power to make her stomach plummet. She would have to get it changed to something a bit cheerier if she stayed in this house, but it was debatable if she would long-term. After all she'd been through, she might eventually look at moving.

She opened the front door and was totally surprised to see Janelle on the doorstep.

God, no.

What the hell does she want?

"Hello Janelle." She really didn't want to invite her in.

"Hi Kathryn, I'm sorry for calling round uninvited. Is it possible to have a quick word?"

It better be quick.

I can't bloody stand you.

"Yes, but I haven't got long I'm afraid, I've got an appointment at two," she lied.

"It won't take long."

"Okay, come in then."

Janelle walked inside and wiped her boots on the

doormat, "Shall I take my boots off?"

"No need, honestly. Come through, can I get you a quick drink or anything?"

"That would be nice, if you've got the time."

Blast, I was only being polite.

I didn't expect you to say yes.

She led Janelle into the kitchen, "What can I get you, tea, coffee, or do you fancy something stronger, I've got a bottle of wine open in the fridge?"

"A small glass of wine will be lovely, thank you."

"Right, have a seat and I'll get us both one." She nodded to a seat at the kitchen table, there was no way she wanted her to get too comfortable in the conservatory.

Kathryn took the cool bottle of white out of the fridge and selected a couple of glasses. As she poured the wine, she asked, "How's things, any surprises going to greet me when I get back to work tomorrow?"

"No, nothing much. Oh, Alison's coming back at the beginning of next month, so it will be all change then."

"Yes, she rang me, that is good news."

"Nobody wants her to come back really, everyone prefers you being in charge," Janelle took the wine from her, "thank you."

No need to creep,

I've got your number.

Kathryn sat down opposite her, "It's really nice of them to say that, but it will be much better for me with Alison back, it'll take the pressure off a bit."

"I'm sure you'll be fine once you're back. You've worked there so long, it won't take you five minutes to get back into the swing of things."

"I'm certain you're right, I'll have to see how things go." She took a sip of her wine, "Anyway, what brings you here?"

Janelle opened her bag and passed her a beautifully wrapped gift box with a huge ribbon on the top, "I called to bring you this."

Bloody hell.

Beware of Greeks bearing gifts.

"What is it? You shouldn't be buying me gifts, you've already sent flowers."

"It's nothing much," she shrugged, "open it."

Kathryn tore open the wrapping and was surprised to see a tub of Jo Malone body cream, "This is far too expensive, I can't take this."

"Don't be daft," Janelle dismissed, "it's no more than you deserve. You've had a double whammy losing your husband and your best friend. A lot of people would be off for months following that sort of trauma."

"Maybe so, but you shouldn't be spending your money on me. I really do appreciate the gesture, but I'd rather you kept it for yourself."

"No, it's for you. My cousin works at the Beauty Bazaar, so gets discounts. Please, I got it for you."

Kathryn couldn't be bothered to argue, she'd give her it back before she left. There was no way she was keeping a gift from her.

What was she doing here anyway?

I really don't want her in my house.

She glanced at the clock. "Well, it's very kind of you to call round, especially when I'm seeing you at work tomorrow, but I do need to get ready for my appointment."

"Oh, right, yes, you did say. I'll not keep you. I just need to tell you something."

"That sounds ominous, is everything alright?"

"Sort of," she pulled a face, "this is more of a confession visit."

"Confession visit?" Kathryn frowned.

"I'm afraid so. You know when I told you about the night of the ball and Mr Dey taking me home?"

That would be when you broke my heart.

You'd had sex with Fin.

"The thing is," she took a sip of her wine, "it didn't really happen quite like that."

The knife was back.

Twisting in her tummy.

"It really doesn't matter to me how it happened," she shrugged her shoulders, "that's between you and Mr Dey. It's none of my business."

"I know, but Mr Dey and Melons are insisting that I put the record straight, that's why I'm here. I've spoken to everyone else."

"Record straight, what about?"

"Him and I," she moistened her lips, "I made it all up. We never really had sex that night."

"What! It never happened?"

God, no.

She can't have made it all up?

Kathryn could hardly believe what she was hearing.

"Why would you lie about something like that? That's a terrible thing to do."

Janelle winced, "I'm sorry, I didn't think. It flew off my tongue and once I'd said it, it seemed to gain momentum."

"But you said he was circumcised," Kathryn needed to be careful, she shouldn't be able to prove or disprove that, "how could you possibly have known such personal information?"

"Easy," Janelle shrugged, "when he came to theatre for that operation on his knee, his venflon leaked from the back of his hand and the blood went everywhere. Dr Greg asked Lee to change his theatre gown and elastic pants, so he shouted me to fetch clean ones from the ward. I gave him a hand and we changed them in the anaesthetic room before he came into theatre for his op."

Good Lord!

The lying bitch.

Kathryn shook her head, "I can't believe you'd make up a lie about having sex with him. You say Mr Dey knows?"

"Yes, but I've no idea who told him. Melons obviously knows now though. They had me in the office and made me write a letter of apology, and tell the truth to everyone."

"What, you've told this to the others in theatre?"

"I might have let it slip, yes."

"Oh, Janelle, how could you?"

"I know it was wrong," she grimaced, "that's why I'm here now, to put things right."

"You could have told me all this at work tomorrow."

"I know, but I'm scared Mr Dey's going to sack me."

"Why, has he said he's going to?"

"He implied he might, but I don't think he can really. I've been to the Citizens Advice Bureau and they said he can't."

"No, I wouldn't have thought it was a sackable offence, but what were you thinking? What were you hoping to gain by making something up like that?"

"I don't know. He did take me home that night, but nothing happened. It was something I said and it got out of hand."

So why are you here?

Telling me?

"So if you know he can't sack you, what do you want from me?"

"I wondered if you would put a word in for me. Even though I don't believe he can sack me, I wouldn't put it past him. If you could perhaps tell him about my work, you know that I'm hard working and a good time keeper. You said all that at my appraisal."

"I would have told him that anyway, but I am still so shocked about what you've done."

"I know but I have apologised. I just want to put it all behind me now. Please say you'll help me; he said he's going to ask you about my work."

"I will tell him the truth, and I hope for your sake you hang onto your job, but it was a pretty horrible thing to do. He must be furious."

"He is," Janelle nodded, "and I truly am sorry, so if you'll speak up for me that would be a help, I'm sure."

"I'll do my best, but I'm not excusing what you've done."

"I don't expect you to. It was wrong, I know that."

Kathryn glanced at her watch, "I'm going to have to rush you now, I've got to go out."

"Oh right, yes, you did say," Janelle stood up and looped a scarf around her neck, "it'll be great to have you back tomorrow, I'll not see you until lunchtime as I'm on a late shift."

They walked into the hall together and Kathryn clutched the gift she'd brought. She wanted rid of her now, and the wretched Jo Malone cream.

Janelle turned at the door, "I do feel bad about what's happened, but with him losing his wife I don't suppose he's involved with anyone, so nobody really got hurt."

Yes they bloody did.

I got hurt.

"You don't know that, but I hope for your sake you're right. And just so you know, you didn't need to bring me a present to get me to speak up on your behalf," she opened the front door, "some of us have integrity so don't need buying."

"Please don't say that, Kathryn, it wasn't meant like that honestly. I bought you a present because I value your friendship and after all you've been through, I wanted to cheer you up. That's all it was, nothing more."

"Well I'd much rather you kept it. I'm afraid using it would remind me of what you've done. Like I said, I'll speak to Mr Dey on your behalf, but that's it."

Janelle hesitated for a second before taking the box from her. Kathryn hoped she wouldn't say anymore, but she did, "I don't understand why you're getting so twitchy about it all, anyone would think you liked him yourself the way you're carrying on."

"I am not going to even respond to that, Janelle; I'll see you at work tomorrow. Bye."

As she closed the door, she fastened the bolt and realised her action was symbolic. She needed to shut her out. Although they had never been great friends as Janelle had always been a bit intense for her liking, she hadn't ever thought she could be quite so devious. In future, she would keep well away from her. She was dangerous.

She walked back into the kitchen, and for the first time in months, the butterflies were back in her tummy. Janelle said Fin was going to speak to her.

He hadn't had sex with her.

He hadn't betrayed her after all.

52

It was early evening and Fin was in his lounge staring at Elsa's leather-bound shocking-pink diary. For some peculiar reason before she died, Elsa had left it at his house. Elaine, his housekeeper said she had called round and sat in his lounge for ten minutes making a phone call, then left. He thought it odd at the time as there was no reason for her to call on that particular day as she knew he wasn't there. His intention had been to give the diary back to Nick but he'd forgotten about it until today.

He stroked the cover and fanned the pages. Only Elsa could have a garish pink diary, most people wouldn't have even considered something that was essentially private to be displayed quite so boldly.

He wondered if he should read it before giving it to Nick. It was personal, written by his cheery big sister and he wasn't sure if he wanted to encroach on her privacy, but there was a part of him that ached to know her last thoughts.

He missed her desperately and still found it hard to believe she was no longer with them. No more quizzing about his love life ... no more matchmaking ... no more chastising ... no more anything. She was gone, and her death still remained a mystery.

He knew he shouldn't, but he couldn't resist. He turned to the first page and started reading.

It was full of typical entries of appointments, birthdays, where she'd been, and what she'd done. The regular weekly meetings with Paul DuToit, a local antique dealer came as a surprise as she'd never mentioned him in any of their conversations. Elsa had always loved beautiful antiques but there was only so many you could buy. Even refurbishing his house which she'd done splendidly wouldn't require a weekly meeting, and looking though the diary it appeared she'd been seeing him each Wednesday. He turned back to the beginning of the year, yes, every Wednesday since January.

The thought he could have been her lover crossed his mind. Elsa had always wanted reassurance about her beauty. Nick loved her, he was sure of that, but maybe it wasn't love that Elsa desired. Possibly it was an appreciation of her beauty and Paul DuToit provided that. He hoped not, but there was nothing to be gained in finding out now. It was better left.

He slowly began to turn each page, digesting each note and scribble she'd written. How had he not realised that she was never on the treatment she'd told him about? Or maybe he had. He'd certainly had an inclination that all wasn't well. How quickly she'd dismissed him when he questioned her, the vagueness about consultant appointments, and the lack of a treatment plan which he'd asked on several occasions to look at. He'd berated himself for not delving deeper, but he'd been distracted by the renovation of the house, St Anne's, and the topsy-turvy weeks with Kathryn. He chastised himself for being taken in, but Elsa was a cunning woman and had been a master at evasion.

He turned to the final scrawled entries in the diary.

Friday 16th December

I'm so tired now. Although I fear death, I fear staying and deteriorating even more. I feel guilty for deceiving everyone when I know they have my best interest at heart, but I couldn't go through all that horrendous treatment again, so I've chosen to lie. I want them to remember me as happy, loving them, and loving life, opposed to the sick woman that I've sadly become. I hope they find it in their hearts to understand and not judge me too harshly.

I'm not deeply religious, but recently I've found great comfort in these beautiful words, 'death is nothing at all, I have just slipped away into the next room.' I can only hope my passing will not be seen as final, but as a temporary parting until we meet again.

My only desire now is for the three most important people in my life to be happy.

Nick, my dear husband, my wish is that he will eventually meet someone and remarry. He's a good man, but not good at being on his own, so I hope there will be some gorgeous lady out there who will cherish him and make him happy.

Fin, my precious baby brother, I've seen how tortured he is, and he's been through so much losing Saskia and Christiaan. His admission that maybe he was in love with Kathryn but couldn't have her, tore me apart. I want him to have a relationship with a woman that would love him as much as I do because he deserves that. I think my dear friend Kathryn is that woman, and I want her to be happy too, and she can be once her cheating husband is out of the way. The only thing is, she wants children so Fin would have to get that vasectomy reversed to fill their house with lots of them.

Saturday 17th December
I love Nick, Fin and Kathryn with all my heart. Be happy Fin and Kathryn, and please forgive me.

What the hell had he just read? *Be happy Fin and Kathryn,* what was that all about and why would she be asking for forgiveness?

He placed the diary on his lap and stared at the coal fire. Why had she left the diary at his house in the first place, she must have wanted him to read it? As the colourful flames danced and roared up the chimney, a shudder ran through him.

The police said there was a witness that saw someone with Philip before he died, but despite numerous appeals in the media for that person to come forward, nobody had. He thought back to the description given by an eyewitness. It was quite vague, the person was medium height, wearing jeans and a thick parker coat with the hood pulled up. The assumption was that it was a fellow walker, and everyone including himself has presumed the person had been male. Could it have been a woman that lured Philip to his death?

No ... that was too ridiculous for words. Elsa couldn't possibly have done that, how could she? Philip would have thought it odd if she'd asked to join him on a walk, but what if she'd conned him in some way? What if she said she needed to speak to him urgently about Kathryn? Would he have met her then? She could have easily driven up to the top of Gannet Heights and met him, but surely someone would have seen her car?

He thought back to the coroner's verdict on Elsa's death and the amount of analgesia found in her system. He knew it was no accidental overdose as the coroner had concluded. Elsa had fully intended to take her own life; even Nick had agreed that privately. They both knew Elsa didn't want them to see her deteriorate and have to support her. But could she possibly push someone over a cliff? His much loved older sister carrying out something so heinous? Could she do that? God, no, it didn't bear thinking about.

He closed the diary and secured the elastic strap around it. He lifted it to his face and inhaled deeply, savouring the floral fragrance of his beloved Elsa as he kissed the last year of her life. Nobody else needed to witness the final scribbled ramblings of a frightened young woman on the verge of death.

He tossed the diary into the fire. The flames sucked it in and the diary began to burn, just like Elsa's body had burned with the terrible disease which had taken her from them.

It was monstrous to imagine she would kill Philip. Yes, the cancer would have affected her brain cells there was no doubt about that, and that could well have circumvented the rational thought process, but she was no cold-blooded killer. That was too abhorrent to even consider.

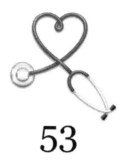

53

Kathryn eased her car into the parking space at St Anne's and turned off the ignition. She stared at the familiar hospital building which for some would be imposing, but for her it was like coming home.

Her tummy was in knots, and the small hairs on her arms felt like they were standing on end, and all because today she was going to see Fin. How was he? She knew nothing anymore as her beloved Elsa was no longer around to keep her up to date with everyday things.

Since Janelle had visited and admitted that nothing sexual had happened between her and Fin, she'd not stopped thinking about him and endured a sleepless night tossing and turning.

Images of the last time she'd seen him at Elsa's funeral were at the forefront of her mind, and she vividly recalled the stunned expression on his face when she'd accused him of having sex with Janelle. She thought he was shocked that he'd been exposed, how was she to know that evil Janelle had made the whole thing up?

Fin had soon sorted that out though and she needed to apologise to him for believing the lies.

She took a deep breath in.

Right, this is it.

The next chapter of my life.

She was earlier than the others, and as she was getting changed into her theatre blues, the door adjacent to theatre opened and Rosa came in and flung her arms around her, "Ah, Sister, welcome back. So pleased to see you."

"Aw, thank you Rosa, I'm pleased to be back. How are you?"

"We fine. Dino bought us new puppy, Tesoro. He keep us up all night crying," she rolled her eyes, "I think he want to be in bed with us."

"I'm sure he does," Kathryn grinned, "you'll have to start as you mean to go on though and don't allow that. You'll never be rid of him."

"I try, but Dino, he soft and Tesoro get away with murder."

"Oh dear, I can see you're going to have your hands full with the dog and Dino."

"Si, you right." They laughed, and then Rosa reached for her hand.

I don't want to hear any more predictions.

Scratch that, yes I do. Tell me about him.

Rosa spoke in almost a whisper, "You had the tears and pain, Sister, that gone now. Her lips curved into a smile, "Soon you be 'appy and 'ave the babies."

If only that was true.

He might not want me anymore.

The changing room door opened and Rosa quickly dropped her hand as the other theatre staff wandered in one by one. Each of them gave her a welcome hug and made encouraging noises about having her back.

She left them getting changed and made her way into the theatre prep room and was surprised to see Erin already there. Erin gave her a big hug also, "So pleased you're back, we've missed you. Are you okay?"

"I'm good thank you. What are you doing here so early?"

"Steve's had to drop me off on his way to work as my car is in the garage."

"Oh right, do you need a lift home later?"

"No thanks. He's coming back when I've finished today and we'll go to the garage to get my car."

"Fine, long as you're okay."

Kathryn picked up the theatre list. She knew Erin had

307

been acting up as sister in charge supported by the Matron, so didn't want to stand on her toes on her first day back. "It's a busy theatre list this morning; shall I leave you to allocate the staff?"

"Course, if you're sure."

"Yes, definitely. I've got to see Matron first thing anyway so don't put me down to scrub or anything."

"No, I'll not do that. Matron told us that you had to do a phased return for the first few days back and to try not to include you in the numbers."

"That's really kind of her, she's been very good. That's why I came back today, Helen said not to return on a busy Monday."

Liar. You'd told her Tuesday would suit you better.

You didn't want to see him when you thought he'd been with Janelle.

"I'll help you get set up," Kathryn continued, "and then we can grab a coffee before the mayhem begins and you can tell me all about what's been going on while I've been off."

Erin smiled, "Sounds like a plan. It really is great to have you back."

"Thank you, it's great to be back," and she meant it. It felt right. She loved working in theatre and it would be a massive upheaval to leave her job. Maybe she just needed to do as her dad said and not make any hasty decisions. His favourite expression sprung to mind, *one step at a time.*

The morning meeting with Matron passed off as normal. It was all routine stuff she'd heard loads of times before. The good news was that business was increasing. Seemingly her and Fin were now advertising cosmetic surgery at St Anne's on local radio, and that was boosting business, and the new NHS contract that the hospital had secured was generating more work. If it carried on, they may have to increase the staffing levels to cope with the additional demands.

"So," Helen concluded, "I think that's about it for now. I don't want to overload you on your first day back. There are some things I need to go over with you, but they can wait."

Kathryn smiled at her thoughtfulness, "Thank you. I'll be on full pelt as soon as I get this week over, I'm sure."

"Well there's no need to rush it. Losing a loved one is always hard, but when it's someone so young and a spouse, then that is even harder."

She didn't want any more sympathy. She'd overdosed on it and wanted to return to normal, "Yes, it has been difficult, but I'm absolutely fine. I'm keen to move forward with my life now."

"Okay, as long as you're sure. Please say though if things are getting too much. Fin has asked me to keep a watchful eye on you."

Has he?

Has he really?

Her heart fluttered.

"Oh, yes, before I forget," Helen continued, "we need to have a chat about Janelle some time."

"Regarding the allegations she's made about her and Fin?"

"Ah, you already know."

"Yes, she came to see me yesterday and told me all about it."

"Did she now. She's no business bothering you while you're off," she paused for a moment, "but thinking about it, Fin did say she needed to speak to everyone to put the record straight. It could have waited until today though."

"That's what I thought, but she's frightened he's going to sack her and wants me to put in a good word for her."

"I'm quite sure she does, the silly girl. I don't think it'll come to that though," Helen lowered her voice, "and between you and I, I'd like to know who told him about it." She lifted an eyebrow, "I can't imagine anyone from theatre would be bold enough to walk up and say, *I hear you slept with Janelle,* but he won't say how he knows."

That's because it was me,

I told him.

Kathryn shook her head, "I'm not defending her in any way, I think it's dreadful what she's done, but I'm guessing it started out as showing off a bit, you know, *guess who took me home*, and escalated from there."

That's good, Kathryn, showing your impartiality.

Quite professional when you can't stand her.

"You're probably right. I never should have left him alone with her that night really, it was ill-advised, but you don't expect a nurse to behave like that. Fin's letting her stew a bit. She's written a letter of apology, and told everyone it didn't happen, so I think she's humiliated enough for now."

"Yes, I think she is. Right then Helen, if there's nothing else …"

"Just one other thing, there's a heads of department meeting today at two. I don't know how you feel about attending on your first day back? You don't have to."

I'll go.

To see him.

"That's fine, of course I'll attend." She stood up to go.

"Hang on," Helen opened her desk drawer and handed her a folder, "here's the minutes from the last meetings. You have them and I'll get one of the admin girls to copy some more off for me."

Kathryn smiled, taking them from her, "That's great, thank you. I'll see you later then."

She closed the door behind her and glanced through the window in Fin's adjacent office to see if he was sitting behind his desk. The office was empty.

Phew, I'm glad he's out.

Liar.

Kathryn sat in the tearoom with the others and picked at her lunch. Food was the last thing on her mind. She was counting down the minutes until two o'clock when she'd see him.

"I bet it's strange being back at work after all the time off isn't it?" Amy asked.

"Yes, but there's only so much cleaning I can do each day, and I'm definitely all shopped out. So the sooner things get back to normal the better."

"Have they come to a conclusion about whether Philip was pushed or not?" Lee asked.

"Lee!" Erin chastised, "I'm sure Kathryn doesn't

want to be discussing that right now on her first day back."

Kathryn smiled, "It's okay Erin, I don't mind talking about it," she turned to Lee, "there's no proof he was pushed, just a witness saying he was with someone before he died, but whoever that was, never came forward. The police did all these footprint samples and measurements, and the position Philip was in at the bottom of the ravine, but it doesn't sound as if anything was conclusive."

"That must be hard," Erin chipped in, "you really want some closure."

Kathryn shrugged, "To be honest, as far as I'm concerned, he slipped. It's hard to think he would as he was so careful and knew every inch of the cliffs, but the pushing theory has never been one I've believed."

Amy joined in, "It's all up in the air though isn't it?"

"Yes, it is, and the case is still open, but I can't imagine there's anyone that would have gained from Philip being dead, so as far as I'm concerned, it is closed really. I think it's the police being a bit overzealous."

Thankfully none of them mentioned Gary Hicks and Philip's relationship, which was common knowledge because of the local media. It would of course have been the topic of great discussion amongst them, but for now Kathryn didn't want to go there.

"Hey, on a lighter note," Erin piped up, "I forgot to ask, who left the Ferrero Rocher chocolate in the office this morning on the keyboard, does anybody know?" Nobody answered so she continued, "What's that in aid of? I wouldn't have minded if it had been a full box, but it was just a measly one on its own."

Lee shook his head, "Only one? Who'd do that, the mean git?"

"That's what I thought," Erin laughed, "but I ate it anyway."

Kathryn's heart flipped. She knew who'd left it. No-one else would have any idea about the significance, but she did. She'd glanced at the clock. In less than twenty minutes she'd be seeing him. Warmth spread through her tummy. *He'd* left the chocolate for her.

The changing room door adjacent to the tearoom

opened interrupting their chatter, and Janelle came in for her late shift, "Hi Kathryn, welcome back."

"Thank you." She didn't get up. The last thing she wanted was a welcome back hug from Janelle. The others yes, but not her.

"How's the morning been?" Janelle asked, putting some fruit she'd brought into the fridge.

"Busy," Erin said, "and it is this afternoon, so I'd put your old clogs on and not your new ones for Mr Barr's list as you're likely to be stood for a while."

"Oh, right, just what I need," Janelle sighed and sat down, "How's your first morning back been, Kathryn?"

She forced herself to be polite in front of the others, "Fine, I haven't done much though. I've only had a meeting with Matron and nipped round to each department to say hello."

"Is that it for today then, are you going home now?"

"No, I've got another meeting to attend and then I will do."

"A meeting with Mr Dey?" Janelle couldn't hide the concern from her voice. She must have thought it was a meeting to discuss her.

"No, a heads of department meeting."

The relief on her face was evident, "Oh right."

Bitch. The trouble you've caused.

You deserve to be sacked.

"Will you be okay going home on your own after work, Kathryn," Erin asked, "you know, to an empty house?"

"Yes, but I'll be fine, I've got to get used to it."

"Don't struggle with anything will you," Janelle said, "we're all here to help."

Oh yes, I can see what a help you'd be.

If you're a friend, I'd hate to be your enemy.

"I'll be okay, honestly. Right, I better get ready for the meeting. Are we alright staff-wise for this afternoon's list Erin, you don't need me, do you?"

"No, there are plenty of us about. Amy can crack on with some ordering."

"Okay, I'll leave you to it then."

She rinsed her mug and went into the changing room

to put on her theatre sister's uniform. She wanted to look nice for seeing him and always felt her uniform was flattering. A bit more makeup wouldn't go amiss as well.

After changing, she applied some lip gloss and attached her frilly hat with a couple of grips. With a pounding heart and butterflies swirling around her tummy, she left theatre and headed towards the boardroom.

This is it.

I'm finally going to see him.

54

Kathryn entered the boardroom and a quick glance at the table confirmed she was the last to arrive. She felt she needed to apologise to those already seated, "I'm not late am I?"

Fin turned, and the first words he'd spoken to her in months came with a kind tone, "No problems Kathryn, grab a coffee and we can get started."

His gorgeous deep voice still had the ability to make her legs turn to jelly.

She put the sachet of hot chocolate into the sophisticated coffee machine and listened to the chattering as it delivered a drink which was supposed to rival leading named brands, but it looked weak and limp to her.

Her eyes were drawn towards him at the head of the table. She knew seeing him was going to be difficult, but maybe she'd underestimated how she would feel. Her tummy flipped just being in the same room as him. His hair was shorter than usual so he must have recently had a haircut.

How is he?

I've missed him.

After adding a little cold milk to her drink, she took the only spare seat at the foot of the table. Why did people always leave the seat opposite the chairperson empty? Each time she'd gone over in her mind seeing him at this meeting, not once had she pictured herself sat directly opposite him with a huge oblong table separating them.

She removed her papers from the folder Helen had given her and selected the last month's minutes as she knew Fin would go through those first before today's schedule. She studied the agenda which was placed in front of them all. Most of it was mundane, but the last agenda item made her curious, *Secondments to the Eastleigh*. What was that all about? She quickly flicked through the minutes of the last monthly meeting and saw that several of the department heads had been asked to contact Fin directly if they would be willing to work at the Eastleigh for short secondments to try and improve standards there.

I wonder if he'll ask me if I want to go?

She looked at Fin. The last few months on compassionate leave, and even her week on holiday had not lessened the impact of being around him. The familiar longing was thudding away inside of her, more so now she knew he hadn't been with Janelle. Maybe she should explain to him how she felt, and see if he still wanted her. But what if he didn't? What if he'd moved on and got someone else now? Surely not though. The Ferrero Rocher chocolate he'd left proved she meant something to him; he wouldn't have done that if he didn't care about her. He wasn't to know Erin would be in early and would get to it before she did.

The meeting droned on. There was to be a Health and Safety inspection of all departments, and they were due a visit from the CQC sometime within the next two weeks. They already knew, but Fin reiterated that the CQC wouldn't give a specific date as they liked to conduct their inspection unannounced.

He was so practiced and slick. She watched him moisten his lips when he'd been talking for a while which caused her heartrate to increase. He paused before reaching the last agenda item about the secondments, and poured himself a glass of water. She looked at his hands, those same hands that had brought her such pleasure, and her inactive pussy twitched. He lifted the glass of water to his lips and she watched his Adams apple move as he slugged the water down. How she'd loved to kiss his neck. His eyes met hers briefly, and she saw puzzlement there. She didn't look away though.

He looked down again at his agenda, "Next, onto discussion point five, the secondments for the Eastleigh. Kathryn, you weren't here last time this was discussed, so to bring you up to speed, I've asked if any of the heads of departments would be willing to go and spend some time at the Eastleigh so we can move that hospital into the twenty-first century." He paused and jotted something down, "Thank you to those of you that have expressed an interest. I'm thrashing out the finer details, and I'm hoping by next week to be able to announce who will be seconded first, and who in the interim will be taking over their roles."

"Can senior staff here that deputise in the absence of their particular manager express an interest in going?" Dinah the ward sister asked.

He squeezed his bottom lip with his fingers, "I'd prefer senior managers with a track record of managing departments for a period of time as opposed to a staff member covering for an annual holiday. For example, you all know Alison is returning on the first of next month after almost a year off. In her absence, Kathryn has done a sterling job acting as theatre manager," he paused for a moment as if considering whether he should say anything, "so if either Alison or Kathryn wanted to go to the Eastleigh, then that would be helpful so we can utilise their managerial skills."

She looked at him, what were those old sayings; *Life is for the living, grasp each opportunity with both hands.*

The new assertive Kathryn Knight was lurking. Dare she?

She cleared her throat, "Is that what you think I should do?"

He looked taken aback, "That was only an example I was giving."

"I wouldn't rush anything, Kathryn," Matron interjected, "you've only just got back. I think you're better here where we can support you."

"Yes," Fin agreed, "there's no need to rush into

anything, but also to throw into the pot, there will be a theatre manager vacancy coming up in March at the Eastleigh when the current manager retires."

"Really?" She was on a roll now, "That presents a bit of a dilemma then as I'll be redundant here in terms of my managerial skills when Alison returns. I wonder if perhaps I could progress further at the Eastleigh. I'd hate to let an opportunity like this slip through my fingers and regret it."

Don't you want me to go?

Away from here, away from you?

He took a sip of his water, "The vacancy won't be there forever, that's for sure."

"Do you think I should move on then," she asked, "is that what you're saying?"

Say you want me here.

Beg me to stay.

He looked uncomfortable, "No, I didn't say that, but I'm not sure this meeting is the best place to discuss this," he shuffled in his seat, "maybe you can speak to Helen afterwards." He reached for the meeting agenda, "Shall we continue ... "

"You're right," she turned and addressed the others sitting around the table, "I am sorry. This isn't really the place to be discussing my future career options, but if you wouldn't mind if I just clarify," she turned back towards Fin, "so, do you think I'd be better off staying here, or should I look at other opportunities and move on? I'm thinking there's no point in staying here if there isn't anything for me."

Heads moved around the table as if they were watching a tennis match at Wimbledon. It would be quite clear to them all now that they weren't discussing secondment opportunities to the Eastleigh at all, but something much more interesting.

He looked unsure, "Considering what you have been through, then yes, possibly a fresh start might be a good thing for you, however it is entirely your decision," he glared.

The ball was back in her court, "Yes, but what do *you* think I should do?"

There was a stunned silence around the room. The

old saying *you could hear a pin drop*, sprung to mind. No shuffling of papers, no tapping of pens, only her looking at his striking brown eyes which were turning darker by the second.

I want to stay here.

Tell me you want me to.

She watched his chest rise as he took a deep breath in, "*I* think this meeting is now closed."

He never lost eye contact with her as the chairs shuffled back and the females hastily reached for their handbags, while the males collected their papers and put pens back into their pockets. The expression on his face would tell them they weren't going to be privy to anything more.

The only person remaining was Helen, "Don't forget we have a meeting at four o'clock with procurement."

He didn't turn towards Helen, but answered keeping his eyes firmly fixed on hers, "I won't. Please close the door on your way out."

The boardroom door slammed shut. *It sounds like Helen's pissed.*

The huge boardroom table separated them, "What on earth was all that about?" he demanded, "Why you are behaving like that in front of everyone?"

She raised her eyebrows, "I was merely asking if you wanted me to go to the Eastleigh or stay here, that's all."

"No you weren't," he dismissed, "you were playing games. What do you want from me? I've kept my distance and tried to be respectful," his voice faltered, "you're not the only one suffering here you know."

Now he'd drawn attention to himself, she could see that. He'd lost weight, and had dark circles under his eyes which she hadn't noticed before. The death of his sister would no doubt have brought back the trauma of losing his wife and son, and her heart ached for him.

She lowered her voice, "I was asking if you want me to stay, or if you want me to go?"

The frustration that had been in his voice disappeared and his tone softened, "Surely you know the answer to that?"

"No, I don't," she whispered.

He shook his head slowly from side to side, and his gorgeous eyes held hers as he stood up and kicked his chair away. Her heart was hammering against her ribs as he walked around to her side of the boardroom table and pulled the chair next to her out and sat down. He looked at her with such tenderness that she felt her breath catch. "I hate what we did, and I am so sorry about the way things have turned out, but I'm not going to apologise about us. So ... in answer to your question, of course I want you to stay," his eyes looked so gentle, "more than anything." He reached for her hand and stared at it as he stroked her fingers, "What I'd really like to do now is start again from the beginning; take things a bit slower this time and get to know each other properly. How does that sound?"

"It sounds wonderful," she smiled as her eyes began filling with tears. Not sad tears this time though, she'd shed far too many of those lately. These were joyful tears, "I'd like that too."

Relief flooded his face, and he tilted her chin with his hand, "You've been through so much and we need to make sure you have time to grieve properly. The last thing I want is to be some sort of rebound man."

"Never," she shook her head, "you could never be a rebound man."

His eyes glistened with tenderness as he leant forward and kissed her lips gently, "It's a relief to hear that," he breathed.

Warmth flooded her entire body, but at the same time her throat tightened, "I'm sorry I believed Janelle. I should have known you wouldn't have done anything like that."

He placed his finger on her lips, "Shush, forget about that now."

"You're not going to sack her are you?"

"No, but she'll be going on a long secondment to the Eastleigh and it will be quite a while before she comes back here, if ever, that's for sure."

"It's probably the best place for her to be honest," she agreed, knowing that it would be hard for both of them to work with her now after all that had happened.

There was something else she needed to say, "I'm

sorry about Elsa too. I had no idea she wasn't having any treatment. I blame myself for being too wrapped up with you and not noticing the signs."

He shook his head dismissively, "There were no signs. She was my sister, but she was a devious monkey. Even now, I question what was going on in that head of hers. She certainly had a hidden side that she kept from us all."

"You're right," she agreed, "I wonder what she'd make of the two of us."

A wave of anguish passed across his face, "I think it could have been what she wanted."

"What do you mean?"

"Nothing," he said, "only that she loved us both and would want us to be happy."

"Yeah, she would. Let's hope she's looking down on us right now and smiling."

He squeezed her hand, "Oh, I'm quite sure she will be."

She took a deep breath in and winced, "I'm still a bit screwed up."

He titled his head, "I like screwed up ... in fact, I *love* screwed up." A look of vulnerability passed across his face, "You're sure you want to be with me?" he questioned softly.

Another tear escaped down her cheek. God, she was so emotional lately. She sniffed and nodded her head, "For as long as you want me."

He pressed her hand against his warm lips and his eyelids closed for a second. When he opened them again, he gave her the most gorgeous smile, "As long as that, eh?"

Epilogue

Rosa had finished for the day and she opened her locker for her handbag. Amy came through into the changing room, "All done, Rosa? Are you going straight home, or have you got shopping to do?"

"I just going down the Avenue. Dino trying to teach new puppy, Tesoro, so will get him some chocolate treats from pet shop. He must 'ave sweet tooth, as last lot I bought gone already."

"He's not the only one with a sweet tooth then?" Amy nodded her head towards the open locker and Rosa's eyes followed her to the top shelf and a box of Ferrero Rocher chocolates.

Rosa lifted the box out, "You want one?"

"Yes please, thank you. I love these. They're much nicer than ordinary chocolate."

"Dino buy me chocolate still after forty-five years bin married."

"Aw, that's so sweet. Fancy that. Your Dino could teach my boyfriend a thing or two in the romantic stakes, he's rubbish."

Rosa shrugged her shoulders, "The men, they all need some 'elp with that. Chocolate the way to a woman's 'eart, and this little one," she held a chocolate up, "is a tiny 'idden gem."

"Gosh, what a little romantic you are, Rosa, I had no idea."

Rosa tapped her nose, "Ah ... si, there's lots people

321

don't know 'bout me."

About the Author

I released my debut novel *For the Love of Emily,* in 2015. At various book signings, readers would ask me if my book was about nursing as they'd read in the local newspapers that I'm a nurse.

I started to think that maybe readers would like a romance based around a nurse, so that's where the idea for *Knight & Dey* initially came from.

I sincerely hoped that you've enjoyed reading is as much as I've loved writing it. Any feedback would be greatly appreciated, I'd love to hear from you.

joymarywood@yahoo.co.uk

Printed in Great Britain
by Amazon

76507591R00194